Mates, Dates

Absolutely Amazing

Cathy Hopkins is the author of the incredibly successful *Mates, Dates* and *Truth, Dare* books, as well as the highly acclaimed *Cinnamon Girl* series. She lives in North London with her husband and cats.

Cathy spends most of her time locked in a shed at the bottom of the garden pretending to write books, but she is actually in there listening to music, hippie dancing and talking to her friends on email.

Apart from that, Cathy has joined the gym and spends more time than is good for her making up excuses as to why she hasn't got time to go.

Find out more about Cathy and her books at
www.cathyhopkins.com

Cathy Hopkins

Mates, Dates

Absolutely Amazing

PICCADILLY PRESS · LONDON

This edition first published in Great Britain in 2009
by Piccadilly Press Ltd,
5 Castle Road, London NW1 8PR
www.piccadillypress.co.uk

A catalogue record for this book is available from
the British Library.

ISBN: 978 1 84812 028 0

1 3 5 7 9 10 8 6 4 2

Cover design by Simon Davis
Printed in the UK by CPI Bookmarque, Croydon, CR0 4TD

Mixed Sources
Product group from well-managed
forests and other controlled sources
www.fsc.org   Cert no. TT-COC-002227
© 1996 Forest Stewardship Council
FSC

Mates, Dates & Pulling Power

Thanks as always to Brenda Gardner, Yasemin Uçar and the ever fab team at Piccadilly Press. To Rosemary Bromley at Juvenelia. To Steve Lovering for all his help and support. To Peter Ziderman for his input about dentists and braces. And to Georgina Acar, Scott and Jack Brenman, Alice Elwes, Rachel Hopkins and Olivia McDonnell for answering all my questions about what it's like being a teenager these days.

Chapter 1

Ghastly Ghoul
Face Packs

'Pah,' I said. 'I wouldn't go out with Adrian Cook if he was dipped in gold and covered in fivers.'

Izzie gave me a disapproving look. '*Nesta*. Covered in fivers? You mean, if he was loaded. So what? I don't think how rich or poor a boy is should make the slightest bit of difference. It's who he is, if he's interesting, good company that counts.'

I pulled a silly face back at her. She can be a real priss queen sometimes. 'Yeah, but he has to be *reasonably* cute,' I said.

'So what if he's cute,' asked Izzie, 'if he's boring to be with? Just good looks don't count for much after a few dates. You always judge by externals.'

'Do not.'

'Do.'

'Not.'

The four of us were sitting in a line on the edge of the bathtub in the bathroom at Lucy's house. TJ, Izzie, Lucy and me. We were covered in some homemade facial gloop that Lucy and Izzie had concocted in the kitchen and were discussing the local boy talent in North London. Pretty short on the ground in my opinion. And I *don't* only judge by externals, I thought. Of course I care what a boy's like inside.

'Beauty is only skin deep,' said TJ, peering at herself in the mirror opposite.

'Yeah, but not today,' I replied, looking at our reflections. 'We look like ghastly ghouls. What is in this stuff, Lucy? It feels very sticky. Are you sure you were meant to put so much honey in it?'

Lucy reached for her natural beauty book, which was on the windowsill. 'I think so,' she said. 'Yeah, egg yolk, yeast and honey.'

'Sounds disgusting,' I said. 'I wish you hadn't told me.'

It was Sunday and sometimes there's not a lot to do on a Sunday, especially if it's raining like it was today. Lucy suggested we have an afternoon of beauty treatments round at her house and as none of us were that well off in the pocket money department, she decided to make DIY face masks. Think I'll stick to nicking Mum's posh ones when she's out from now on,

I thought. Egg on my face? Never a good idea at the best of times.

'Well, if it doesn't work, no problem, you can always eat it,' said Lucy, sticking her tongue out and licking her top lip.

'I wouldn't if I were you,' said Izzie. 'Raw egg can give you that salmonella disease.'

'That's quite rare,' said TJ. 'And I think the egg has to be off.'

TJ's our resident medical adviser on account of the fact that both her parents are doctors and some of their medical knowledge rubs off on her.

Lucy quickly put her tongue back in her mouth. 'Yuck,' she said.

Izzie took her trainers off, put a towel in the bath, then got in and lay down with her feet resting up on the taps. 'Honestly, the things we girls have to do to look beautiful,' she said. 'I bet boys never do anything like this.'

'Don't you believe it,' said Lucy. 'Steve and Lal are always slapping moisturiser all over them. And they take an age in the bathroom getting ready. Boys can be just as vain as girls.'

'At least we don't have to shave,' said TJ.

'Well, not our faces,' I said. 'But we do our legs and under our arms. Waxing is better than shaving though, it lasts longer.'

'My gran does her chin,' TJ added, laughing. 'She said it's one of the awful things about getting old. Hair starts sprouting everywhere, from your ears, your nose, your chin.'

'Oo, sexy,' I said. I took a close look at my nostrils in the mirror. 'I hope that never happens to me.'

After we'd rinsed off our face masks, we resumed our discussion in Lucy's bedroom about the local boys. What Izzie had said about me judging by externals had irked me. I wasn't so superficial as to only go out with boys because of what they looked like or if they had money or something. My last long-term boyfriend had been very rich, but that wasn't the reason I went out with him. I liked him for who he was. That is until he dumped me because he was going to university in Scotland and wanted to be free to date any new girl that he fancied up there. Maybe the girls think I only dated him because he was loaded. I decided to find out what they really thought about me, but planned to ask them in a really subtle way.

'So Izzie, about what you said before. Were you saying that you think I'm shallow?' Oops, I thought. I knew before I'd finished the question that it hadn't come out the way I intended. Subtlety was never my best trait.

Izzie laughed. 'No Nesta, not shallow, but image is very important to you.'

'Like it isn't to you?' I asked. I looked at my three friends all busy painting each other's toenails. Lucy's petite and blonde, TJ and Iz are tall and dark and all three of them are gorgeous in their own ways, but they all work at it, forever trying new things and new looks in an attempt to improve on nature. I am *not* the only one. 'And Iz, you did a whole makeover on yourself just before term started in September.'

'I know. It's important to all of us,' she said as she began to paint TJ's toenails a purple shade called Vampire. 'All I was saying is that there is other stuff that's important as well. Like, what's inside a person.'

'I know that. TJ, Lucy, do you think I'm shallow?'

'I never said I thought you were shallow,' said Izzie. 'You did.'

'Yeah, but you think it,' I said, looking at TJ and Lucy.

Lucy looked uncomfortable. She hates confrontation, but I had to know what my friends really thought of me.

'I wouldn't use the word shallow,' she said after a few minutes, 'but I know a certain sense of style and looking good is important to you.'

'TJ?'

'Um. God. I don't know,' she said. 'You've obviously got a good brain or else you wouldn't do so well at school.'

'Yeah, but am I shallow?'

'Depends what you mean by shallow,' blustered TJ. 'I mean, I wouldn't say you're deep . . . but you're not shallow either.'

'Who wants to be deep,' I said lowering my voice. '*Bor*-ring.'

'I think Izzie's deep,' said Lucy, 'and she's far from boring. She's always thinking about things and asking questions about stuff like why we're here and what it's all about. You're not boring, Izzie.'

Oh, here we go. Now I've managed to insult one of my best friends. Me and my big mouth, I thought. I didn't mean to say that Izzie was boring. I'd better try and say something to make it clear what I really meant.

'Yeah and where does that get you, Izzie?' I asked. 'Who knows the answers to questions like that? You could drive yourself mad asking about life, the universe and everything. Perhaps that's why you are a bit mad. I reckon, we're here, you get on with it. End of story.'

Oops, I thought as Izzie's face fell. I don't think that helped. Maybe I should shut up for a while.

'That's it,' said TJ. 'Pragmatic. That's what you are, Nesta.'

Bugger, I thought. I don't know what pragmatic means. But no way am I going to let on or else they really will think that I'm shallow. Whatever it meant, I felt I was being got at. Huh.

'Right, pragmatic, I guess that's OK.'

'Yeah,' continued TJ, 'you just get on with life without questioning it too much. You like to have fun, do girlie things, enjoy life, you're not a complicated person and you're not that bothered about educating your mind or anything.'

'I am too. I read. I keep up with what's happening.'

TJ and Izzie burst out laughing. 'OK, what have you read lately?' asked TJ.

'*CosmoGIRL! Bliss. OK!* magazine.'

TJ and Izzie exchanged glances.

'What's wrong with that?' I asked.

'Nothing,' said Izzie. 'We all read the mags and they're great. But when did you last read a book?'

'All the time. We read books every day at school. There's a time and a place for everything. And school is the place for books. Out of school is the place for fun.'

'But some books *are* fun,' said TJ. 'They can take you to different places, let you in to different people's experiences, how others think. Don't close your mind to them just because they're not all glossy with photos of celebrities in them.'

I was definitely being got at. TJ is a regular bookworm. She reads everything and anything and Izzie's dad lectures in English at some university in town and is always giving her heavy-looking books to read. Not my cup of tea at all, I'd rather watch a good soap on telly, but she dutifully reads everything her dad gives her.

'OK,' I said, 'so I'm not a bookworm. That doesn't make me shallow. Lucy doesn't read a lot, do you Luce?'

Lucy looked more uncomfortable than ever now. 'Actually, Steve passes on some of his books to me and I quite often read late at night.'

'Hah! Closet reader,' I said. 'I never knew that.'

'You never asked,' said Lucy blushing furiously. 'And I didn't think you'd be interested.'

'Hhmmm. So you think I'm too shallow to have a discussion about books.'

'No,' TJ and Lucy chorused.

'Well, I didn't know I had such nerdy brainbox friends,' I said.

'See, that's just it,' said Izzie. 'You think that because someone reads that they're a nerd. You couldn't be more wrong.'

'Huh,' I said.

'I think,' said TJ, 'you have different people for different parts of yourself. Like I can talk to Izzie about books, astrology and stuff like what life is all about, I can talk to Lucy about fashion and design and I can talk to you about . . . er, make-up and . . . or . . . I know, advice about boys. Nobody knows more about boys than you, Nesta.'

Well that's true, I thought. I suppose it helps having an older brother. Boys have never phased me. I sussed out pretty early that all of them, no matter what age or how cool they act, are little boys underneath. They are as nervous and unsure about girls as girls are about them.

'So,' I said. 'We have here, Izzie the seeker, TJ the thinker, Lucy the designer *extraordinaire* and me, the what? The airhead?'

'Course not,' said Lucy. 'No one said that. What's got into you today? You always come in the top ten in exams at school, so how can you think that you're an airhead? You're the one putting yourself down.'

'And you are the boy expert,' said TJ.

'OK then,' I said, 'when it comes to boys. Fact. The cute ones often don't read because they have got a life. Fact. The nerdy ones bury their heads in books because they haven't got a life.'

'*Noooo*,' said Izzie. 'No way. You couldn't be more wrong. I mean, take Ben. He's cute and reads loads.'

Hmm, I thought. Ben is Izzie's ex and although really nice, not someone I'd call a babe magnet. Definitely not my type.

'Well, I think there are two types of boys,' I said. 'The hot babe magnets who, OK, might be trouble and break your heart, but are fun and great to be seen out with. And there's the other type, not quite as attractive, but cosy and good company and you know where you are with them, because they don't mess you around, basically because they know that if they did, they might not get off with anyone else.'

Izzie laughed. 'You always see things in black or white. Nothing in between.'

'So?'

'You can't always generalise, especially about people,' said TJ. 'I don't think everything is black or white. I think there are shades of grey as well. Like take Steve, he's really clever and also attractive.'

I kept my mouth shut. Steve is one of Lucy's brothers and he's been dating TJ for ages now. But once again, like Ben, yes, nice, a laugh, but babe magnet – no way. I didn't want to insult TJ by saying that her boyfriend wasn't a babe, nor Lucy by saying that I didn't think her brother was attractive. People can be very defensive about their family. It's like they can say the worst possible things themselves about brothers and sisters, but God help anyone else who says anything bad. I guess I'm the same about my brother, Tony. I slag him off something rotten sometimes, but I won't hear a word against him from anyone else. I dutifully kept my mouth zipped about Steve, but sometimes it's difficult holding in what I really think. Sometimes I worry that I might be getting that disease, Tourette's syndrome or something. I read about it in a magazine. Instead of blood leaking out or people being sick, people puke out their thoughts instead and they shout awful things in public or on the tube or somewhere. They can't help it apparently, like the 'What not to say and when not to say it' filter is missing from their brain. I'd be forever in trouble if my thoughts leaked out. I wonder if it's possible to have inner Tourette's syndrome. Sometimes I think awful things about people before I can stop myself. Mad things just pop into my head. Sometimes my thoughts shock even me. In school sometimes, I want to shout 'knickers' at inappropriate moments like school assembly when our headmistress is droning on. Or if I see someone really unattractive in the street, I think, 'Woah, there goes a fat ugly one,' then I feel awful because some people can't help the way they look. Or when Dad is giving me a hard time about something, I think, 'Hhmm. Take your advice, Pater, and stick it up your bum.' Luckily, most of the time my brain filter works and I manage to keep my thoughts to myself. Maybe I'm secretly insane? It is a worry.

'So you reckon the choices are gorgeous and dangerous versus safe and secure, but not so gorgeous?' asked Lucy.

'Yeah,' I said. 'That's your choice. One or the other.'

'I reckon you can get boys who are both,' said Izzie. 'Gorgeous and safe and secure. Not all gorgeous boys mess you around.'

'They might not at first,' I said, thinking about Simon dumping me, 'but they do in the end, basically because they know they can.'

TJ shook her head. 'I agree with Izzie,' she said.

'Lucy?' I asked.

She's had this on/off thing with my brother Tony for over a year. Even though he's my brother, I can see that he's the first type, ie: is v.v. attractive even though a little arrogant with it. There's always a queue of girls after him and he never gets serious about any of them. Except Lucy that is. He really likes her, but half the reason that he stays interested is because she doesn't fall over herself wanting to be with him. She keeps him on his toes. I know for a fact that if she wasn't messing him around, he'd be messing her around. It's like they're doing a dance, he steps forward, she steps back. She steps forward, he steps back. Right now, in the dance, Lucy is stepping back and Tony is stepping forward.

'Um, I also agree with Izzie,' said Lucy. 'Oh, I know Tony's not exactly Mr Commitment, but at least he's honest about who he is.'

'Yeah, course,' said Izzie. 'There are all sorts of types. There are boys who are deep *and* gorgeous. Cute boys who think about things. Cute boys who will commit and not mess you around. People are different depending on who they're with, so maybe you just haven't brought out the deeper side of the boys you've been with.'

'What do you mean?' I asked.

'Well, like we're different with different people,' said Izzie. 'You're one way with your parents, another way with teachers, another way with your friends, another way with boys.'

'Yeah. So?'

'Well, like TJ was saying, she talks to Iz about some things, Lucy about others and you about others.'

'Yeah,' said TJ. 'Like I go to Iz for advice and I come to you for a laugh.'

I had to think about that. Was that a compliment or an insult?

'Are you saying you don't think I can give advice?'

'No . . . yes,' said TJ looking flustered. 'I was trying to say something nice about you. Not many people are as much fun as you. Oh, I don't know. I think you're being over sensitive today, Nesta.'

'Yes, don't be a drama queen,' said Izzie.

I'm not even going to reply to that, I thought. Drama queen! *Moi?* As *if*.

'All I was saying,' continued Izzie, 'was that we're probably totally different with different boys too. With some, you don't feel yourself at all and have nothing to say, with others, you can't stop talking. People bring out different sides of you. Maybe you've never brought out what you call the nerdy side of a boy, because you've never talked about anything to bring it out.'

'So you *are* saying I'm shallow and I bring out the shallow part of people, boys included. *And* I can't give advice. *And* I'm a drama queen.'

'*No*,' said Izzie. 'Oh, I don't know. Just maybe, next time you like a boy, try talking about a book you've read or ask him what he feels about the purpose of life or something.'

Huh, I thought, not exactly a fun chat-up line in my estimation. I was feeling peeved by what the girls had said. I don't want to be thought of as an airhead-type drama queen bimbo. I'm not. I do well at school. I *do* think about things. Like, what to wear, how to do my hair, which is my favourite boy band and so on. But maybe I should talk about 'deep' stuff. Books. Um. Maybe I'd better read one – a grown-up one, that is. I used to read a lot when I was younger, but I went off it. I don't know why. I'll start again when I get home, I decided. I'll pick a really intellectual, impressive-type book and that will show them, when I start quoting bits off by heart. Then I'll find a boy and knock his socks off with my brainy brain-type brain as well as my looks. I shall show them all that airhead, I am not.

Lucy's DIY Face-masks

Egg and Yeast Mask

1 egg yolk

1 tablespoon of brewer's yeast

1 teaspoon of sunflower oil

Mix into a smooth paste. Apply to face and neck and leave for fifteen minutes then rinse off.

NB: *The yeast can stimulate the skin and draw out impurities, so not the best one to use before a big party in case it brings out any lurking spots.*

Nourishing Mask

1 whole egg

1 teaspoon honey

1 teaspoon almond oil

Mix together then apply. Leave on for fifteen minutes then rinse off.

Rejuvenating Mask

2 tablespoons of ripe avocado

1 teaspoon honey

3 drops of lemon juice

Mash the avocado, add the lemon juice, add the honey and mix into a paste. Apply and leave on for at least twenty minutes. You may have to lie on the floor with a towel behind your head and neck for this one as it can be a bit runny.

Banana Mask *(especially good for dry skin)*
Half a ripe banana
1 tablespoon of honey
1 tablespoon of double cream
Mash the banana. Mix with the honey and cream and apply.
(This one's OK to eat as well!)

Chapter 2

War Zone

When I got home later that afternoon, I intended to go straight to the dictionary and look up pragmatic then go and find myself a 'deep' book from the shelves in our sitting room. However, as soon as I'd stepped into the hall of our flat, I heard raised voices coming from the kitchen. Oops, war zone, I thought as I went in to see what it was all about.

'But Dad,' Tony was saying, 'everyone in our year is taking their test and Mark Janson has even got his own car.'

Dad looked tight-lipped. 'I said no, and that's final. We'll talk about it again when you're nineteen.'

Ah, I thought, I know what this is about. It's Tony's birthday tomorrow. September 22nd. He'll be eighteen and he wants to do a course of driving lessons in the hope of getting a car when he passes his A-levels. He did ask if he could learn to drive last year when he was seventeen and I remember that there were fireworks then. It's weird because Dad is usually pretty cool about most things, but when it comes to talking about driving, he clamps up and becomes totally unapproachable. Poor Tony, he really thought Dad would give in this year and had even saved all his cash Christmas presents to go towards lessons.

I decided to step in and help.

'Don't be a meanie, Dad. It *is* his eighteenth birthday, that's a really special one.' Well that clearly didn't help, I thought as Dad's expression turned from frosty to ice. However, I don't believe in giving up easily. 'Loads of people Tony's age drive, Dad. And Tony would be very careful, wouldn't you?'

'Yeah, course.'

'He may be careful, but there are some maniacs out on the road,' said Dad.

'But . . .' Tony began.

'I *said* end of story,' said Dad, then he got up and left the room.

'Sorry,' I said as Tony sat at the counter and put his head in his hands.

'It's not fair,' he groaned.

'You sound like Kevin,' I said laughing and went into my impersonation of the teenage character that Harry Enfield plays in the film *Kevin and Perry Go Large*. He's a really obnoxious fifteen-year-old who is always telling his parents, 'It's not fair,' and 'I hate you.' It usually makes Tony laugh when I do it, but this time he wasn't going for it.

'It makes me look like a right dork,' he said. 'Three of my mates have been driving for six months already. I hate being the one who has to act like a kid – oh my dad won't let me. It sounds so pathetic.'

'So what *do* you want to do on your birthday?' When someone is feeling low, my philosophy is to change the subject to something cheerful.

'Not much I can do, is there? On a Monday? Mum says we can do something special at a later date, maybe a weekend when everyone's a bit more chilled.'

'But you have to do something on the day and although, yeah, you have to go to school, there's always the evening. You could do something nice if Mum hasn't already got something planned.'

'Actually she did say we could go out for dinner tomorrow, but who wants to go out with old misery Dad? Not exactly exciting. I'll probably meet up with some mates after school. You can come if you promise not to drool on any of them.'

'As if. Anyway I've got a dentist's appointment after school tomorrow,' I said. 'I might not be up to eating out if I have to have a filling or something. Why don't you have a party later? It is your eighteenth after all.'

Tony shook his head. 'That's what Mum said. I'll think

about it, but if Mum and Dad want to supervise, I'd rather not.'

'So what would you really like to do?'

Tony was quiet while he thought. 'I know what I'd like to do,' he said finally. 'I'd like to go out with Lucy. Just the two of us. Not actually on my birthday necessarily, but some time soon after. But I don't suppose she'll be up for a date either, you know what she's like, always blowing hot and cold.'

'Ahh,' I said, putting on my moany groany voice. 'Poor Tony. Itthh noooot faaiiirrr.'

At least this time he laughed. Or grimaced, sometimes it's hard to tell with Tone.

A few minutes later Mum came through. 'Ah good. I'm glad to get you both together as I wanted to have a bit of a chat.'

Tony and I looked at each other and tried not to laugh. Quite a few of our mates' parents have been doing this lately, so we knew what to expect by 'a bit of a chat'. It was a talk about sex, drugs or drink and how we mustn't do any of them.

'So,' she began, 'just to let you know how things are at the moment.'

Ah. Maybe I was wrong, I thought. Maybe it's not the 'It only takes one time and, before you know it, you're pregnant' sex lecture. Maybe it's the 'We have to tighten our belts' lecture.

'As you know,' Mum continued, 'my contract at the station was renewed last year . . .'

'Oh, they're not talking about letting you go again are they?' asked Tony.

Earlier this year, Mum thought she was going to be out of a job. She works as a news presenter on Cable and her position, as with all the presenters, is precarious as the producers like to try out new faces or, as Mum says, younger faces.

'No, they aren't talking of getting rid of me, no, just cutting down my hours. The producers are doing it to all us diehards and, to give them their due, they do have to keep trying out new people. So. This is the situation. Dad's got a new film to direct and that's going well, but there's not an enormous budget on this one and he's doing it mainly because of the prestige, not the money. It will look good on his CV and hopefully lead to other things. So money's going to be a bit tight, plus we'll have a big tax bill coming in January. So. What does this mean for all of us? Bit of budgeting. Pulling our belts in a little and no money for extras I'm afraid. I know there was a skiing trip you fancied going on with the school, Tony, but that's out for the time being. But we can live, that's the main thing.'

'That's cool,' said Tony. 'I wasn't that bothered about skiing to be honest. Not since Mark Crawley broke both his arm and leg on the last trip. Seeing him lumber about in a plaster cast put me off a bit.'

'And I'm sorry, Tony,' said Mum. 'About the party for your eighteenth. Do you mind waiting a while? Until things have improved a bit?'

'No problem,' said Tony. 'I wasn't sure I wanted one anyway.'

He's great with Mum. They have a really good relationship, much better than he has with Dad, which is interesting seeing as Dad is his real dad, but Mum is his stepmum. His real mum died when he was tiny, then later Dad married my mum. She's always been there as long as he can remember. Our family confuses a lot of people, because Dad is Italian – dark-haired, dark-eyed, olive-skinned. (Actually he's three-quarters Italian and a quarter Spanish to be precise as Granddad is half Italian, half Spanish and Grandma is Italian.) Tony's inherited his European good looks, complete with Dad's movie star type dimple on his chin. Mum's Jamaican, dark skin, dark hair, green eyes and, although I take after her, I'm not as dark, more kind of coffee coloured. When new people meet Tony and me, then find out that we're brother and sister, you can see their minds working overtime trying to work out why we look so different.

'OK, Nesta?' asked Mum.

'Yeah. You know me,' I said. 'I don't care in the least about material things.' Mum did a double-take and Tony burst out laughing. What a cheek. I am clearly one of the most misunderstood people in the history of time. Still, at least what Mum had said explained why Dad was being funny about Tony having driving lessons. Clearly he couldn't afford them, but didn't want to admit it. Men or boys, the whole male species are weird about some things and can't just come out and say stuff like they're lost or broke or something. As if to admit you're hard up means you've failed in some way. Huh, I thought, I have no problem admitting when I have no money.

'So we're poor again, are we?' I asked.

'Not poor, Nesta,' said Mum. 'Just not rich at the moment.'

We're always going through these phases – spare money, no spare money. Dad says working in the media is often feast or famine. When I'm an actress, I'm going to make sure I'm mega rich all the time by getting into every play and film going, as I don't reckon it's much fun having no dosh. I can see what a strain the ups and downs of finances put on Mum and Dad.

'Anything you want to ask?' asked Mum.

Tony shook his head.

'Nah,' I said. I planned to go upstairs and learn my audition part for the end of term play at school. We're doing *West Side Story* this year and I want to go for the part of Maria.

'Good,' said Mum. 'So you both understand? No extras for a while?'

I nodded. It's funny, I quite like the fact that Mum

treats Tony and me like adults and keeps us informed as to what's going on, as I know some people's parents don't. It makes me feel accepted as a grown-up. On the other hand, I don't want to know, because I reckon all that stuff is their job, being parents, paying the bills and all that and I want to just be a teenager and not think about any of it. Mum says she tells us about the finances so that we don't think that 'Money grows on trees'. As if.

'Er, Matt, wasn't there something you wanted to say?' Mum called into the hall, then turned back to us. 'And your dad had something he wanted to say as well.'

Ah. Now the sex talk, I thought, sneaking a glance at Tony. He raised an eyebrow as if to say, this should be interesting.

There was a cough from somewhere in the vicinity of the sitting room, then we heard Dad's footsteps approaching.

He shuffled about on his feet for a few moments. 'Right,' he said. 'Ahem. Yes. Er . . . I . . . I wanted to talk to you about contraception.'

'What! *Again?*' Tony groaned.

I rolled my eyes. 'Mum, Dad. We do all this stuff at school.'

'Yeah,' said Tony as he leaned back on his stool and put his hands behind his head in that arrogant 'You can't teach me anything' way of his. 'But it's cool, if you want to talk about it. So . . . Dad. Contraception? What would you like to know?'

I creased up laughing. So did Mum and Dad. Phew. War zone safe for a few more days.

Pragmatic: dealing with matters according to their practical significance or immediate importance.

Chapter 3

Count-down to Clamming up

Fifty-eight, fifty-nine, sixty. Four minutes left. One, two, three . . . I counted as I lay on the couch at the dentist's the next day after school. About four more minutes and I should be out of here, I thought, then it's all over for another six months. Dental surgeries are *not* my favourite places: the persistent buzz of drilling behind closed doors, the smell of polished wood mixed with antiseptic mouthwash, the anguished screams of despair as patients beg for mercy . . . OK, maybe the screams are in my head, but it doesn't help that my dentist, Mr Saltman, has a poster of Steve Martin in the film, *Little Shop of Horrors*, on his ceiling. Everyone that lies back on the chair has no choice but to see the poster as Mr Saltman works on their teeth. In the film, Steve Martin plays Orin Scrivello, the demented and sadistic dentist. Hhmm? What is Mr Saltman trying to say to his patients, I wondered.

'Scange choich of poh – er,' I mumbled as I pointed up at the ceiling. I was trying to say, strange choice of poster, but it was somewhat difficult with Mr Saltman's thumb and index finger in my cheek and my top lip stretched almost up to my ear (not my most alluring look). As he tapped my teeth with some cold metal implement, I closed my eyes and tried to think of nice relaxing things. Izzie had briefed me as we were leaving school. 'Think soothing thoughts,' she'd said, 'positive visualisations to distract you from the pain.' She'd suggested waterfalls, flowers, dolphins. Sadly dolphins don't do it for me, nor waterfalls, *bor*-ring. I decided to try and think up some soothing visualisations of my own. Things that made me happy to think about. The perfume counters in Selfridges. Rails of fab clothes in Morgan. The lingerie department in Fenwicks. Snogging Brad Pitt. Oh, I'm being shallow, I suddenly thought. Clothes, underwear, snogging. No, I can do better than that. I can do deep visualisations or else the girls would have been right yesterday, all I think about is my appearance, boys and clothes. No, I'll try again. I *will* think deep meaningful things. I imagined myself going on a protest march to save the environment. Hhmm, I wondered, what does one wear for a demonstration? Green or brown? Something that looks like you're serious about the cause, but casually alluring as well in case there's a hot eco-warrior boy there. Oh *no*. I was back to clothes and boys. I tried again. Think uplifting thoughts, uplifting, *deep* thoughts, I told myself. Something to distract from the fact that my jaw has locked and my neck muscles have gone into spasm. No. The visualisation stuff wasn't working. All I could see now was Steve Martin with his drill in his hand, an evil look in his eye and he was coming closer. I was never very good at getting the right visualisation for the right moment, I'm not like Izzie, she's so into all that New Age hocus pocus and it seems to work for her.

I opened my eyes to see if Mr Saltman had finished. No. He was still nose to nose with me, only with a mask over his nose and mouth. And glasses over his eyes. He looked like a giant insect hovering in my face and suddenly I had the urge to laugh as the words to Steve Martin's song from the film rang through my brain, 'to beee a dena-tist . . .' Gulp. Arghh, I thought as I struggled to swallow.

'Ow,' I cried as Mr Saltman pulled my mouth to the left. Real person down here, I thought, skin may be elastic, but it's not *that* stretchy. Sadly he didn't seem to be picking up on my thoughts and continued to yank my bottom lip as though it was made out of plasticine.

'So Nesta, have you been flossing regularly?' he asked.

'Urg, argle oof,' I attempted to say. I mean how ridiculous? Asking people questions when they're lying on their backs with their mouths full of fingers, metal things and cotton wool. I think it may be one way that dentists make their jobs enjoyable. When they get bored or something, they wait until someone is in their chair with their mouth full of dentisty type stuff, then they ask them questions and secretly laugh as they watch their patients struggling to answer.

I nodded, then tried to swallow again. Not long to go now, surely? Two more minutes. One, two, three, four . . .

Finally Mr Saltman stood back. 'OK, you can rinse now,' he said as he pressed a button on the side of the chair causing it to suddenly jerk up from horizontal to vertical and so throwing me forward. That's the other way that dentists get their laughs, I decided. Playing around with their chairs. Most of them have some way of lowering you down or pushing you back up. I wonder if they have ejector buttons for really difficult patients or nasty kids who bite them. They can just press a secret button and the patient flies out of the chair and back into reception. I know I'd have one fitted if I were a dentist. But then, I'm not going to be a dentist. I'm going to be an actress, which is one of the reasons I do actually turn up regularly for this torture. It's v. important to have good teeth. Which reminds me, I ought to be going over my audition piece for *West Side Story*. I'd decided to do Maria's song, 'There's a Place For Us'. Pah, I thought, I could have been doing that as a distraction. It would have been a great visualisation, imagining that I'd got the lead part and I was there, on stage, singing my heart out as everyone looked on in admiration.

As I rinsed with the disgusting bright pink liquid in the plastic cup on the stand next to the chair, Mr Saltman went to look at the X-rays of my teeth that he'd taken earlier. He started whispering to his assistant, a girl who looked younger than I do. No way she's coming anywhere near my mouth, I thought, she's clearly only just got her second teeth herself.

'So do they all have to come out?' I asked. I thought I was being very funny, but Mr Saltman wasn't laughing.

'No, none will have to come out, I don't think,' he said. 'But I *am* concerned about the slight overcrowding in your mouth. It might cause a crossover on the top two teeth as you get older and possibly on the bottom ones too. It won't be evident for a while but will happen . . .'

What is he talking about, I wondered? Crossovers. Overcrowding. 'Uh?' I asked.

'We'll need to get an impression of your teeth,' he said.

'There you go.' I beamed, giving him my widest smile.

Mr Saltman laughed. 'No, not that kind of impression. I need a moulding to send to Mr Schneider, the orthodontist.'

'For what?'

'You need to have a brace fitted, Nesta.'

'A whadttttt!!?'

'Brace,' said Mr Saltman. 'There's a chance if we leave them that some of the front teeth will grow crooked. A brace will soon correct that, then you'll have picture perfect peggies for when you're older.'

'But I'm fifteen, Mr Saltman.'

'I know,' he smiled. 'Perfect time for the corrections.'

Perfect time to ruin my life, I thought. Perfect time to ruin my appearance. My pulling power. My social life. My snogging skills. My . . . ohmigod, my *part* in *West Side Story*. No way can I go for the part of Maria. I'd be the laughing stock as soon as I opened my mouth to sing. In fact, instead of singing, 'There's a Place For Us', I'd have to sing, 'There's a Brace For Us'.

'No. I can't have a brace,' I said firmly. 'No, take all my teeth out and give me false ones. At least that way, I can still smile.'

Mr Saltman laughed again. 'It will only be for a year, Nesta. And so many people your age have them these days.'

Yes, but I'm not so many people, I thought.

'It won't be so bad,' continued Mr Saltman, 'and Mr Schneider will keep a close eye on you. You'll need to go for regular check-ups every few weeks.'

Nooooooooooooooooooooooooooooooo, I moaned inwardly. I thought I was through with dentists until the next check-up in six months. As I lay on the chair inwardly going through how my life was going to change, Mr Saltman's assistant had been out, then come back with what looked like a piece of plasticine on a tray. She put it in front of me.

'Oh dinner? No thanks,' I said holding my hand up. 'I'll pass.'

Mr Saltman held the gloop close to my mouth.

'Now bite in,' he said, 'and we'll get a nice imprint of your teeth.'

Dutifully I bit into the minty flavoured putty.

'Good girl,' said Mr Saltman. 'Now hold still until I say.'

That's it, I thought. My life is over. I shall never go out again. I shall do a Harry Potter and I don't mean go to Hogwart's and become a wizard. No, I shall voluntarily move into a cupboard under the stairs and not speak to anyone. Never show my face. Not for a year. Not until I can smile again. So the girls were right, I thought. I am shallow. I *do* care a lot about my appearance. I can't help it. I like boys noticing me. I like looking good. And now what? Who's going to give me a second look except to say, oh how awful. Have you SEEN that girl's metal teeth? And as for my stage career, this has put an end to all that for a while. No way I'm putting myself in the spotlight now. Huh. Life stinks.

As I waited for the impression to take, I glanced up at the poster of Steve Martin. I could swear he gave me a satisfied smile.

Izzie's Visualisation To Take Your Mind Off Bad Times

1) Lie back, close your eyes, uncross your legs and arms. Take three deep breaths right into your abdomen.

2) Think of a time when you were totally relaxed, confident and happy, perhaps by a beach or a river or in the garden in summer.

3) Visualise the colours in your scene, now turn them up, make them brighter in your mind.

4) Imagine the sounds: birds singing, leaves rustling or waves breaking on the shore. Turn the sounds up in your mind.

5) Imagine the smells: fresh cut grass, the scent of roses or the salty air at the sea. Turn the scents up in your mind.

6) Bring all the sounds, scents and sights together into a whole picture in your mind.

7) Fix this picture with a physical sign, ie: when you have the picture clear in your mind, make a gesture with your hands, either touch the thumb and index finger together or clench your fist. Every time you do this gesture in future, it will remind you of your positive feel-good visualisation and take you to a cool state of mind quickly.

Nesta's Visualisation For Relaxation

Forget Izzie's version. *Way* too complicated.

1) Lie back, close eyes. Imagine snogging your fave boy band pin-up and he's the best kisser you've ever come across in your whole life. May also help to imagine that you look your tip-top best at the time.

Chapter 4

Tragic
Heroine

Waiting for the date for the brace to be put in was like waiting for exam results and three very looooong weeks later, the dreaded deed was done. On Monday afternoon I went, like a man doomed to the guillotine, resigned to my terrible fate and, though I tried to be brave, even my snogging fantasy didn't help. I emerged from the orthodontist's looking to the world a normal teenager, but inside I was a wounded soul, cut down in the prime of my life. I returned home to take refuge in the only place where I would find solace for the next year. Under my duvet.

As soon as school was out, the crowds had gathered to mock.

'Come on, let us in,' called Izzie through my bedroom door.

'Yeah, you can't look that bad,' said Lucy.

'Yeah, come on Nesta,' said TJ. 'It's no big deal, honestly. Loads of people in school have them nowadays.'

'Yeah and loads of people have spots,' I called back. 'Doesn't mean I have to join them.'

Suddenly I heard a scuffle in the corridor outside my room, then Tony's voice, some stifled giggles, then footsteps retreating. Well, it didn't take them long to give up, I thought as I lay back on my bed in my best tragic heroine pose. When things are bad in my life, I sometimes try and pretend that I'm a character in a film and act through the feelings I'm experiencing. I racked my brains for an appropriate role. Heroine with a brace? Julia Roberts? Sandra Bullock? J-Lo? Hhmm? Parts with braces? Parts with braces? No, the only role that kept coming back was Anthony Hopkins as Hannibal Lecter in *Silence of the Lambs*, when he's in prison and has to wear a metal contraption over his jaw to stop him eating people.

I got up and went to the door to listen for clues as to what my mates were up to. Silence. Huh, I thought. Abandoned in my hour of need. I know I wouldn't let them in my room, but they should know well enough by now that I would have done in a few minutes. I just wanted them to appreciate how upsetting this all was. I'd been putting on a very brave face for the last few weeks since I heard I had to have a brace. Laughing it off, saying it was no big deal, I didn't care, etc. All lies, so that they wouldn't think that I was vain or shallow. But now it was in, on, or whatever, I couldn't keep up the act. I needed my mates to commiserate with and tell me that it was all going to be all right. I did care. It *did* hurt. Not so much when it was fitted, but afterwards. Strange and sharp in my mouth. Uncomfortable for a few days is what Mr Schneider had told me it would feel like. *Uncomfortable!* I think he needs to check his dictionary definitions. This isn't uncomfortable, it's agony, my gums ache like anything. And it didn't help that the first person I bumped into when I came out of Mr Scheider's surgery was Michael Brenman from Year Twelve. We had a very brief thing once (a snog) and he gave me a big flirty smile when he saw me. Course, all I saw were his perfect, white, straight teeth. I clamped my lips together and ran. Oh misery, I thought, is this what it's going to be like for the next year? Year. *Year?* That's three hundred and sixty-five days. Twelve months, fifty-two weeks of not being able to open my mouth when a cute boy is around. If ever there was a hell on earth, *this* is it.

I could hear footsteps returning, so I unlocked my door then leaped back on to the bed. Someone tried the handle, then on seeing that the door wasn't locked any more, Izzie stuck her head round. When she saw me lying there, she opened the door wide. Lucy, Izzie, TJ and Tony all stood in the frame of the doorway giggling like five-year-olds. Then they smiled. They all looked like they had no teeth.

I cracked up. Even though I'd been determined to keep up my tragic heroine act a little longer, I had to laugh (though I made sure I put my hand over my mouth as I did).

'All for one and one for all,' a toothless Lucy said with a grin.

'How did you do that?' I asked from behind my hand.

'Drinking chocolate,' said Tony. 'You put some in your mouth then sort of mush it up a bit, then put it on your teeth with your tongue.'

'Just to show that you're not alone,' said TJ.

'Hey, come on,' I said. 'I still have my teeth! It's only a brace.'

Izzie rubbed her tongue along her front teeth, turning them back to white. 'Exactly,' she said, then came over to sit next to me on the bed. 'So come on, give us a look.'

The others crowded round and stared at me, like they were waiting for a circus freak to begin his act. I shook my head.

'You're going to have to open your mouth sometime,' said Lucy. 'Come on, put your hand down.'

I shook my head again. 'It's horrible.'

'OK, then we'll all have to start talking like you, with

our hands over our mouths,' said Lucy. 'We'll start a new craze.'

They all started messing about, talking with their hands over their mouths. Maybe it's not so bad, I thought as I watched them all having a laugh. Maybe I can risk it.

'OK, I'll give you a quick look,' I said. I moved my hand away from my face, then attempted a smile.

Mistake. Not even Izzie was fast enough to cover her shocked reaction. '*Woah*,' she said.

'Wow,' said Lucy coming closer and staring at my teeth. 'Did it hurt a *lot*?'

'More now than when he put it on. It's kind of sore,' I said as I put my hand back over my mouth. 'My whole mouth aches. Does it look like . . . totally awful?'

By now Izzie had recovered. 'No, not *totally* awful. Just a shock at first as we're not used to it. But it's OK. And it's not the end of the world . . . You still look fabulous . . .'

'As long as I keep my mouth shut?'

Izzie nodded, then burst out laughing. 'Sorry, sorry,' she blustered, 'just people are always telling you to keep your mouth shut and now you're going to. Sorry. I wouldn't laugh if you were really hurt or something . . .'

I gave her arm a light slap. 'It's OK. I guess I wouldn't want you lying to me. I know it looks weird. They're called railway tracks because that's what they look like. I could have got coloured ones if I'd wanted, but I didn't want to draw more attention to them than necessary.'

'I don't know,' said TJ, 'Mary O'Connor has got pink and purple ones, I think they look really cool.'

'There's a brace for us,' sang Lucy to the tune of 'There's a Place For Us' from *West Side Story*. 'Somewhere . . . a brace for us.' They'd all thought it was really funny when I'd told them of my version of the song and hadn't stopped singing it since, whenever they saw me, in fact.

'A brace is a brace is a brace, whatever colour it is,' I said.

'Not necessarily,' said Tony. 'Henry, a guy at our school, has a Tom Cruise.'

'Which is?' I asked.

'An invisible brace, transparent. Apparently Tom Cruise had one but they cost a fortune. Henry's parents are loaded though.'

'It will be all right,' said Lucy. 'You'll get used to it soon. It's like when you have a bad haircut, you feel you can never go out again but you do.'

'That's because your hair grows again,' I said.

'No,' Lucy insisted. 'It's because you get used to it.'

'Yeah,' said Izzie, 'and you have so much else going for you, great legs, great body, great hair. No one will ever even notice your teeth.'

Their words of support weren't helping. 'No boy will ever fancy me again,' I said with a groan. 'I will have to live the life of a nun for a year like Julie Andrews in *The Sound of Music*.'

Lucy picked up a towel from the chest of drawers and

put it over her head. 'Cliiiimb eveeeery mountaaaain, follow eeeeery streeeeam . . .' she warbled in a soprano voice.

'We thought you might want to go to Hampstead. Cruise the shops,' said TJ. 'Cheer you up a bit.'

'Can't,' I said, lying back on the bed. 'My former life is over.'

'Nah,' said Lucy. 'Something will happen. As Mum always says, life never closes a door without opening a window.'

I shook my head. 'Yeah, right. And there's light at the end of the tunnel.'

'That's the attitude,' said Izzie.

'Yeah. The light at the end of the tunnel is an oncoming train.'

Izzie laughed at our old joke. 'Oh, it will be all right,' she said.

'No it won't. From now on, I'm going to be a recluse.'

'OK,' said Izzie, lying next to me. 'We'll be recluses with you.'

Tony went to make hot chocolate for all of us (part of his trying-to-impress-Lucy act), then we lay around listening to sad songs about loneliness and generally feeling dejected. Even though I was really the only one who had anything to feel tragic about, it was nice that they tried to share it with me. Tony brought in an opera CD, which he said was about a real tragic heroine (as if I wasn't) singing about despair. However, by this time, I was beginning to get bored with moping about, and listening to the opera singer screeching away was the last straw.

'What I don't understand about opera,' I said, 'is why, just when the heroine discovers that she's about to die of some terrible lung disease, she sings her head off for another hour. Get on, die and put us all out of our misery, I say.'

'I'll second that,' said Lucy.

'So does this mean that you've had enough of being a recluse then?' asked TJ.

'Dunno, maybe,' I said. 'Yeah. Brace or no brace, this being tragic lark's a bit boring.'

'So what shall we do then?' asked Lucy.

'Movie,' said Izzie.

'Movie,' chorused TJ and Lucy.

Half an hour later, we were coming out of the local library with the DVD, *Godfather II*. TJ loves this film. She's seen it five times already, mainly because she's in love with Robert de Niro. Hmm. Each to their own, I thought, he's not my fave fantasy babe, *way* too old! Next stop was the pizza shop. This is more like it, I thought, as we made our way through the entrance hall of the library, you've got to still have fun, no matter what life throws at you.

Izzie stopped to look at the notices on the board. They advertise all sorts of the stuff that she's into. T'ai chi, crystal healing, astrology, massage.

'Hey, check this out,' she said as she scanned the board. 'It might be just the thing for you, Nesta.'

I went over to join her and read the notice.

Acting for All. *Wednesday nights, 7–8.30. A fun and relaxed class given by a professional actor. Improvisation, drama games, vocal technique and script work. Everyone welcome from beginners to working actors wanting to refresh their skills. £5 per session.*

'Five quid,' said Izzie. 'That's cheap.'

'A lot of the council-run courses are,' said Lucy. 'My mum said they try to make them accessible for everyone.'

'Yeah,' I said, 'sounds good. And it would be good use of my brace time. I mean, no way I can perform in publico like in *West Side Story*, but to do a class away from school where I don't know anyone, that would be cool.'

'I still think that you should go for the part in *West Side Story*,' said Izzie.

'And I think you should stand on your head and wave your knickers in the air,' I replied, 'but neither of us are going to do it, are we?'

Izzie went to do a handstand right there, up against the wall in the library, but I pulled her back. 'No, no, I didn't mean it. But no way am I going for the part. I told you. I don't want anyone looking at me, but . . .' I glanced back at the noticeboard, 'this course looks interesting.'

'Yeah,' said TJ, 'but the people that do these courses are usually middle-aged and decrepit . . .'

'Exactly,' I said. 'No chance of humiliating myself in front of any cute boys of our age then. No, I think it will be brilliant. Just the thing. Excellento.'

Izzie laughed. 'You know what I love about you?'

'What?'

'The way you can go from total misery to total elation, all in the space of a day.'

'All in the space of five minutes sometimes.' I smiled back at her from behind my hand. I was feeling a million times better than earlier this afternoon. 'My mum says that when life throws you a lemon, you have to make lemonade. My brace is the lemon, doing this course would be making lemonade, if you know what I mean. It would be a way of using my time constructively. Only one thing would make it better . . .'

'What?' asked Lucy.

'If one of you guys would do the course as well.'

'Not me,' said TJ. 'I have to work on the school magazine Wednesday nights.'

'And I said I'd help Dad restock the shop on Wednesday nights this term,' said Lucy. Her dad runs the local health food shop and putting in some hours there is one way Lucy can pick up some spare cash. 'Sorry, Nesta.'

'No prob.' I turned to Izzie.

'But I don't want to be an actress,' she said heading for the door. 'I want to be a singer songwriter.'

'Ah,' I said, 'but think Kylie, think Madonna, think J-Lo.'

'What about them?'

'They're all actresses as well as singers. My dad's always saying that working in any part of the media can be feast or famine until you make it big. It's good to have a few strings to your bow. And loads of singers have acted in films as well as pursued their song writing. Come on Iz, it would be another thing that you can offer when you're famous.'

I could see Izzie was thinking about it. One of the things I like about her is that she is into learning about so many things. She's totally open-minded . . . which made me think, I know just how to persuade her . . .

'Thing is, with learning,' I began, 'you can never stop. You can never think that you're there. It's like, you can always improve your performance skills whether it's for stage, singing or acting . . .'

Izzie sighed. 'OK. Enough. You're on. I'm in.'

'Excellent,' I said. 'See Lucy, your mum was right, life never closes a wotsit without opening another wotsit.'

Life never closes a door without opening a window.

Chapter 5

Ding
Dong

'Sorry, Nesta love, I thought you understood,' said Mum when I got home and told her about the classes.

'But it's only five pounds for each class. That's pretty good value.'

'I know, but add that up over a term . . .'

'Don't worry,' I interrupted. She looked sad and I didn't want her to feel like that. 'It doesn't matter.'

I went to my room to mope, but I wasn't in the mood for being miserable. Been there, done that. Got the T-shirt. I found it a humongous waste of time in fact. I lay back on my bed and had a good think. Ways of getting money. Hhmm. Well, I know one thing not to do again and that's gamble. Earlier this year, I spent all my savings on Scratch cards. Lost the lot, so I won't be doing that again. No, there must be some job I can do, babysitting or something. Suddenly a light switched on in my head. Course, that's it, I thought as I quickly dialled Lucy's number.

'Hey, Nesta,' said Lucy when she picked up the phone. 'What can I do for you?'

'Actually, Luce, more like what can I do for you? Or more, for your dad that is. Does he need any other workers to do restocking in the shop.'

'He does actually. On Fridays.'

'How much?'

'He pays me five quid an hour. Two hours ten quid.'

'Ask if he'll give me a job.'

I heard Lucy yell at the other end of the phone. 'Dad, can Nesta have a job restocking on Friday nights?'

I heard a distant voice yell back. 'Yes. The more the merrier.'

Lucy came back on the phone. 'Sorted, mate.'

'Excellent. Another string to my bow. Shelf stacker.'

'I'll do some hours with you as well as my Wednesday,' said Lucy. 'Be fun if we're both doing it.'

Ha, I thought as I put the phone down. Where there's a will, there's a way. And it's part of the process according to my dad. He says that loads of great movie stars start out working in dead end jobs, so that they can pay their way before their big break.

★ ★ ★

The following Wednesday, Izzie and I pitched up for our first acting class. It was to be held in Muswell Hill in a place that was an ordinary school in the day time and used for adult education in the evenings.

'That has to be it,' said Izzie as we approached a four storey building. 'It looks like a school with all those windows.'

'And it looks like ours isn't the only night course being held here,' I said. Music was pounding out from every level and we could see girls in leotards ballet dancing on one floor, another bunch jazz dancing on another, others kick-boxing on the ground floor. 'Looks like lots of girls come here, hope there won't be too many boys.'

'Speak for yourself,' said Izzie. 'You may be having a year off boys, but I'm not.'

After signing in at reception, we made our way up to the first floor where our class was to be held. As we waited for the ballet class to finish, a group of people began to assemble outside the door.

Excellent, I thought as I watched them arrive and, like Izzie and me, smile apprehensively at the rest of the group. A bald guy with a beard, a petite white-haired lady, two curly-haired twenty-year-olds, maybe sisters, a chubby guy with glasses, probably in his forties. A couple more middle-aged ladies. Couple more guys, probably in their thirties. Excellent, I thought. Not one cute boy in sight.

Our teacher was a slim red-headed woman in her late twenties called Jo. She started us off with a few introduction games. First we had to say our names and five things about ourselves. I was third.

'Nesta. Star sign Leo. Fave band, Red Hot Chili Peppers. Fave TV programme, *The Simpsons*. Fave food, pizza. Live in Highgate.'

The introductions were a bit of a blur and, by the end of it, I'd only got about four people's names.

Then we had to say our name again and do an action that started with the same letter as your name.

'Make it as mad as you like,' said Jo.

Everyone seemed a bit shy at first, so I decided to start us off as we've done stuff like this in drama at school.

'Nesta. Napping,' I said, then closed my eyes and put my head on one side.

Izzie went next. 'Izzie: itching.' That got a laugh as she played out scratching herself all over. After that the others were off.

'Jan: jumping.'

'Dave: drawing.'

'Catherine: canoeing.'

There were twelve of us in all and the game seemed to do the trick as, afterwards, most of us found we could remember most people's names.

I'm going to enjoy this, I thought as Jo asked us to stand anywhere in the room.

'Choose a character,' she said, 'male or female, any age, then walk round the room as you imagine they would.'

I decided to do a bloke I'd seen walking down Archway Road last week. He walked like a gorilla with a swagger. A real tough man. After we'd swaggered, minced, strode, tiptoed round for a while, Jo asked us to lie on the floor and go to sleep in the manner of our character. I lay in the corner and started snoring. After a while, Jo said, 'OK, now it's six a.m. What's your character doing now?'

I heard a few people get up but I stayed where I was. No way, my character would be out of bed yet. He was a yob. Probably didn't even know that there were two six o'clocks in a day.

Jo went on. 'And now it's seven a.m.' I could hear more people get up. When she said, 'Eight,' even more got up. As she said, 'Nine,' then, 'Ten,' then, 'Eleven. What's your character doing now?' I could hear that everyone was up. I opened my eyes and sneaked a look. My fellow luvvies were acting their socks off, miming driving, typing, on the phone, eating, talking, having a life.

'OK, twelve o'clock and what are your characters doing now?' said Jo. 'Er, on the floor, Napping Nesta isn't it? Is there a problem? I see your character hasn't done anything? Are you stuck about what to do?'

'Oh no,' I said. 'My character's a lazy yob and never gets out of bed before one.'

In the corner, Izzie cracked up.

'OK,' said Jo. 'Maybe your yob could get up a bit earlier today so that you get something out of the exercise.'

'OK,' I said. I got up, mimed having a fag, lay about, scratched a bit, watched telly and studied the others. Some people were really going for it. Bet they're sorry they picked such overactive characters, I thought as I mimed having another fag.

When we'd all finished our day, everyone had to say what character they'd been doing. Izzie, poor thing, had played her mum and had had to get up at six-thirty to go to work. She had her mum's walk down really well though.

'People think that acting is about learning lines,' said Jo, 'and to some degree of course, it is. But there's so much more to it than that, which is why I wanted to start with this exercise. Think about it. Before someone has even opened their mouth, other people have made an assessment or a judgement. Why is it, we steer away from certain people on the street, others we feel are OK?'

'Clothes, image,' I said. 'Your choice of style says a lot about you.'

'Yes, but even more than that,' said Jo. 'Any ideas?'

'Body language,' said Jan, the white-haired lady.

'Exactly,' said Jo. 'How people walk, how they sit, how they hold themselves, says infinitely more than what they choose to verbalise or choose to wear. In the same way, if you want to act, your audience has to know who your character is the second you walk on the stage, way before you begin to say your lines. It's not enough to just put on a costume. You can't just walk on as you in another person's clothes and expect to be believed as someone else.'

What Jo said was very true, I thought. One of the things I love doing is sitting in cafés watching people go by and I've always thought that you can tell so much about them by how they walk, whether they scrunch their shoulders up, if they stride or dawdle. Like even at school, without visuals, you can tell which teacher is coming along the corridor by the sound of their footsteps. Mrs Allen's are really quick, confident, like she doesn't have time to waste. Click, clack, click. Miss Watkins' are slower, more considered, sort of ploddy, like she is. I'm going to really watch people and how they walk from now on, I decided, so that I can put it into practice for different roles in my acting career.

After the 'character' exercise, we played some games where we had to close our eyes and wander round the room trying to work out where other people were by the sounds they made. At first I couldn't see the point of it, but afterwards Jo explained that one of the first things you had to learn on stage was awareness of other actors. 'So many people are so concerned about doing their bit, their moment in the spotlight, that they forget that they're part of a team.'

By the end of the class, I was well impressed. I felt I'd learned loads in just over an hour and still had much, much more to discover.

'That was five quid well spent,' I whispered to Izzie as we got our coats to leave at the end. She nodded and, as I turned to the windowsill to get my scarf, I was aware that someone had walked in behind us.

Izzie nudged me. 'Eyes left,' she said. 'Ding *do-nnggg*.'

Ding dong is our new alert for when there's talent around. Lucy's brother Lal started it after he'd watched the movie, *Carry On Nurse*. Leslie Phillips plays a character called Jack Bell in the film and he says, 'Ding dong' whenever he sees someone he fancies. We've all started saying it now along with, 'Oo, matron!', an expression used by the character played by Kenneth Williams in later *Carry On* films. People at school think we're mad, but we all think it's hysterically funny especially if Mrs Allen is reading out something really serious and Lucy, TJ, Izzie and I all turn to each other and mouth, 'Oo, matron!'

I turned to see a boy going up to Jo. I couldn't see his face, but from the back he had dark hair and was wearing a calf-length tweedy coat and a red scarf. Trained up as I was now, I could tell just by his body language that he was flustered. Izzie and I strained to hear what he was saying.

'I'm *so* sorry,' he said. 'I went to the wrong place. I thought the class was at the Institute so I went there then by the time I discovered I was in the wrong place, the class here had already started. I tried to get here, but I had to wait ages for a bus and . . .'

Jo smiled at him. 'No problem. At least now you know where we are for next week.' She checked her list. 'You must be . . . Luke.'

'Yeah. Luke De Biasi.'

'Well, it's a bit late to introduce you now,' said Jo indicating the rest of us, 'as we're all just leaving, but these are the people who will be in the class with you.'

As Luke turned round to look at the group, I quickly turned away, so that he wouldn't catch me staring. Izzie wasn't as cool. She dug her elbow into my back and whispered, 'Hubba hubba.'

I couldn't resist, so turned for a quick peek at him. When I saw his face, my peek became a look that lasted . . . and lasted . . . I couldn't help it. I knew that I ought to look away, but something in his eyes held me like a magnet. Time slowed down and my heart seemed to speed up. It was like Luke and I were the only two people in the room. Finally I broke his gaze and ran.

Ding *dong*: – talent in the vicinity.
Hubba bubba: – cor! He's tasty.
Oo, matron!: – oo, *er*!

Chapter 6

Oo, Matron!

Aghhhhhhhhhhhhhhhhhhhhh. Ugggggggggg. *Arghhhhhhhhhh*. That's all I can say, I thought, as I stared at my reflection in the wardrobe mirror before I got into bed later that night. Sometimes life is so unfair. Why, oh *why* would I have to see the boy of my dreams when I look like a tin opener? We haven't even met properly. We haven't *even* spoken and yet I know that he's special. I felt like I'd seen him before, then I remembered where. TJ's house. There's a painting in their hall. TJ said it's by a Pre-Raphaelite painter called Edward Burne-Jones and it's called 'The Tree of Forgiveness'. Anyway, Luke looks like the man in it. Dark eyes, high cheek bones, wide mouth and I loved the coat he wore to the drama class. It looked like vintage American, like the ones that men wore in old black and white movie classics. Really cool. I smiled at my reflection again. The killer shark from the film *Jaws* grimaced back at me. No. There was no getting away from it. I looked horrible. The girls may say I have other things going for me but, when I open my mouth, all you see is the brace. It's like, you can have a huge fifty foot white wall but, if there's one black dot on it, that's what your eye will be drawn towards. So agh. Ug. Argh. And, as Izzie would say, poo.

Luke. I could still see him in my mind's eye. Aristocratic-looking. Roman-looking in fact. His name is Italian. Luke De Biasi. Probably called Luca at home. He was very good-looking, but more than that, and I know Izzie would laugh at me for saying it, he looked intelligent. He did. There was something in his eyes. And I don't mean contact lenses.

Anyway that's the last time I'll see him, I thought, because no way can I go back to that class if he's going to be in it. I'll have to wait a year and bump into him when I've had my brace off and can smile at people and talk to them again.

Izzie said I was being stupid when I told her that I wasn't going back. Honestly, and she has the cheek to say that I'm blunt sometimes. Calling me stupid. Huh! That's not exactly tact city. She doesn't understand. I could never relax in class knowing that he was there, watching me, thinking nice face, shame about the metal munchers. No,

I couldn't possibly. I know that boys imagine snogging as well as girls, but I can't believe that braces figure highly on the fave fantasy girl requirement list. Like: nice hair, good legs, great bod, attractive mouth, brace.

I don't know. Maybe I *could* go back to class. I could be a quiet member of the group. An observer. There to learn. I could be silent. Never open my mouth. I could be mysterious. Enigmatic.

Hah! Who am I kidding? Gobby is my middle name.

I spent a few minutes practising my closed mouth smile in the mirror as I considered my options.

Forget him? Not an option.

Postpone meeting him until the brace is removed? No. Can't do that. He might have a girlfriend by then. Yikes. He might have a girlfriend *now*! Of course he might. Probably does. All the more reason for *not* postponing meeting him. I have to find out where I stand.

Go to class but disguise the fact I have a brace in. Hhhmm. Maybe. Yes. I think that's the best plan. Is it? Isn't it? I know! I could get one of those head-to-toe tent dresses that some Muslim women wear to cover themselves. I could pretend I'm a new girl in class and I *am* Muslim. Yes! That's it. No one would ever know. Izzie could just say that Nesta decided not to do the class any more, but another friend of hers has come instead. Her *Muslim* friend, Mustapha Bracein. Then I could watch him from inside my dress. Burkas, I think they're called.

Yeah. Brilliant idea. Or is it? Hhmm. Best sleep on it, I thought, I can't decide now and if I try to, I think I may well blow a fuse in my brain.

I woke up the next morning with the solution. Or solutions. Disguise, distraction and decoys. My first plan was to wear a balaclava not a burka. Tony's got one for when he eventually gets to go skiing. He is funny. He knows Mum hasn't got the money to pay for him to go and he hasn't got any of the really expensive equipment he needs, but he has got a balaclava. Izzie told him that he had to start somewhere and that sometimes if you make a symbolic step towards your goal/dream or whatever, the universe conspires to make it happen. Yeah, right. Mystic Izzie. She's bonkers. Anyway, Tony let me borrow his strange but symbolic woolly hat, but sadly it didn't go down too well at school.

'Nesta Williams, can you give me any explanation as to why you find it necessary to wear a woolly hat in the art class?' asked Mrs Elwes.

'It's a balaclava, Miss.'

'I don't care what it is. You're not wearing it in my class.'

'Yes, Miss.'

My next tactic didn't go down too well either.

'And what period are we studying in history at the moment, Nesta?' asked Miss Watkins.

'Tudors, Miss.'

'Not the Egyptians?'

'No, Miss.'

'Then perhaps you could explain why you have a scarf wrapped around your neck and face in the manner of an Egyptian mummy.'

'I'm cold, Miss.'

'So get a thermal vest, girl. In the meantime, take off the scarf. I like to be able to see the faces of my pupils when I'm teaching. To make sure that they're still awake.'

Lucy thought it was hysterical. 'You in a thermal vest,' she said as we made our way out of school in the afternoon. 'That I'd like to see.'

'No *way*. So uncool,' I said.

'Thermal vest, so uncool. Course they are, that's why they're thermal. Oh very good, Nesta,' said Lucy laughing her head off. Sometimes I think she takes too many vitamins or something. It seems that all my friends are mad. Apart from TJ maybe, but give it time.

'So what's with all the headgear today?' asked TJ.

'I'm trying a few things out before the next acting class,' I said. 'To disguise my brace.' Of course, I'd filled TJ and Lucy in on meeting Luke as soon as I'd got home last night. They were very sympathetic, but both of them thought I should go back to the class and not consider giving it up for a moment.

'If this guy is worth bothering about,' said TJ, 'he's not

going to be put off by your brace. I think you should be brave. Be who and what you are and if he doesn't like it, forget him.'

'I guess you're right on one level,' I said. 'But on another level, boys are highly visual. They go on what they see and if they like it. The time for being who you are, hairy legs, strange habits, brace or whatever, comes later. First you have to lure them in . . . You know that, TJ.'

TJ sighed and nodded. At the end of Year Nine, she had a crush on a boy who lived next door to her. Only problem was that he saw her as one of the lads, a mate, so she had to seriously reconsider her image and get him to see her as a girl. It worked too except, once he was interested, she realised that he was *really* boring.

'Yeah,' said TJ. 'I think it's sad but true. Boys do like girls who look like girls.'

'Exactly,' I said. And then I had my most brilliant idea.

Half an hour later, we were in the lingerie department of a store at the Mall.

'And are you going to explain why having a brace put in has resulted in a strange compulsion to buy underwear?' asked Lucy.

'Distraction,' I said. 'Obvious isn't it?'

'Yes, shopping is always a good distraction . . .'

'Not for *us*. For boys,' I explained. 'See, it was when TJ said that boys like girls who look like girls that I realised, that's what I have to do. Get boys distracted from my face and the way to do that is . . .' I indicated the racks of gorgeous girlie underwear.

'Show them your knickers?' asked Lucy.

'*No.*'

Lucy laughed. 'Wear your knickers on your head? That would cover your brace.'

'*Noooo.* Don't be mad. I mean, show them my chesty bits. Have you ever been with a boy when you're showing even the tiniest bit of cleavage?'

'The *tiniest* bit of cleavage is sadly all I've got,' sighed Lucy as she eyed the rails.

Izzie nodded. 'Yeah, it's like their eyes are pulled towards it by some magnetic force. They can't help it. When I wore a low top to band rehearsal one evening, it was hysterical. The boys were doing their best not to look, but I could see their cheeks starting to twitch with the effort. Biff didn't even try not to look. He just talked to my chest all night.'

'I hate that,' said TJ. 'It's like you're a walking pair of boobs and nothing else.'

Lucy grinned. 'You know that song by Frank Sinatra's daughter Nancy, "These Boots Are Made For Walking"? We ought to sing, "These Boobs Are Made For Walking".'

TJ patted her on the head. 'Keep taking the tablets, Lucy,' she said.

'Boys can't help it,' I said. 'It's their hormones. I know

sometimes it's horrible being leered at, but it can be used to your advantage. Like my next meeting with Luke. My plan is to buy the most uplifting fab-shaped bra there is in this shop then wear it, so that he will be so busy looking at my marvellous chest that he won't notice that my mouth is full of metal.'

'He's going to look up sometime, Nesta,' said TJ.

'And when he does, I'll shut my mouth. I'll only talk when he's looking at my cleavage.'

'You're bonkers,' laughed Izzie.

No, I'm not. It's simple, I thought. That is until we started to look for the bra. After fifteen minutes I was totally confused. There were rails and rails of them. Not just colours and fabrics but types: bras for total support, egoboosters, minimisers, bras with no front, no back, balcony bras, wired, plunge, moulded, padded, seamed, non-padded, five-way, sheer, strapless, halter-neck, crossover, one-shoulder, bioform, sculptured, push up, multiway, T-shirt, sports, stretch cup. They even had thermal ones.

'Arghhhhhh,' I cried. 'I've seen Hitchcock's film, *The Birds*. But now showing at a store near you. *The Bras*. They're mean, they're keen, they're taking over.'

TJ, Izzie and Lucy cracked up laughing as I swung five bras up in the air and made them fly like birds.

A shop assistant gave me a funny look, so I put the bras back on the rails. 'But how are you supposed to know which one is best?' I asked. 'Do I need a bioform or a five-way push up?'

'I would imagine five-way push ups are for aliens,' said Lucy. 'As they are the only beings who could possibly have five boobs to push up.'

This time it was Izzie who patted her on the head. 'Poor dear,' she said. 'We really ought not to let you out again.'

TJ pointed at a notice on the wall and began to laugh. 'God. Have you seen this?'

We gathered round to read the notice. 'How to calculate your bra size,' it said.

'First you need a degree in maths,' said TJ. 'Measure your ribcage, add four for an even number, five for an odd number. Measure your full bust then subtract the bra size from the full size to give you your cup size.'

There was a tape measure on the wall next to the notice.

TJ got out her calculator. 'You measure and I'll calculate,' she said.

Lucy got out some paper and wrote as I measured my ribcage then round my bust. 'Why are bras sold in inches when the rest of the world has gone metric?' she asked.

'Dunno,' I said. 'But all I wanted was to buy a bra. Not do an engineering class.'

TJ ignored me. 'Thirty-two B,' she said after a few moments. 'Easy.'

'Yeah. That's what my mum always gets me and her method is very scientific. She guesses it. Easy.'

We picked out a few bras, but in the end decided that the 'egobooster' looked like it might give the best cleavage effect. I picked one from the rails, took it into the dressing room and tried it on.

'Oo, matron!' the girls chorused as they stuck their heads round the curtain five minutes later.

'Too much?' I asked as I took in my reflection.

'You could get a leading role in *Lethal Weapon 2*,' said TJ laughing.

'Only it would be called *Lethal Weapons, I Have Two*,' said Lucy.

'Well I think it will definitely distract him,' said Izzie, 'but it might be a bit obvious turning up to class in that when the majority of the other people are middle-aged and dressed in baggy tracksuits.'

I sighed. 'So what next?' I asked. 'I've tried headgear. Bras. Scarves.'

'You could pretend that you're dumb,' said TJ.

'*Brilliant* idea!' I said. 'I could learn sign language.'

TJ looked taken aback. 'I was joking,' she said.

'Anyway, the rest of the class know you can speak from last week,' said Izzie.

I felt miserable. All my good ideas had come to nothing. I would just have to talk with my hand over my mouth or perfect the art of talking through closed lips.

Nope. Even I knew that no way was I going to be able to do that in an acting class. No. It was too sad, but I would have to resort back to option B. Oh cruel world, I thought. I would have to let Luke go and not go back to the class at all. True love was not meant to be mine. I would just have to grow old with my memories of how it could have been. On the other hand, it would make me more beautiful as people would be able to sense my loss, the sadness behind the smiles, the inner wistfulness behind the mask of success. Yes, mine would be a high but lonely destiny.

I sniffed and tried to look noble. 'It happens in all the best movies you know? In *Dr Zhivago*, after many years apart, he sees Lara, the love of his life, at the end. He jumps off a bus to try and catch her but, too late, he has a heart attack and dies on the pavement and she never knows how close he was. And in *Wuthering Heights*, Cathy dies leaving her one true love, Heathcliff, heartbroken forever. Sometimes it's not meant to be . . .'

Izzie raised her eyes to the ceiling. 'Oh for Gawd's sake. Nesta. Luvvie. Dwarling. You've got a *brace*, not a noose around your neck. You are not dead. Luke is not dead. Life is not over.'

'You don't understand the pain of unrequited love,' I said through closed lips. 'Or true passion.'

Izzie turned and grinned at TJ and Lucy. 'True passion? Oh yes I do. And two words sum it up. Chocolate fudge.'

'Yeah, bugger unrequited love and passion,' said Lucy. 'Chocolate never lets you down. And it doesn't care what your teeth look like. Come on. Food department. Now.'

'Best idea you've had all day,' said TJ and the three of them headed off for the chocolate counters like homing pigeons. Huh, I thought as I watched them charge off. Am I misunderstood or what? But what can you do? I thought as I hurried to catch them up. If you can't beat them, join them.

How to Measure for a Bra

1) Measure in inches around the ribcage directly under your boobs.
2) If it's an odd number, add 5 inches, if it's an even number, add 4 inches.
3) This gives you your bra size (e.g., 31 inches + 5 inches = 36 inches, or 34 inches + 4 inches = 38 inches).
4) Then measure the fullest part of your bust. The difference between the full bust measurement and the bra size measurement gives you your cup size. For instance:

1 inch smaller than bra size = AA-cup size
Same as bra size = A-cup
1 inch bigger than bra size = B-cup
2 inch bigger than bra size = C-cup
3 inch bigger than bra size = D-cup
4 inch bigger than bra size = DD-cup
5 inch bigger than bra size = E-cup
6 inch bigger than bra size = F-cup
7 inch bigger than bra size = G-cup
and any bigger that that, you need an
over-the-shoulder boulder holder, not a bra.

Note from Nesta: *Whadttttt*? Forget all that. Most large department stores offer a professional measuring service for bra sizes for free. Sounds good to me.

Chapter 7

Wahey and Hurrahalot

Life is full of surprises.

My brother Tony takes girl chasing seriously. *Very* seriously. Girls are his favourite hobby and he likes to think of himself as the Casanova of North London. The pro. The Master. He who knows about girls. Part of me thinks that it's hysterical as I live with him. I've seen him in the morning when he's just woken up (not a pretty sight). I've seen him when he's been ill and wants his mum (also not a pretty sight). But another part of me has to hand it to him. His dedication to his art does seem to pay off and there's always a queue of girls desperate for his attention. Part of his girl chasing degree has been researching the perfect place to take a girl for a romantic evening. And he thinks he's found it.

'I read a review in the local paper,' he said. 'Family run restaurant, intimate, unpretentious, slightly bohemian, fab food and not too expensive. Voted the area's favourite restaurant by locals for five years running.'

'And?'

'I need you to come and give me your opinion before I book it for . . .'

'You and Lucy?'

He nodded. 'Yeah, if she'll come.'

'Sure.'

So there I was on Friday evening waiting in a restaurant for my brother who, as usual, was late. I didn't mind too much though as I'd spent the last hour stacking shelves at Lucy's dad's shop and it was good to sit down and relax. Quite a funky-looking place, I thought as I scraped some wax off the wine bottle that served as a candle holder in front of me. There were red and white gingham cloths on the tables and the walls were a colourful mishmash of amateur paintings, faded photos of people from times gone by, postcards from all over the world. All were fighting for space and none were winning.

'Would you like to order?' said a voice to my right.

'Um. I'm waiting for someone,' I said looking up. When I saw who it was, I clapped my hand over my mouth. '*You*!'

It was Luke. Even in his waiter's apron, he looked Pre-Raphaelite and gorgeous.

He laughed and placed a basket of bread and a small bowl of olive oil in front of me. 'Yeah. It's me. Why? What did I do?'

'Oh, nothing,' I said from behind my hand. 'Just . . . you're the guy from class the other night. What are you doing here?'

'I work here two nights a week. What's your excuse?'

'Waiting for my brother.'

Ohmigod, ohmigod, ohmigod, I thought, as my heart started thumping in my chest. This is what Iz is always on about. Fate. Just as I'd decided to be all tragic and never see Luke again, destiny decides otherwise. Wahey and hurrahalot. Let's hear it for destiny.

'OK,' he said getting out his note-pad. 'So what would you like while you're waiting?'

I suppose a snog's out of the question, I thought before I could stop myself. I almost blushed then told myself, no relax, Nesta. He can't read your mind.

'Appuchino,' I muttered.

'Pardon?'

'Carperino.'

'Sorry, I can't understand what you're saying. Your hand seems to be superglued to your top lip . . .'

I put my hand down and attempted to speak without opening my mouth. 'Uepurino,' I said.

Luke looked knowingly at me. 'Brace, huh?' he said gently.

Uh? Am I *that* obvious? 'No. Yeah. How did you know?'

Luke pointed behind him to a very pretty dark-haired girl behind the counter. 'Marisa. She had one until last month. She did the same. Hid behind her hand.'

My heart sank. She was gorgeous. Obviously his girlfriend as she smiled when he turned to look at her.

'So she works here too?'

Luke nodded. 'It's our dad's restaurant . . .'

His *sister*?! Yabadabadoo.

'It's well worth it, you know,' continued Luke.

'Owning a restaurant?'

'*No*. Having a brace.' He called Marisa over. 'Hey, Marisa, this is . . . I don't know your name.'

'Nesta,' I said from behind my hand.

'Brace,' said Marisa.

I nodded.

'Just in?'

I nodded again. 'Week almost.'

She gave me a huge smile revealing perfect teeth. 'It's worth it in the end, but it's awful when it first goes in. Feels like everyone's looking at you.'

I nodded.

'People don't even notice,' said Luke. 'I never really noticed Marisa's. I think she was more conscious of it than anyone.'

'So how do you two know each other?' asked Marisa.

Luke looked around as though looking for someone then whispered, 'We're doing the same course.'

'Why the secrecy?' I whispered back.

'You tell her,' said Marisa. 'What do you want, Nesta?'

'Cappuccino, thanks,' I said.

Luke turned to go, but Marisa pulled him back. 'No, Luca, you sit, it's quiet. Explain.'

After she'd disappeared, Luke sat opposite me. As soon as he looked into my eyes, I felt myself getting hot and my insides felt like they were melting. He was amazing looking. Sooooooo beautiful. I hadn't imagined it. It's a weird thing that when I first meet someone, I can remember what they look like for about a day, then it fades, like from sharp focus to blurry. Seeing him again was a real blast back to picture perfect.

Luke looked down at the table. 'I'm supposed to be doing an accountancy course.'

'Oh . . . and?'

'On *Wednesday* nights . . .'

'Ah.' Oh well done on the brilliant conversation, Nesta, I thought. Oh. And. Ah. Yes, riveting stuff. Luckily, he didn't seem to notice.

'Yeah. Ah,' continued Luke. 'Dad's in the restaurant business. He has three now. This one which has been here for years, one in Soho and he's just opened a third up near Harrow, not far from where I go to school actually. It's quite handy for popping into at lunch-time. Anyway, my brother runs the Soho restaurant and Dad wants me to be involved when I leave school after my A-levels, maybe oversee the Harrow one. I want to act. It's all I've ever wanted to do but he's dead against it. So . . . I told him I was going to do accountancy to help with the business when, in fact, I'm doing acting. That's why I was late last week. Dad dropped me off at the accountancy course and I had to dash like mad to get to the acting.'

'But what will happen if he drops you every week? You'll never make it.'

'It was just last week. My car was being serviced, but I've got it back now and can drive myself.'

Hhmm. Is gorgeous *and* has own car, I thought. Not that I am influenced by things like that at all. Not at *all*. I am *deep* and *beyond* material trappings. But . . . hhmm . . . I wonder what kind of car?

'But . . . what are you going to do at the end of the course when you haven't learned anything about figures?'

Luke laughed. 'I shall act dumb. By then, I should have the skills.' Then he shrugged. 'Dunno. I'll think of something.'

After that, we chatted for a while about acting and films and which he liked and which he hated. As we talked I realised that he knew a lot about them. He mentioned films I'd never heard of and he seemed to know who had directed them and who had produced them. As I listened to him, I began to feel out of my depth, because I watch films just for fun. That awful feeling that I might be shallow and boring came creeping back and I resolved to swot up on who was who and what was what in the film industry. Hhhmm, how can I impress you without revealing that I don't know half as much about films as you do, I wondered as I stared at his bottom lip and tried to commit it to memory.

Suddenly what to say was obvious.

'My dad's a director,' I blurted out.

'Really? Wow!' said Luke. 'Lucky you. Films, TV or documentary?'

'TV mostly. Dramas. But I think he'd like to do a film, you know, for the big screen.'

Luke nodded. 'Must be amazing. And there was me rabbiting on about films when you're the real expert with your dad in the biz.'

Yeah, right. Me the expert, I thought as I gave him my lips-closed smile.

'I wish my father did something interesting,' continued Luke. 'I can't tell you how much I don't want to be involved in his restaurant business.'

'But involved how? What does he want you to be? Chef? Manager?'

'Bit of both. That's how it is in a family business.'

I couldn't resist. I stuffed two big bits of bread in front of my teeth in my lower cheeks then attempted my impersonation of Marlon Brando as he was in *The*

Godfather. 'So, Luca, de family needs you,' I drawled in an Italian accent.

He laughed. 'Excellent,' he said. 'Marlon Brando. *The Godfather?*'

I nodded and desperately tried to swallow the bread, praying that it hadn't got caught in my brace. How attractive would that be? Not. I put my hand back over my mouth just in case.

'Can you cook?' I asked.

'I'm Italian. Course I can.'

'I'm half Italian,' I said. 'I can half cook.' Actually that's a lie, I can't cook to save my life, but it made him laugh.

'So you know what it's like then. Life revolves round the kitchen.'

'Er, yeah. Round the kitchen. Curries, pasta, you name it,' I said. 'I can produce a great meal at the drop of a hat.' Not a complete lie, I thought. All it takes is a quick phone call to the takeaway place and hey presto, *voilà*, il supperoni.

Just at that moment, Tony came in so I introduced them along with my quick explanation as to why we look so different. 'Same dad, different mothers,' I said. 'Dad's where we get the Italian genes from.'

'And she doesn't mean Armani jeans,' smiled Tony, then started laughing at his own joke.

Luke slid out of his seat to let him sit down. 'And the gift of cooking, I hear,' he said.

Tony looked at me quizzically.

'Well, no. Mum can cook as well,' I said. 'She's from Jamaica and does a mean curry.'

'Sounds good,' said Luke turning to Tony. 'Your sister was just telling me what a great cook she is.'

Tony looked surprised. 'She *was*?' I could see that he was about to laugh, but I kicked him under the table and he straightened his face. 'I mean. Yeah. She is. Always cooking stuff up is our Nesta.'

Another customer caught Luke's eye. 'Won't be a mo,' he said as he went to take the man's order.

'So what do you think?' asked Tony looking round after he'd gone. 'Romantic or what? Do you think Lucy will like it?'

'She'll feel very at home here. It's kind of a cosy mess, just like the kitchen at her house.' I looked over at Luke and sighed. 'And it is possibly the most romantic place I've ever been in my whole life . . .'

Tony glanced over at Luke. 'Ah. The waiter. That was quick.'

'Luca De Biasi,' I said. 'His dad owns the restaurant. He's doing the acting course I'm doing . . .'

Tony nodded. 'Ah, he's the guy you fell in love with on Wednesday . . .'

I nodded back. 'Fate has given me a second chance.'

'And maybe she'll even give you a third.' Tony smiled mischievously as Luke came back and handed us menus.

'The lasagne is good tonight,' said Luke.

Tony glanced at the menu. 'Hey, Nesta,' he said. 'Why don't you invite Luke to come and try your *unbelievable* cookery skills.'

Whadtt!! I thought, no way. But Luke was looking at me to see my reaction and I didn't want him to feel that I didn't want to see him again. Arrghhh. What to do? Um. I know! Agree to it but don't give a date. Be vague and hopefully he'll forget about it.

'Yeah sure,' I said. 'I'd love to cook for you sometime, Luke.'

'Mum and Dad are out tomorrow night,' Tony said with a grin. 'If you're not busy, would you like to come over then?'

'Yeah. Cool,' said Luke. 'I look forward to it.'

Tony sniggered. 'Yeah. And I can assure you that it will be an experience you'll never forget.'

Tony Costello, you are dead, I thought as I kicked him again under the table.

Tony's Top Romantic Places

- Anywhere candlelit.
- Biasi's Italian restaurant.
- Kenwood on Hampstead Heath on a hot summer's night when there's a concert on.
- Back seat of the movies (still a good one, particularly if it's a horror movie as the girl will need to hold your hand).
- Any funky café with big old sofas to sink into.
- Tony's bedroom.

Note from Nesta: this last one only works for Tony . . .

Chapter 8

Recipe for Disaster

Move over Nigella, there's a new domestic goddess in town I thought as I lay in a jasmine-scented bath the following evening. Everything was sorted. The table was laid. My chicken curry was cooking nicely in the oven. Mum and Dad were out of the way until after their movie finished. My guests would be arriving in half an hour. (I'd phoned Lucy and begged her to come and join us, so that it wasn't Luke and me with Tony sitting in the middle having a right laugh.) All I had left to do was light the candles. This entertaining lark is easy peasy, I thought as I lathered my legs with Mum's Guerlain bath gel.

'Keep it simple,' Mum'd advised earlier. 'You don't want to be in a panic when your guests arrive, so do something you can prepare beforehand and just warm it up when people arrive.'

She'd been fab and offered to help when I told her of my dilemma. Between the two of us, we'd made a Jamaican curry, my grandmother's recipe. I thought Luke'd like something different from the Italian meals he must get every night.

'All you have to do is turn on the oven,' said Mum before she'd left. 'A hundred and eighty degrees centigrade for an hour and twenty minutes.'

After my bath, I got changed into my black halter-neck top and black jeans, put on my make-up then lit the candles.

By the time Luke arrived, the flat looked warm and inviting.

'Wow, this is nice,' he said as I gave him a quick guided tour. I have to hand it to Mum, I thought, as we went from room to room, she really does know how to create a comfortable atmosphere with her use of warm colours, Moroccan rugs and Eastern artefacts. Luke particularly liked looking at Dad's black and white photos that lined the hall walls. And he spent ages looking at Dad's film books on the bookshelf in the sitting room. I made a mental note to have a look at some of them myself as the doorbell rang and I went to let Lucy in.

I felt so grown-up. Like I was playing the part of a hostess at an adult dinner party in a movie. Lucy was a bit shy when she first arrived, as she's not used to having proper dinner here with candles and the big table in the sitting room set and everything. Usually it's a slice of pizza on the knees in front of the telly. She soon relaxed though and I could tell she liked Luke because, when he went to look at our CDs, she did a fake swoon with her hand on her heart then gave me the thumbs up.

I looked at my watch as Luke put my new chill out CD on. 'Supper should be ready,' I said as I showed everyone where to sit at the table.

When I went into the kitchen to get the curry out of the oven, something didn't feel right. Or should I say, smell right. Whenever Mum cooked it, you could smell the spices and garlic wafting out of the oven long before it was ready. I couldn't smell anything. I lifted the dish from the oven. Oh *noooooo*. Cold. It was stone cold. Uncooked. Raw.

'Need a hand?' asked Tony coming up behind me.

'More than a hand. Blooming oven's not working.'

Tony bent over, looked at the oven then laughed. 'It's not broken Nesta. You turned the grill on but not the oven.'

I looked at the switches. The grill symbol was just above the oven symbol. 'Oh *no*! Oh *no*.' I hated things like this happening. Mum had got this posh new oven last year and using it was *really* complicated. It could do all sorts of things if you knew how to work it. It probably even turned into a private plane if you knew what knobs to turn, but I hadn't got the hang of it. I hate reading all those techno manuals that assume that the reader is fluent in domestic appliance speak. Why couldn't it just have an on/off button then simpletons like me could use it.

Tony laughed again and pointed at the dials. 'You have to turn it on. To oven, not grill, and then you have to put it to the temperature you want.'

'Oh don't laugh. What are we going to do?'

'What do you want to do?'

'Dunno. Crawl away and hide. I mean, how's it going to look? I'll be a laughing stock. He'll think, Nesta. Cook? Why she can't even turn the cooker on. Pathetic. He'll think I'm soooo pathetic.'

'We could heat it up now,' suggested Tony.

'Takes an hour and a half,' I said. 'They'll be starving.' I felt like crying. I wanted it all to be so perfect and now it was ruined.

'Can I take anything through?' asked Luke appearing at the kitchen door.

I was about to blurt out that I was a complete idiot and he may as well go home and give up on me right there and then, when Tony pulled on my arm.

'Um, bit of a problem, mate,' he said. 'Fuse has blown on the cooker I think. No heat.'

Oh, bless him, I thought. He can be a real pal when he wants. I made a mental note to back him up in some way when he needed my support in the future.

'Want me to take a look?' asked Luke. 'I'm fixing stuff all the time at the restaurant.'

'Noo*oooo*,' said Tony. 'Best not mess with it. It can be a bit dodgy sometimes. No. We thought we'd . . .'

'Get take-out,' I interrupted, then I remembered Tony and I didn't have much money between us. Oh God, what to do now? It would be rude to ask our guests to pay for their own meals after we'd invited them.

Tony had obviously realised the same thing. He squeezed my arm again. 'No. We don't need to do take-away. We're Italian,' he said. 'So . . . We've er . . . got the microwave. I'm sure we can knock something up.'

He started opening cupboards and pulling out pots and jars. Our evening is turning into a disaster, I thought. Tony's like me and he can't even boil an egg without ruining it.

'Does the top part of the cooker still work?' asked Luke.

Tony switched one of the switches. 'Yeah. The hob is gas, it's only the oven that's electric.'

'Got any pasta?' asked Luke.

Tony nodded.

'Parmesan cheese?'

Tony nodded again.

'Nesta. You've done your bit for the night. You go and join Lucy and I'll knock us something up,' said Luke. 'Give us a hand, Tony?'

Tony nodded, so I went into the sitting room to join Lucy.

'Oh, poor you,' she said, after I'd told her what had happened. 'But hey, a boy who can cook, looks like a Roman god and seems genuinely nice.'

'I know. I think he may be out of my league,' I said.

Lucy's jaw fell open. 'Out of your league? In all the time I've known you, I have never heard you say anything so ridiculous.'

I was feeling miserable. 'I think he is. Like, he is gorgeous, but more than that, he seems to be good at everything. Bright. He's soon going to find out that I'm a total airhead. In fact that's what he must be thinking now. I bet he's worked out what happened and that I can't even work the cooker. God, I'm soooo stupid.'

'Rubbish,' said Lucy. 'I don't know what's got into you lately. You're not stupid and he wouldn't be here if he didn't like you. I bet he's grilling Tony about you right now and trying to find out all he can about you.' Then she laughed. 'Geddit? Grilling Tony. Luke's a chef. Grilling Tony? Hope not. Cannibalism isn't my thing.'

I gave her my Queen Victoria, 'We are not amused' look.

'Sorry,' she said. 'Couldn't resist. But I bet he is trying to find out more about you.'

'Do you think? Let's go and listen.'

We sneaked into the hall and eavesdropped on the

boys. They seemed to be getting on brilliantly. Chatting away about cars. Tony was telling Luke about Dad refusing to let him have driving lessons.

I had to laugh at them when I poked my head round the door. They looked so domesticated. Luke in Mum's Marge Simpson apron and Tony chopping tomatoes.

'You should have your own TV show,' I said. 'Move over Jamie Oliver, Luke and Tony have come to town.'

Half an hour later, Luke brought in a big bowl of pasta. It was absolutely perfect and tasted amazing. Lucy even helped herself to an extra bowlful. Tony chatted away happily, but I didn't say very much as I was still feeling like an idiot because of the cooker.

After the pasta, we cleared away the dishes and it was time for dessert. Well, at least nothing can go wrong with this, I thought as I took a tub of ice cream from the freezer then found chocolate sauce and maple syrup to pour over it.

I found bowls, put everything on a tray and took it all through and put it on the table.

'Help yourself,' I said to Luke. 'It's vanilla. Homemade by Mum.'

'Fantastic,' said Luke digging in with a large spoon. 'You can't beat that homemade flavour.'

'What do you think?' I asked as he took a mouthful.

'Erum . . .' I could see he was struggling to be polite, but it was clear that he didn't like it.

Then Tony took a spoonful. 'Ey*uuck!*' He spat it back into his bowl. '*Nesta!* This isn't ice cream.' He picked up the tub and looked at the label, then he burst out laughing. 'This is the creamed cod that Mum made last Friday night. No one was very hungry remember? She freezed the leftovers.'

By this time I was purple with shame. Luke was going to think I was Queen of Stupid. Reigning bimbo champion. 'Oh, so sorry, sorry,' I blustered. 'I'll get the right tub.'

'Don't worry,' said Tony getting up. 'I'll get it. You stay.'

'I'll give you a hand,' said Lucy getting up to go with him.

I gave Luke a weak smile and tried to gauge what was going on his head. Not sure, I thought. He does look amused. But is this a good thing? Or a bad thing?

And that's when I did my pièce de résistance for the night. I leaned over to relight one of the candles while at the same time giving Luke my best seductive look. I was so busy gazing at him that I didn't notice that as I lit the match and leaned over, the candle flared and next thing I knew, I'd singed the front of my hair.

'Aghh,' I cried as I frantically blew the candle out then poured a glass of apple juice over my forehead.

Lucy came back in with the ice cream. 'What's that strange smell, like something's burning?'

'And why is Nesta trying to drink her juice through

the top of her head?' asked Tony. 'Mm. Great party trick, Nesta. Sorry about my sister, Luke, she has these strange turns. It's probably time for her medication.'

'She just singed her hair,' said Luke as I lifted my head. Juice dripped down my forehead into my eyes causing my mascara to run. I couldn't bear it another moment. They were all looking at me as though I was a clown and they were waiting for the next trick.

'Excuse me a second,' I said, then ran to my bedroom and dived on to my bed. A second later, Lucy came after me.

'You OK?' she asked.

'Yes. Nooooo. I mean, can the evening get any worse?'

'No,' said Lucy sitting on the end of the bed and shaking her head solemnly. 'I don't think it can. But don't worry, everything happens in threes. You've had the three. The supper was raw. The ice cream was actually creamed cod. And you set fire to your hair. So that's one, two, three.' She tried to look concerned, but I could see it coming. Her shoulders were starting to shake. Then she bent over laughing. 'Snnnckkkk,' she giggled. 'Set . . . fire . . . to . . . your . . . hair.'

I began to see the funny side of it as well. 'Well Tony did tell Luke that my cooking would be an experience he'd never forget.'

'Oh you can be sure of that,' Lucy said, laughing. 'And I just knew there was something fishy about that ice cream.'

'Yeah, like, oh my cod,' I said and started laughing as well.

Soon the two of us had rolled off the bed and were on the floor howling, tears pouring down our cheeks. It wasn't long before Tony and Luke came to find out where we were.

At first Tony looked really concerned. Then he realised we were laughing, not crying.

'What's so funny?' asked Tony.

'Nesta is,' said Lucy pointing at me. 'Nesta Williams. The Domestic Coddess.'

And then they started laughing and Luke sat on the floor next to me and interlocked his hand with mine. It felt great. Like a current of electricity coursing right from the tip of my fingers to the tips of my toes.

After that the evening was brilliant. We went back into the sitting room, had ice cream with all the toppings we could find, maple syrup, chocolate sauce, chopped nuts and flakes and we played the chill out CD again. We were having such a good time that, before I knew it, it was ten-thirty and Mum and Dad were back.

Great, I thought. I'd been hoping that Luke would still be here when Dad got back. So maybe I didn't dazzle him with my brilliant cookery skills, but I was sure that Dad would impress him by chatting to him about films.

But something really weird happened instead.

Mum and Dad came in and Dad took one look at

Luke, then did a double take. Then he started staring at Luke with a really hard look on his face. What is the matter with him, I thought? It was like he had seen a ghost.

'Mum and Dad, this is Luke. Luke, this is Mum and Dad,' I said.

Mum smiled. 'Pleased to meet you, Luke. How was the curry?'

That set us all off laughing again.

'Hmm. Slight change of plan,' said Tony. 'Explain later.'

'Oh. OK,' said Mum, looking puzzled.

'And by mistake, I served your creamed cod as ice cream,' I said.

Mum started laughing then, but Dad was still staring at Luke.

'What's your surname, Luke?' he suddenly asked.

'De Biasi,' said Luke.

Dad's face clouded and he turned and left the room.

This wasn't like my dad. Usually he was King of Charm. Even Mum looked surprised by his behaviour. What was going on?

Nesta's Mum's Tips for Dinner Parties

- Keep it simple.
- If possible, have a trial run on a night before the dinner party, so that you know exactly what to do and how the meal will turn out.
- Choose a recipe where you can do most of the preparation beforehand and just heat it up when the guests arrive. That way, you can spend time with your guests.

Nesta's Tips for Dinner Parties

- Remember to turn on the oven.
- Read the labels on tubs in the freezer.
- Try not to burn your hair or eyebrows.

On second thoughts:

Nesta's Tips for Dinner Parties, Version Two

- Go out to eat.

Chapter 9

Old Misery

I confronted Dad in the kitchen the following morning.

'But why not?'

'Because I don't wish to, Nesta,' said Dad. 'And that's the end of it.'

'But Dad, you *have* to give me a reason . . .'

If Dad's face was a weather forecast, it just turned from clouds to thunder. 'I don't *have* to do anything,' he said.

I know teenagers are renowned for saying it's not fair, but this *really* wasn't. All I'd asked was that Dad be friendlier to Luke in future and chat to him about being a film director. But no, Old Misery was being, well, an old misery.

'But Dad, all I'm asking is that you talk to him. I felt ashamed of you last night, I really did. I've been brought up to be polite to visitors and make them feel welcome. Your behaviour was rude and for no reason.'

A loud snigger came from the counter where Mum was peeling carrots for Sunday lunch. She turned and looked at Dad with an amused look as if to say, 'Get out of that one, matie.'

Dad pouted like a sullen teenager. 'I don't wish to discuss it, Nesta. And for once in your life, will you please not question everything.'

'But it doesn't make sense. I don't understand. Give me a good reason. Luke's not a drug addict. Or a creep. Or an alien. So why? I don't understand why.'

'Subject closed,' said Dad, then he picked up his newspaper and held it up to his face.

Mum shrugged her shoulders and pulled an 'I don't know' kind of face. I went into the hall, grabbed my coat and headed for the front door.

'Where are you going?' called Mum. 'Lunch won't be long.'

'Lost my appetite,' I said as I opened the door then slammed it behind me.

As I made my way down the street, I felt tears sting the back of my eyes. I felt angry. And frustrated. And upset. I got on really well with my dad normally and we rarely argued. Why was he being so unreasonable all of a sudden? I didn't understand. I hate feeling like this, I thought, and I hate us not getting on at home. I called

Izzie on my mobile to commiserate. I knew she'd understand as sometimes she doesn't get on with her mum.

'Maybe it's a jealousy thing,' she said. 'Fathers never like to see their little girls with boys. He's always been your number one, then along comes a boy like Luke to steal you away. I mean, I know you've had cute boyfriends before, but Luke is exceptionally good-looking.'

'He is, isn't he?'

'Yeah. As in ding *double* dong. He looks a bit like Tony in fact.'

'Does not.'

'Does. In that he's very good-looking in an Italian kind of way. You know dark and . . .'

'Oh. Do you think I'm being all shallow and just going for looks again?'

'Dunno. Are you?'

'Well, I do like the way he looks, who wouldn't? But I can really talk to him as well. We get on. He knows a lot.'

'There you go then, Nesta. Beauty and brains. What more could you want?'

'Dad to like him.'

'Give him time. Maybe seeing Luke reminded your dad that he's getting older. Who knows what goes on in our parents' warped and twisted minds? Maybe he's going through the male menopause. How did Luke react when your dad gave him the cold shoulder?'

'Disappointed, I think. He'd been really looking

forward to talking to him about movies. I felt such an idiot. I'd given my dad this great build up then he turns up, and blanks Luke. He split soon after Dad got home. He knew that he wasn't welcome.'

'Weird, huh? Your dad's never been heavy about a boy before.'

'I know.'

'So what are you going to do?'

'I'm going to see Luke right now. He told me he was working at Biasi's today, so I'm just going to pop in and check that he's cool.'

'Er, Nesta. Are you sure you should?' asked Izzie. 'I mean, you're always the first to say don't be too available in the beginning of a relationship. You invited him for dinner last night and now you're going to see him again. Might be too much, too soon, don't you think? Might frighten him off.'

'Nah. This is different. I think he needs to know that I'm on his side, not on my dad's. Besides, I know he likes me. Even though he left pretty fast last night, we did have a snog at the door before he went.'

'Out of ten?'

'Ten. He's an ace kisser.'

'Not a brace kisser?' said Izzie with a laugh.

'Nope. I was worried about my brace at first, but it didn't get in the way at all, and he did say to go in and see him if I felt like it.'

'Well, good luck,' said Izzie. 'And I hope your dad chills. Try talking to him again when he's had a bit of space. He probably realises that he was out of order last night and will be more receptive to talking later.'

Good old Izzie, I thought. She's always good to chat to in a crisis. She's sort of calm and wise at the same time. And mad as well, if that's possible. 'Yeah, right, I will,' I said. 'I think that's why I was so upset, as we've always been able to talk about stuff before, but this time, it was like he put up a brick wall.'

The atmosphere in Biasi's was brilliant. The place was packed and buzzing with lunch-time diners and, although Luke was busy serving people, I could tell that he was pleased to see me.

'I'll catch you on my break in about fifteen minutes,' he said as he directed me to a bar counter near the till where a large, glamorous, dark-haired lady was sitting with a glass of red wine.

'Mum, this is Nesta,' he said.

His mum was great. Within minutes she was telling me all about her family, and the village in Italy she came from, and the house that they have there where they grow olives and herbs and make their own pesto. When I told her that I was half Italian, she treated me as if I were a long lost relative and insisted that I have the recipe for their pesto along with a sample jar. After ten minutes or so, we were joined by a very suave-looking older man with silver-grey hair.

'Dad,' mouthed Luke from the other side of the restaurant. He didn't need to tell me. I could see immediately as they were the spitting image of each other.

Like Mrs De Biasi, Luke's dad was very friendly and charming. He insisted that I have a drink on the house and sample the olives and freshly baked bread while I waited for Luke.

As I sat there munching, Marisa came out of the kitchen in the back carrying a birthday cake with loads of candles. Complete pandemonium broke out as Mr and Mrs De Biasi led the waiters with trumpets and tambourines in a chorus of 'Happy Birthday' sung to a white-haired old lady who was dining with her family. I felt so at home and it seemed that everyone who came into the restaurant felt the same way. Most of the diners knew the De Biasis personally and Mrs De Biasi relished filling me in on all sorts of gossip and who was who and who did what.

Luke came and sat with me in his break and his mum and dad made themselves scarce, but not before his mum gave me a huge wink.

'I really like your parents,' I said. 'Meeting them makes me feel extra bad about last night and my dad. He's not usually like that.'

Luke shrugged. 'Maybe he wasn't feeling well. Another time. In fact, bring your mum and dad down here for a meal. As you can see it's pretty informal and relaxed around here.'

'That's a great idea,' I said. 'Dad's bound to love it. I mean, he *is* Italian. He loves good pasta. He'll love the atmosphere in here and so will Mum.'

'Any time,' said Luke.

I glanced over at his dad. 'Your dad seems really nice and approachable. Why don't you try telling him about wanting to act.'

Luke put a finger up to his mouth as if to hush me. He indicated a few of the other waiters and waitresses busy rushing about dealing with the Sunday lunch crowd. 'I have tried, believe me. But see the staff. A few of them are actors. Like William over there, he hasn't worked since last year . . .'

'I thought I recognised him,' I said. 'He was in . . . oh, I can't remember the name of it, a soap on ITV?'

Luke nodded. 'Yeah. His face was everywhere, but since then nothing has come in.'

'Yeah, but he was, like, *really* famous. I'd have thought producers were queuing up for him.'

Luke shook his head. 'He says that so many of his actor friends are resting. Basically that means out of work.' He pointed at a girl with short red hair busy carrying plates of tiramisu. 'That's Sophie. Also an out of work actor. See, Dad gets to see so many of them here as they come and ask for work whilst they're in between jobs. He doesn't want that for me.'

'But hasn't that put you off?'

'Nope. I understand that you don't get every job and that there are periods when you don't work. I'm not under any illusion that you become an actor and, hey presto, everyone wants you. No. I will help out in Dad's restaurants, it's just . . . I don't want it to be my whole life. My only career. Acting will always be my number one, but I'm well aware that you have to have backup as well.'

What he said made me think. Dad was always saying the same thing – that work in the media often meant feast or famine, our family had enough experience of it ourselves, but I hadn't related it to myself before and thought about a backup career. I'd just presumed that it would be different for me, that I'd have loads of work when I hit the stage, but maybe it wasn't going to be as easy as that.

'So you see why Dad isn't that enamoured when I tell him that I want to be an actor when I leave school?'

I nodded. 'Yes, but I guess it's because he cares about you. Wants you to be secure and all that . . .'

'Yeah. But I want to be happy as well.'

'Dads, huh?'

Luke nodded. 'Yeah. A pain.'

'Yeah. But it's not usually a pain with my dad. He's great most days. In fact, I'm going to go home and have it out with him. And I think you should with your dad, too.'

'Yeah, right,' said Luke. 'How about you go with yours first and you can tell me how it went next Wednesday.'

Mum, Dad and Tony were just finishing lunch when I got home over an hour later laden with presents.

'What's all this?' asked Mum as I emptied my carrier bag out on the kitchen table.

'Cool,' said Tony as he picked up a packet of almond biscuits.

Mrs De Biasi had given me a huge Panettone, biscuits, jars of anchovies, a bottle of olive oil, a jar of pesto.

'From Luke's mum,' I said. 'She's amazing. When she found out that I was half Italian, she wouldn't stop giving me things. I tried to refuse, but she insisted, saying that it was all from the restaurant so not expensive. And Mr De Biasi said that I must bring you all there'

Dad looked up from his plate.

'Look Dad, all your favourites . . .' I continued.

'So you met Mr De Biasi?' interrupted Dad.

'Yeah. He's really nice. You'd really like him. He's very handsome like you. Luke's mum's very good-looking as well. Glam in a Sophia Loren kind of way. So when shall we go?'

Dad got up from the table. 'I'd prefer it if you didn't see Luke or go there again,' he said, then he left the room.

I was gobsmacked. I looked at Mum and Tony. They

looked surprised as well, but neither of them said anything. The silence felt really uncomfortable.

'What *is* going on?' I asked. 'What's the matter with Dad?'

'Beats me,' said Tony.

Mum sighed and looked after Dad. 'I think . . . I think your dad should tell you.'

'Tell me what? You're not getting divorced are you?' I gasped.

'No, silly.'

'Is it because there isn't much money at the moment?'

Mum shook her head.

'So what then?'

Mum sighed. 'Look, I'll tell you part of the story, but then you must ask your dad.'

I sat down at the table. 'OK. Listening.'

'Your dad knew Luke's dad. Years ago. I never met him, it was long before we were together, but I've heard him talk about him. Gianni De Biasi. Apparently they were mates when they were lads, in fact, more than mates from what I can make out. They were like brothers.'

'Ohmigod! It's true what they say, it's a *small* world. Well that's *brilliant*, isn't it? They can meet up again. It will be soooo fantastic.'

Mum shook her head. 'No. Something happened . . .'

'What?'

'That's the part I think your dad should tell you,' she said.

Mrs De Biasi's Homemade Pesto
(serves four)

3 handfuls of fresh basil (finely chopped)
1 handful of pinenuts (lightly toasted)
1 handful of Parmesan cheese (grated)
Quarter of a clove of garlic
Lemon juice
Extra virgin olive oil
Sea salt and freshly ground black pepper

Pound the garlic, a pinch of salt and the basil in a bowl. Add the pinenuts and pound again. Add half the Parmesan. Stir, then add just enough olive oil to bind the sauce.

Season with salt and pepper to taste, then add the rest of the cheese. If you're not happy with the consistency, keep adding oil and cheese until you are. Add a squeeze of lemon at the end.

Delicious mixed into pasta.

Chapter 10

Oh, Brother!

'So what *did* happen with them?' asked Lucy.

We were sitting in the playground at break the next morning. TJ, Lucy, Izzie and me, squashed on a bench trying to keep warm as it was a cloudy day with a bitter wind blowing.

'Still don't know. I was about to go charging in to Dad and find out the rest of the story, but Mum asked me to let him tell me in his own time. Somehow I got the feeling she was right. It wasn't the time to start demanding answers. I've never seen Dad like this before and it wasn't so much that he was angry, more like upset.'

Lucy nodded. 'I think you were right. Mum says you can't force people to talk until they're ready. In fact, forcing an issue that is very painful may only make someone bury it deeper.'

'I guess I just have to wait then,' I said.

'Poo,' said Izzie.

'I know.'

'But we don't know it was painful,' said Izzie. 'All we know is that something happened.'

'Sounds a biggie whatever it was,' said TJ. 'A mystery. I wonder what it is.'

'So do I,' I said. 'The suspense is killing me and patience is not my best virtue.'

'Maybe they were both in love with Luke's mum,' said Lucy looking dreamy. 'You said she was glamorous. If she still is now, then she was probably even more stunning when she was younger. Maybe she was your dad's childhood sweetheart then Luke's dad stole her away and your dad has never forgiven him.'

'You've been watching too many romantic videos, Lucy,' I said.

'Or maybe it was *your* mum that they both wanted,' said TJ.

I shook my head. 'No. Mum said they knew each other before she came on the scene.'

'Maybe Tony's mum then,' said TJ, then gasped. 'Maybe he murdered her! That would give your dad good reason not to want to see Luke's dad.'

'She died in hospital, bozo,' I said. 'She was ill. And if

he'd murdered her, er, don't you think he might be in prison? Not running a chain of Italian restaurants.'

'Oh yeah, sorry, got carried away,' said TJ. 'Well, whatever the reason, I reckon it must have been about love. Most of these types of things are.'

'Or money,' said Izzie. 'Maybe they were in business together and one of them did the dirty.'

'I don't think so,' I said. 'My dad wouldn't and Luke's dad looks pretty decent.'

'It might have been something really small,' said Lucy. 'A misunderstanding that was never resolved.'

'It's just like *Romeo and Juliet*,' said TJ. 'Remember? The Montagues and Capulets, they were both Italian, just like you, both families hated each other and Romeo and Juliet were forbidden to see each other, just like you and Luke.'

'Thanks a lot, TJ,' I said. 'They both end up dead if I remember right.'

'Only because everything went wrong with their getaway plan,' she said. 'Juliet pretends to be dead and Romeo thinks that she actually is, so he kills himself, then she wakes up, sees that he's dead and kills herself as well.'

Lucy rolled her eyes. 'Not a comedy, then?' she asked.

'No,' I said. 'And I can't stand all that boring thee, thou and forthwith stuff.'

'*Nesta!*' said TJ. 'It's one of Shakespeare's most famous plays. It's a fab story. There's a movie with Leonardo Di

Caprio as Romeo that's worth watching if you don't want to read the play itself.'

Oh, here we go again, I thought. I'm being got at just because I don't read as much as the others. 'Shakespeare schmakespeare. Sorry, TJ, I just don't think me and old Willie speak the same language.'

'You don't know until you've tried,' said TJ.

'Poo,' I said.

'Maybe Luke will remember something,' said Lucy. 'Maybe he's heard your dad's name when his dad has been talking about the past.'

'But your dad doesn't want you to see Luke,' said TJ. 'Are you going to disobey him?'

'Well, I'm going to go to my acting class and oh, *quelle surprise*! Luke just happens to go as well. Tony knows I met Luke at acting class, but Mum and Dad don't. What they don't know, won't hurt them.'

'Text us as soon as you find out anything, oh Juliet,' said TJ as the bell for classes rang summoning us back to lessons.

It was great to see Luke again on Wednesday in the acting class and this time he was there right on time.

'I need to talk to you later,' I whispered to him as Jo asked us all to stand in the centre of the room for warm-up exercises.

After a few stretches and a bit of limbering up, we went

on to an improvisation where we had to get into groups of three, then act out a scene showing two people that got on well and didn't like the third person. First, Jo asked us to do the scene with dialogue and then again showing the same scenario with mainly body language. It was soooo interesting as, like the last class, it showed that the way people hold themselves can reveal more than what they say. It made me more determined than ever to walk upright and not slouched over like some saddo. I might not be able to smile with confidence any more, but I can at least walk as though I believe in myself.

Following that, we played games where we had to throw out suggestions for creatures and actions. Izzie said, 'Bees buzzing,' and we all had to pretend to be bees. Then, someone else said, 'Sheep grazing,' and we all had to do that. It was a real laugh, especially seeing all these middle-aged people acting like five-year-olds and rolling on the floor. It felt more like playschool than an acting class.

Then, Jo started putting newspaper on the floor.

'Twelve pieces,' she said, then counted the people in the class. 'Twelve of you. Go and stand on a piece of paper and I'm going to play some music. As the music plays, move around the floor only stepping on the paper. As you do so, I'm going to remove some of the paper, then I'm going to stop the music and I want you to freeze where you are. Anyone who has a foot on the floor is out.'

Definitely playschool, I thought as I found a piece of paper and the music started up. It was hysterical as, when the music stopped, we found that there were only eight pieces of paper left on the floor. Panic broke out as everyone scrabbled to stand on a piece of paper. A few people were out as they lost their balance and stood on the floor. And so it went on until there were four of us left and only two pieces of paper. Izzie, Luke, Jan and I. We had to really hang on to each other so that one of us didn't lose our balance and put a foot off the paper. For me, it was a great excuse to wrap myself around Luke. He didn't seem to mind at all and held on to me tightly. He smelled divine, sort of citrusy and warm and it felt great to snuggle into his neck with a legitimate excuse. Then Izzie started laughing as she had her leg wound around mine and was losing her balance and threatening to topple all of us over. That started me laughing as well and soon all four of us were giggling like idiots, desperately trying to hang on to each other at the same time and not lose our footing. As the music started up again and people began to unfold, I found that I couldn't. I seemed to be caught in Luke's jumper.

'Oh *no*!' I cried as Luke tried to move away. A strand of wool from his jumper had got caught in my brace, so I was attached to his neck like a Siamese twin. 'Enuheraahh . . .'on't 'ove.'

Jo saw what was happening and rushed over to separate

us, but I felt so embarrassed. All the rest of the group was standing laughing. Even Luke thought it was hilarious. 'My animal magnetism,' he said grinning, as Jo carefully extricated the wool I'd caught on from my brace. 'Girls just can't bear to be apart from me.'

I felt stupid. I had spent most of my time trying to talk through half closed lips so no one would notice my brace, then I went and did something that brought it to *everyone*'s attention. Like me saying, er, just in case you missed the fact that I have railway tracks on my teeth, watch this!

The rest of the class went without a hitch and it was fun, but I couldn't help checking my watch. I was looking forward to the end, so I could get Luke on his own.

At last it was over and, as we all trooped out of the school, Luke offered to give Izzie and me a lift home.

'Nice car,' said Izzie as he held the door open for us five minutes later. 'I like these Volkswagen Passats.'

I hadn't even noticed the car as I was so impatient to talk to Luke. Amazing that Izzie knew what type it was, I thought as I got into the front seat. When did she become a car expert? Up until recently, if you asked her about a car, she'd say, 'Oh, er . . . it was a green one.'

'So what was it you wanted to say to me?' asked Luke as he started up the engine.

'You won't believe it,' I said and quickly filled him in on my dad's weird reaction to hearing that I had met his dad and what my mum had told me about my dad and his being old friends.

'Wow,' he said. 'Small world, huh? And at least that explains why he did that double take on Saturday night. Like he'd seen a ghost.'

'I suppose he had in a way, if he used to be mates with your dad. You do look like him. But have you ever heard him talk about my dad? Matt Costello.'

'Don't think so.' Luke shook his head.

'Nan used to call Dad Matteo not Matt. Maybe your dad will know him as that.'

'I'll ask him when I get home. Try and find out what happened.'

After we'd dropped Izzie, Luke drove up to Highgate and we stopped in at Café Rouge for a late night hot chocolate. We soon got talking about films and, once again, I felt aware of how much he knew about them and I didn't. I decided to tell him about how I pretend I'm a character in a film if I'm in a stressful situation.

'So what character would you be now?' he asked.

'But I only do it when I'm stressed.'

'Yeah. So what character would you be now?'

'But what makes you think I'm stressed?' I asked.

'You're still holding your hand over your mouth. You *can* relax with me you know, the brace doesn't bother me.' Then he smiled. 'Except that is, when you fasten it to my left shoulder.'

I tried putting my hand down, but he was right, I couldn't relax. I couldn't help but be aware of my metal mouth.

'So what character?' he asked.

My mind had gone blank. 'Dunno,' I said.

'OK. Who are your top favourite characters in films then?'

I wanted to distract him. I felt really awkward. He was sitting so close and doing that lovely thing that some boys do – looking into your eyes and then at your mouth, then back at your eyes. Only I couldn't enjoy the sensation as I was so aware of how *un*attractive my mouth was. 'Don't you ever think about anything else besides movies?' I asked through closed lips.

He looked hurt for a moment. 'Yeah. Sorry. Was I being boring?'

'*No.* Just . . .'

'No, sorry . . . I know I can go on,' he said leaning back slightly and crossing his arms over his chest. 'I tend to get carried away. So. What would you like to talk about?'

I felt a sinking feeling in my stomach. I've blown it, I thought. I've cut him off when he was in full flow about his major passion in life. I've made him feel ill at ease. I can tell by his body language and the way he's crossed his arms, like closing off from me. I read somewhere that people do that when they feel uncomfortable. Maybe the girls were right when they said that I don't give boys a chance to show the true side of themselves. Right. That's it, I thought. I have to change and be able to hold a conversation about films without being intimidated by my lack of knowledge or else he's going to get bored with me. And I have to learn not to be inhibited about my teeth.

'No, sorry. I *am* interested in films just . . .' I glanced at my watch, 'Just . . . oh dentists. Look at the time, look I'd better . . .'

'Er, *dentists*?' Luke said, laughing. 'What have they got to do with anything?'

'It's my new swear word,' I said. 'Look. Sorry, but I'd better go. Mum thinks I've only gone to class so, if I'm any later, she'll worry.'

'And we don't want your dad to suspect you're out with me until we've got to the bottom of why my family is a no-go zone.'

'Exactly,' I said standing up, 'but he won't know that I'm out late. He's away at the moment, on location in Bristol. He's filming a two parter for the BBC there.'

'Cool.' Luke stood up and helped me put on my jacket. 'Let me pay for the drinks, then we'll go.'

While he was away at the counter, I took a look around the café and spotted Jade Wilcocks and Mary O'Connor from our class at a table on the far side. Jade caught my eye and waved me over.

'Hey, Nesta,' she said when I went to join them.

'Hey.'

'Is that the divine brother I keep hearing about?' asked Jade, jutting her chin in Luke's direction.

I shook my head. 'No. His name's Luke. Why would you think he's my brother?'

'Looks a bit like the guy I saw Lucy with in Hampstead once in the summer,' said Mary, 'and I knew she was seeing your brother off and on so . . .'

Then it hit me. That had to be it! The reason why Dad wanted me to stay away from Luke. Lucy had been right. It was a love thing. It was *obvious*. Izzie was right too, Luke did look a bit like Tony. Mary was right in mistaking them for each other. Which explained why Dad didn't want me to see Luke any more. Dad had clearly had a love affair with Luke's mum. Luke *was* my brother!

'Are you OK?' asked Mary. 'You look a bit faint all of a sudden.'

'Umf . . .' I said. Ohmigod. I'd snogged my own brother. And given him ten out of ten. Told Lucy that he was an ace kisser.

Now what, I asked myself as Luke came over to join us. My brain was about to explode.

'Luke,' I said. 'Sorry got to go.'

'Yeah. I'll give you a lift . . .'

'*No*. Can't see you any more. Sorry.'

Luke looked around the café. 'Did I just miss something? *Why* can't you see me any more?'

'Because you're my brother!' I blurted out.

'You just said he wasn't,' said Jade, who seemed to be enjoying every moment.

I headed for the door. 'Well he is,' I called over my shoulder. 'Sorry, Luke.'

And with that, I ran out of the café. As soon as I was outside, I dialled Dad's mobile.

Top Tip for Brace Wearers

When snuggling into a boy's neck or shoulder,
if he's wearing anything made of wool,
keep your mouth shut.

Chapter 11

Oops!

'Where's Mum?' I asked as soon as I got home.

'Having an early night. She's doing the morning shift tomorrow,' said Tony, who was slouched on one of the sofas in front of the telly in the sitting room. He was watching the sci-fi channel, currently his favourite.

I raced down the corridor into Mum's room, but the lights were out and I could see she was in bed.

'Mum,' I whispered in case she was still awake. No response, so I gently closed the door and went back to the living room.

'Tony . . .'

'Shhhhhhhh,' he said and turned up the volume on the remote.

'I need to . . .'

'*Nesta*. Don't be annoying.'

'It's *really* important . . .'

Tony's eyes didn't leave the screen. '*So* is this. Talk to me after. It's a *crucial* moment.'

'Can't you record it? I really need to talk to you.'

Tony turned up the volume even higher. '*Later.* Now *shut* up.'

He was starting to look cross, so I thought I'd better be quiet or else he'd get me back when I was watching *The Simpsons* or something that I like. Plus, I know how it feels when you're really stuck into a programme and someone comes in and starts talking away as though the telly's not even on. It's Dad usually.

I went to look on the kitchen notice board to see if Mum had put Dad's number up there. No. Nothing. Only taxis, pizza places and plumbers. This is really bad, I thought. No one seems to realise, this is an emergency and I can't get hold of my own father.

Finally, *finally,* Tony's programme ended and he turned to me and leaned forward. 'OK. You've got two minutes before the next episode starts. What's so important?'

'Luke. I think he's our brother. I need to talk to Dad.'

Tony fell back on the sofa laughing. 'Right. Yeah. Everyone's our brother, everyone's our sister. In fact, the world . . .' he began to sing, 'is just a great big family . . .'

'No, I'm serious Tone . . . Our half-brother. I think Dad had an affair with Luke's mum, then Mr De Biasi came along and pushed Dad out of the way and now they hate each other.'

'Are you on *drugs*?'

'No.'

When Tony saw that I wasn't laughing, he tried to make his face go straight. 'OK. Just what exactly makes you think this?'

'It's obvious, Tony. Think about it. Dad doesn't want me to see Luke. He blanches when I mention that I've met Luke's dad . . .'

'Exactly,' said Tony. 'I was there. He went weird when you mentioned Luke's dad. Not his mum. Don't you think if he'd had this great affair with Mrs De Biasi that there might be some kind of reaction when you mentioned her?'

That stopped me for a moment. 'Yeah. No. The fight was with Mr De Biasi as he was the one who took Mrs De Biasi away from Dad. Maybe. Anyway. I need to speak to Dad.'

'He's in Bristol somewhere.'

'I *know*, dingbat. But where's his number? He always leaves his contact number.'

'Mum will have it.'

'Mum's asleep,' I said.

'Good, as it's probably not a good idea to call Dad out of the blue and tell him that you know about his secret *lurve* child.'

'It's not funny, Tony.'

'It is.'

'Isn't.'

'*Is*. You're mad to think that about Luke. Lost the plot. Away with the fairies. Barking. Woof. Woof.'

'Don't be horrible. What am I going to do?'

'You'll just have to wait, Nesta.' He flicked the volume back up for the next episode of his programme and stretched out again. 'Call him in the morning. In the meantime, get us a Coke will you?'

I threw a cushion at him, then got up to go to the kitchen. Sometimes I think Tony thinks I'm nothing more than his private slave. Two brothers? I don't know if I could cope.

I didn't sleep well that night. I dreamed that Dad was having supper with Marlon Brando. Both of them had braces on their teeth and kept singing that song that goes something like, 'We are familee, look at all my brothers and me . . .' All sung in a thick Italian accent.

As I staggered into the bathroom the next morning, I contemplated as to whether to ask Mum about Luke. It might come as a blow to her. She might not know anything about Dad having a secret child. I'd ask Dad to do the right thing and tell her himself. Yes, I thought. That would be best.

Mum and Tony were both already in the kitchen

having coffee and chatting when I went to grab some breakfast. I gave Tony a filthy look and turned to Mum. 'I need to talk to Dad. Can I have his number in Bristol?'

'Sure,' she said. 'It's on the pad next to the bed in my room. Give him my love, won't you.'

When I found the number, I sat on Mum's bed and dialled.

A female voice answered. 'Hello, Hogarth Hotel.'

'Can I speak to Mr Costello, please?'

The phone went quiet for a moment, then I heard a ringing, then the receptionist came back on again. 'I'm afraid there's no reply,' she said. 'Would you like to leave a message?'

'No thanks,' I said, then put the phone down. My heart was thumping and I realised that I hadn't really thought about what I was going to say and needed to plan how to put it. Like, hey, Dad about your secret son? I don't think so.

I was about to try his mobile when Mum came into the room and sat on the bed beside me. She was trying not to, but I could tell she was having a hard time not laughing.

'Nesta,' she said. 'Tony's just been telling me what you think about this boy Luke that you've met. Um, listen love, I can't let you go into school with this on your mind. He's not your brother, I can tell you that much. As I said on Sunday, your dad does have some history with Luke's dad and . . . he should have told you what it was all about himself.'

'Well, you tell me . . .'

Mum hesitated for a moment, then shook her head. 'Let your dad tell you when he gets back at the weekend. I'll have a word with him. I promise he'll tell you the whole story and, in the meantime, I can assure you that what he'll have to say is *not* that Luke is your brother or his son.'

'Promise?'

'Promise.'

'Because I *have* kissed him you know.'

I could see that Mum was struggling not to laugh and I could hear Tony sniggering in the corridor behind the door.

'Did you tell Dad he's been a very naughty boy and we know all about his love child?' he called through.

'You shut up, Tony pig face,' I called back.

He opened the door and leaned in. 'You've been watching too many soaps, Nesta. Now the *real* truth is that Mrs De Biasi is actually a transexual, but when she was a man, she fathered Lucy behind Mr Lovering's back. TJ is an alien and Izzie, well, we all know that she's had three babies and is trying to hide them from her mother. And Izzie's mum, well, she's actually a lesbian who's afraid to admit it and Mr Foster is on drugs but trying to reform.'

I went to throw one of the pillows from Mum's bed at Tony, but Mum stopped my arm. 'Now *stop* it, both of you. Enough of this nonsense. Nesta, you've got an over-vivid imagination. Tony stop winding her up. And *both* of you, off to school NOW.'

I got up and pushed past Tony, but not without sticking my tongue out at him and standing on his right foot with all my weight.

'Owwwww,' he cried. 'Muuuuum.'

'Baby,' I said.

'*Enough*,' said Mum getting up from the bed.

I went into the kitchen and grabbed a piece of toast off a plate on the breakfast bar, put on my jacket and headed off for school. Sometimes I hate having a brother. I'm glad I haven't got two, I thought. Ohmigod. What must Luke have thought? Oh dentists. I checked my mobile in the hope that there was a message from him. Nothing. Oh double dentists. I'd better phone and grovel. Apologise. Explain that . . . what will I say? That aliens came to Highgate last night and took over my brain for a couple of hours? Oh dear. I suppose it was a bit mad thinking that he was my brother, but it made sense at the time. Triple dentists. I must work on my excuses and come up with a really good one if I'm to get him back. Oh, knickers. Sometimes it's very difficult being me.

Nesta's Excuses for Having Acted Crazy

1) Aliens landed and took over my brain for two hours.
2) No! That wasn't me. That was my psychotic twin. We don't usually let her out, but she escaped last night for a short while. Soooooo sorreeeeeeeeeeeeeee.
3) Pretend to be an actress and say: 'I was researching a role for my new movie where I have to play a mad girl and I wanted to get into the character for a while.'

Chapter 12

Mental
Makeover

I dialled Luke's mobile on the way to school. It was switched off.

I tried again when I got to school. Still switched off.

In the break at school, I made my way into the girls' cloakroom, found a cubicle then dialled his number again. Luckily it was break at his school as well, as he picked up.

'Hi, this is Nesta,' I said.

'Oh. Yeah. Hi.' His voice sounded cold. Uninterested.

'I er, just wanted to say three things. First sorry, the aliens got me. Not my fault I was weird last night, they interfered with my brain.'

There was silence at the other end.

'OK. Not aliens. Um . . . I was researching for a film role where I have to play a schizophrenic. That's someone with a dual personality. No, you weren't. Yes, I was. Shut up. No, you shut up.'

Still silence.

'OK, you got me,' I said. 'I have to tell you the real truth. I have an evil and psychotic twin. It was her you saw last night.'

Still silence.

'Oh Luke, listen, I guess, I . . . I wanted to say, sorry. I guess I acted a bit strange last night. This thing with our dads has got to me more than I thought and my mum always said I had an overactive imagination. I guess it ran away with me. I know what I thought was mad especially now in the light of the day, having slept on it and . . .' I realised that I was doing all the talking. 'Are you still there, Luke? Join in anytime . . .' There was a very loooooooooong silence. Oh dentists, I thought, I'm going to be dumped before we really got started. And it's all my stupid fault. 'Are you still there, Luke?'

'Yeah.'

'Right. So . . .' But I didn't have anything else to say. My flow of bad apology and mad excuses had dried up. 'Um, OK then. See you around maybe . . . Sorry, sorry . . .'

'Look, Nesta,' said Luke, 'I think you have to make up your mind what you want. I felt a total idiot last night, being left in that café with two of your mates watching it all . . .'

'Not my mates. They're in my class . . .'

'Whatever.'

'Yeah. Sorry. Whatever.'

'And what were you on about? Me being your brother?'

'I know. Oops. Big mistake. Velly solly.'

I heard the bell go in the distance at his end. 'I have to go to class. Look, Nesta. I think we got involved a bit fast. Let's slow down a bit and take some time. Think about what we want, OK. *You* think about what *you* want. I get the feeling that you don't really know.'

'Oh . . . OK.'

'Just take some time . . .'

'Yeah,' I said. 'I heard you. Take some time. OK. One, two, three. OK. Ready.'

At last Luke laughed. 'Bit longer maybe. Look. Call me later,' he said. 'Maybe we could meet up tomorrow?' This time his voice sounded warmer.

'OK. Later.'

Hurrah, I thought as I switched my phone off and went to find the girls. Once again, life never closes a wotsit without opening another wotsit.

Tomorrow, he'd said. That's Friday. In that case, I decided, I was going to take full advantage of the next twenty-four hours and put myself through a mental makeover and crash course on films and all I could find to do with them. When I saw Luke next, I was going to astound him with my tip-top knowledge of everything to do with movies and not just the entertaining kind that I liked. I was going to be Miss Film Critic of the year.

At lunch-time, I went to the library and piled all the books about films that I could on to the desk. I poured through them trying to remember who'd directed what and who'd produced what, so that I could name-drop and impress Luke. In the evening, I pulled all Dad's movie books out on to the dining table and continued my swotting up.

'What's going on?' asked Tony when he found me nose to page with *Halliwell's Film Guide*.

'Need to know about movies,' I said, indicating the books.

'But you do already,' he said. 'Don't tell me that having a director as a dad hasn't rubbed off on you? I think you know more than you realise.'

'Not as much as Luke. He knows about ones I've never heard of.'

'And you probably know about ones he's never heard of. Don't put yourself down, Nesta.'

'But there's so many, hundreds, thousands, I'm beginning to think that there aren't enough hours in the week to mug up on it all. I don't know where to begin.'

'Well what genre are you looking at?' he asked. 'You do know what a genre is, don't you?'

'Yeah. Course,' I said. 'It means type. Like romance or comedy. There are loads of different genres. Like thriller, horror, detective, sci-fi, war, cartoon . . .'

'See. You're not as stupid as you look,' said Tony.

'But I'll *never* have enough time to swot up on all of them,' I said, groaning. 'It's so complicated.'

'So why are you looking at all this stuff? For a school project?'

'No way. For Luke.'

Tony laughed. 'Ah well, there's only one film you should talk to him about,' he said.

'Which is?'

'The Coen brothers movie. *O Brother, Where Art Thou?*'

'Oh ha ha, you're so funny,' I said. 'I'm trying to forget about that minor brain blip. But seriously, I need to impress Luke with my knowledge of movies.'

'Why?'

'It's his passion and I think I blew it the other night by dismissing him when he was talking about them.'

'Ah. You've forgotten the rules.'

'What rules?'

'How to be a brilliant conversationalist.'

'I know how to be a brilliant conversationalist, least no one's ever complained before. Why? Do you know something I don't?'

'Actually, yes I do,' said Tony. 'Or something you've forgotten.'

'OK, Mister Know It All. What?'

Tony shook his head and looked at me sadly. 'Wow. This guy has really got to you, hasn't he? I don't think I've ever seen you lose it like this before. It's like your brain has gone dead. You don't talk, you *listen*. Ask a few pointed questions, then listen some more.'

'Duh? Explain?'

'What's the most flattering thing in the world?' asked Tony.

'To be told you're totally beautiful, I guess.'

'Wrong. Well, that's OK, but actually, it's when someone is like, totally interested in what you have to say. Often in conversations, people don't listen to each other. Not really. Often, all the time one person is talking, the other person is planning what they're going to say, often not even really listening . . .'

I couldn't resist. 'Sorry. What were you saying? I was too busy planning what I was going to say next.'

'If you're not going to pay attention . . .'

'No, Tone, I was just having a laugh. Sorry. Listening.'

'Well, that's it really. There's nothing more flattering than someone really listening to you. People *love* to talk about themselves and what they think. Course, this tactic won't last for ever, as you might get bored out of your brains listening to someone else's opinion all the time, but in the beginning it can really sway things in your favour. I do it all the time. Makes girls feel really special. A lot of boys haven't cottoned on to it yet. Ask girls what they think about things they're into and really listen like you're fascinated.'

I pointed to all the books I'd been studying. 'So you're saying that I don't have to study all this stuff?'

'You can if you want to but, if the only reason you're doing it is to have a conversation with Luke about movies and make him feel good, then you don't need to read up. All you need to do is listen to what he thinks, ask him his opinion about a few films and really listen to his replies. If you do it right, he won't even notice that you haven't said much.'

'Thanks Tony, you're a star,' I said. How could I have forgotten the golden rules, I asked myself? I already *knew* what he'd told me. Clearly falling in lurve had not made me blind but *stupid*. But then, I guess this is the first time that the tables have turned on me. Usually it's boys who are trying to impress me. I've never felt that I had to work hard to impress one of them before. And now Tony's reminded me how easy it is. Just let them talk and I listen. I put away the books and settled down to watch *EastEnders*. Bliss.

The Bluffer's Guide to Good Conversation, by Tony

1) When you can, bluff it.
2) When you can't, don't be afraid to say that you don't know about a subject or else you can end up looking a prat.
3) Third option is to feed lines to the person you're interested in and listen to their replies. Remember it only works in the short term. If you're really interested in someone for the long run, it's best to be honest, as communication has to be two-way for it to work.
4) Before you try option 3, practise until perfect, the kind of facial expression that says that you know exactly what he/she's talking about (a cross between glee and constipation).
5) Study your subject and start off with a few general openers that will spark off areas of interest eg, for film: 'And who do you think should win Best Actor at this years Oscars?'
6) Learn to feed lines that get him/her going on his favourite subject.

For example, for a boy who's into movies:

Right approach:
He: Are you into movies?

You: Oh yes. What are your top three favourites and why?

Him: Ten minutes animated reply.

You: Mmmm. *Fascinating.* Tell me more.

Him: Another ten minute animated opinion.

You: *Exactly!*

He: (thinks) What an impressive girl!

Wrong approach:

He: Are you into movies?

You: I prefer telly. Let me tell you what I think . . . (ten minutes of you talking.)

He: But I don't watch those things . . .

You: Really? Well let me fill you in on what you've been missing. (Ten minutes about the soap.)

He: (thinks) We have nothing in common, plus I can't get a word in. I'm outta here now.

Note from Nesta: Of course, true communication is two-way with talking and listening on both sides, but this is an excellent method when you are trying to pull, especially if you have a brace in, as it means you can just nod and look interested (and beautiful).

Chapter 13

Revelations

By Friday night, I was ready to try out my tip-top conversation skills on the lovely Luca. He called me on my mobile at lunch-time and asked if I'd like to go over to his house that evening.

'Mum will be here for a while,' he said, 'then she'll go to join Dad at the restaurant and Marisa's out with her mates, so I thought we could watch a movie or something.'

I'd like to do 'or something', I thought and almost said so, but I managed to restrain myself and put my 'How to be a brilliant conversationalist' into practice instead.

'I have to work for an hour or so at Lucy's dad's shop after school, but I could come over after that. A movie sounds great. But what genre? Sci-fi, Horror? War? Which do *you* prefer?'

Woah! Did that get Luke going! He was off and didn't pause for breath for five minutes.

'Mmmm. Exactly,' I said when he'd finished.

'I'm really looking forward to seeing you again,' he said. 'It's not often I meet a girl who knows about films and who I can talk to like this.'

Bingo, I thought. Hoho haha, yep yeppity yes.

After my shelf stacking stint at Mr Lovering's shop, I dashed home to get changed to go to Luke's. Black jeans, black polo neck, black kohl on my eyes, so that I looked like one of those Frenchie bohemian intellectual types. I made sure that I wore my high black boots though, so I didn't look too brainboxy.

I was ready to leave at the same time as Mum, who was going to pick up Dad from the station, and she offered to drop me on her way. She wasn't too happy when I gave her Luke's address.

'What's all this about then?' she asked as we followed the directions he'd given. 'I thought your dad asked you not to see him.'

'I know, but you haven't forbidden me, have you? And anyway, it doesn't make sense. Surely you can see that?'

'I guess.' Mum shrugged as if to say she didn't understand Dad's ultimatum either.

'Don't tell him where I am, will you?' I asked as we reached Luke's road and Mum stopped in front of a semi-detached house with a neat lawn in the front.

'Not if you don't want,' she said, 'but I think you two have got some talking to do over the weekend. I don't like all this going behind each other's backs and not telling the whole story . . .'

'He started it.'

Mum sighed. 'He has his reasons.'

'So why doesn't he tell me them?'

Mum sighed again. 'Just be back around ten, OK?'

'OK. Luke will probably drop me.'

'Well, give me a ring if he can't.'

Two minutes later, a smiling Mrs De Biasi opened the door of their house, then showed me into the sitting room. It was a Mediterranean-style room, modern with marble floors and light sofas dotted with turquoise and sea blue cushions. I did 'Polite Visitor' for a while and asked questions about the décor, how her week had been and so on, then she went to call Luke and get us some juice. As soon as Luke came down, I quickly asked if he had any update on the story of our two dads.

He shook his head. 'Not really, the time hasn't been right. There's either been people around or, I dunno . . . we don't exactly communciate very well at the best of times and I thought it might be weird if I suddenly asked about his past, especially if it's something awkward. How about you?'

I shook my head. 'Dad's only getting back this evening and I didn't think it was a question for the phone. But

Mum said she'd make him tell me the whole story. I'll let him have a lie-in tomorrow then see how it feels . . .'

Luke nodded. 'I know. Waiting for the right time can take forever sometimes . . .'

Suddenly I spotted a group of framed photos on the bookshelves at the back of the room and got up from the sofa to go and have a closer look. One of them was of a boy, who looked about ten. 'Ah sweet,' I said to Luke. 'It's you, isn't it?'

'It is,' said Mrs De Biasi coming back in with a tray of drinks and almond biscuits. 'He was such a sweetie.' She showed me another photo of a baby. 'And this is him as a baby.'

Luke looked really embarrassed. 'Muu*um*,' he groaned. 'What time are you going? I'm sure Nesta isn't in the least bit interested in looking at photos of me.'

I laughed. 'Oh, but I am. I love looking at photos and you were sooooo cute.'

'My lovely Luca,' said Mrs De Biasi, giving Luke's cheek a pinch. 'He was so beautiful as a child. A little cherub.'

'Muu*um*,' groaned Luke again.

'You like to see some more, Nesta?' asked Mrs De Biasi pulling out some huge photo albums out from the shelf.

Luke went over to his mum and put a cautionary hand on her arm. '*No*, Mum. *Please*.'

'But I'd love to see them,' I said. 'Honest.'

Luke sighed and stepped out of the way. 'She does this all the time. Ma, I'm sure Nesta isn't in the slightest bit interested.'

Mrs De Biasi ignored him and laid two albums out on the coffee table. Soon we were sitting side by side and she was flicking the pages, showing me photos of Luke at six months, as a toddler, a little boy . . .

'Mum has photographed every event for every year since . . . the beginning of time,' said Luke indicating the shelves. 'See – all that bookcase is full of her albums, photos of relatives, friends, the milkman, the newspaper boy, everyone goes in.'

'People are what make life special,' smiled Mrs De Biasi. 'And now I am going to photograph you. It's not often Luke invites a girl home. Hold on, I'll just get my camera, I think it's upstairs . . .'

'Have you told your mum anything about my dad recognising your name?' I asked when she'd gone.

Luke shook his head. 'Didn't want to until we knew what it was about ourselves.'

'Probably best,' I said and went to look at the other framed photos on the bookshelf. 'Hey, are all these albums your mum's? Or is there one of your dad's?'

'Most of them are mixed,' said Luke getting up. 'But I seem to remember that there is one of Dad's from when he was young. Oh right. You think there might be a photo of your dad in there?'

I nodded.

'Smart thinking,' said Luke. 'Here. Let me find it.'

He found a tattered red album on the bottom shelf and hauled it on to the table. As he turned the pages, old sepia photos were revealed.

'Old aunties and great grandparents . . .' he said as faces from another era gazed out at us. About a quarter of the way through the book, the sepia pictures turned to black and white, then colour, then there it was.

'Ohmigod!' I gasped and pointed to a man in a photo. 'That's my dad.'

'And that's mine standing next to him,' said Luke.

The picture was of a couple of teenage lads sitting on a wall outside a terraced house. They looked about seventeen. Both had their arms round a teenage girl in the middle.

'Shhhh,' I said as we heard footsteps coming back down the stairs. 'Don't say anything. Let's see if she can tell us anything.'

'Hey Ma, who's this?' asked Luke, pointing at the photo. 'Not you, is it?'

Luke's mum came and stood next to him and looked at the picture. 'No,' she said, then smiled sadly. 'That was Matteo's sister, Nadia Costello.'

I looked closely at the photo. I'd seen pictures of Nadia, but not this one. I was almost named after her. She died when she was eighteen in a car accident, which is why Dad didn't want me to have the same name. Nesta was a sort of compromise to keep his mum happy.

'And who was Matteo?' asked Luke acting innocent.

Mrs De Biasi sat down at the table. 'He was your father's best friend. They grew up together. Like brothers they were.'

'Did you know him?' I asked.

'Oh yes,' she said. 'In those days, all the Italian families knew each other. We all lived close. We were in and out of each other's houses. We worked and played together. It was a very close community.'

'So how come I've never met him?' asked Luke playing it perfectly.

'Ah . . .' sighed Mrs De Biasi. 'They fell out.'

'Why?' asked Luke. 'What happened?'

'Nadia died,' said Mrs De Biasi, closing the album and putting it back on the shelf.

'But why would Matteo and Gianni fall out over that?' Luke asked.

'Matteo blamed Gianni for her death.'

'But why?' I gasped. 'What did he do?'

Mrs De Biasi sat on the sofa and looked out of the window for a moment, then she turned back to us. 'He didn't do anything. That's what is so sad. When Gianni was young, all the young Italians hung out together, all local . . .'

'Including Matteo's sister, Nadia?' I asked.

Mrs De Biasi nodded her head. 'One night, we'd all been to a club in Soho, Matteo was supposed to see Nadia home safely, but he'd just met some new girl. I can't remember her name. Oh, he was a one for the girls was Matteo . . .'

Like Tony, I thought. Like father, like son.

'He didn't want to be landed with his younger sister for the night,' continued Mrs De Biasi. 'He wanted to go off with his new girl. Anyway, he and Gianni argued about taking Nadia home and, as Gianni didn't have a girl that night, it was just before we dated, he agreed that he'd see her home. She had just passed her driving test and insisted on driving. I think Gianni had a bit of a crush on her and so he let her. Plus, she was a strong-willed girl was Nadia, I remember, liked to get her own way . . .' She was quiet for a few minutes and looked sad as though remembering something painful.

'So what happened?' I asked.

Mrs De Biasi let out a deep sigh. 'On their way home, some lunatic drunk driver ploughed into them. Nadia was killed instantly and Gianni taken to hospital. We didn't know if he was going to make it as it was touch and go for him for a while. But Matteo never came to see him. He blamed Gianni and never spoke to him again.'

'But it wasn't Gianni, I mean Mr De Biasi's fault,' I exclaimed.

'No, it wasn't,' said Mrs De Biasi. 'But Matteo blamed him all the same.'

'Guilt,' I said. 'He was supposed to see her home, but went off with the other girl.'

'Yes.'

'What happened to him?' I asked. 'Do you know?'

'We heard that he married later,' said Mrs De Biasi, her eyes filling with tears. 'Had a son, then his wife died. So sad, so much loss in his life.'

Seeing Mrs De Biasi on the verge of tears caused tears to spring to my eyes. Poor Dad. Even though I knew about Nadia and of course about Tony's mum, I'd never really thought about how it must have been for him before. And now I felt really sorry for him. It must have been awful losing two people he was close to in such a short time.

'What was he like when he was young?' I asked.

Mrs De Biasi's face lit up. 'Oh he was a joy. So full of life. So charming. All the girls had a crush on him.' Her face clouded again. 'He moved away, to Bristol I think. That's the last we heard.'

I looked at Luke. I was dying to tell her that Dad only lived around the corner.

'Has Dad ever tried to contact him?' he asked.

'At first,' said Mrs De Biasi, 'but Matteo wouldn't have anything to do with him. I often wonder what happened to him. Gianni would dearly love to re-establish contact and heal the past.'

She pulled a tissue from her sleeve and had a good

blow. Then she sat up straight as though pulling herself together. 'Best not to dwell on the past. And anyway, why are you two so interested?'

I couldn't hold back any longer. 'Mrs De Biasi,' I burst out. 'I have something to tell you.'

Nesta's Top Tips for the Intellectual (But Sexy) Look

Clothes:

All black, tight fitting. Think Audrey Hepburn in the 1957 film classic, *Funny Face*. (Get my movie knowledge! Impressive or wot?)

No girlie pinks or pastels.

Accessories:

Pair of specs: even if you don't need them (preferably tortoiseshell and v. trendy frame).

Heavy-looking Russian novel (don't worry, you don't have to read it!).

Shoes: black chunky workman-type boots, but only if worn with ultra short skirt and black tights.

Packet of Gauloise cigarettes, but don't even think about lighting one up as they taste *dégoûtante* (disgusting).

Chapter 14

Surprise, Surprise!

I couldn't wait to tell Dad. Mrs De Biasi's reaction to discovering who I was had strengthened my resolve to get him and Mr De Biasi back together as soon as possible.

When she had grasped the fact that I really was Matteo's daughter, she laughed and hugged me, then cried, then rang her husband and cried and laughed all over again.

'Very emotional, my ma,' said Luke as we listened to her telling her husband the whole story over the phone. 'She cries at everything.'

'I think it's lovely,' I said. 'People shouldn't be afraid to show what they feel.'

'Gianni can't believe it,' said Mrs De Biasi after she'd put down the phone. 'We're both so pleased to know Matteo is well and happily married after so much tragedy early in his life. And so happy to know he has you and your brother Tony, but I fear that he won't have changed his mind about Gianni. I hope so, now that we have met you, Nesta, but don't get your hopes up, we have to respect his feelings too. We may want reconciliation but he may not.'

Luke nodded. 'Yes, it's really up to your dad,' he said.

'Well, what are your feelings, Mrs De Biasi?' I asked.

'Ah, Nesta. I feel that life is too short to hold these stupid grudges and those boys had a true friendship. Too precious to lose.'

Exactly my feelings, I thought. I couldn't imagine life without Lucy, Izzie and TJ to share everything with and talk things over with.

When Mrs De Biasi had gone off to the restaurant, Luke and I sat down to watch a movie. He'd already told me that he liked war films and, although they're not my favourite, I decided that, as part of my movie education, I had to expand my viewing and watch a few new genres. He'd picked out one called *Saving Private Ryan*. Should be OK, I thought, Tom Hanks is in it so it must be a feel-goody of a sort.

'It's really cool that you want to watch this,' said Luke as he put the DVD in the machine. 'Not many girls would, but I think it's important to know that these things went on.'

'Oh so do I,' I said as I took my boots off, then curled up on the sofa. I was feeling very pleased about everything. Happy happy. It was all going to turn out brilliantly. Even though Mrs De Biasi and Luke had their reservations, I was certain I was going to prove them wrong. I was going to reconcile Dad and Luke's dad. I could see the grand reunion now. It would be like those smaltzy programmes on telly that bring together people who have lost each other and they hug and cry, like Mrs De Biasi had, then clap and laugh and generally feel good and smile a lot. And it would all be down to me. Fab. And now, here I was with Luke ready to watch a serious-type film. Yes. I was definitely changing. Growing up. No one could accuse me of being shallow any more. Oh no, I reunite people, help heal troubled pasts and watch war films. You can't get more unshallow than that. Yeah. As the credits to the movie rolled, I wondered if I should get a pair of glasses to wear to complement my new persona. One of those pairs with square frames that make you look really cool and intelligent. I don't need glasses, but I'm sure I could get a pair without a prescription, just for the effect.

Luke and I snuggled up on the sofa and began to watch the movie. First five minutes, yeah, it was OK. Ten minutes, not really my cup of tea, but I'll sit through it for Luke. However, as it went on, I found I couldn't even do that. It was *horrible*. The war scenes were unbelievable, or rather they were totally believable. Awful. Graphic. People getting blown up and killed left, right and centre. I tried to make myself carry on watching, but it was too upsetting, so I made an excuse that I needed to use the bathroom and got out double quick.

As I splashed my face with water, I tried to tell myself that, as Luke had said, I ought to watch to know what went on. History and all that. Part of my education, etc. Then I thought, but I *do* know what went on. I do. Maybe I don't know names and dates and countries, but I do know what goes on in war. Hell on earth, that's what and it makes me *really* depressed. More than anything. Whatever nationality, I know mothers lost sons, sisters lost brothers, children lost fathers. Boys like Tony, Luke, Steve and Lal, hardly older and all sent to early graves. And I thought, why do people have to fight and kill like that? What for? Where's it got anyone? I truly believe that the majority of the world, of all races and beliefs, want to live in peace. They want to watch their pot plants grow on their patios, enjoy the summers, their families, their pets. I hate war. And I've just realised that I hate war films too.

After a few minutes, Luke came and knocked on the bathroom door.

'You all right in there?' he called.

I opened the door. 'Yes. No. Just . . . I'm really sorry Luke, but I can't watch any more of that film. I hope you don't think I'm shallow, but . . . I think there's so much

147

bad news in the world, when I watch a movie I want to be entertained not freaked out . . .'

'Found it upsetting, did you?'

I nodded. 'Yeah. Sorry. Can't do it.'

Luke smiled. 'That's OK and I don't think you're shallow. Everyone likes different stuff, that's all. Look, I'll find you a feel-good movie instead. Ever seen *It's a Wonderful Life?*'

At last some of my swotting up came in handy. Only last night, I read about it in one of Dad's books. One of the great classics, the book had said. 'I haven't seen it, but it was directed by Frank Capra wasn't it? Starring James Stewart?'

Luke looked well impressed. 'Yeah. Hey, you know your stuff. Come on, I'll put it on for you.'

Ten minutes later we were back on the sofa and this time I got well stuck in. It was a fantastic movie. All about a man who feels his whole life has been a waste, until an angel takes him back through it, showing the effect he'd had on people and what would have happened if he hadn't been there. It was a really uplifting, amazing film and left me with a warm glow. Much better than seeing people get their heads blown off, I thought.

In their different ways though, both films made me think the same thing – that life is precious and it's really important to let the people that you love know it. Friends, family, whoever. Not to let any petty arguments or misunderstandings get in the way. By the end of the evening, I was certain that it was fated that I'd met Luke. It was my destiny to bring our dads back together. I couldn't wait.

Mum was sitting on her own in the sitting room when I got home. 'Where's Dad?' I asked.

'Oh, hi love. Bit of a crisis with the film. He had to go straight into the editing suite to sort it out. He'll be back later. There was some problem on the first rushes.' My face must have fallen as Mum looked at me anxiously. 'What is it, Nesta? What's happened?'

I went and sat beside her and the whole story poured out. 'You knew about Aunt Nadia, didn't you?' I asked.

'Some of it,' she admitted. 'Your dad told me about it once when we passed the place in North Finchley where they all used to live. I could tell it was a very sore subject for him. Look, I can see that you're dying to talk to him about it all . . . but not tonight sweetheart, please, he's got a lot on his mind with the film and probably won't be back until late. Let him sleep and you can talk in the morning.'

I did as I was told, but made sure I was up bright and early ready to break the news to him. Mum was right. I couldn't wait. I knew he'd be overjoyed that Mr and Mrs De Biasi wanted to see him and heal the past.

When I got to the kitchen, Mum was already making coffee.

'Can I take Dad's in to him?' I asked.

'Oh Nesta! You've missed him again. They didn't sort the problem last night, so he had to go in first thing. He was up at six. He said to say hi and he's sorry he missed you last night and he'll see you later. He'll probably be back before lunch.'

'Did you tell him that I know about the De Biasis?'

Mum shook her head. 'No, I didn't. Talk to him later . . . but Nesta, don't get your hopes up. I know you're excited about it, but your dad might not have the same reaction.'

'I bet he will,' I said. 'It's going to be fab. It all happened a long time ago. He's bound to want to see them again.'

Mum gave me a strange look, then went back to making toast.

Over breakfast, I told Tony the latest news and together we went to meet the girls and Luke in Costa in Highgate for mid-morning coffee and a general Saturday hang-out. We got there first, so bought some cappuccinos and pastries and looked for somewhere to sit.

'It's all starting to make sense now,' said Tony as he bagged our favourite seats in the window.

'What is?' I asked.

'Why Dad didn't want me to have driving lessons. Remember, he went over the top about it?'

I nodded. 'Yes, of course. Nadia had only just passed

her test when she was killed. I guess he didn't want anything like that to happen to you.'

Tony gazed out of the window for a while in silence. 'If he'd only told us what had happened, I would have understood. I really would. Instead, I thought he was being totally unreasonable . . .'

'I know,' I said. 'It's mad that we don't communicate properly. I mean, he's our dad. He ought to be able to tell us what he's really thinking. Oh, I do hope he'll see the De Biasis. I mean I understand he was freaked at the time, it was his responsibility to see Aunt Nadia home and he blew it, but he shouldn't blame it on Luke's dad.'

'No,' said Tony. 'But I guess you never think anything is going to happen like that. It's like, Mum and Dad are always asking me to watch out for you and yet the number of times I've gone off and left you to get home on your own or asked one of the girls to make sure you get home . . .'

'I know. It could happen so easily. Dad lost his sister. He couldn't prevent that, but he needn't have lost his best friend.'

A moment later, Luke came in to join us and Tony went to get him a drink from the counter. Luke sat in the chair next to me and took my hand. I was about to tell him that I hadn't had a chance to speak to Dad yet, when a familiar car drove past and slowed down for the lights at the pelican crossing. It was a black BMW. Our car. And

Dad was in the driving seat. He glanced in the window at Costa and his face lit up when he saw me. He waved, then he saw Luke next to me and his face clouded. He pulled over at the kerb, much to the annoyance of whoever was behind him, and beckoned for me to come out of the café.

'Dad's out there,' I said to Luke. 'Won't be a moment. Maybe he'll come and join us.'

Outside, Dad waved at me to get into the car, so I slid into the passenger seat and gave him a big hug.

'Hi, Dad.'

'I thought I asked you not to see that boy,' he said.

'It's OK,' I said. 'I know everything.'

'What do you mean, you know everything?'

'Luke's mum told me the whole story. About Nadia . . .'

Dad looked like he was going to explode. 'She *what*? She had no right doing that. It's not her business.'

'I saw photos, Dad. In her album. She didn't know who I was. There was a picture of you and Luke's dad and Aunt Nadia. Luke asked who the girl in the photo was.'

Dad took a couple of very deep breaths as though trying to calm himself.

'It wasn't Mrs De Biasi's fault it all came out, but it did,' I blustered. 'And then I watched *Saving Private Ryan* and it made me realise that life is too short to have any kind of war, big or little and . . . and then I watched *It's a*

Wonderful Life and I realised that your friends and family are the most important thing . . .'

But Dad didn't seem to be listening. He was staring ahead with a grim look on his face.

'Come and meet Luke again,' I said. 'He's in there with Tony.'

'With Tony?'

I nodded.

'You tell him to come out at once. I don't want you mixing with that family.'

'Why not, Dad? You're being totally unreasonable. What happened was a long time ago. It's all in the past . . . And it wasn't Gianni, I mean Mr De Biasi's fault Nadia died. He almost died himself. You must see that. It might have been you in that car with her and she would have still died. You just feel guilty about it. It's mad. It was the fault of the drunk driver who drove into them. No one else's fault.'

'We'll continue this discussion at home,' said Dad and he started up the engine. I quickly got out of the car. Dad leaned over and wound down the window. 'Nesta. Back in the car. Now.'

'No. I'm going back into Costa, then I'm going to the De Biasis' restaurant and I'm not coming home until you come and talk to Luke's dad.'

'Nesta, get in the car.'

I turned my back and walked towards Costa, where I

could see Luke and Tony looking out of the window with concern. Behind them, I caught a glimpse of TJ, Izzie and Lucy in the queue at the counter. They must have arrived while I was in the car with Dad. It wasn't meant to be like that, I thought as I went back in to join them. It was meant to be one of the best moments of Dad's life. I'd wanted to make him really happy after all he'd been through, but instead I'd never seen him look so mad. Or sad.

'Well that went well,' I said as I rejoined Tony and Luke.

'You OK?' asked Luke.

'Yeah, course,' I said, then sighed. 'Parents, huh? You try your best to keep them on the right track, but sometimes they won't listen . . .' I tried my best to smile and make light of what had just happened, but instead, I burst into tears.

Big Realisation

People don't always want what you want for them.

Chapter 15

Stand Off

'I'd never dare defy my dad like that,' said TJ as we made our way down Jackson's Lane on the way to Biasi's. 'He'd throw me out or something.'

'Dad would never do that,' I said, 'but he did look upset.' Privately I was wondering if I had pushed my luck a bit too far. I didn't know what had come over me as I'm not usually that disobedient, but then Dad and I don't usually argue.

'I think you should go home,' said TJ. 'Give him time to adjust to the idea that the whole story about your aunt is out. It's a biggie for him. He must have felt he let everyone down at the time and now you know about it. He probably wants to be the hero in your eyes. You need to tell him he still is and that everyone makes mistakes and has regrets.'

'I did, sort of. I told him that the only person responsible for Nadia's death was the drunk driver. But he wasn't listening. What do you think I should do, Lucy?'

'God, I don't know. Go home and give him a hug. I feel really sorry for him.'

I felt such a failure. Giving Dad a big hug is exactly what I'd meant to do. Part of my fantasy of organising the great reunion. Hah. So much for my mediator, peace-making, healing-the-past skills. Me and my big mouth. Nothing ever comes out right.

Luke and Tony had walked ahead of the rest of us. They seemed to get on really well and I couldn't help but think that Dad and Luke's dad must have looked just like them when they were younger. I was really chuffed that Tony had decided to come with me and support me. He didn't always take my side, but I think he wanted to get this sorted. Or it may be because he thinks that, if Dad doesn't come round, then he'll never let him drive. On the other hand, it may be because Lucy is coming with us and it's a chance for him to hang out with her a bit more. At that moment, he turned and caught Lucy's eye and they smiled at each other. Yeah, he's definitely come along because of Lucy.

As we walked on, I considered my options. Should I go home and give Dad a hug and say I was sorry? Should I let the reunion with Mr De Biaisi go and not push him? Then I remembered the Frank Capra film last night. The whole story seemed to be saying that things happen for a reason. We meet the people that we meet in life for a purpose. Of all the families, in all of London, I meet the De Biasis. It *had* to be fate. I decided to ask the destiny expert.

'What do you think I should do, Iz?'

'Hmmmm,' said Izzie. 'I think you should . . . I dunno, er . . . be prepared to be flexible. Prepared to bend. Yeah, that's it. I read in one of my books that you have to be like a branch on a tree. You know, it bends in the wind. Whereas stuff that doesn't bend or resists, gets broken.'

'Right,' I said, feeling none the wiser. Sometimes I don't quite get Izzie's advice. 'Yeah. OK. I'll be a branch on a tree. You got any last bits of wisdom to pass on, TJ?'

'Don't ask me,' she said. 'You have to decide.'

'Well I'm going to Biasi's,' I said, 'and I'm going to stick to my guns and not budge until Dad comes to talk to them.'

'Then I hope you like pasta,' said Lucy.

'Why?'

'Because you might be there for a very long time.'

Ten minutes later, we all trooped into Biasi's. It was still early and there weren't any customers for lunch yet, so Luke took advantage of the quiet time to do introductions, then fill his mum and dad in on the latest. Seeing their reaction, my reunion fantasy faded even more. They were horrified.

'Oh *no*. Oh Nesta, I'm so sorry,' said Mrs De Biasi. 'I remember how stubborn your dad could be. When he'd made his mind up about something, there was no shifting him.'

Tony laughed. 'One of the many traits he's passed down to his daughter. They're both as stubborn as mules, so this stand-off will be interesting. See who backs down first.'

'Well, it won't be me,' I said.

'No please, Nesta, go home,' said Mrs De Biasi. 'We don't want to come between you and your family. It's the last thing we want.'

'I can't. Not now.'

Mr De Biasi came over and stood in front of me. 'Nesta, go home,' he urged. 'Your father blames me for enough as it is. I don't need this on top. It will only stir everything up again. If he doesn't want to see us, then we must respect that.'

Lucy put her hand on my arm. 'He's right,' she said. 'This might hinder rather than help. Remember what Mum said about not pushing people before they were ready.'

Tony nodded. 'Yeah. Best leave it, sis. It's Dad's call, not yours.'

I was just starting to think that maybe they were right when I saw our car draw up outside the restaurant. Dad was driving and Mum was in the passenger seat. 'Ohmigod! They're here,' I gasped.

I saw Dad glance in at the window, then quickly look away. It must have been quite a shock for him seeing all of us staring back out at him.

'Come away from the door,' said Mrs De Biasi bustling everyone to sit at a table. 'Don't stare at him.'

Two minutes later, the door opened and Mum came in.

I quickly introduced her to Luke's mum and dad and she was very sweet to them, although she gave me a 'Just wait till I get you home, madam' look. 'I'm so sorry about all this family stuff,' she said to the De Biasis, 'You seem to have got caught up in the middle.'

'No, please, we were so happy to hear that Matteo is well,' said Mr De Biasi, 'and to meet Nesta . . .'

'She's so like her father,' said Mrs De Biasi, glancing out of the window with a wistful look.

'Well, I've come to take her home,' said Mum. 'It's lunch-time and Matt wants to spend some time with her and Tony before he has to go back off to Bristol.'

I wasn't fooled. 'So why did Dad come here with you? You could have come on your own.'

Mum sighed. 'Don't be difficult, Nesta. He offered to give me a lift.'

'I think he wants to see the De Biasis more than he's letting on,' I said. 'He needn't have driven you to come and get me. He doesn't usually. It's the unconscious mind thingee, oh you explain Izzie, you know, where your subconscious makes you do what your conscious mind won't let you.'

Suddenly Mr De Biasi got up. 'Enough,' he said and he walked out and got straight into the car with Dad.

'Ohmigod, ohmigod,' I said and dashed to the window to try and see what was going on. I could see that they were in the car and were talking, Mr De Biasi gesticulating and Dad staring ahead. Everything that Jo had told us about body language on the acting class was so evident. I couldn't hear what was being said, but it was clear that Dad was closed off and Mr De Biasi was trying to reach him.

It was Mum who called me away. 'Let them have their privacy,' she said.

'But Mum, this is the big moment . . .' I started.

'Your mother's right,' said Mrs De Biasi. 'Let them be.'

It was agony having to tear myself away from the window. If I'd had my way, I'd have gone and sat in the back seat and stuck my head in between them, so that I could have heard *exactly* what was being said and witnessed every facial expression and *every* shift of body language. But no, Mum made me sit with my back to the window and sip Diet Coke. My mum and Luke's made an effort to get on despite the strange circumstances and everyone else was chatting and laughing and having a good time, but for me the next fifteen minutes seemed to go on forever. It seemed like the dads had been out there for hours.

After what seemed like an eternity, I got up.

'Nesta,' warned Mum. 'Leave them.'

'Yeah. Will,' I said. 'Just going to the ladies.'

As I got up to go to the cloakrooms, I turned and had a quick peak out of the window. They were getting out of the car. Ohmigod, I thought, I hope it's OK and they're not going to fight or anything embarrassing like that. But no, Dad seemed to be dabbing his eyes and . . . yes . . . now he was smiling.

'Nesta,' said Mum, 'I *said* to leave them.'

'But . . . but they've got out of the car,' I said. 'Something's happening.'

Now even Mum couldn't resist looking. She stood up and peeked out, then everyone else did as well. Mr De Biasi was saying something to Dad and Dad creased up laughing. Then the two of them started walking towards the restaurant. For a brief second, I saw the boys that they were, Luke and Tony grown older. The moment after that was hysterical, as everyone dived for their places and tried to look nonchalant, like they hadn't really been gawping outside watching the dads' every move.

The door opened and they came in. Dad was still laughing as he turned to look at me. 'Gianni has just been telling me that you thought Luke was my long lost son . . .'

'Der . . . um, wah . . .' I started, then turned to Mr De Biasi. 'But how did you know?'

Mr De Biasi glanced at Luke, who looked sheepish for a moment. 'Well, I had to check out that it wasn't true, so I asked Mum,' he said, 'and she told Dad.'

Mrs De Biasi had been standing there silently beaming and suddenly she couldn't contain herself any more. 'Ciao, Matteo,' she said, rushing forward with open arms.

Dad turned to her and beamed back. 'Catarina,' he said, then he was enveloped in a huge hug.

Then Mr De Biasi couldn't hold back either and he and Dad looked at each other and gave each other a huge bear hug.

At last, it was the Kodak moment, but of course no one had a camera. Mum's eyes had misted over. Mrs and Mr De Biasi both had their arms around Dad. Tony, Luke, Lucy, Izzie and TJ were grinning like idiots. It was fab.

Chapter 16

Roses and Garlic

'I think friendship is the most important thing in life,' I said as I smeared aloe vera gel over my chin. It was a couple of weeks after le grando reunioni and Lucy, TJ, Izzie and I were lined up on the bathtub doing our Sunday morning monthly beauty routine. This time, I'd been down to the chemists and bought four gel face packs. Proper ones that didn't dribble down your neck or have raw egg in them. *Au naturel* dribbly gloops may be homemade and healthy, but they really aren't my style.

'So do I,' said Lucy. 'We must all make a pact that nothing will ever come between us, like it did for Nesta's and Luke's dads. They wasted years.'

'Each of them had their families,' said TJ, 'so it wasn't totally wasted time.'

'Yeah, but there's that saying, you can't pick your family, but you can pick your friends,' said Izzie. 'Friends are like a chosen family.'

'But whether it's friends or family, you have to keep talking,' I said. 'Say how you feel, even if it's a bit confrontational.'

Seems I started a craze with the De Biasi thing. Confrontation. Tony confronted Dad about driving lessons and, although he hasn't exactly said yes, he didn't say no either, so there's hope. Luke confronted his dad about wanting to be an actor and his dad said he'd think about it. Again, it's a start. And Mum confronted her bosses at work about cutting her hours and they said they'd do what they could to give her more time and reassured her that she had a secure job with them no matter how many younger faces they brought in. And I wasn't left out of the loop. Dad had a go at me about butting into other people's business. 'You don't always know what's best for everyone all the time, Nesta,' he said. 'Yes, I'm glad to see Gianni again, but I would have preferred to have done it in my own time.' I did apologise, but privately I think it's a good job that I pushed him. I know what 'in his own time' means from having him as a dad all these years. It's like when Mum asks him to mend a door or change a light bulb. He says he will, 'in his own time', which means never. He probably even means to, but Mum has learned that if she wants something doing, it's often quicker to do it herself.

So, all in all, there's been a lot going on, but I think it's all been for the best. Our family is certainly talking about stuff more openly than we did before. On top of all the confrontation and communication, the girls and I have decided that we have to have lots of jobs when we grow up, so that all our eggs aren't in one basket career-wise. Tony said he thought I ought to be a journalist as well as an actress and when I asked him why, he said because I speak in headlines. Huh! I don't know *what* he means.

Dad never did tell us what he and Mr De Biasi said in the car, but whatever it was, it mended the rift between them and we've been invited for Sunday lunch with them. We're also having a big birthday bash there as a late celebration for Tony's eighteenth. I get the feeling that the De Biasis are going to be regulars in our lives from now on. Hhhm. Don't know how I feel about that. My parents being chummy with my boyfriend's parents. Is it a good idea? Tony's removed himself from the cosy set-up already. He's taking Lucy out next weekend, but he's taking her to some place in Hampstead. 'Somewhere where no one knows us, so no one will be watching us and seeing what we're getting up to.' Hhmm, I thought, sounds like he has something in mind. I'd better warn Lucy, but on second thoughts, she can handle herself these days.

After we'd rinsed off our face packs, we got down to the serious business of painting our nails. Izzie pulled out a bottle of her favourite colour and a pack of stick-on diamonds.

'Want any of these?' she asked.

Looking at them gave me a brilliant idea.

'Yes please,' I said and took the sheet she was holding out to me.

I went to the mirror and stuck the diamonds on my brace, then I turned and smiled. 'Designer braces. What do you think?'

Izzie and TJ cracked up. 'Excellent,' said TJ. 'A million dollar smile.'

'Yeah,' I said. 'I decided I can't go round for the next year hiding behind my hand. I decided I'm going to wear my brace with pride.'

'Does it still hurt having it in?' asked TJ.

'No. It hasn't hurt for ages,' I said. 'It's like it's hardly there now.'

Lucy came back in with a tray of Cokes, so I smiled for her too. 'Cool. Mouth jewellery,' she said as she handed me a Coke. 'You'll start a trend.'

'I've also been thinking,' I said. 'All that stuff about being shallow, well, I've decided that it's not a bad thing and, actually, I like being the way I am. So,' I raised my Coke, 'here's a toast to frivolity.'

'What's brought this on?' asked TJ.

'I've been thinking about it a lot over the last few weeks. I was really worried that you all thought I was lightweight, you know, shallow, but I realised something the other night when I was at Luke's house watching his war film. I'll never be into heavy stuff like politics or war. I'll never be into reading literary-type books with clever words that only brainboxes understand. But I've realised that it doesn't matter. There's room for everyone and that includes people who are lightweight, in fact there are times people *want* lightweight. There's room for all types of films, for all types of books and for all types of people. And one sort shouldn't make the other sort feel unworthy or inferior. This is my new philosophy. There's a place for black and there's a place for pink. Room for garlic *and* for roses. Garlic smells um . . . garlicky, roses smell sweet. There's a time and place for both of them, but imagine if the rose suddenly developed a complex because it smelled flowery and not pungent. It would be really sad. No. As I said, everything has its place. Same with people. We're all different and that's what makes life interesting. You can't *be* everything and *know* about everything nor can you be what you're not. Shouldn't even try to be. Um, a rose shouldn't try to be garlic, nor the other way round. Um . . . what am I trying to say? Um . . . that all you can be is true to yourself.'

Izzie was giving me a really strange look, then she cracked up laughing.

'What? I asked. '*What?*"

'Just . . . wow,' said Izzie. 'That's *really* deep.'

'Is it?'

'Yeah,' said TJ. 'And it's exactly what Shakespeare wrote in *Hamlet*. "To thine own self be true, And it must follow, as the night the day, Thou canst not then be false to any man.""

'Really? Then he sounds really cool, does old Shakespearie dearie,' I said, feeling really chuffed that Izzie had said I was deep. 'Yeah. Yo! Shakespeare. My man.'

'To thine own self be true,
And it must follow, as the night the day,
Thou canst not then be false to any man.'
From *Hamlet,* by Shakespeare

'Be true to yourself. (Unless your roots need doing.)'
Nesta Williams (deep person)

Thanks as always to Brenda Gardner, Yasemin Uçar and the ever fab team at Piccadilly Press. To Rosemary Bromley at Juvenelia. And to Steve Lovering for all his help, input and for trekking round all the locations in the book with me.

Chapter 1

Wombat

'You go on in, TJ,' said Lucy looking up at Kenwood House.
'I'll walk the dogs.'

I burst out laughing. Lucy's tiny, not even five foot, more like
the dogs would walk her than the other way around. 'Yeah
right,' I said. 'I can see the headlines now. Have you seen this
girl? Blonde. Small   '

'Petite,' interrupted Lucy.

'Sorry, right, petite. Last sighted, Hampstead Heath being
dragged off by three wild animals.'

Izzie, Lucy, Nesta and I were standing shivering outside the
entrance to Kenwood House on Hampstead Heath on Saturday
morning. We had Ben, Jerry and Mojo with us. Ben and Jerry are
the Labradors who belong to Lucy's family and Mojo is my dog
(breed, er . . . somewhat mixed but he's very cute, black with a
white patch over one eye and he's my best friend, apart from
Hannah, Lucy, Izzie and Nesta that is).

'Yeah,' said Nesta, pushing stray dark hairs back into the
woolly hat that she had pulled down over her ears. 'Isn't the
saying supposed to go, mad dogs and English men go out in the
midday *sun*? Not the November rain. What are we doing out

here anyway when we could be in the café like sensible people, hogging the radiators and drinking big mugs of hot chocolate?'

'If you're cold, you go in and have a look around with TJ,' said Izzie. 'I'll stay with you, Lucy. I've been in. It's dead boring. Dark old rooms filled with paintings of people with glum, ugly faces staring down at you. They look like they've got plums in their mouths and pokers up their bums.'

'I've been in too,' I said. 'Many times. And those boring paintings, some of them are by Rembrandt, Gainsborough, Reynolds, there's even a Turner. I think it's a fabulous old building.'

Izzie looked at the white house and pulled a face. 'Looks like an enormous wedding cake in my opinion. Not my style at all.'

'It's neoclassical,' I said.

Nesta looked at me with amazement. 'God! How do you know this stuff?' she asked.

'Dunno,' I said, shrugging. 'Read it somewhere, I guess.'

'Well, you must read a *lot*,' said Nesta. 'You always seem to know about everything. Brains *and* beauty. It's not fair.'

'I am not beautiful.'

'Yes you are,' said Lucy. 'Remember when that journalist Sam Denham visited our school when we were in Year Nine and he called you Lara Croft? Not many people can claim to look like Angelina Jolie. Your trouble is that you have no confidence about your looks.'

'Yeah,' said Nesta, 'you could be one of those girls in the movies who wears specs, no make-up and has her hair tied back and works in a science lab or something. Then she meets the hero, lets her hair down, takes off her glasses and reveals that actually she's a total babe.'

'And the hero falls in love with her saying, oh but Miss Watts! You are *beeeooodiful*,' said Izzie, laughing.

'Stop it,' I said. I was getting embarrassed though it was cool to be compared to Angelina Jolie.

'It is awesome though,' said Lucy. 'As Nesta said, you do seem to know about all sorts of stuff the rest of us don't.'

'Only what I find interesting. I mean, don't you think it's amazing that there are paintings by all these famous artists right on our doorstep? Like, ten minutes away from where we live. Some people pay fortunes to go to Venice, Amsterdam, Florence and Paris to look at the great masters and we only have to pop down the road. Don't you think that's brilliant?'

Izzie gave me a blank look. 'No,' she said.

'There's one called *The Guitar Player* by Vermeer. I'd have thought you'd have loved that, Izzie, seeing as you're into music. She's got such a look of delight on her face. It's not like so many other paintings of the period where, you're right, the expressions are glum. It's like she was the first of many teenagers to get a guitar and you see how it never changes through time. Even back then they were . . .'

'Whatever. So she's got her guitar? I bet she's still dead ugly. All those people in old paintings are,' said Izzie with a playful squeeze of my arm. 'I went in there years ago with Mum. Not an experience I care to repeat. Nah. Looking round stuffy old houses isn't my thing at all.'

'I *love* looking around old places,' I said. 'The sense of history, imagining how it was in days gone by, who lived there, what they wore . . .'

'You're weird, TJ Watts,' said Izzie.

I pulled my best weird face (cross-eyed with a squiffy mouth). 'But don't forget it's also famous as a location in the movies. You have to admit that's pretty cool.'

'What movies?' asked Nesta.

'*Mansfield Park*. Some of that was filmed here and . . . and, it's in *Notting Hill* as well. Remember near the end when Hugh Grant goes to visit Julia Roberts' character when she's starring in a historical drama. That scene was filmed here. You can see the house in the background.'

'Still a stuffy old place,' said Izzie. 'But whatever turns you on.'

I rolled my eyes. 'Oh such philistines as friends. I don't know if I can bear it.'

'Well, at least you don't have to hang out with a brainbox like we do,' groaned Izzie.

'Neanderthal,' I said.

'Swot box.'

'Airhead.'

'Clever clogs.'

'Ignoramus.'

'Wombat.'

'*Wombat?*'

'Yeah,' said Izzie with a wide grin. 'Neoclassical wombat.'

This time Lucy rolled her eyes. 'For heaven's sake. I'm freezing. When you two have finished slagging each other off, do you think you could possibly make your mutually mad minds up what you're going to do?'

'And actually, if anyone's an airhead or whatever, it's me,' said Nesta. 'Izzie, you're as much of a bookworm as TJ and don't pretend otherwise. I'll go inside and look with you, TJ. Part of my education programme.'

Nesta recently went through this phase when she was worried that we all thought that she was shallow. Then she started going out with a boy called Luke and got paranoid that he might think she wasn't very bright. As if. She's really clever, just not into reading much if she doesn't have to. She's the original good-time girl. Good times to her being boys and, well . . . more boys. A few weeks ago though, she declared that she's going to learn about 'everything.' I wouldn't care if I had her looks. Even with her brace in she still looks fantastic and boys would fall at her feet whatever her IQ.

I looked around at my friends. Lucy's teeth were chattering. Izzie had a red nose from the cold, her dark hair was hanging in wet strands round her face and her head-to-toe black outfit made her look more Goth-like than ever. Only Nesta didn't look like an iceberg, but maybe that's because being half-Jamaican, half-Italian, her fudge-coloured skin doesn't fade to lily white like the rest of ours in the English winter.

As Nesta and I went inside the house, Lucy and Izzie were hauled off by the dogs in the direction of the café. Once we got in, however, Nesta spotted the room to the right of the entrance hall.

'Just a quick look,' she said, as she made a beeline for the gift shop where she spent fifteen minutes smelling all the bath gels on sale and then trying all the lip balms. She finally settled for a cherry-flavoured one.

'We don't need to go round the house,' she said, as she gave the lady at the counter her money. 'There are loads of books here that tell you all about the place and have photos of the rooms. We can have a quick flick through and we'll have seen all that there is here easy-peasy and without having to trudge round.'

I give up, I thought. I like to go from room to room and sit and look at the paintings and soak up the atmosphere. Not much chance of that with Nesta, I don't think.

'OK, quick flick through the books then we'll join the others,' I agreed.

'Cool,' said Nesta.

It was then she spotted the guest book and began to write

in it. I went to sign my name after hers and saw what she had written.

'*Queen Victoria was 'ere with her husband. We woz not amused.*'

If you can't beat them, join them, I thought as I wrote, 'Kenwood rocks, signed Mick Jagger' underneath Nesta's writing.

<u>Kenwood House</u>: an eighteenth century neoclassical villa on Hampstead Heath, North London.

<u>The art collection</u> features work by Rembrandt, Vermeer, Turner, Reynolds, Gainsborough, Van Dyck and Frans Hals.

<u>Movies</u> in which it was used as a location include *Mansfield Park* and *Notting Hill*.

Chapter 2

Dog Heaven

Hampstead Heath is dog heaven. Miles and miles of grounds and woodland for them to run about in while their owners collapse on benches and watch them work off their boundless energy. The rain had stopped, so we let Ben, Jerry and Mojo off their leads and away they were, tails wagging, tongues out, grinning all over their faces as they greeted other dogs. And their owners.

'Pretend they're not with us,' said Lucy, as Ben enthusiastically sniffed the bottom of a rather surprised looking poodle.

As we sat overlooking the hill rolling down to the lake at the bottom of the field, our conversation soon turned to one of our favourite subjects. Boys. Although we all have different interests, Izzie into all her New Age stuff, Lucy into fashion, Nesta into acting and me into books and writing, we have one thing in common: the subject of boys and relationships.

'Luke's taking me to see some weird arty film tonight,' said Nesta. '*Seven Samurai*, I think it's called. Supposed to be a classic.'

'It is. You'll love it,' I said. 'It was remade later into *The Magnificent Seven*, you know, the cowboy film.'

Nesta stared at me in amazement. 'See. There you go again. Something else you seem to know all about and I've never heard off. And seeing as my dad's a film director, if anyone should know about movies, it's me. You're awesome, TJ. How come you *know* this stuff?'

I shrugged. 'My brother Paul went through a phase when he was into all those old films. He never stopped talking about them. But I don't know loads of stuff. Honest. I'm not a Norma Know It All or anything.'

Lucy put her hand on my arm. 'We don't think you are,' she said.

'No, just a . . .' started Izzie.

'Neoclassical wombat,' Lucy finished for her.

'But hey, TJ,' said Nesta. 'You shouldn't try and hide that you know loads or apologise about it. I'd be proud of it if I were you.'

I grinned sheepishly. I've only been hanging around with Nesta, Izzie and Lucy since June. They adopted me after my best friend, Hannah, went to live in South Africa leaving me here on my own. They've been great mates and I really want to stay in with them. I don't want to make them feel like I'm showing off or anything, like trying to prove that I know more than them. I've got an uncle like that. Whenever anyone mentions any subject, politics, religion, books, whatever, he has to let everyone know that he's better informed than the rest of us, usually by giving us a ten-minute lecture. He's *really* boring, like his opinion is the only one that matters and the rest of us should be honoured that he takes the time to fill us in.

'So when's your sister getting married, TJ?' asked Lucy.

'Christmas Eve,' I replied.

'That's *so* romantic.'

'Nah. It's the only night Marie can get off from the hospital where she works,' I said.

'I'd love to design a winter wedding gown,' continued Lucy. 'I've always envisaged a white velvet one with a long cloak.' Lucy wants to design clothes when she leaves school. She has a great eye for fashion and has made some fab outfits. Shame she's not making my sister Marie's dress. Marie isn't romantic at all. She's totally disinterested and hasn't even been for a dress fitting yet.

'Oh, I'll just dash out and buy any old thing nearer the day,' she said last time she was up from Devon, where she's started a new job so that she could be near her fiancé, Stuart. 'I'm *so* not into having a white wedding. What's the point of forking out a fortune for some bit of fabric that you're only going to wear on one day.'

'You will *not* dash out and buy any old thing,' said Mum. 'It's your big day and you're going to look fabulous whether you like it or not.'

I laughed at the time and wondered whose big day it was really going to be, Mum's or Marie's. Either way, we're all going down south next weekend to, as Mum put it, 'talk wedding dresses'.

'Are they still arguing over whether to do it in a church or registry office?' asked Izzie.

I grimaced. Discussions had been going on for weeks now. 'Yeah, and still nothing's been decided. Marie favours a registry office, but she has got some place she wants to show us for the reception. Mum and Dad want her to do it in a church. And Paul thinks she should never have told anyone about it and flown off to Hawaii in secret to get married on a beach, barefoot under the stars with some ageing hippie type conducting a service that they'd written themselves.'

'That sounds fab,' said Izzie. 'Your brother has the right idea.'

'I read about a couple that got married at the bottom of the sea, in scuba-diving outfits,' said Nesta.

'Did they have a dolphin doing the service instead of the priest?' I asked.

'Or a whale?' asked Lucy. 'Then they could have sent invites saying – have a whale of a time at our wedding.'

'Keep taking the tablets, Lucy,' said Izzie.

'You can do anything you want these days,' said Nesta. 'Get married bungee jumping if you like.'

'No thanks,' I said. 'I think taking the leap to get married would be scary enough, never mind having to jump off a bridge into the bargain. Anyway, we're going down to discuss it all next weekend.'

'It is a big commitment,' said Nesta. 'I mean, saying "I do" to one person for the rest of your life. Like, how exactly do you know if he's The One?'

'Or number thirty-one?' said Izzie. 'In your case, with the way you go through boys, that's probably the number you'll be on by the time you get to Marie's age. Twenty-six isn't she, TJ?'

I nodded.

Nesta pinched Izzie's arm. 'Cheek. I haven't had many boyfriends.'

'More than the rest of us,' said Lucy.

'Not *serious* ones,' said Nesta. 'Not like Luke.'

'What about Simon?' said Izzie.

'Simon was OK, but it's different with Luke. We're really in love.'

'How do you know that?' asked Izzie. 'How do you know when it's really love? I mean, do you want to marry him?'

'Give me a break,' said Nesta, laughing. 'I'm only fifteen. And you don't want to marry everyone you love.'

'In some cultures, girls marry or choose a partner when they're twelve . . .' I started, then immediately regretted it.

'Yeah, you're right, in some cultures some girls get paired off really young,' said Nesta.

'But you didn't answer my question,' Izzie insisted. 'How do you know when you're really in love? What do you think, TJ?'

'Oh God. I don't know. Ask me when I'm older. When I've had a bit more experience. I've only had one proper boyfriend.'

I've been dating Lucy's brother, Steve, for just over three months and although I really like him, no way can I say that I'm in love. We like hanging out. Having a laugh. Lucy was looking at me curiously. Oh please don't ask me what I think you're going to ask me, I thought.

'So. Do you love Steve?' asked Nesta before Lucy could open her mouth.

'Er . . . We get on really well and . . .'

I think Lucy sensed my discomfort. 'Don't embarrass her,' she said.

'OK, you then. Do you love Tony?' asked Nesta.

Lucy blushed. Tony is Nesta's elder brother and he and Lucy have been seeing a lot of each other lately, although both of them insist that it's only casual.

'Dunno,' she said. 'I . . . like him more than any other boy that I've ever been out with. And as you all know, that's not many. Um. Two in fact. So it's hard to tell. I like him a lot, but I always imagined that with true love, you'd really know it. Both of you. Not all this on off stuff Tony and I do. Neither of us can make up our minds what we want.'

'Oh, I think Tony knows exactly what he wants,' said Nesta.

'Which is?' asked Lucy.

'To get you to do the horizontal shoe shuffle.'

'*Whadttt?*' asked Lucy.

'You know, sex.'

Lucy blushed furiously. 'You're probably right,' she said with a sigh. 'But I'm sure if I did the, er . . . horizontal shoe shuffle, he'd lose interest in no time.'

'Not necessarily,' said Nesta.

'Oh he would. Anyway I'm not ready. I don't want to be pressurised into it. I want to do it when the time feels right. It was enough worrying about whether I was a good kisser or not. I don't want to get into worrying about whether I'm good at sex as well.'

'I believe in soulmates,' said Izzie. 'That somewhere on the planet is someone who is perfect for you and if you meet him, then sex and all the rest of it will be perfect and you won't have to worry.'

'Somewhere on the planet?' I asked. 'What if your soulmate lives in Outer Mongolia and you never meet?'

'I believe in soulmates as well,' said Lucy, 'and, if he lived somewhere remote, fate would bring you together, at an airport or somewhere, like two magnets drawn together irresistibly. You'd just be about to get on your plane to Paris and he would be dashing down an escalator and your eyes would meet . . .'

'And he'd trip and fall over someone's suitcase,' said Izzie, 'bang his head and when he woke up, you'd be standing over him . . .'

'With choirs of heavenly angels singing hallelujah,' I added laughing. 'Oh, get real guys. You've all been watching way too many slushy films.'

'Well maybe not like that,' said Lucy. 'But I reckon that if you met your soulmate, there would be some kind of recognition. You'd be on the same wavelength and maybe even know what each other was thinking without having to say anything.'

'Maybe,' said Nesta, 'but who's to say you only have one soulmate? You might have loads.'

'You wish,' said Lucy. 'I read somewhere that soulmates have been together through many lifetimes. So I think that Izzie is right, there would be some kind of recognition. It would be like meeting a long lost friend and there would be something familiar about them, because actually you've been together time after time.'

'God, I hope not,' said Nesta. 'Sounds awful. I mean marriage to one person sounds bad enough, but a whole eternity with the same guy. You'd have to love him one heck of a lot. Whatever happened to having fun? Never mind finding Mr Right. I'll settle for Mr Right Now.'

'If it's meant to be,' said Izzie, 'it's meant to be.'

Nesta pulled a doubtful face. 'Hhhmm. You'd have to believe in reincarnation and I'm not sure I do. Only way to know is die and find out. Then you'll know for sure. Like with soulmates, if I meet one, I'll let you know.'

'I agree,' I said. 'I think the notion of soulmates is just a romantic way of saying that there are some boys you click with or fancy more than others. End of story.'

'Well I hope you meet your soulmate in *this* life,' said Izzie, 'then you'll be proved wrong.'

'Yeah right,' I replied with a grin.

'But nobody has answered Izzie's question,' said Lucy. 'How do you know if you're really in love?'

'Can't sleep. Can't eat. It's like having a nasty virus and feeling insane,' said Izzie. 'That's why I like being celibate. It's nice. Peaceful. No having to worry about will he phone me. Is my bum too big and all that crapola.'

I cracked up. 'How can you be celibate when you haven't even had sex yet?'

'Easy. Celibate means an unmarried person or someone who isn't having sex,' said Izzie. 'So I've been celibate for fifteen years now. But going back to love, I reckon it does your head in. All the great love songs say so. Like having an itch that you can't scratch. The love bug. I got a fever etc, etc. Count me out.'

Lucy nodded. 'But it's a nice itch.'

'Yeah,' agreed Nesta. 'Like you can't stop thinking about him. Can't wait to be with him. Time is slow when you're apart, yet it passes quickly when you're together. It's like that with Luke.'

'Bit of an old romantic yourself, hey Nesta,' I teased. I hoped nobody would ask me about being in love with Steve again. I mean, I really liked him, but there was no way I thought about him *all* the time.

'I think you know it's love because you feel all tingly when you're with him,' said Lucy. 'Like you're really alive, energised.'

'You can get that feeling from drinking a drink from the health shop,' said Izzie. 'Try one with ginseng in it.'

I laughed. 'So who needs love?'

'I think that if you meet The One then you'd be able to be your best self with him,' said Lucy. 'Talk to him. It would feel right, easy. You'd be able to be yourself without having to put on an act or feeling like you have to impress him.'

'That sounds cool,' I said. 'I reckon Mojo must be The One then, because that's how I feel around him. I can talk to him about anything and he always looks really interested.'

'I said you were weird,' said Izzie. 'But seriously, this One. Would he be like you, with lots in common? Or would it be a case of opposites attract?'

'Maybe it's just chemical,' I said, as I watched Mojo chasing a border collie then do the doggie 'hi' by smelling its rear end. 'Pheromones. Purely animal. Like dogs. You like the way they smell.'

Nesta laughed as she watched the dogs. 'Imagine if we did that! It would be hysterical. No way am I going round smelling bottoms. Not very romantic! There has to be a more dignified way to know if he's The One.'

'I guess we'll know whether it's love when the time comes,' I said.

'Yeah,' said Izzie. 'Like when it's hot or cold. You just know it.'

'And in the meantime, we can have lots of fun along the way,' said Nesta.

Around lunch-time, we rounded up the dogs and tied their leads to our bench. I stayed to keep an eye on them and make sure that they didn't drag the bench down the hill while the others went to the Ladies.

'So how was that?' I asked Mojo, who was sitting at my feet looking up at me adoringly. 'Did you make any new friends?'

'First sign of madness, talking to yourself,' said a male voice to my right.

I looked up to see Nesta's boyfriend smiling down at me.

'Er, nihi . . . I was talking to my dog,' I blustered.

'Oh. He speaks English does he?'

I laughed. 'Do you know that had never occurred to me. Maybe I ought to try French?'

'Or Italian,' added Luke, laughing, and leaned over to say something to Mojo in Italian. Mojo leaped up, put his paws on Luke's shoulders and licked his face with great enthusiasm.

'Ohmigod,' I said. 'I think you might be right. Mojo is clearly Italian. Oh no. Now I'll have to learn how to speak it.'

Luke laughed again. 'Hey, is Nesta with you? She called me on her mobile and asked me to meet her here.'

I jerked my thumb towards the Ladies. 'She'll be back in a mo.'

Luke sat down beside me and turned to look at the house on the right, behind us. 'Did you go inside?'

'Only for a minute,' I said. 'None of the others were too keen. I'm going to come back and do it properly another day. I love looking round places like this.'

'Me too,' said Luke. 'It's one of my favourite things. I like imagining what the people were like who lived here . . .'

'Me *too*,' I said. 'Yeah. Like who were they? Were they happy?'

'Yeah. Did they get on? Have kids? Is there a good vibe or a bad vibe in there. I like reading books about places like this, sometimes they have photos of the inhabitants and their families. As I look at their faces, I wonder, what were you thinking the day you were painted? Like what did you have for breakfast?'

'*Yeah*. I like to sit and soak up the atmosphere, see if I can somehow be transported back . . .'

'Yeah,' said Luke. 'And don't you think it's amazing that this place is here? Some people go all the way to Paris or Rome to see works of art and we have some amazing ones right on our doorstep.'

I turned and had a good look at him. I couldn't believe he was saying exactly what I thought. I'd only met Luke once before and then it was only briefly with a crowd of others at his parents' restaurant. They're Italian and knew Nesta's dad when they were younger and there was some drama going on about a falling out they had years ago and Nesta was told she couldn't see Luke. All sorted now, but I hadn't really talked to him as it was neither the time nor place. Or looked at him beyond a glance. And now that I did look, there was something about him that looked . . . sort of familiar. I felt myself flush as he looked back at me.

'Have we met before?' he asked.

I nodded. 'Yeah. With Nesta at your parents' restaurant.'

He shook his head. 'No. Before then. I remember *that* night No. It's just . . . you look kind of familiar.'

I shook my head. 'No I don't think so.' I would have remembered meeting someone as striking as Luke. He wasn't your average tall, dark and handsome, although he was all of those things with a mane of black hair. It made him look like a poet from a bygone era. But there was something else about him. He looked interesting. Intelligent. He was still staring at me and I felt myself turning pink. I stood up and started playing with the dog's lead. When I looked at Luke again, he was smiling, like he was amused. Was it because he'd felt my embarrassment and was laughing at me? He probably had this effect on loads of girls. Or was he amused because I'd got the dogs' leads all tangled and almost tripped over Jerry? Oh hell. Whatever, I thought, Nesta's lucky to have such a gorgeous boyfriend. I'd love to talk to him more about old houses and paintings. I glanced at him again as he kneeled on the ground by the bench and tried to untangle the leads.

'I'd love to talk to you more some day about old houses,' he said as he looked at me. 'Not many people are that interested.'

I gulped. 'Er nihi . . .' I muttered, as Izzie, Nesta and Lucy came bouncing up the steps behind us and put an end to our conversation.

Meeting The One

Who says you get only one One? If you're lucky, you will meet The One, The Two, The Three . . . and so on. Nesta

The One will be your soulmate for life. Lucy

If it's meant to be, destiny will bring you together in this life as it has in past lives. Izzie

It's all chemical. The One is just a way of saying you fancy someone and your pheromones are mutually attractive. TJ

Chapter 3

Our Father
Who Art in Devon

'Typical Marie.' Mum said as we drove down to Devon the following Saturday. 'She always was a contrary one.'

'I thought Paul was your difficult child, Mum,' I teased from the back. My brother Paul freaked my parents out in the summer by dropping out of medical school to travel the world. He's in Morocco at the moment and flying back on Christmas Eve for the wedding before going on to Ethiopia in the New Year. Dad calls him a drifter as he hasn't decided what he wants to be yet.

'You're *all* difficult,' said Dad as he steered our car down the A381 towards a place called Bigbury Bay in Devon.

'But honestly, a *sea* tractor!' said Mum. 'What is the girl thinking of?'

'Well, we'll have a look and try and talk her out of it,' said Dad. 'You know, take the line of going along with it all, then try and make her see sense.'

I thought the location sounded fab and wondered if I should warn Marie about their 'let's go along with it' strategy.

Apparently Marie's found this hotel on an island that caters for weddings and the only way to get to it, when the tide is in, is by sea tractor. Excellent, I thought, when I heard the news. Makes a change from arriving at a wedding in the usual boring limo.

Mum hadn't finished her rant. 'How on *earth* does she think she's going to get all the guests across to the hotel? No. The idea is ridiculous.'

'It was good enough for royalty,' I said. I'd looked the place up on the Internet last night. It sounded just my kind of thing, an old hotel steeped in history. Apparently anyone who was anyone used to go there in the summers of the 1930s. Edward, Prince of Wales, Mrs Simpson, Noel Coward, Amy Johnson, Winston Churchill to name a few. According to the website, it was flapper heaven with an orchestra playing on a platform in a natural swimming pool called the Mermaid Pool.

But on they went, moan moan moan. I tried making them laugh with Lucy's joke, our father who art in Devon, Harold be thy name, but they didn't find it funny. No, they were having much more fun having a groan.

'London would have been much more convenient for the guests from the North,' said Mum.

'And what if the weather's bad? It will be a nightmare if no one can get there,' said Dad. 'No. It doesn't bode well.'

'And it's not cheap either,' said Mum.

I decided to close my eyes and try and sleep. Burgh Island Hotel sounded the business to me and, anyway, it was Marie's wedding not Mum's or Dad's. As I drifted off, I found myself thinking about Luke. I wonder if he knows about this place. Sounds like his sort of thing too. He's been popping into my head all week, on and off. I kept replaying the moment he turned and asked if we'd met before over and over in my head.

It was amazing as usually when I meet a good-looking boy, my brain turns to mush and my vocal cords paralyse. I get taken over by this alien girl I call Noola who can't say anything except *uhyuh, yuneewee* and *nihingyah*. But I'd managed to have a conversation with Luke. Actually spoken words that formed themselves into meaningful sentences. It was like I'd known him for ages. And the moment he talked to Mojo in Italian – it was so funny . . . But I mustn't think about him. He's Nesta's boyfriend. Steve. *Steve* is my boyfriend. I ought to be daydreaming about telling him about Burgh Island, not Luke. He likes places with interesting histories too. So why didn't you think of telling *him* about it first? asked a prissy voice in the back of my head. He's not as good-looking as Luke, said another voice. Steve is cute in his own way. He looks like an eighteen-year-old Harry Potter, whereas Luke is a total babe with his wide mouth, thick eyelashes and . . . Oh shut up, I thought. Shut up, shut up, shut up. I made a resolution to tell Steve all about Burgh Island the moment I got back.

Mum and Dad's moaning and groaning continued as we parked in the car park on the mainland opposite the hotel and unloaded our overnight bags from the boot. I looked across the bay and there was the hotel, exactly as the website had described it: 'A white art deco cruise liner beached on dry land.' I couldn't wait to get there.

The sea tractor was brilliant. I'd never seen anything like it. It was like travelling on an open-air bus with ginormous wheels and, before we knew it, we were across the bay and a man was taking our bags and loading them in a car to drive us the short distance up to the hotel.

'All this palaver,' Mum droned on as we passed a little pub called The Pilchard Inn. 'And what if it snows?'

We'd been in the hotel about five minutes and I could see that Mum and Dad's objections were fading fast.

'Well I suppose it is rather nice when you get here,' said Mum as she took in the fabulous art deco interior.

'Hhmmm,' said Dad approvingly as he strolled into a room called the Palm Court that had a stunning, domed, stained glass roof in vibrant peacock colours.

'*Nice?* Mum, it's awesome,' I said as Marie came out from the Palm Court to meet us.

'Awesome,' she said. 'I take it that you approve then?'

'I do,' I said.

'What about the wrinklies?' she whispered after hugs and enquiries about the journey, and Mum and Dad busied themselves with signing in and getting our room keys.

I laughed. Marie's picked up on my nickname for Mum and Dad. I started calling them the wrinklies, because they're so much older than most people's parents. Probably not for Marie and Paul as they're both in their twenties, but I came along later. A surprise baby I think I was. Probably *was* a surprise as both Mum and Dad are doctors and should know better about contraception and the like. It was funny when Mum gave me my first 'sex' talk and lectured me about, 'How it can only take one time' and, 'Mistakes do happen', I asked her if I was a mistake and she didn't know where to look.

'They'll be OK,' I said. 'Just give them time.'

After a fabulous lunch in the Sun Lounge, Mum and Dad seemed to be doing a total about-turn.

'Winston Churchill came here, you know,' said Dad as he puffed on a cigar.

Mum sipped her coffee. 'And Edward Prince of Wales, and Mrs Simpson.'

Dad smiled. 'You can almost see them in their whites can't

you? Running through the corridors calling "anyone for tennis" to each other.'

'And Agatha Christie wrote here,' I added. 'In fact, it was used as a location for the film *Evil Under the Sun*.'

Mum sighed contentedly and looked out of the window. 'It *is* lovely. How did you find it, Marie?'

'Stuart brought me here last month and we both fell in love with the place,' said Marie. 'Then when we realised that they had a licence to do weddings, well . . .'

Hah. I thought. Sorted. Everybody happy.

'Just don't make me wear pink on the day,' I said.

Marie laughed. 'Oh I thought a bright *candy* pink might be nice. With lots of ribbons and bows. Gimme a break. You can be my bridesmaid in your jeans and trainers. As long as you're here, that's all I care about.'

'Talking of outfits,' said Mum, rooting in her bag and producing a wad of brides' magazines, 'I brought these for us to look through.'

Nice try, I thought as I looked at Marie sympathetically.

A little later, we went back over to the mainland and that's when the real trouble started. It was a lovely afternoon with a bright blue sky and Marie drove us around the area. It was incredibly pretty. Idyllic in fact. Thatched cottages, winding roads through hedgerows, quaint little villages. After a stop for a cup of tea in a roadside tea shop, Marie set off to find a bank and Mum and Dad headed down the High Street and started gazing in estate agents' windows.

'What are you looking for?' I asked as I caught them up. 'Somewhere to rent for the summer?'

Mum glanced at Dad. 'Er, not exactly,' she said.

'Just getting an idea of the prices,' said Dad as he continued looking in the window.

'Why? Are you thinking of going into real estate?' I asked.

'No,' said Dad and looked at Mum. 'Um. Er. You tell her, Maureen.'

Mum took a deep breath. 'We've been meaning to talk to you about it for some time, TJ. We've been thinking of moving.'

'Moving! Why? When? What for?'

'Now don't panic,' said Mum. 'Actually we've been talking about it for some time now . . .'

'Not to me, you haven't. This is the first I've heard.'

'We didn't want to say anything until we were more sure, but your father is thinking of going part-time and commuting. We've always liked this part of the world and after looking around today, well . . .'

'But why can't you go part-time and stay in London, Dad?'

'We could. That is . . . was an option. But we fancy a change of pace. And it won't be long before we come up for retirement. We always wanted to retire by the sea and now that Marie's down here as well . . .'

Noooooooooooooooooooooooooooooooooooooooooooo,   I thought as alarm hit the pit of my stomach. 'But what about me? What about school? What about my friends?'

Dad hesitated for a while. 'A change of pace might do you good as well,' he said finally. 'I'm not sure that London's the best place for you and . . . well, that new crowd you've got in with . . .'

'New crowd? You mean, Lucy, Nesta and Izzie? But you hardly know them . . .' He didn't either, as I hardly ever took them back to my house. Dad never liked me bringing friends home that much and, when I did, he always complained about the noise. It was much simpler to go and hang out at their houses.

'I do know them, TJ. What about that time I caught you all having a pillow fight and jumping up and down on your bed? Not very mature. Not the behaviour of nice young ladies. You're going to be fifteen on Monday and it's time you started acting your age.'

'But we were just being silly that day. We're not usually like that.'

'What about that Izzie then? Remember that incident with her? I think she might be a bad influence.'

'*Izzie!* But . . . Why Izzie?'

'Even her own mother was worried about her in the summer. She was round at our house and she'd been out with some strange boy and drinking . . .'

I snorted back laughter. 'That was a one-off. Izzie is Queen Organic. She's so into health stuff. Honestly. She's *not* a bad influence. No way. I could show you girls at our school who are a bad influence, but not Izzie.'

Wrong thing to say.

'Exactly,' said Dad. 'So you admit that there are girls at your school who are a bad influence?'

'No. Yes. But I don't hang with them. No. Mum. Dad. No. We can't move. My whole life is up in London. I *can't* leave.'

But Mum and Dad had spotted another estate agent's on the opposite side of the road and were making a beeline for it.

No. No. Nooooooooooooo, please God, I thought. I mean, I like Devon and all, but live here? Noooooooooooooooooooo.

Burgh Island Hotel is on Burgh Island, which is a twenty-six acre tidal island, two hundred metres off the south Devon coast between Salcombe and Plymouth.

Famous people who have stayed there include Noel Coward, Agatha Christie, Edward Prince of Wales and Mrs Simpson, Amy Johnson, Winston Churchill.

Movies in which it was used as a location include *Evil Under the Sun*.

Chapter 4

School
Project

'But you can't go,' said Lucy as we went into assembly the following Monday. 'Steve was gutted after you told him last night.'

I stuffed the birthday cards and presents that they'd just given me into my rucksack. Lavender bath gel and soap from Nesta, glittery nail polish from Lucy, a scented candle from Izzie, plus Lucy had brought me a card and present from Steve – a CD collection of love songs from the last decade. Somehow, their gifts made the fact that I might have to move away even worse. Even though they were birthday presents, it felt like they were leaving presents.

'Never mind Steve,' said Izzie linking her arm through mine. 'I'm gutted. We'd really miss you.'

'Maybe you could come back at weekends,' said Nesta. 'You can stay in my room with me.'

'And we'd come down to visit in the holidays,' said Lucy. 'I like Devon.'

'So do I,' I said as we took our places in our class line up.

'But that doesn't mean I want to live there.' I felt utterly miserable. Some birthday, I thought. Fifteen and it felt like my life was over. I wouldn't know anyone in Devon. Starting a new school would be horrible, like reliving what it was like when Hannah first moved abroad. And I know what Hannah went through when she first got to South Africa, although she's made friends now. But I didn't want to make new friends. I didn't want to go through all that again. I liked Lucy, Izzie and Nesta. I'd never find mates like them again. And no matter how much they insisted they'd come and visit and stay in touch, I knew what would happen. It was happening with Hannah already. We'd promised to email every day, keep telling each other everything, but she hadn't been in touch for weeks now – not even an email wishing me happy birthday. But come to think of it, I hadn't been in touch either. It was too awful to think that the same thing might happen with my new friends. No. Mum and Dad couldn't be serious. It was a mad idea.

'You could always run away,' Nesta whispered in my ear. 'We'd make sure you had food and stuff . . .'

'Quiet at the back,' called Mrs Allen looking pointedly in our direction.

After the usual boring announcements, Mrs Allen suddenly beamed. 'Now girls, I have something special to tell you about today. An exciting project is to be launched by the mayor and it's one that I think many of you will be very interested in . . .'

Nesta turned and feigned a yawn to me. I grinned back at her.

'The aim of the project is to produce a book detailing our city's heritage,' continued Mrs Allen, 'that has been written and researched by the city's students. The final version is to go on sale at the British Museum. The project is open to all pupils from Year Ten upwards who wish to take part. The mayor has asked that those involved research London as it is today and London as it was in the past. Areas such as its history, its famous landmarks, buildings, costumes through the ages, contributions from its inhabitants, artists, writers, architects . . . and the list goes on. Schools have been chosen from each of the four areas of London: North, South, East and West. Our school has been fortunate enough to have been asked to be one of the schools representing the North. Each school within each area will obviously focus on their particular area . . .'

Sounds brilliant, I thought. I'd love to be involved, but I'll probably be living out in the back of beyond in some backwater with people who've never even been to London.

'The mayor has asked to see an initial presentation just before Christmas, so that only gives us until the end of term,' Mrs Allen continued. 'So we need to get ourselves in gear immediately. The first meeting for the North London area, for those of you who'd like to contribute, will be tomorrow evening at the Institute of Science in Pond Square in Highgate, so . . . all those budding journalists, historians and artists out there, take note. All the head teachers of the schools taking part are meeting tonight and we're going to appoint one pupil to oversee the project with the help of a number of teachers. But essentially, this is your project and I hope that you will rise to meet the challenge and make this particular school proud of your efforts. At the end of term, there will be an open day featuring the work so far and school governor, Susan Barratt, and Sam Denham, the celebrity journalist, whom I believe some of you know from his visit here last year, will be attending. Details have been posted on the noticeboard in the hall. Pupils involved will be given time to work on the project and can arrange this with their head of year.'

Cool, I thought as Mrs Allen continued. Even though we might move to Devon before the project is completed, Mum said it might be ages before they find the right house, so I've got at least one more term here, and then they've got to sell our house. I'd have time to take part in the initial stages at least. 'Well you can count me out,' said Nesta as we made our way to first lesson. 'We get enough homework as it is.'

'Might be fun,' said Lucy. 'I'm going to volunteer. I could research costumes through the ages. It's an excuse to go and look round places like the Victoria and Albert Museum. I've been meaning to do it for ages and you never know, it might give me inspiration for my own designs. I like combining the old with the new.'

'What about you, TJ?' asked Izzie. 'You up for it?'

I nodded. 'Think so. I'd like to do something on the old houses in Hampstead and Highgate. You know, like Kenwood House. There are plenty of other places I've been meaning to get round too. Like Lucy said, it's a good excuse to do it and it might be my last chance if we move.'

'And you could do something on the spiritual side of London,' suggested Lucy, turning to Izzie.

'Maybe,' she replied. 'Yeah. I'll have a think about it.'

Nesta pouted. 'I hate you all. Now I feel left out, or at least I will if you all take part and I don't.'

'Then choose something interesting to you,' I said. 'You could look at theatre through the ages. Or great love affairs.'

Nesta didn't look convinced. 'I guess,' she said. 'And Mrs Allen did say that there'd be time off to do it. So maybe. Certainly no harm in going to the open day at the end of term. That Sam Denham was a bit of a dish. I wouldn't mind seeing him again.'

I laughed. Typical Nesta, I thought, as Lucy, Izzie and I signed our names on the board and wrote our area of interest.

On Tuesday night, we met at Nesta's house near Highgate and got changed and made up.

'Just in case there are any boy babes there,' said Izzie as she wriggled into a denim mini with a zip down the front.

'I thought you were going through a celibate phase,' I said.

Izzie laughed. 'I like to keep an open mind on all matters.'

'And I've decided I'm not going to do it,' said Nesta. 'It's not my thing.'

'So why are you coming?' I asked.

'Luke's going to be there. His school is one of the ones chosen as well.'

'So is Steve's,' I said. 'He called earlier. He wants to do photography.'

'What about Lal?' asked Izzie.

Lucy laughed. 'Not interested. Too much like hard work he said. What about Tony, Nesta?'

'His headmaster turned it down. Said that the pupils there had to focus on their exams. But then Luke's doing A-levels as well, but his headmaster didn't seem to mind. Apparently he said it would look good on their CV if their material gets used.'

'More like the school's CV,' I said. 'Smart headmaster if you ask me.'

The hall was already full when we got to the Institute and Nesta spied Luke on the other side of the room at the front. He gave us a friendly wave and I watched as Nesta made her way over to him and he put his arm around her and steered her towards a seat. He looked gorgeous in a big overcoat with a red scarf knotted round his neck. I looked around for Steve, but couldn't see him in the crowd.

The meeting soon got underway with one of the teachers from a school in Cricklewood taking the chair.

'My name's Miss Longbottom,' she started, and immediately I noticed Lucy's shoulders begin to shake in front of me. It doesn't take a lot to make Lucy laugh, only trouble is that it's infectious. Especially in a place where you're not supposed to be laughing. Izzie's shoulders started to shake next and I missed the list of categories that Miss Longbottom was reading out as I battled not to laugh as well. I caught the end of what she said though. Some girl called Marie Nash was to be the overall co-ordinator and the different areas of interest had their own co-ordinators who we were to report to.

Lucy took note of who was in charge of costume and who was in her group. Steve was put in charge of photography with a team of three other pupils and Izzie was put with a boy called Trevor in charge of the spiritual development of North London. I wondered if he knew what he was in for. He looked very straight and probably envisaged looking at churches and the development of Christianity. With Izzie by his side, he'd be looking at witches, mysticism and lines of energy if she had her way. There were other groups for science, music, geography, architecture and finally Miss Longbottom got to the famous houses and their inhabitants.

'And now we come to the inhabitants and historical houses in North London. Luke De Biasi will be co-ordinating this area along with . . .' she glanced down at her list, 'Theresa Joanne Watts, Sian Collins and Olivia Jacobs.'

Nesta turned and gave me the thumbs up. I smiled back at her. Cool, I thought. I'll get a chance to talk to him properly about old houses.

'OK everyone,' said Miss Longbottom, 'now, if you can all divide into your areas and introduce yourselves, we'll reconvene in about twenty minutes.'

As everyone got into groups, Nesta caught up with me as I made my way over to meet Luke, Olivia and Sian.

'It's so top, you'll be working with Luke,' she said. 'You can keep an eye on those two other girls while you're at it. I saw the way that little blonde one looked at him. I'm sure she fancies him.'

'I don't think you've anything to worry about,' I said, as I glanced over and Luke beckoned me to go and join them. 'She's not a patch on you.'

'Well, report back if there's any funny business, won't you?'

'Course I will,' I said. 'Just call me Watts, Private Detective.'

Email: **Outbox (1)**
From: babewithbrains@psnet.co.uk
To: hannahnutter@fastmail.com
Date: 25th November
Subject: Londres

Aloha Hannah ma petite fruitcake
    Sorry I haven't been in touch lately, it's been mad here. How you doing? I still miss you. Life is major crapola at the mo. Mum and Dad have had a nasty turn and decided they want to go and live in Devon. Yes, Devon. No thank you.
    Still hanging with Izzie, Lucy and Nesta. They are great mates which will make it even harder if I have to leave London.
    Cool news is that we're doing a big project (loads of schools involved) about London's history. I'll be working with Nesta's new boyfriend Luke who is a total dish. And really nice.

Luv
TJ

Email: **Inbox (1)**
From: hannahnutter@fastmail.com
To: babewithbrains@psnet.co.uk
Date: 25th November
Subject: Moving

Bernando fernando octiposie
    God! Poor vous. Major whammy in the problemo stakes.
    OK. Listen to Auntie Hannah.
    Re moving:
    Plan A: when the estate agents send people to view your

house, volunteer to show them round. As you do, let it slip that you have psychotic neighbours with very noisy children who all have criminal records.

Plan B: tell prospective buyers that the house has a ghost. A really horrible ghost, who likes to wander round with an amputated arm and hit people with the soggy end. Tell them, he's 'armless enough apart from that one habit. Hahahahaha.

Plan C: get a load of rotting garbage, hide it in every room, then tell the prospective buyers that there is a bad damp problem in the house.

That should sort them. Am I a genius or wot?

What happened to Steve? You didn't mention him. Are you still dating?

Over here we're going into summer sizzler time and it's fab. It's probably no consolation, but remember how I felt when I heard we were moving. I thought my life was over. Now I love it here and have made good friends. Things change. You might actually like Devon. I know that's probably not what you want to hear at the moment, but things might not be as black as they seem.

Yours truly
Agony Aunt Hannah.
PS: Write back soon.
PPS: Ohmigod. I've just seen the date and realised. It was von birthcake yesterday. Oh er. Bad girl Hannah. Um. Card in the post. Present in the . . . in the shop. I am soooooo sorry. I will make it up to you. Please don't hate me forever. Happy happy birthday even if it's late. And sorreee sorreeee sorreeee am bad friend. Smackgirlnaughty.

Please email back instantly and say you forgive moi.

Email: **Outbox (1)**
From: <u>babewithbrains@psnet.co.uk</u>
To: <u>hannahnutter@fastmail.com</u>
Date: 26th November 26th
Subject: Birthday

You ees forgiven. My birthday was no big deal this year. For one thing it was on a Monday and school day. Mum and Dad took me for a special cream tea when we were down in Devon which was nice, but then I am anti Devon at the mo (haha, you're Auntie Hannah and I'm anti Devon, geddit?) so couldn't really enjoy it. Got loads of fab pressies from the girls though and lovely CD collection from Steve. Next year, however, I will be sixteen and expect you to fly over and make a personal appearance.

Love
Anti Devon

Chapter 5

Funny Business

'So what role would you like me to play, Luke?' asked Sian.

Luke looked thoughtful. 'Hamlet,' he said.

Sian threw her head back and snorted a weird loud laugh. Like a donkey braying. Woah, I thought. What Luke said was funny, but not *that* funny.

We were having our first meeting the following evening in one of the art prefabs at the back of our school. It had been allocated as a make-do office for our part of the project. It was lucky for me that it was at our school as the others had to travel to different areas. Lucy to a school in Kilburn and Izzie to one in St John's Wood.

Luke got up and stood on one of the desks. 'So,' he said, grinning down at the three of us. 'Here we are team. Without further ado, I now declare this meeting open.'

He stepped down and the meeting got going. He'd clearly already put a lot of thought into it as he had leaflets, brochures and details about old houses printed out from Net sites.

'We have a huge area to cover, so I suggest that we break it down. If we focus on Hampstead and Highgate up to Christmas for the first presentation that will give us lots to work with in the initial stages. We can do the rest of North London later. So. I'm going to allocate places for each of us to visit. Best we start this weekend as we don't have a huge amount of time. I suggest at this stage, we visit the places, make our notes, then meet again early next week to see which we want to keep in and which we want to keep out.

'OK, Kenwood House. Olivia, you take that one, OK?'

Olivia nodded and took the brochure that he handed her. I liked the look of her. She was tall and skinny with bright red hair cut in a short bob, and was attractive but not in the conventional sense, as she had a large nose but it kind of fitted her face. I thought that if I was in her class at school, I'd have picked her to be a friend – she looked interesting.

'Sian, you can do Burgh House. It's at the back of Hampstead village. I think you'll like it there.'

Sian nodded. 'OK, boss.' In contrast to Olivia, Sian was short and blonde. She had a thin face and a long body with a large bottom and short legs, typical pear shape. She seemed nice enough though, eager to get on with us all and to please. Especially Luke.

'Now Miss TJ Watts, or would you prefer me to call you Theresa Joanne?' asked Luke with a wicked smile.

'TJ will do just fine, thank you very much,' I said, sounding like a real priss queen. 'Everyone calls me TJ.'

'TJ it is then,' he said. 'Now, where shall I send you?'

'I was looking on the Internet last night and I found that there are loads of companies that do guided tours of the area. There's one leaving from Hampstead tube at two o'clock on Sunday. Might be worth doing as it sounds like they cover a lot of ground and they'll probably be brill on the history of the area.'

'Excellent,' said Luke. 'In fact, I'll come with you. I've heard about that walk and always meant to do it.'

Sian looked disappointed. 'Maybe we should all do it,' she suggested.

Luke shook his head. 'No, two of us will be enough.'

I felt chuffed that he wanted to go with me, and I might have imagined it, but Sian gave me a funny look and appeared to be going into a sulk. However, she seemed to shake off her mood and the rest of the meeting was really productive.

'There's Avenue House on East End Road in East Finchley,' said Olivia, 'that might be worth a visit. It's an interesting old place with lovely gardens.'

'And Lauderdale House in Highgate,' I said. 'And, of course, Highgate Cemetery. That's fabulous and there are so many famous people buried there including Karl Marx. In fact, some people say it's a communist plot.'

Luke and Olivia laughed, but Sian looked at me as though I was mad. I don't think she got the joke.

'Excellent suggestions, TJ,' said Luke. 'And we must include the house where the poet John Keats lived, and Fenton House at the top of Hampstead. Yeah, we're going to have our work cut out, but it's going to be great. Really interesting.'

His enthusiasm was infectious and I felt really pleased that he was our co-ordinator. Unlike poor Izzie. She'd been put with a boy called Trevor from Steve's school, who not only looked boring, but Steve told me that he really was. Izzie wasn't looking forward to spending much time with him.

At the end of the hour, we all had a good idea what we had to do and I felt fired up to get started. I felt sure that we were in with a good chance of our contributions being used if we could present all our findings in an interesting manner. With Luke in charge, I didn't think that would be a problem.

As I wandered out to the gate with Olivia after the meeting, once again I thought how lucky Nesta was to have a boyfriend like Luke. Good-looking, a nice guy and a born leader. We were going to be a good team. I could see already that Sian would do anything Luke asked and Olivia was really cool.

'Luke seems like a laugh,' I said as we went and stood at the bus stop.

'Oh yeah, he is. He's always been fun,' she replied.

'Oh, do you know him, I mean apart from . . . ?'

'Yeah. I've known him for ages. He used to live in the same street as us. He's a mate of my brother William.'

'What's he really like then? He seems very confident, you know, knows exactly what he wants.'

Olivia shrugged. 'Yes and no. He wasn't always like that,' then she laughed. 'Bit of a late developer if you know what I mean.'

I didn't. 'No,' I said.

'He was never such a looker. He's kind of grown into himself in the last few years, but back when he was thirteen or fourteen, he was a bit gawky and could never get off with anyone. But now, he's a babe magnet. They're queuing up for him. And he loves it.'

'Oh really?'

'Yeah. But he never stays with anyone that long.'

'Really? Oh dear. He's going out with my mate.'

'Oh God, sorry. Maybe I shouldn't have said anything. And who knows? Maybe he's grown up a bit. Like, who's to say when true love will strike? Just he messed a mate of mine around. I still don't know if she's really over him.'

'God. Why are some guys like that? You know, notching up girls . . .'

'I reckon it's because of his dad.'

'His *dad*? His dad wants him to have loads of girlfriends?'

213

'No dummy,' Olivia said, laughing. 'It's like he's trying to prove something to himself. His dad is really heavy sometimes. I know because Luke takes refuge at our house with William. He reckons Luke's dad has knocked his confidence. Like nothing is ever good enough, if he gets A, why hasn't he got an A plus sort of thing. Now Luke has discovered something that he excels in. Pulling girls. It's an area where his dad can't interfere. And he's going for the A star.'

'So you're saying that underneath Luke is insecure?'

'I guess,' she said, then smiled, 'but then aren't we all dwahling?'

I laughed. I was about to say something back when I realised that I'd left my rucksack behind.

'Oh bummer,' I said as a bus came round the corner. 'Forgot my rucksack.'

'See you next week then,' she called as she stuck out her hand to stop the bus.

When I got back to the art prefab, the door was locked. That's strange, I thought as I'd left before Luke and Sian. I knocked then peeked through the window and could see Luke and Sian sitting close together. Very close together. And Luke was holding Sian's hand. Luke looked up, saw me at the window and his face clouded. A moment later, he came to the door with my rucksack.

'Forget this?' he asked as he handed it to me. It was very clear that he didn't want me going inside. He looked uncomfortable, like he couldn't wait to get rid of me and, behind him, Sian's face looked a picture of guilt.

'Er . . . thanks,' I muttered, then dashed away.

Ohmigod, I thought. Poor Nesta. Oh, poor poor Nesta.

On the bus, I agonised over whether to call Nesta immediately and tell her what I'd seen. But what had I seen? I felt confused and I didn't want to stir trouble unnecessarily. I'd only been back home about ten minutes and was about to have supper when the phone went.

'TJ, it's for you. Shall I tell him to phone back later?' called Mum from the hall.

'Who is it?'

'Someone called Luke.'

'No, I'll take it,' I said. I got up immediately. Maybe I should confront him and see what he says, I thought as I dashed to the hall.

'Hi.'

'Hey, TJ,' said Luke cheerily. 'Just confirming Sunday. How about you come here to my house and I'll drive us into Hampstead.'

'Um, OK. Yeah.'

'And . . . I wanted to put you in the picture about Sian.'

'Oh. Yeah. Sian,' I said, wondering how he was going to get out of it.

'Bit of a screwball, little Sian,' said Luke. 'A mixed–up kid. She wanted to talk to someone and I guess I was nearest. I was trying to make her feel better.'

'Oh right,' I said.

'I don't know what impression you got when you looked through the window . . .'

'I . . . er . . .'

'All innocent. At least it is on my part. Between you and me, she's got a bit of a crush on me. Don't really know what to do about it. Got any ideas?'

Well, at least he'd come clean, I thought.

'Dunno. Um. Wear a bag over your head.'

Luke laughed. 'And pick my nose. Reckon that will put her off?'

I laughed as well. 'Maybe.' I felt flattered that he'd opened up to me and wanted my advice. I liked that. Like in the meeting, whenever I made a suggestion, he made me feel as if my opinion mattered. On some projects I've worked on in the past, some people are only interested in what they have to contribute.

'And hey, no need to tell Nesta about her. I don't want her causing any trouble. As I said, Sian's a bit mixed-up. She doesn't need anyone coming down heavy on her when there's nothing going on.'

'Sure,' I said.

'So. Just between us?' he asked.

'Just between us.'

After he'd hung up, I felt relieved I didn't have to tell Nesta. She'd have confronted Sian for sure. And if there was nothing in it, no point. Luke sounded nice, like he wanted to help Sian but not upset Nesta at the same time.

Some Houses of Interest That Are Open to the Public in the Hampstead and Highgate Area

1) Burgh House, New End Square, Hampstead, London. Built in 1704.
2) Fenton House, Windmill Hill, Hampstead, London. Built around 1693 (one of the earliest and largest houses in the area).
3) Kenwood House, Hampstead Heath, London. An original smaller building was remodelled into the existing one in the 1700s.
4) Avenue House, East End Road, East Finchley. Built in 1859.
5) Lauderdale House, Waterlow Park, Highgate. Built around 1580.
6) Keats House, Keats Grove, Hampstead, London. The poet John Keats lived there from 1818 until 1820.

Chapter 6

Guided
Walk

'*Exactly* what I wanted!' said Steve as he pounced on a book in the local library in East Finchley after school on Friday.

I went and looked over his shoulder. It was a book with old pictures of how Hampstead village used to look at the beginning of the last century.

'Top,' I said as I watched him flick through. 'Why don't you borrow it, find the locations, then you can take some up to the minute photos of exactly the same places? Then exhibit them side by side so people can see the difference.'

'Excellent idea,' he said. 'My team thought we might do some of the local characters too and show them alongside those of people from the past. You know, the lollipop lady, policemen . . .'

'Traffic wardens,' I said. 'You see them more than you do policemen. They always remind me of wasps hovering around waiting to strike and sting.'

Steve laughed. 'And they do sting too. Mum got a ticket the other day. Cost her a fortune. She was major miffed.'

'Must have been amazing in the old days,' I said. 'Imagine how it must have been before all the cars and traffic.'

'Yeah,' said Steve. 'Must have been fab.'

After we'd looked at photography books, we searched for other books about the area and Steve found me one that listed all the famous writers and artists that had lived there.

'Just what I need,' I said as I glanced through it.

'And if you can find the places where they lived,' said Steve, 'then I'll take photos of the houses for you. For instance, the painter, John Constable, lived in Hampstead and I'm pretty sure I've seen one of those blue plaques they put up on the outside wall of the house to say someone famous lived there, I just can't remember where.'

'He lived in two places in Hampstead, one of them is on Well Walk,' I said as I leafed through the book. 'And according to this, there are loads of other famous people who either lived there or wrote about it. I know Charles Dickens is one of them as I often pass the house where he stayed on my way up to Nesta's. Maybe there will be a plaque outside her house one day when she's famous. Nesta Williams lived here. Actress and general fabster.'

'Don't sell yourself short. Maybe there'll be one outside your house,' said Steve, 'when you're a famous international journalist and novelist.' Then he laughed. 'Lal wanted to make some of those plaques and sell them at Christmas. His latest marketing idea. He wants to make them look the same as the genuine article, you know blue with white writing, but instead of them being made of plaster or whatever they use, he wants to make them out of some kind of self-adhesive thin plastic so that people can stick them on their inside walls.'

'But if no one famous lived in your house, what's the point?'

'Ah but that *is* the point, or so Lal says. They wouldn't be plaques commemorating famous people, they'd be tributes to us lesser people and people could choose what was written, like, Mrs Jones lived here, the best mum in the world.'

'Or Lal Lovering lived here, he was a total nutter,' I suggested.

'Er no, I think Lal had something more like, Lal Lovering lived here, the world's greatest lover. You know what he's like.'

I laughed. 'It is a brill idea. I'd buy some. One for Izzie saying, Mystic Iz lived here. Astrologer, witch and seeker. For Lucy, Dress designer extraordinaire. And Nesta . . .'

'Show-off and drama queen,' said Steve. Unlike most boys, he had never fallen for Nesta, whereas Lal had the most ginormous crush on her and went gaga whenever he saw her.

'She's not really a show-off,' I said. 'She's just . . . an extrovert.'

'Yeah right. A show-off,' said Steve.

When we went our separate ways later on in the afternoon, my thoughts turned to Luke and how I'd thought how lucky Nesta was to have him as a boyfriend. I should have thought how lucky *I* was to have a boyfriend like Steve. He's so easy to be with, a real friend and I know he'd do anything for me, like with the project, he's so supportive and as interested in what I'm doing as he is in his own part.

On Sunday morning, I felt nervous about going to meet Luke. I guess I was a little intimidated by him. I spent ages trying to decide what to wear, as I didn't want to look like I'd made too much effort, but I didn't want to look like I'd just crawled out of bed either. After trying on half my wardrobe, I settled on my usual uniform of jeans and a jumper. Really boring, I thought as I checked my watch and realised that I'd better get going. I put on my denim jacket and checked the mirror again. Too much denim, I decided and changed the denim jacket for my black one. God I hate this, I thought, I can never get that 'just threw it on and look fabulous look' that the others seem to have down pat. I always end up with the 'just threw it on and look ordinary' look. My style is the no-style style. I'd be the perfect candidate for one of those before and after makeovers that they do in magazines, only I'd be the before. And my after would look the same. I rummaged around in my chest of drawers and found the rainbow striped hat and scarf set that Marie bought me last Christmas. Hhmm, brightens me up a bit, I thought as I checked the mirror again, but now I look like one of those cheery people who present children's programmes on telly and dress in really bright colours. Too bad, I thought as I headed for the door, I'll have to do. And why am I even worrying about impressing Luke anyway? With a girlfriend as stunning as Nesta, I don't reckon he even notices other girls, never mind what they're wearing.

I arrived at the road where Luke lives about ten minutes early. I didn't want to seem too eager so I stepped into a phone box to kill some time and reapply my lip gloss. After a while, I felt like a stalker watching his house from the phone box, so I took a deep breath and walked to his gate, up the path and rang the bell.

'Be right there,' called a voice from somewhere inside. A few moments later, Luke opened the door. 'Come on in, I'm in the kitchen.'

He led me through to the back of the house where he resumed ironing a shirt.

'Want anything to drink before we go?' he asked as he whipped off the T-shirt he had on.

Wow*zola*, I thought as I looked at his naked torso. I felt like Jim Carrey in that film *The Mask* when he sees Cameron Diaz for the first time and his eyes be-doiing out of their sockets and on to the floor and back again like they're on springs. *Then* I realised I was staring, so quickly looked at the door. Then I realised I might look seriously uncool, like I'd never seen a boy without his shirt on before. I was sure I was blushing. I made myself look up and meet his eyes. 'Unyah, na, nah, no thanks,' I stuttered. He had a fab body. And I mean *fab*, like he regularly worked out. His shoulders were broad, his skin a lovely olive colour and his upper chest was nicely toned, not muscly just . . . perfect. I've seen my brother Paul loads of times running around in his boxers, but he's a skinny thing and his chest kind of sinks in. I've even seen Steve almost naked when he's been changing for tennis – to say that he's not a contestant for the Mr Universe competition is an understatement, as he's kind of thin in the chest region, like Paul, and he's very very pale. But Luke, he was like one of those Calvin Klein models modelling underwear that you see on posters on the sides of buses sometimes. As Izzie would say, hubba hubba. Get a grip, I told myself, you're acting like a stupid teenage schoolgirl. But I *am* a stupid teenage schoolgirl, said a voice in my head.

'Won't be a mo,' said Luke, as he donned the ironed shirt then grabbed his big overcoat and scarf from the back of the kitchen door. 'OK, Watts, let's get ready to rumble.'

'Er, right, rumble,' I said as I followed him out through the house and to his car.

We arrived in Hampstead about fifteen minutes later and made our way up to the tube station.

'I'm really looking forward to this,' said Luke as we joined a small crowd of tourists buying tickets, from a man with a shaved head outside the tube. There was the usual bunch by the sound of their voices, a couple of Americans, couple of Japanese, couple of Australian students, couple of Germans.

After a few minutes, more tourists poured out of the tube station, paid their money and we were away.

'My name's Peter and I'm your guide for the day,' said the man with the tickets, as he headed towards the traffic lights. 'The tour will last about two hours. Now stick together and careful crossing the road . . .'

'I feel like a kid in junior school,' I whispered to Luke as the group of about twenty of us swarmed after him across the road.

'I know,' laughed Luke. 'And make sure you wipe your nose before you talk to anyone.'

I was just about to get a tissue out when I realised that he was joking. Get a *grip*, Watts, I told myself. You're acting like a no-brain.

The tour was fascinating from the beginning, when Peter told us that the name Hampstead came from a word that meant the old homestead when there was nothing but a farm in the area. It became more popular later when people used to come up to the area for the clean air and the waters.

'Both polluted now,' laughed Luke as an old van spluttered past blowing fumes out of its exhaust pipe.

'Even King Henry the Eighth made use of the waters here,' continued Peter. 'He had all his laundry sent here and the royal undergarments could be seen for miles drying on gorse bushes. The popularity of the waters and the area waned after a doctor declared that actually sea air was the best and everyone took off for the coast. After that, the area became very popular with artists and writers . . .'

Both Luke and I had to scribble notes madly to get down what Peter said as he led us down a lovely street full of Georgian houses called Church Row, named so because there was a church at the end of it. We had a quick look round the church, then went out into an old graveyard. This doesn't feel like London at all, I thought, as we strolled amongst the trees and old graves that were overgrown with ivy.

'This doesn't feel like London at all,' said Luke. 'It feels like the countryside.'

'Just what I was thinking,' I said.

'Go to the far end of the cemetery,' said Peter pointing to a quiet corner, 'and you'll see the grave of one of Hampstead's most famous residents.'

The group moved over to where he had indicated under the trees and there, to my amazement, was a raised large stone coffin on the side of which were engraved the words, John Constable.

I felt inexplicably moved. 'I can't believe it,' I said. 'It's so unostentatious. No signs, no notices saying who's here. It makes it so much more impressive just to come across it. I'd have thought a painter as famous as he is would have been buried in one of the grander cemeteries or in a cathedral with a huge gold plaque.'

Luke nodded. 'Just what I was thinking.'

'Great minds think alike.' I grinned back at him.

'Constable painted the Heath more than any of the other painters who came here,' said Peter. 'He really loved the place.'

'Kind of right that he should be buried here then,' Luke whispered to me.

After the graveyard at the back of the church, Peter led us over the road to another part of the cemetery. 'It's claimed that the writer Jackie Collins and her sister Joan have already bought plots to be buried in here.'

'No doubt, Jackie'll have, "A plot at last" written on her gravestone.'

Luke laughed. 'I never realised that people could reserve where they wanted to be buried though.'

'Yeah. It's kind of morbid, don't you think? You know, planning your death?'

Luke nodded. 'Yeah, but I guess it's going to happen to all of us at some time or other. Probably not a bad idea to think about how you'd want your send off to be.'

'I'd like a choir singing something cheery like, "Wish Me Luck as You Wave Me Goodbye",' I said.

'Luke laughed again. 'I might have "Cold As Ice", or something appropriate like that. Or maybe "Voodoo Child". And afterwards, I'd like to be stuffed and put in the corner of someone's hall and used as a hatstand.'

I pinched his arm. '*Stop* it. I'm sure you'd make a very nice hatstand, but it's too spooky talking about death in a graveyard.'

'They say that DH Lawrence's wife had him cremated, then mixed his ashes with concrete-type stuff and had him made into a fireplace.'

'No way!'

'I read it somewhere, I swear,' said Luke.

As we wandered through the back lanes, we learned so much from Peter about the previous inhabitants of Hampstead: John Constable, George Du Maurier, George Romney. But it was also rumoured that a major Hollywood star had bought a house in the back lanes just round the corner from a famous film director, and there was even a celebrity chef living near the Holly Bush pub.

'Don't know if they're still here,' said Peter, 'as I'm not from this area and it could just be gossip.'

I couldn't wait to tell Nesta. Even if it was just a rumour that there were celebrities in the area, she'd still want to come and have a look. I felt a twinge of sadness about the imminent move to Devon as we wandered on. North London was so full of interest and I'd be leaving it all behind me, when there was still so much I wanted to explore.

At the top of Holly Hill, we stopped outside a grand-looking house called Fenton House. 'This is one of the earliest houses in Hampstead, built in 1693,' said Peter. 'Now have you noticed anything odd about the windows?'

'Some of them are bricked up,' said one of the American tourists.

'Anyone know why?' asked Peter.

I put my hand up. 'Um . . . in the sixteen hundreds, a tax was declared saying that the more windows you had, the more tax you had to pay. A lot of residents didn't want to pay the extra taxes and had their windows bricked up. They declared the tax as robbery, daylight robbery.'

'Hence the origin of the saying that is part of our language today,' said Peter. 'Well done. Couldn't have put it better myself. It was during the reign of Queen Anne.'

'Show-off,' whispered Luke, then he pinched my arm and grinned. 'I love finding out about things like that.'

'Me too,' I agreed.

Up and down and round the lanes we walked as Peter filled us in on history interspersed with gossip. 'The pond at the top of Hampstead was where travellers used to stop to water their horses on their way in and out of London,' he informed us. 'It was also where highway men used to hide, so that they could pounce on the travellers as they tended their horses. It is said that Dick Turpin was one of them and to this day he haunts the Spaniard's Inn just down the lane. The pond area was also where highwaymen were hung as examples to others.'

'Do you think that's where the term hanging out came from?' asked Luke.

I laughed. 'Doubt it somehow. Maybe the expression, hanging out to dry, is more like it.'

As we proceeded down past the pond and into East Heath Road, there was a house where Elizabeth Taylor lived with

Richard Burton, over the road from them, a fab Gothic mansion where Boy George used to live. I made a note to ask Steve to come and take photos of them for the open day presentation.

Luke and I chatted easily as we followed everyone round and discovered that we had loads in common: books, our interest in history, old films, theatre. At one point, he took my hand to lead me across a road and, for a moment, I let myself imagine what it would be like if he were my boyfriend. It was only for a moment, then I felt really bad. He was Nesta's boyfriend. How could I even consider it, even for a second? Plus Steve. I had Steve. I don't think he'd be too happy if he'd been passing and seen me holding Luke's hand, no matter how innocent.

'So you're dating Lucy's brother?' Luke asked as if he'd picked up on my thoughts once again.

I took my hand out of his immediately. 'Um yes. Since the summer.'

'I've seen him around, but never really spoken to him. What's he like?'

'Nice. Sweet. He's a real mate.'

'Sweet, huh?' Luke gave me a strange look as if he were waiting for more, but I didn't feel comfortable talking to him about Steve. Instead, I pretended I wanted to hear something that Peter was saying to one of the Japanese tourists and moved away from Luke.

The tour finished off as we walked down Well Walk, which we learned was so named because that was where the wells of water used to be. Then on to Flask Walk, which is where the water was put into flasks to be sold. On the way, we passed Burgh House, which Peter told us was one of the oldest houses in Hampstead.

'I asked Sian to do that one,' said Luke, 'so we don't have to go in. Let's go and get a drink instead. I think we've earned one.'

After the tour, we went and sat outside the Coffee Cup café in the village and chatted about what we'd learned and what we might put in our presentation. It was then I started to feel uncomfortable. Walking round with Luke had been OK, but sitting opposite him and looking straight into his eyes and he into mine, I felt strange, like my brain was going to fuse and I was sure I was blushing madly. I didn't want to be feeling what I was feeling, and the more I tried to push the sensations to the back of my head, the more they seemed to want to be in the front. In the end, I didn't look at him. Instead I watched the passersby as Luke continued talking and World War Three started in my head.

You're in danger of becoming like Sian, said one voice at the back of my mind, and you know what Luke thinks of her. A mixed-up kid. Someone with a sad crush on him. You'll be another on a long list.

But he is very attractive, said another voice. Not only looking, but personality-wise as well. There's nothing wrong in appreciating beauty. It would be mad not too. Chill.

And on the voices went:

But he's Nesta's boyfriend.

So? You're not planning to steal him or anything.

No. I'm not. But I shouldn't flirt either.

Don't kid yourself that he'd flirt with you. Someone like Luke would never look twice at someone like you, not in a fancying kind of way.

But I think he does like me.

So? There's a difference between liking someone and fancying them.

Erk! How many people are there inside my head?

228

'Are you listening to me, TJ?' asked Luke. 'You look like you're miles away. What are you thinking about?'

'Oh! Nothing. Er. Sorry,' I said, getting up. 'Look. Better go. Just realised the time.'

He looked disappointed. 'Sorry,' he said. 'I've been boring you haven't I? Was I going on?'

'No, no . . . I just have to go.'

Luke didn't look convinced. 'OK. See you Tuesday then and we'll compare notes.'

I started to head off.

'Hey, sure you don't want a lift?' Luke called after me.

'Nope. Thanks. Got to run,' I said over my shoulder, then hurried on. I must be mad, I thought. A lift would have been brilliant. Now I have to make my own way home. But I needed time on my own to think. Blow away the madness that seemed to be taking me over.

OK, I told myself as I made my way home, OK, so Luke is class A, five star attractive. So is Orlando Bloom. Fine. I can appreciate them. It's fine. That's OK. Only looking. It would be insane not to acknowledge beauty and appreciate that someone is nice and interesting. Yeah. Madness not to. So no big deal. No problem. Maybe I'm getting a bug. Yeah. That's it. Probably a virus going round making me feel funny. Being out in the cold with all those strangers. Lot of bugs going round at this time of year. Flu, colds, fevers. Nothing more than that.

By the time I reached home, I felt calmer. More rational.

Got a bug. Sorted. Yes. No prob.

Some of the Famous People Who've Lived in Hampstead

Kingsley Amis, writer

WH Auden, poet

William Blake, artist

Richard Burton, actor

Agatha Christie, writer

John Constable, artist

Dame Judi Dench, actress

Charles Dickens, writer

Daphne Du Maurier, writer

George Du Maurier, cartoonist and novelist

Sigmund Freud, psychoanalyst

Thomas Hardy, writer

William Hogarth, artist

Aldous Huxley, writer

John Keats, poet

DH Lawrence, writer

AA Milne, writer

Florence Nightingale, nursing reformer

George Orwell, writer

George Romney, artist

Dante Gabriel Rossetti, artist and poet

Peter Sellers, actor

Sting (Gordon Sumner), musician

HG Wells, writer

Chapter 7

Worst Person in the World

We were in the graveyard at the back of the church on Church Row. It was snowing and everywhere looked white and magical.

'You're freezing,' said Luke as he took off his red woollen scarf and wound it round my neck. Then he took the ends of the scarf and pulled me towards him. I could feel the warmth of his body through his coat. He reached up with his left hand and stroked the side of my cheek gently, then slid his hand down to my chin and tilted my face up to meet his. I looked into his eyes as his face moved towards mine and our lips . . .

'ARRRRGGHHHHHHHHHHHHHHHHHHHHHHHHH HHHHHHH!'

I sat up in a cold sweat. Where was I? Oh. Home. Bed. Warm. I lay back down and pulled the duvet up to my neck. Ohmigod. I dreamed I was snogging Luke. Ohmigod. Sorted, huh? Got it all under control? Got some kind of a bug? Yeah, right. I might have my conscious mind under control, but my unconscious clearly had ideas of its own. And those ideas were getting up close and very personal with Nesta's boyfriend. I am clearly the worst person on the planet.

At school later, I felt even worse. Nesta was so nice to me, but then why shouldn't she be? She didn't know that I was having X-rated kisses with her boyfriend in my dreams.

'Luke said you had a good time on the walk,' she said at break-time as we made our way down towards the hall.

'Yeah. We did. There was so much to take in. We've got a ton of work to do. I knew there were a few famous people who lived in the area, but nothing like the number we've discovered.'

Nesta put her arm through mine. 'Luke thinks you don't like him,' she said.

'*Whadt?* Why? What on earth gave him that impression?'

'Dunno.' She shrugged. 'I guess you can be cool with people sometimes. A bit aloof sort of thing.'

'No. It's not that. I'm . . . I'm shy . . .' Actually I'd heard people say that I was aloof before, but I never mean to be. It's when I don't know people very well, I go quiet. But I didn't think I had been with Luke. I thought we'd got on great. Too great.

'Is that what he said. I was aloof?'

Nesta nodded. 'Something about you running off as soon as the walk was over, like you didn't want to hang out with him more than was necessary. He said that you're a bit of a mystery and don't give anything away. He was asking a lot about you.'

Izzie raised an eyebrow. 'Maybe he fancies her. Watch out Nesta, you've got competition.'

Nesta laughed so I joined in, probably a little too hysterically.

'Numpf. Er . . . As if . . .' I said.

'I do think he rates you though, TJ. He said he thought you

were really smart. I told him you were. The smartest person I know.'

'Neeyuh, thanks.' I felt lost for words. And a little hurt. He rates me because I'm smart. But he dates Nesta because she's beautiful.

Nesta put her hand on my arm. 'TJ, for me, be nice to Luke. I mean, me, Iz and Lucy know that you're a fabster but when people don't know you, they might be intimidated by your distant cool manner. Maybe make a bit more of an effort to be friendly?'

I gulped. Me, distant? Cool? Hah! If only she knew the turmoil that went on in my head sometimes. And wanting me to be more *friendly* to Luke, she clearly didn't have the slightest idea what she was asking. And amazing! Luke thought I didn't *like* him. I thought it was written all over my face that I did.

'I think it's because you're cool that Steve likes you,' said Lucy. 'He said that you're not like other teenage girls, who shriek instead of talk and are always getting hysterical.'

'Did he?' I asked. It's strange how other people see you and how you see yourself, I thought. This person they were describing didn't sound like me one bit. Cool? Aloof? Distant? More like totally mental. Mental girl from Mental land, that's me.

'Steve said he's going to help you,' said Lucy, linking my other arm. 'Take photos.'

'Um, yeah,' I mumbled. Oh God. Steve. I felt like I'd betrayed him. I ought to have been dreaming about kissing him, not Luke. For a moment, I had a real ache to talk to Hannah. We'd been friends for so many years and talked over *everything*. She'd know what to say. How to play it. I looked at Lucy, Izzie and Nesta. I'd *thought* I could talk to them about everything, but no way could I mention this. They'd hate me forever and think I was the worst person in the world, and maybe I was. Like, hey guys, guess what I dreamed last night. I was snogging Luke and I think I fancy him. It's an unspoken rule: Thou shalt keep thy hands off other people's boyfriends.

After school, Nesta and Lucy were going up to Highgate to meet Luke and Tony and they asked if I wanted to join them and bring Steve. No *way*, I thought, too many highly intuitive people in one small space. Despite my apparent cool demeanour, one of them would be bound to suss out what was going on in my head, so I made my excuses and headed for home.

Got to keep busy, I thought, once I was on the bus. Stay out of Luke's way. Never be alone with him again. Be nice to him in company to keep Nesta happy. Then it will all be fine.

I spent the evening compiling a list of the famous people that lived in Hampstead, then I pulled out the photocopy of the map of the area that I'd done earlier at school and spent the evening putting stars on the map to show where they all lived. Luke will like this, I thought as I surveyed my work. It looked really good. Names of people, what they did, and the dates they lived in Hampstead on one side. The map with the stars showing where they lived in the middle, then the names and addresses on the right-hand side. It would look great when it was blown up. On a board next to it, I'd put the photographs of the houses where some of them lived that Steve was going to take for me. Yeah, it would look cool. Yeah. Cool. Like me. Not.

Outbox (1)
From: babewithbrains@psnet.co.uk
To: hannahnutter@fastmail.com
Date: 1st December
Subject: Boys. Urgent.

Dear Hannah
Please reply to this as soon as you get it. No. Actually please read it first then reply. Haha.

Actually, not funny. Nothing funny about my situation. I think I may be the worst person in the world. I fancy Nesta's boyfriend, Luke. I dreamed I was snogging him last night and now I feel really bad. And Nesta's being really sweet and telling me to make an effort to be more friendly to him. More friendly?!!!!

What shall I do? Shall I quit the project? I wish you were here really badly.

Email back soon.

Luv TJ
PS: By the way, do you think that I'm aloof or distant?

Email: **Inbox (1)**
From: hannahnutter@fastmail.com
To: babewithbrains@psnet.co.uk
Date: 2nd December
Subject: Boys urgent

Ma petite little TJ

Chill. I fancy loads of my mates' boyfriends. Everybody does. What's the big deal? It's totally normal especially if they are cute, babe type boyfriends. What are you supposed to do, cast out your eyes or something madly biblical? It's sooooo typical of you to get in a tizz over something like this and it's because you are a nice person with a conscience. So you dreamed about him? Doesn't mean you snogged him in real life. So my advice, is chill. Chill like a chilled thing. Don't quit the project. Why don't you tell Nesta? It's always nice to hear that a mate rates your boyfriend and I bet you'll have a laugh about it.

Lots of love and I miss you too
Hannah
PS: No, I don't think you're aloof, but I know other people at school, when I was there, were sometimes intimidated as you're such a mega brain. And you can be shy sometimes, so maybe people who don't know you take it as indifference or think that you're bored cos you don't say anything. Stuff 'em I say. As the song goes: 'Don't go changin' . . .'

Outbox (1)
From: babewithbrains@psnet.co.uk
To: hannahnutter@fastmail.com
Date: 2nd December
Subject: Guys. Urgent.

No way can I tell Nesta. Much as I love her, she has a big mouth. If I tell her I fancy Luke, yeah, we'll probably have a laugh, then she'll tell Izzie and Lucy. And Luke. They've already been talking about me. And if she told him, then I'd be too embarrassed to work on the project with him. So no way. But I will try and chill.
    Chill. Chilling. Chilled.
    Yours, the Ice Queen of Norf London. Gawd it's cold over here. And not just cos I'm chilled. Tis cos tis winter.

Chapter 8

Skiving

By Wednesday evening, I felt like I'd got myself together again. I'd be professional, competent and detached. I'd be that person that people saw. Distant, cool. I could do it and not let any silly feelings get in the way.

Luke, Sian and Olivia were already in the prefab when I got to the project meeting and we launched into all our findings straight away. Sian had obviously been doing her homework and she showed us the brochures that she'd picked up over the weekend.

'And there's another guided walk,' she said looking at Luke hopefully, 'only this time it's round Highgate. Sunday afternoon at one forty-five.'

'Excellent,' said Luke. 'Can you do it?'

Sian nodded.

'OK, you and Olivia do that,' he continued. 'There really is a lot of ground to cover, so I reckon it's best if you two cover Highgate and TJ and I will focus on Hampstead.'

'Oh, I don't mind doing Highgate,' I said, 'if Sian wants to do Hampstead with you.'

Luke shook his head and looked at my lists and maps. 'After this great start you've made? No way. In fact, TJ, I'd like to go down right now and look at DH Lawrence's house in the Vale of Health if that's OK with you.'

'Um, sure.'

'OK. Sian, Olivia. You hold the fort here and TJ and I will nip down there. There's plenty for you to do. Sort out which places you want to highlight in Highgate.'

'Yes, sir,' said Olivia with a mock salute.

Sian nodded but didn't look very happy. 'But I wanted to go over what angle to take,' she said indicating all her findings.

'We will,' said Luke as he put on his coat. 'I'll give you a call and we'll get together. OK?'

This time when she nodded, she looked happier.

'In fact,' said Luke, 'let's step things up a bit. Meet here again tomorrow night?'

'Yeah,' said Sian. 'Great.'

'In fact,' Luke continued, 'we should meet as many times as we need this week until we've got things really sorted. We need to get on top of this, put our other homework on the back burner until we know exactly what we're going to present, then we can kick back and relax a bit.'

I think Sian thought he meant meetings just with her and looked delighted, but then Luke turned to Olivia. 'You in?'

Olivia nodded.

'TJ?'

'I'll do my best.'

Poor Sian. Her face had fallen again. It looked like she was never going to get Luke on his own.

We drove down to the Vale of Health and Luke parked the car

at the top of the lane. It's a remarkable place, just off East Heath Road and a lot of locals don't even know that it exists. It's like a countryside village hidden away at the bottom of Hampstead Heath.

We soon found the house where DH Lawrence lived as there was the typical blue plaque mounted on the outside wall.

'I didn't realise it was privately owned,' said Luke with disappointment as he looked at the terraced house. From the bike in the front garden and computer at an upstairs window, it was clearly inhabited.

'Me neither,' I said. 'I thought it would be like the one at Keats Grove where it's a shrine to Keats. Ah well, never mind. I'll get Steve to photograph it anyway.'

'I guess we could go and check out Keats House,' sighed Luke, then he grinned and checked his watch, 'or we could go and have a skive.'

'Skive, like how?'

'Movie.'

My first instinct was to say no, but then I remembered what Nesta had said about being more friendly.

'Yeah, sure. Where?'

'Ever been to the Everyman cinema in Hampstead village?'

I shook my head. 'I've walked past a few times, but never been in. We always go to the one up near Finchley.'

'Then you're in for a treat. And it's on me. I got some good tips last week working in Dad's restaurant.'

'This is awesome,' I said, as an usherette showed us to our seats twenty minutes later.

Luke looked really pleased. 'I know.'

He'd paid top price so that we could sit upstairs in the

private balcony, where there were a small number of plush leather chairs and sofas.

'Sit where you like,' said the usherette. 'It's quiet today.'

'So where would madam like to sit?' asked Luke after she'd gone.

I sprawled in an enormous chair at the back. 'Everywhere looks great,' I said.

'This is my favourite,' said Luke as he sat on a sofa on the second and back row.

I went and sat beside him. It was amazing. Totally luxurious and it felt like we were the only people in the cinema having a private viewing. A few minutes later, the lights went down and the trailers started up. Luke curled up happily in his corner of the sofa.

'Cool, huh?' he said.

'Major.' I nodded back.

As the movie started, I found it hard to concentrate. I was so aware of Luke's proximity. At one point, he sat up and our knees were touching and just the pressure of his leg against mine was enough to send my head spinning. I moved my leg away then, a few minutes later, our arms touched and it felt like heat from him was burning into me. Then Luke slipped his shoes off and stretched out. 'Sit back,' he whispered. 'Make the most of it.'

I did as I was told and he put his feet up and over my knees and grinned at me. 'Heaven, huh?'

'Unuh . . .' I whispered back. 'H . . . heaven.'

Well Nesta, I thought, as I glanced down at Luke curled up comfortably like a cat, at least I'm doing as you told me. You can't get more friendly than this!

After the movie, Luke suggested we have a cappuccino in the

bar downstairs. Once again, my first instinct was to say no, but I'd run off last time we'd had coffee and I didn't want him reporting back to Nesta again. And I remembered what Hannah had written. Chill. Everyone fancies their mate's boyfriend, especially if they're cute, babe types. Well, Luke was definitely that. And we did get along and have loads in common. I decided to chill and enjoy the moment. There was nothing wrong with that.

As Luke went to the bar, I sat in one of the armchairs and looked around. Fab, I thought, I really like it here. The atmosphere was a mixture of sophisticated and bohemian, with low lighting, dark walls and velvet sofas and chairs and there were framed black and white photos from old Bollywood films on the wall. I felt very grown-up, sitting there with the other people sipping their wine and picking at bowls of olives.

'Very posh,' I whispered to Luke, when he came back with the drinks. 'I see they do olives here, not your common old popcorn.'

A couple of teen girls came in and eyed Luke up, then looked enviously at me. I couldn't help but feel great to be the one that was with him.

As on the walk, Luke was interesting company and we chatted about films we liked and ones we wanted to see. Just as I was starting to relax and enjoy myself, Luke went quiet for a few moments then looked at me intensely. No one had ever looked at me like that before, like he was really looking into me. I felt myself getting pinker and pinker.

'It's easy being with you, TJ Watts,' he said finally. 'I wonder what would have happened if I'd met you before Nesta.'

'Uh . . . nyah . . .'

That was me gone. I mean, what was I supposed to say? He'd completely thrown me. 'Um, er . . . dunno, um. Like another coffee? No? Um. I would.' And I was up and off to the counter before he could say anything else to blow my mind.

When I returned, Luke didn't press me for an answer. He glanced at his watch as I bolted back scalding coffee then he began looking at me again. My heart started to palpitate madly in my chest.

'Better get going I guess,' I said and stood up.

Like at the Coffee Cup café on Sunday, he looked disappointed but he didn't object. 'Sure,' he said as he got up and put on his coat. 'Yeah. I'll drop you.'

As we made our way back to the car, the traffic was busy and, for a brief moment as we crossed the road, he took my hand. I ran with him towards the pavement on the opposite side of the road and, when I glanced to my left, I noticed that someone had stopped and was staring at us. It was Lal. Lal, as in Steve and Lucy's brother Lal. And he had a very quizzical look on his face. Then he turned on his heel and stomped off round a corner.

Outbox (1)
From: babewithbrains@psnet.co.uk
To: hannahnutter@fastmail.com
Date: 3rd December
Subject: Heeeeeeelp!!!!!

Dear Hannah
Oh God am I in trouble Nesta told me to be more friendly
so I was and when Luke suggested a skive to the movies I
went and he took my hand when we crossed the road and
Lal Lovering saw us and Luke asked me what I thought
would have happened if he'd met me before he'd met Nesta
oh God, what did he mean? Maybe nothing and he took my
hand (the second time by the way) does that mean anything?
Maybe not as he is Italian and I think he's a naturally
touchy-feely type person maybe I'm imagining things oh
God Hannah, come back to England all is forgiven I have
no one to talk to over here and it's driving me mad. I'm
beginning to think that a move to Devon might be best after
all.
 Tell me what to DOOOO! I neeeeeeeeeeed you.

Love your friend
Mad person

Email: **Inbox (1)**
From: hannahnutter@fastmail.com
To: babewithbrains@psnet.co.uk
Date: 4th December
Subject: Heeellppp

Hohohahaha. My little percorini. What a merry old state you is in back there in Britland. First thing. Breathe. Second thing. Breathe again.

Sounds like this guy Luke is flirting with you. He's checking you out for definite. Yes, the holding hand thing may be innocent, but I don't think the question was. Think about it. Would you have ever in your wildest dreams have asked him what he thought would have happened if you'd met him before you met Steve? No. Exactly. Comprendi? This guy sounds like trouble. Be mucho mucho careful.

Try to avoid situations where you're alone with him. And don't give anything away, cos then he's gotcha.

Still sweltering here. Don't fancy anyone big time at the mo which is quite nice as there's a group of us that just hang out.

Luv and kisses
Auntie Hannah

Chapter 9

Week from Hell

'Lucy phoned,' said Mum as soon as I walked though the door after the movie with Luke.

'When?'

'About five minutes ago.'

'Did she leave a message?'

'Only to phone her as soon as you get back.'

'How did she sound?'

'What do you mean? Like Lucy. Why? Is something going on?'

'No.'

I raced up the stairs and stared at the phone. How was I going to get out of this? Mojo was scrabbling outside my door, so I let him in and he jumped on the end of my bed where he lay wagging his tail.

'God I so wish you could talk, Mojo,' I said as he rolled over and I tickled his tummy. 'Come on, talk to me. What's on the top of a house? Come on . . .'

'Rufff,' barked Mojo.

'That's right! A roof. And how am I feeling?'

'Rurrf,' he replied. 'Rfff, rrfff.'

'Right again, I *am* feeling rough,' I said. Mojo looked so pleased with himself that he rolled back on his legs, sprang up and gave my face a huge lick. 'See, you can talk if you try,' I told him.

By the eager expression on Mojo's face, he was doing his best, but I decided to ask someone who spoke proper English instead. I emailed Hannah, then lay back on my bed and stared at the ceiling. Two minutes later, the phone rang again. I let it ring and didn't pick up my extension.

'TJ, it's for you,' Mum called up the stairs. 'Lucy.'

I took a deep breath and picked up the phone.

'Hey Lucy,' I said in my most cheerful voice.

'So what's going on?' asked Lucy.

Lal obviously hadn't wasted any time reporting back.

'Oh same old same old,' I replied, trying to avoid the tone in her voice. I knew exactly what she meant by 'going on'.

'You and Luke,' said Lucy. 'Lal said he saw you.'

'Oh *that*.'

'Yeah that. Lal said you and Luke were holding hands.'

'Not really.'

'Well you either were or you weren't.'

'We were, but not as in holding hands holding hands if you know what I mean. He took my hand when we crossed the road, that's all. Traffic safety. He was probably a boy scout trained to steer old-age pensioners across. Nothing's going on. Lucy, you know I'd never . . .'

'Do you fancy him?'

'*Noooo*. No way. Course not. I mean, yeah, he's really attractive, but he's not my type. And anyway, Lucy, you know

I'd never do that to Nesta. Or Steve. Hey, Lucy come on, you guys are my friends.'

'Well OK. Just checking, because I know Steve would be gutted and so would Nesta if you were carrying on with Luke.'

I felt near to tears. I really wanted to tell her everything, but I didn't dare in case it came out wrong and made things worse than they were. 'But I'm *not*. Honestly. Lucy, you've *got* to believe me.'

'So where had you been?'

'Movie. Luke wanted to skive and I was going to say I couldn't go, but Nesta *told* me to be more friendly to him. Remember? You were there. You heard her. I would never ever *ever* take anyone else's boyfriend. Especially Nesta's. You've *got* to believe me.'

There was a pause for a few seconds. 'I do. Sorry. It's probably just Lal, you know what he's like, he came in all flustered about what he'd seen. You know what a crush he has on Nesta. He was probably hoping you were going to run off with Luke, then he could step in and comfort Nesta. Sorry. I should have known it was innocent.'

After she'd put the phone down, I lay back on the bed. That's done it, I thought. I've lied to one of my best friends. It was true that I wouldn't be disloyal to Nesta and nothing was *really* going on. It was in my head though. And I did fancy Luke. Like crazy. Oh hell. What a week. The week from hell. And it was only Wednesday.

At school on Thursday, Lucy was fine, her usual sunny self and Nesta didn't mention the hand–holding episode, so I presumed that Lucy had thought it best to keep quiet about it. I felt relieved as our friendship carried on as normal. I only wished my head did. Try as I might, I couldn't stop thinking about

Luke, over and over again, how he'd looked at me when he'd asked what might have happened if he'd met me before he'd met Nesta. How it felt when he kicked off his shoes in the cinema and put his legs over my knees like we were the oldest and easiest of friends. How it had felt when he'd taken my hand when we crossed the road. And I couldn't help but imagine what it would be like to kiss him. The thought of it made me tingle from my head to my toes. I tried to put him out of my mind, but he wouldn't go and I couldn't help but look forward to the meeting after school and seeing him again.

However, at the project meeting later, it was clear that Luke wasn't feeling the same way. He blanked me, that is, he talked to me, told me what to do, but he didn't look at me. Not properly. Not once. It was as if he couldn't meet my eyes. I wondered if maybe he felt bad about last night and felt like he'd been disloyal to Nesta. I was disappointed on one level but, on another, I felt relieved. It made it easier to deal with and, once again, I told myself to get over him and get a grip.

When I arrived at the meeting on Friday, Luke was already there and he was totally opposite to how he was the day before. He looked right at me, then started complaining about his neck and asked me to give it a rub. At first I was going to refuse, but what excuse could I give? That I daren't touch him? He might have thought I was mad, or a sad case, like Sian with a pathetic schoolgirl crush on someone she can't have. Or maybe I should have come clean and said I felt a bit weird because of Nesta. But then he might have thought I was a prude. He'd only asked for a neck rub. It wasn't like he'd asked me to snog him. And if anyone else had asked for a neck rub, I wouldn't have thought it was any big deal. I'd just have done it. My anxiety soon faded as I started to massage him. It felt amazing just to touch his shoulders and his neck and he sighed like he was enjoying it too. I know I wasn't imagining that the air grew charged and at one point he put his hand up on top of mine and left it there for a few moments, then he leaned back against me and we stayed like that for a while. Nothing said. I felt this strange feeling – a mixture of sadness and closeness as I knew we couldn't go any further than an innocent neck rub. I'm sure he was feeling the same, because he said this weird thing out of the blue. 'Unspoken but not unknown,' he said. And that was all. I knew what he meant. Only a neck rub, only a neck rub, I kept telling myself, but it felt like much more. But when we heard Sian and Olivia approaching, he leaped up quickly and started looking busy. He wouldn't have done that if it was innocent, would he? Maybe my feelings were not as one-sided as I thought. What the hell is going on? I asked myself for the hundredth time that week.

On Saturday, we were due to have another quick meeting in the morning, but I was late as my bus got held up in traffic. I peeked through the window before I went in, and this time when I arrived Sian was alone with Luke. I could hardly believe my eyes as she was massaging his neck. I felt sick at the thought that he'd asked another girl to do it for him and looked like he was enjoying it. Olivia arrived a few moments after me and saw me looking in the window. When she saw them together, she glanced at me and raised an eyebrow as if to say, what's going on here then? I wondered myself and, all through the meeting, my head was all over the place. Yesterday I'd thought that there something special between Luke and me. Had I imagined it? Not from my side I hadn't. I had no doubt that I felt a lot for Luke and, although I had no intention of ever acting on it, I couldn't deny those feelings. It must happen to people all the time. You meet someone, you go out with them, then you meet someone else you fancy. Doesn't mean you leave your first boyfriend. But then, was it all in my head? Maybe I *was* just like Sian? Another girl on a long list of people who had a crush on Luke. I so wished I could talk to my mates about it all, especially Nesta. If it had been about any other boy, she'd have been brilliant to talk it over with, as boys are her speciality. But because it was Luke, her boyfriend I reminded myself for the umpteenth time, I could never bring the subject up. I felt miserable and mixed-up. I didn't want to be feeling any of it but, every now and then, Luke would catch my eye in the meeting and not look away for a few seconds, and the look in his eye was so tender. My stomach did backflips and somersaults. There was something there. There was. I *couldn't* be imagining it, could I? For a brief moment I felt like thumping him and yelling, 'Don't *look* at me like that! Stop *playing* with my head!' But then he might have thought I was bonkers. And Sian and Olivia definitely would! One time Olivia noticed Luke and me looking at each other and I looked away quickly. Got to get out of here quick, I told myself, but then another part wanted to stay and look into his eyes one more time.

After the meeting had ended, try as I might, I couldn't make myself walk away when Sian and Olivia left. I fussed about with my coat, shuffled my papers, packed and repacked my rucksack until finally Luke looked up.

'Did you want something?' asked Luke as he gathered up his things.

I felt uncomfortable. I should have gone. Left. Got the bus. I felt like I had the wrong body on. The wrong clothes. My head didn't fit the rest of me.

'Er . . . we need to talk . . .' I started, then, as Luke rolled his eyes, I remembered that Nesta had told me that those were the four words that most boys dread. 'Er, it's nothing really,' I continued trying to make my voice light. 'Um . . . How's your neck?'

Luke rotated his chin. 'Better actually.'

'Yeah, I noticed that you got Sian to give you a rub earlier.' It was out before I could help it and I knew my tone sounded jealous.

Luke stopped what he was doing, sighed heavily and looked at me. 'You're not going to go weird on me, are you?'

I felt my heart sink. 'What do you mean?'

'Sian. Neck rub. It's all innocent, you know.'

'Yeah. I know.'

'Good. Because I credit you with more intelligence than reading things into things that aren't there.'

'Yeah. Right.' The atmosphere felt heavy, all wrong. I was doing a saddo. Needy. Hanging on where I wasn't wanted in the hope of another look, a word of encouragement, anything to let me know that I wasn't alone in what I was feeling.

Luke pulled his jacket on. 'See you then.'

'Yeah. See you.'

Arrghhhhhh, I thought as I watched him walk off. Don't read things into things? Did he mean between me and him or between him and Sian? Hell. I was dying to ask him, but then I might make myself look a *real* fool. Desperate. Clingy. And I know how much boys hate that. And besides, there was Steve and Nesta to think of. Luke might be a totally innocent party and, if I blabbed out all my feelings, he might think I was the most crapola girlfriend in the world and the lousiest friend. Don't give anything away, Hannah had said.

I was losing my mind and desperately needed someone to talk to. But who? Nesta was off the list because of Luke. Lucy was off the list because of Steve. Mojo was no good and emailing Hannah wasn't enough any more. She was too far away. I needed someone who knew everyone involved. Someone who could give me some good advice.

Forget looking a fool, I thought. You've got nothing to lose.

I decided to take a chance, got out my mobile and dialled.

The four words boys most dread: We need to talk.

Chapter 10

Yogis

'So what's up, doc?' said Izzie with a smile as she let me into her house, then we made our way up the stairs to her bedroom.

'Oh nothing,' I said when we got to her room and I flopped on to the bed.

'Want some lunch?'

I shook my head. 'Not hungry.'

Izzie sat at her desk. 'You said you needed to talk to me. Sounded urgent.'

'Yeah. No. I mean . . . just to catch up. How's it all going? You know, your side of the project?'

Izzie smiled mischievously. 'Cool. In fact, I'm having a total gas with Trevor. He's slowly coming round to my way of thinking. I told him that no way could we concentrate only on the Christian development of the area. Now we're looking at all sorts of stuff. All the religions. The persecution of witches, mysticism, magic . . . He's getting into it. And I even persuaded him to have his hair cut into a decent style.'

'You'll be persuading him to get a tattoo next,' I said, laughing.

'Not a bad idea. But it's been good. We've discovered loads of interesting stuff, like, you know that place in Highgate, Pond Square?'

I nodded.

'Well there aren't any ponds there any more, but there used to be. Two of them. And one of them was used to duck women in . . .'

'Witches?'

'No. Just women who nagged their husbands! I'm going to suggest that they bring the tradition back for parents who nag their children. My mum will be a regular.'

I laughed. Izzie's relationship with her mother was tempestuous at the best of times. They were total opposites. Her mum was neat, organised and mega straight. Izzie was into everything, curious and open-minded. They often clashed when Izzie discovered some new fad, religion or therapy and decided to change her life for the umpteenth time.

Izzie pulled her chair closer to the bed. 'You know if you *do* need to talk TJ, I'm happy to listen and not just about project stuff.'

'I know. I . . .' I *desperately* wanted to talk to her. Spill it all out. But there was still a part of me that was worried that she'd hate me. Izzie and Lucy went back a long way, mates in junior school and best mates ever since. And both had been friends with Nesta longer than I had. And then there was the fact that Steve was Lucy's brother and she was very protective of him. I didn't want to get on the wrong side of Lucy, as the wrong side of her would include Izzie. But then again, Izzie was my friend too and, apart from all her mad ideas, she was good at giving advice. 'God it's so complicated . . .' I began.

'Try me,' said Izzie.

'It's nothing really, just . . . oh . . . I don't know . . . I don't know where to begin . . .'

'Something's obviously bothering you and it's always better out than in.'

I decided to trust her. I was going to crack up if I didn't. 'If I tell you, promise you won't tell anyone else?'

'Promise.'

'OK. I . . . I just feel like I'm going totally mental. See, this thing happened recently and I can't stop thinking about it and I don't want to think about it, but I can't stop myself. And the more I try and stop myself the more I think about it . . .'

'Ah,' said Izzie. 'Thing. A boy.'

I nodded. I knew she'd understand. 'Not just any boy.'

'Not Steve?'

I shook my head. 'Not Steve.'

'Ah. Who then?'

'Er . . . um . . . er . . .' I looked at the carpet. 'Luke.'

'*Luke?* Oh!'

'I know. Oh.'

'Has anything happened between you?'

'*No.* It can't. Won't. No. It's all in my stupid, stupid head.'

'Well he *is* a bit of a dish,' said Izzie.

'Do you fancy him?' I asked.

'I think he's stunning, but no, the chemistry's not there and no matter how gorgeous someone is, if the magic's not there, it's not there. And it ain't with us.'

That got me thinking again. Chemistry. It was definitely there between Luke and me. Whenever we saw each other, he was like a magnet and I was an iron filing. I had no choice but to be drawn towards him. I couldn't help it. It was chemistry.

'It's . . . look, I know he's Nesta's boyfriend,' I said, 'and I respect that. I would never go after him. It's just . . . As you said, chemistry.'

'Yeah, but you can feel chemistry with loads of people, even people you don't fancy or know it would never work with. I felt it with this complete dork on holiday a couple of years ago. He worked on the beach and was so full of himself, running about like he was some lifeguard stud when actually he had skinny legs, was lily-white pale and his job was to collect money for the deckchairs. The chemistry was really strong but no way would I have followed it through. It was weird. Feeling an attraction and a repulsion at the same time.'

'I know. I *know*. And some people are out of bounds. I've been thinking about it a lot. Like when people get married. Doesn't mean they stop feeling attracted to other people, but they have made a vow to be faithful, so if they feel chemistry with someone else, most times, they let the chemistry go.'

'Right,' said Izzie. 'But Luke and Nesta aren't married.'

'But she is my mate. To me that means hands off her boyfriend. My mates mean a lot to me.'

'Likewise,' said Izzie.

'And my mates are mainly why I don't want to move to Devon. Or didn't. I don't know any more. Now with this thing with Luke . . . maybe it would be for the best . . .'

Izzie looked surprised. 'That bad, huh? So. I take it that you've felt some vibe with Luke then?'

'I think so. I mean, yes. Definitely, most definitely, but I'd never act on it. Honest. It's just difficult having to do the project with him and all. It's so *strong*. It's like I'm caught in a powerful current in a river and it's carrying me along, but I know I can't go with it so I'm swimming the opposite way. It's wearing me *out*.'

'Hhmmmm,' said Izzie, then she grinned. 'So get out of the river!'

'What? *How*?'

She turned to her desk, picked up a leaflet and read from it. 'If you want uncomplicated love, follow me.'

I waited for her to continue. Which she didn't.

'What's that supposed to mean?'

'Buddhism,' she said. 'I've been reading about it. See, there are many kinds of love, although we use the same word for all of them. We love our pets, we love our parents, we love our brothers and sisters, we love our friends, we *love* chocolate. All the same word, love, but very different levels of it and each level has its own complications. We love some boys. That's the most complicated kind of love of all. It brings insecurity, jealousy, loss of focus, madness.'

'Tell me about it.' I thought about the range of emotions I'd been through over the last few days – excitement, insanity, highs, lows, tenderness, expectation, disappointment, sadness, elation, despair . . .

'Buddha says that the source of all unhappiness is desire,' continued Izzie. 'One desire always leads to another, which is why we're never content. We get one thing, we want another. We get a new top, great, hurrah. Next week, we don't like it any more and we see one we want even more, and on and on it goes, with us always thinking that getting these things will make us happy. But it doesn't. It makes us agitated. We fancy a boy. We want to hold his hand, we want to snog him and on it goes . . .'

'Yeah. So? All that stuff's totally normal. How do you stop it?'

'By going beyond desire. Buddha calls it a wheel, always turning. What you have to do is go to the centre of the wheel through meditation and there you'll find peace and stillness.'

She made it sound so simple. Then she got out one of her yoga books and showed me a meditation where I had to block my right nostril with my thumb and breathe in through the left nostril, then block the left nostril, with my middle finger and breathe out through the right one. Over and over. By the end of my visit, I did feel slightly calmer, mainly because I kept losing track of which nostril I was supposed to be breathing in or out of and which finger or thumb was where, so my mind was distracted from Luke for a brief time.

'We can be yogis,' said Izzie.

'Mmm. Maybe. Not sure I've got the hang of this,' I said.

She reassured me that practice makes perfect, so I decided to give it a go. I was going to be a yogi, get out of the river and find the centre of the wheel. Or something like that.

Centred, peaceful, focused. Off the cycle of desire. I am free, I told myself as I went home. In one nostril, out the other. Then I wondered what you did if you had a cold and your nose was stuffed up. Was that the end of your inner calm?

On Sunday, all the gang arranged to meet up at Costa in Highgate for our usual Sunday morning natter. Lucy was there first with Tony. Then Izzie arrived with her nostrils. Soon after her, Nesta came in the door with Luke and, as soon as I saw them, I went into my meditation. Block one nostril, breathe in the other . . .

'Do you need a tissue?' asked Lucy.

'No,' I said. 'I'm meditating.'

'Then do it in private,' laughed Lucy. 'It looks like you're picking your nose.'

'My most alluring look.' I grinned back at her. Izzie smiled over at me. It was going to be OK.

As we caught up on the week and what we'd all been doing, I made sure that I didn't look directly at Luke. However, I couldn't help but notice how friendly he was with everyone. His hand on Izzie's arm as he enthused about the project, hand resting on Lucy's shoulder when he got up and asked if anyone wanted anything from the counter. Yes, he's definitely a touchy-feely kind of person, I thought. Him holding my hand the other day was just another example. It meant nothing. At least, not to him. A few more nostrilly-breathing things and I'd be fine. A blip. A minor setback. No biggie.

But then Nesta got up to help Luke fetch drinks and, when they were in the queue, they started fooling around and soon the whole café was witnessing an Oscar winning snog. Nesta never was one to be shy about who was watching her. I tried to look away but I couldn't. It was awful. I felt like someone had stabbed me with a knife. Jealousy. It can hurt like hell. It was so clear. Luke was totally into Nesta and I had a sad schoolgirl crush on him. It was all in my head. And always would be. I was pathetic. Sad. Pitiful.

Then I noticed Lucy looking at me.

Then Izzie looked at Nesta and Luke, then back at me.

Then Lucy looked at Izzie looking at me.

Then Lucy looked at me. At Nesta and Luke. Back at Izzie. Then back at me.

I felt like a rabbit caught in the spotlight as both of them stared me. Izzie with concern. Lucy with questions.

Lucy knows, I thought. She *knows* that something is going on in my head. I tried my nostril breathing without the aid of my thumb, but it looked like I was holding back a sneeze. So much for me being a yogi, I thought, as I got up and headed for the Ladies at the back of the café, where I kicked the wall and almost broke my toe. I can't go on with this, I thought. Everyone can see right through me and, any minute now, Steve and Lal are going to get here as well. Lal who already suspects something is going on and Steve, who is like Lucy, as sharp as a knife and would suss me out in no time.

There was only one thing for it.

Yoga Meditation

1) Sit comfortably with the spine straight.
2) For this technique, you are going to inhale and exhale through alternate nostrils. First put your right hand up to your face. Lightly rest your right thumb on the right side of your nose.
3) Rest your index finger on your forehead and have your middle finger ready by the left nostril for when you need it. The hand fits quite comfortably into this position.
4) When you are ready, apply a slight pressure with the thumb, closing the right nasal passage.
5) Now slowly inhale through the left nostril, hold for two counts then apply gentle pressure on the left nostril with your middle finger (releasing your thumb from the right nostril as you do so) and exhale slowly through the right nostril.
6) Then, with the middle finger still resting on the left nostril, inhale through the right nostril, slowly, hold for two counts, then lift the middle finger from the left nostril and exhale through the left, closing the right nostril with your thumb again.
7) Try a few times to get the movements right, then do it slowly up to ten times. Once you have mastered the technique, you can sit and do it for ten minutes or longer and it will bring about a sensation of calm and focus (unless you're TJ).

Chapter 11

Another Level?

'Mum, I have something I want to say to you.'

'You're back early, TJ,' said Mum, looking up from the chair where she was doing the *Telegraph* crossword. 'I thought you were out with the girls.'

'I was, but I've been thinking and I wanted to tell you something straight away.'

'What is it?'

'About Devon. I've changed my mind. I want to go.'

Mum smiled and put her paper aside. 'I thought you might come round in the end but . . .'

'When are we going?'

'But what's brought on this sudden change?'

'Nothing. Be good to have a new start. Er, I want to be a writer. New experience, fresh fields, etc. That sort of thing. So. When are we going?'

'Oh, TJ. There's so much to sort out and we've only just started thinking about it. We haven't even put the house on the market yet and there's so much your dad has to sort out with his position at the hospital.'

'OK. So, how about I go and live with Marie in the meantime? Get used to my new school.'

Mum took off her reading glasses and peered at me. 'TJ. What's going on? Sit down for a moment. Has something happened?'

I hovered behind the chair by the fireplace. 'No. Why do you always have to think something's happened? I've simply changed my mind and now I think that Devon is a great idea. The sooner the better. So. Shall I call Marie?'

'No. You won't call Marie. She's got enough on her plate at the moment, what with starting her new job and wedding plans. Something's going on. What is it, TJ?'

'*Nothing*. Honestly,' I replied as I headed out of the sitting room. 'I'd tell you if there was.'

Mum looked like she believed every word of it. Not. But what would I say to her? I've got a crush on one of my best friends' boyfriend and I'm going slowly mental. What would she say? What could anyone say, except get over it, saddo.

Must rethink the plan, I thought, as I lay on my bed ten minutes later and stared at the ceiling as if I was going to find the answer magically written there. Must rethink the plan. My mind had gone into overdrive. What was I going to do? I couldn't face school if they all knew. What if Izzie had told Lucy what I'd told her. And she'd told Nesta. And Nesta had told Steve and Luke. And . . . oh God oh God oh God . . .

A moment later, I heard the phone ring. Oh no, I thought as I put a pillow over my head. It's probably one of the girls and I'm to be hauled in front of the judge and jury. It wasn't me guv, honest, I'm innocent.

'TJ,' called Mum. 'Phone for you. It's Luke.'

Luke? What on earth does he want? I wondered as I reached for the extension. Oh please, God, Jesus, Buddha, Krishna, in fact anybody who's up there and might be listening, please don't let anyone have told Luke that I fancy him.

'Hey, Watts,' he said. 'What you doing?'

'Not much,' I said. Going totally bonkers would be the correct answer, but I wasn't going to tell him that.

'How about we go and check out Keats House in South Hampstead?' he asked. 'It's open this afternoon.'

He sounded cool enough. Maybe it was OK and no one had said anything. 'I thought you were doing something with Nesta,' I said.

'Yeah, I was, then Lucy was in a panic about the project and asked Nesta if she could give her a hand. So, she went off with her. So how about Keats House?'

'Sorry. Can't.'

'I thought you said you weren't doing much.'

'Er . . . got homework, you know . . .'

The tone of Luke's voice suddenly changed from cheery to more serious. 'Please TJ. I . . . I . . . look, I think I . . . you were right the other day, we *do* need to talk. Meet me in half an hour?'

Need to talk? Oh hell. Someone *has* said something.

'What about?'

'Not on the phone. Please come.'

He sounded so serious that my curiosity got the better of me and I agreed to go. As I quickly got ready and headed out, my mind was spinning. Needed to talk? What about? The project? Somehow I doubted it. Maybe Sian again? What?

As I made my way down the front path, I noticed that Mum was watching me through the window.

'Bye, back later,' I mouthed and gave her a wave. Her

expression looked concerned. I hoped that she wasn't going to do an inquisition later. There was nothing I could tell any of them. I didn't know what was going on myself.

Luke was waiting for me outside the bookshop in South End Green. He looked up and smiled when he saw me and my heart missed a beat.

'Hey,' he said. 'Thanks for coming. Grab a hot chocolate before we go?'

'Sure,' I said. 'Yes. Chocolate. Good.'

Luke led us towards the café where he took a quick look inside. 'Bit crowded in there. Shall we sit outside? More private?'

I nodded. *Private?* My earlier instinct that he didn't just want to talk about the project had been right. Eek. It was freezing outside but, if he wanted privacy, then I wasn't going to argue and, with a bit of luck, the cold weather might stop me blushing every time he looked at me. As he went inside to get drinks, my brain went into overdrive again. What on earth would he need to talk to me about that he didn't want anyone to overhear?

He came back a few minutes later and we sat in silence. I sensed that, whatever it was he wanted to say, he wasn't finding it easy and tried to give him a reassuring smile. I could listen. I could be like Izzie. Maybe I should tell him about Buddhism and the nostril-breathing thingee. Then again, maybe not. Izzie can get away with New Age self-help advice. Not me. He'd think I was mad. The waitress brought us two big mugs of hot chocolate and we sat and drank them for a while, once again in silence. Funny thing silence, I thought. It can be comfortable, uncomfortable, peaceful, tense, long and drawn out, concentrated, dreamy, amicable. This one felt awkward.

In the end, I couldn't stand it any longer. 'So what did you want to talk about?'

Luke looked at the pavement, then into the café, then over the road at the trees. 'Nesta,' he said after a few moments.

'Nesta?'

Luke nodded. 'Nesta.'

So far, it's a riveting conversation, I thought. He says a name, I repeat it back.

'Has she said something?' I asked as paranoia took grip and I tried to mentally prepare myself for Izzie having spilled the beans.

Luke looked confused. 'Said something? Like what?'

'I don't know. Um. Let's skip back a few moments. So. Nesta?'

'Yes, Nesta. I need to talk about what to do next.'

Oh *no*, I thought. He's going to ask me for advice about Nesta. I should have known. I'm her mate, he probably wants some inside information. Lucy once told me that it happened all the time with boys and Nesta. They were always approaching Lucy to ask how to get off with her or get a date or something. But then Luke was already dating her, so what could he want from me?

'OK,' I said. 'What to do next. In what sense?'

Luke sighed and looked back at the pavement. 'It's not working out.'

Not working out? *Noooooooo*. That's not part of the script. Not the one in my head anyway.

'I mean, she's really great,' Luke continued, 'it's just . . . I'm not sure I want to be as involved as she does. It all happened pretty fast and . . . oh, I don't know . . .'

I don't know either, I thought. Why tell me? What does he want from me? How to tell her? How to break the bad news?

'I . . . er . . . does she have any idea?' I asked.

Luke finally looked at me and as always my stomach did a somersault. 'No. No idea, I think. And I don't want to hurt her. I like her. She's great.' He smiled. 'High maintenance, but great. With you, it's much easier . . .'

'What do you mean? High maintenance?'

'Oh, you know Nesta. She's a star and stars need to be the centre of attention all the time. And she wants me full-time and I'm not sure that I want the same thing, at least not with her anyway. I know most blokes would think I was mad. She's stunning but, in the end, well, there's got to be something else, hasn't there? Chemistry.'

'But I thought you did have . . . chemistry,' I said, thinking about the Hollywood snog they'd done earlier in the queue at the café and everything Nesta had said about them being in love.

'So did I. But then I . . . It's like at school. There's chemistry and then there's advanced chemistry, if you know what I mean.' At this point he gave me a searching look. 'I can talk to you. It's easier with you, well in one way it is, in another, it's more complicated. Steve. Nesta. I don't want to hurt anyone, but . . .' He reached over and took my hand and stroked the back of it gently with his thumb. I pulled it back.

'Don't.'

Luke looked hurt. 'Why not?'

'Because . . . I . . .' I wasn't exactly clear what he was saying about Nesta. Or me. It's hard breaking up with someone and he might just need a hand to hold, I quickly told myself. Even so, I couldn't handle the effect it was having on me. I couldn't sit there holding hands, comforting him because things weren't working out with Nesta. Even if he was going to finish with her. It felt disloyal.

'Because you what?' Luke asked and reached for my hand again.

It was too much for me and I pulled my hand back once more. 'Because I can't handle it,' I blurted. 'You might only be holding my hand but . . . to me . . . I can't help but . . . I . . .'

Luke put both of his hands over mine and held on to them so that I couldn't pull away. 'I think you know it's not just me holding your hand.'

'But you hold *everyone's* hand. I've seen you, arm round this person, having a massage from that . . .'

'Oh, you mean Sian? I told you, there's nothing there. Not like with us. I think you know that what we have is on another level.'

Don't give anything away, said Hannah's voice at the back of my head. I was longing to ask him what he meant, on another level? Did he mean a special friendship? Platonic? What kind of level? Chill, I told myself. Don't make a fool of yourself. He wants advice as to how to finish with Nesta and thinks that he can talk to me. One of the lads, that's me. Scott next door used to tell me that he liked me for that reason, because I was non-threatening. One of the boys. Not fanciable, that's what he meant. That's a level of sorts. Luke wants advice and I'm easy to talk to. That's all. Don't read anything into it, I told myself. He's clearly upset about having to finish with Nesta and that's why he's holding my hand. I mustn't *mustn't* give anything away about the madness in my own mind. It's the last thing he needs on top of everything else at this moment in time.

I put my 'one of the boys' hat on. 'Luke, I think you ought to be talking to Nesta about this, not me. I'm sorry, but she's one of my best friends and I feel disloyal. I can't tell you what to do or say and I can't be a go-between. I know it's hard, but if it's not working out then you have to tell her. Let her know before anyone else. It's only fair on her.'

Luke let go of my hand, drained his cup, nodded then looked at me sadly. 'Yes, of course. I understand,' he said. 'Of course.'

He stood up and gave himself a shake as if shaking off his mood. 'OK, Watts,' he said in a more cheerful voice. 'Let's go check out Keats' place. Apparently he was in love with some woman who lived there called Fanny Brawne.' He laughed. 'All these people pining for people they can't have. Round and round we go. Tough old life, isn't it?'

And off he went in the direction of Keats Grove. Phew, I thought as I followed him. I think that was OK. I think that was the right thing to do, to say. But poor Nesta. She's not going to be happy about this, not one bit. I'll have to do everything I can to help and see her through it.

As we walked around Keats House, Luke reverted to his usual self, talking about the project, and it was easy to respond to him on that level. I told him what I'd read about the poets from Keats' era and he seemed impressed. He didn't mention Nesta again. My mind, however, couldn't let go so easily and kept replaying and replaying the things he'd said, the way he'd looked at me, how it had felt when he stroked my hand. What had he meant? People pining for people they can't have? Keats? Sian? Nesta? Or *me*? Could he have meant me? And what did he mean by saying that what we had was on another level? Good-friends level? Bonded-over-our-shared-interest-in-history level? We-can-talk-to-each-other-easily level? Or what? Don't go there, I told myself. Don't go into, 'Or what?' If by any miraculous chance Luke did feel the same way about me as I felt about him, then this time was even worse than before. No one must ever know. To fancy Luke, when he was going out with Nesta was one thing, but to act on it even in the slightest way when he was about to break up with her

269

would be even worse. She's going to hurt enough without one of her best friends doing the dirty on her. No, I thought, as Luke bent over a display to read an ancient book then beckoned me over to read what it said, it can never happen. Never. Never. Never.

Quote From a Letter John Keats wrote to Fanny Brawne:

'I love you too much to venture into Hampstead. I feel it is not paying a visit but venturing into a fire.'

Chapter 12

Unrequited Twins

I was dreading the next project meeting on Wednesday and, in the meantime, watched Nesta closely for clues that Luke might have said something to her. Clearly not by the way she behaved and talked, as though everything was normal. Lucy on the other hand seemed concerned about my relationship with Steve.

'He really missed you when you dashed off on Sunday,' she said at break on Monday.

'Yeah, sorry, I wasn't feeling too good,' I blustered. 'Got a bit of a bug.'

'I thought you didn't seem your usual self, didn't I, Izzie? Remember I said to you.'

Izzie raised an eyebrow but didn't say anything.

'Are you OK now? Are you cooling off towards Steve?' asked Lucy. 'He says you haven't been around much lately.'

I shook my head. 'Been busy. There's so much to do on the project and so little time.'

Unseen by Lucy, Izzie raised her other eyebrow. Was this a

new type of meditation? Eyebrows now instead of nostrils or was she trying to say something? You never knew with Izzie.

Lucy nodded. 'Yeah, I know what you mean. It has been full on. But you will tell Steve if you're going off him, won't you? I'd hate to see him hurt and I want to be prepared for any reactions.'

'Yeah. Course. But my feelings for him haven't changed. Honest,' I said. It was true. They hadn't changed. I still really liked Steve, always would, but I couldn't deny that what I felt for Luke was on another level. Oh hell. There's that expression again. Did Luke mean what I mean by another level? As in fancy-like-mad, never-felt-this-way-before-in-my-life type level? Oh shut up, shut up, shut up, I told myself as we went into maths.

By the time Wednesday came round, I was feeling marginally saner. Everything was OK with the girls, clearly nobody had said anything and I had it clear in my mind that if I could just get through the project and see Nesta through the break up with Luke then I wouldn't have to see him again. It would all blow over. And then we'd move to Devon where I'd definitely never see him again.

I geared myself up to seeing Luke at the meeting and being really cool but, when I arrived in the prefab, Sian was the only one there, bent over some notes at one of the tables.

'Hey,' I said as I walked in. 'Others not here yet?'

Sian shook her head. 'Not coming,' she said. 'Luke wants to go over some things with Olivia. I guess we're not wanted.'

I felt a mixture of relief and disappointment. 'Oh, OK,' I said and put my rucksack down next to hers on the table.

Sian looked agitated. 'Do you think he fancies Olivia?'

'*Olivia?* Er, I don't think so. They've been mates a long time. She told me. He's a friend of her brother.'

Sian sighed, then shifted some papers around. After a few moments, she looked up at me. 'TJ. Can I talk to you?'

'Sure.'

'Promise you won't tell anyone?'

Oh no, I thought. She's going to tell me about her crush on Luke. I shook my head. 'No, I won't tell anyone.'

'It's about Luke,' she started. No surprise there, I thought as I sat at the desk and waited to hear all about her unrequited love. 'He . . . well, we . . .'

'You like him, don't you?' I asked. I thought I'd make it easy for her. We were in the same situation after all. She was clearly mixed-up, wondering if Luke was coming on to every girl he spent time with. She was worried about Olivia. I was worried about her.

She nodded. 'I don't expect you to really be able to understand . . .' she continued.

Hah! I thought. Little do you know but you couldn't have picked anybody more perfect to understand. Emotionally we were twins. Both experiencing unrequited love. I decided that I'd hear her out and give her the same advice that Hannah had given me. Luke was a babe. Loads of people had crushes on him, but she had to try and get over it. Stay cool. Move on.

'See, it's really difficult . . .' Sian continued.

'Yes . . .'

'I know Nesta's a mate of yours, so you mustn't tell her that I know, but he's going to finish with her. It's not working out with them.'

'Really?' I was surprised that he'd told her. Strange, I thought. But then maybe I was so unhelpful on Sunday that he felt he had to go somewhere else for advice or a shoulder to cry on.

Sian nodded. 'Yes. I do feel bad about it but then, what's

happening with us is so strong that, well, he couldn't carry on with Nesta, it wouldn't be fair to her.'

D'oh, I thought. Am I missing something here? 'Er . . . what do you mean what's happening with you?'

'Me and Luke.'

Poor Sian, I thought. She really imagines that she has a chance but, after what he said to me about her, she's going to get badly let down.

'Sian,' I said. 'I know Luke is lovely, but I reckon he gets a lot of people fancying him. And he's so open and friendly with everyone, sometimes it's possible to get the wires crossed, if you know what I mean. Read too much into things. You have to take care of yourself. You don't want to get your hopes up, then get hurt when nothing happens.'

'Oh I'm sure I've not got my wires crossed . . .'

God, she has it bad, I thought. She really has been reading a lot into the time she's spent with him.

'Sian, Luke's a very touchy-feely kind of guy. It doesn't always mean anything and it has to be a two-way thing for it to work.'

'I know. And it is.'

'But how do you know that, when nothing's happened between you?'

'But it *has* happened. He came over on Monday night. Now I've no doubt that he feels the same.'

I felt a horrible lurch in the pit of my stomach. 'But how?'

Sian looked coy for a moment. 'He kissed me.'

That shut me up. He *kissed* her? But . . . but, I thought, he told me that she was a poor mixed-up kid. That he could *never* fancy her.

'Oh sorry TJ, you looked shocked. I know Nesta's your friend. Sorry. We didn't mean for anyone to get hurt. But he is

275

going to finish with her. He's just waiting for the right moment to tell her, then we can be together.'

I felt like my brain was going to explode. Could this have been what he wanted to talk to me about on Sunday? I asked myself. Not just finishing with Nesta, but starting to go with Sian . . . ? No, surely not. But then . . . maybe. Oh God. How could I have been such a *fool*? Talk about getting your wires crossed, misreading the signals. I get the prize. All ready to tell Sian what an idiot she was with her unreciprocated love and how it was all in her head, when all along it was me that had it in *my* head and I couldn't have been more wrong about everything. Oh God. I'd been so sure that there was something special between us. All those longing looks he gave me. Then again . . . maybe he's playing everyone along. Me, Sian, Nesta. All of us. No. He's not like that. It's all in my stupid head. He'd kissed Sian, hadn't he? But then . . . it can't be that special between them if she's worried about him spending time with Olivia. She can't be that sure of him. Maybe he's just notching girls up, seeing how many he can score. Olivia did warn me in the beginning. He likes to prove to himself that he can have anyone. No. No. He's a nice guy. Oh God I feel confused.

Email: **Inbox (1)**
From: hannahnutter@fastmail.com
To: babewithbrains@psnet.co.uk
Date: 8th December
Subject: Dishy dude

Hey dingbat features
What's happening over there? Hope all is OK with the Lukieminukie. Let me know.

Yours
Hanahlulu

Email: **Outbox (1)**
From: babewithbrains@psnet.co.uk
To: hannahnutter@fastmail.com
Date: 10th December
Subject: Re Dishy dude

Hi Hannah
This is the worst day of my whole whole life. I've never felt so totally down and confused. Turns out Luke isn't into Nesta. Or me. He's into this strange-looking girl called Sian. At least I think he is. She just told me, they've kissed already. I was all ready to tell her that she was misreading the signals and was on a lost cause when she confessed that they'd snogged. You can misread someone holding your hand but a snog's a snog. No misreading that. I feel a fool. Miserable. Stupid. Can't trust my own feelings, don't know if I can trust the signals I'm getting from Luke. Who can I trust?

Yours truly
Foolish in Finchley

Email: **Inbox (1)**
From: <u>hannahnutter@fastmail.com</u>
To: <u>babewithbrains@psnet.co.uk</u>
Date: 10th December
Subject: Re Dishy dude

ME! Idioto. You can trust me. Nothing is over until the fat lady sings or something like that. Listen. I've snogged people I don't fancy. Wrong place. Too much sun. Temporary loss of sanity. All sorts of reasons.

I think you ought to go and have it out with dishy dude. See what's really going on in his head regards you, this Sian girl and Nesta. You've got nothing to lose by the sound of it and, knowing you as I do, you aren't one to let your imagination get the better of you.

Keep me updated. Sounds like life over there is much more exciting than over here. Nothing's happening. Don't fancy anyone.

Tres boooring. I feel like a nun. Nun of this, nun of that, geddit?

Love
Sister Mary Conceptua Hannah

Chapter 13

Life Before Boys

Horrible. Life can't get more horrible, I thought after I'd got home. The hour spent with Sian had been excruciating with her going on and on about Luke, not realising that her every word was like rubbing salt in a wound.

'Supper's on the table,' called Mum from the kitchen.

'Not hungry,' I called back. 'I'll have something later.'

Much later, I thought. I felt sick, like I never wanted to eat again. I threw myself on my bed. I hate this feeling, I thought. I so want to be back to normal. Before Steve. Before Luke. Back when I was about eight and all I thought about boys was that they were noisy creatures who picked their noses, had smelly socks and were to be avoided at all costs. It's rotten fancying boys. It's rotten being a teenager. It's rotten being me.

I replied to an email from Hannah bringing her up to date on my latest nightmare, then I tried to do some homework, but my mind wouldn't concentrate. I attempted Izzie's meditation to calm myself, but peace of mind seemed a million miles away and I couldn't get the image of Luke kissing Sian out of my head. I needed something to relax that was easy to do. An aromatic bath, I thought, that's supposed to be effective. Last time I'd seen her, Izzie had given me a list of oils from her essential oil book that you could add to the water to combat stress. I went and looked at my lotions and potions and found the one with lavender in it that Nesta had given me for my birthday. Lavender's one of the oils on the list, so I went and ran a bath then poured in a few drops. It smelt delicious, but when I got in, I felt guilty lying there inhaling a lovely scent given to me by a friend who I knew I'd let down.

After my bath I checked my emails and luckily Hannah had replied quickly. Talk to Luke, she said. At first I thought, no way, I can't and emailed her back saying so. What's the point? I had my chance to talk to him on Sunday and I blew it. I had the conversation with him in my head instead, imagining what he'd say. Over and over again. Each time, I changed the script. Maybe I should talk to Nesta? Tell her about Sian. She deserves to know. No. I can't do that. That's Luke's responsibility and besides, I don't really know what the story is or what's going on with them at all.

This is mad, I thought after a while, why don't I just have it out with Luke? Hannah's right. I've got nothing to lose, not any more. My sanity went weeks ago. Talk to him. Find out for once and for all what's going on, with Sian, with Nesta, with me.

I went to the phone, picked it up then lost my nerve and put it down again.

After a few deep breaths, I picked it up again and dialled. My heart was thumping in my chest as it began to ring at his end.

'Hello,' said an Indian-sounding voice.

'Um, is Luke there?'

'I'm afraid you have the wrong number, my dear,' said the voice and the phone clicked off.

I checked the numbers, picked up the phone and dialled once more. I can do this, I can do this, I told myself as the phone began to ring at the other end. Just as I heard someone pick up, my bedroom door opened and Mum came in with some cheese on toast on a plate. I almost had a heart attack and quickly slammed down the phone.

'*Mum!*'

'Sorry, love, were you talking to someone?'

'*No.* I mean yes, I mean . . . finished.'

Mum put the plate on my desk, then sat on the end of my bed. 'Is everything all right, TJ?'

'Yeah. Course. Why?'

'Just you haven't seemed your usual self lately. Is something bothering you?'

'No. Fine, everything's fine. Been busy. School project. And course, thinking about Devon. But yes, everything's fine.'

Mum sighed and got up. 'Eat up your supper and I'll bring you a cup of tea,' she said as she went to the door where she paused. 'If you need to talk to me about anything, I'm always here.'

For a brief moment, I thought I would talk to her. She'd been a teenager once, many lifetimes ago. Maybe she went through something like this. Maybe she'd understand. I was just about to open my mouth when the phone rang causing me to jump again.

'Are you going to get that?' asked Mum.

I nodded and picked up the extension. It was Luke.

I put my hand over the receiver. 'For me,' I whispered to Mum.

Mum nodded and left me to it.

'Hey, Watts,' said Luke. 'Did you just ring me?'

'Er, no, that is yeah . . .'

'Thought so. The phone went but when I picked up there was no one there, so I rang one-four-seven-one and it gave me your number.'

'Oh yeah, just my m . . . I got disturbed.'

'So what can I do for you?'

I took a deep breath and decided to go for it. 'I just left Sian,' I said, then waited for him to tell me what had happened with them.

'So?' he said after a pause.

'So, she told me what happened between you.'

Luke laughed or rather snorted at the other end. 'I bet she did.'

'So you're not denying it.'

'Hey, Watts,' said Luke. 'I *told* you that she had a crush on me.'

'Yeah, but she says you feel the same way.'

'Yeah, right,' Luke snorted again.

'She said you kissed her.'

'Oh *did* she now?'

'Well did you or didn't you?'

'Would you care either way, Watts?'

'Me? No, course not. Just after what you were saying the other day, about Nesta . . .'

'Listen,' said Luke in a serious tone, 'Sian kissed *me*. There's a difference. No way was it a two-way thing if you get what I mean. She took me unaware, invited me round saying she wanted to go through the Highgate side of things on the project and me, like a total fool, fell for it. I told you, no way would I fancy Sian. She's just not my type. No way. It's all in her head.'

'She thinks you're going to go out with her after you've finished with Nesta.'

I could hear Luke sigh. 'Bugger,' he said. 'I'm going to have to tell her straight, aren't I?'

'Dunno,' I said. 'I guess.' My mind was reeling. I *wanted* to believe him. It did sound like he was telling the truth, but there was a niggling feeling at the back of my mind telling me that something wasn't right.

'I really didn't kiss her,' said Luke as if picking up on my need for more reassurance. 'I let her kiss me for like . . . a nanosecond. I didn't want to . . . you know, like . . . push her off. That would have been cruel. It can be hard knowing how to play it sometimes. How do you let someone down? I mean, she's a sweet kid and I didn't want to hurt her. You must know how it can be. Sometimes you do the kissing, sometimes you are kissed, sometimes it's totally mutual. But no way was it with Sian.'

I felt weird talking about different types of kisses with Luke. It brought too many images up in my mind. Which I *did* like. So there was nothing to the kiss with Sian. Once again, Hannah had been right and it was possible to get into a situation where you ended up snogging (or being snogged by) someone you didn't want to be with. So he didn't fancy her, but I still didn't know what he felt about *me*. I should ask him, I thought, but I didn't know how to begin. I needed time to think about how to phrase it, without dropping myself in it and looking a total prat. But I needed to know. I needed to know really badly if what I'd been feeling over the last few weeks had all been in my imagination or whether he felt the same way.

'Listen Luke . . .'

'Yeah?'

'Um . . . tomorrow, after school . . . er . . . could you, could we meet up?'

'You asking me on a date, Watts?'

'*No*. Course not. No date. Talk.' Then I wondered when my use of English had disintegrated to Tarzan speak – like me

Tarzan, you Jane. Me TJ. You Luke. Ugabuga. I am beyond help, I thought.

Luke laughed. 'Oh. No date? Talk,' he said. 'Why can't we talk now?'

'Um . . . not on the phone. I . . . I want to see you in person.'

'Hmmm. Sounds serious, Watts. OK. Yeah. I can do that. Be good. What time?' His voice sounded warm.

'About seven? Under the trees in Pond Square.'

'I'll be there,' he said.

Essential Oils to Aid Relaxation

Add six to eight drops to the bath water as it is running. Swish the oil around so that it doesn't all stay in one spot.

Camomile
Cedarwood
Clary sage
Lavender
Marjoram
Neroli
Patchouli
Petitgrain
Rose
Rosewood
Sandalwood
Ylang ylang

Chapter 14

Earth to Planet Watts

The following day at school I felt like I was floating on a cloud. A dark cloud full of thunder, rain and lightning maybe, but a cloud none the less and my state of mind didn't go unnoticed.

'Are you with us, Theresa Joanne?' asked Miss Watkins in PSHE.

'And what's so exciting out there, Miss Watts?' asked Mr Johnson in English, when he caught me gazing out of the window.

'Calling TJ Watts, TJ *Watts*,' said Mrs Elwes in art. 'Earth to planet Watts. Come back.'

I had so much to consider. Moving to Devon was still on the agenda and my life and all its complications here might soon all be behind me. I wasn't sure how I felt about that. It kept changing. And Steve. I'd hardly seen him since the project began and although we usually only met at the weekend, we did generally talk on the phone in the week. We'd both been busy and he had a lot on with his photography team, but I wondered if he'd minded that I hadn't been calling as often as usual. And then, there was Luke. Part of me felt anxious about the meeting with him tonight, and part of me felt a rush of excitement. In case any of the girls sussed my strange state of mind and started asking questions, I made my excuses at lunch-time and buried myself in research in the library. They were cool about it. Everyone involved in the project was under pressure as the presentation of our work so far was next week, so we had to get everything finished.

After school, I dashed home to get ready. I felt so nervous. I'd never felt like this when I was going to meet Steve. It was like I'd drunk about six cups of strong coffee and I was buzzing.

I decided to wear my combats, a T-shirt and my parka jacket as it would be cold outside. Then I combed my hair loose instead of wearing it like I usually did – scraped back in a plait. A quick slick of lip gloss, a squirt of perfume and I was ready.

About ten minutes before leaving, I heard the doorbell go then, a few moments later, Mum called up the stairs.

'TJ. Steve's here for you. And Dad and I are off to our concert now. See you later.'

Steve! Ohmigod! I thought as I heard his footsteps coming up the stairs. What am I going to say? A moment later, my bedroom door opened and in he walked.

'Hey, you look nice,' he said as he stooped to give me a kiss, but I had leaned in to give him a hug and turned slightly so that his kiss landed on my cheek. I turned my face back so that he could kiss me on the lips but, by then, he'd backed off.

'Oh. Thanks.'

'Going out?'

I nodded.

'Where?'

'Um, Highgate. Um, project stuff.'

'Want me to come?' asked Steve. 'Keep you company?'

I felt like a fly caught in a web. 'Um. Nah. It will be boring. You know, meeting schmeeting.'

Steve looked disappointed. 'Meeting Luke?'

I nodded again. Steve shrugged then reached into the bag he was carrying and pulled out a postcard and a photo. 'Thought you might like to see these.'

I bent over to look as Steve laid them out on my desk.

'The painting is called *Work* and it's by Ford Madox Brown,' he explained as I looked at the postcard of an old-fashioned painting showing some men with rolled-up sleeves digging. 'It's really famous.' Then he pointed to the photograph. 'And *here* is the place he painted.'

'Oh wow,' I said as I compared the two. 'It's on Greenhill, just off Hampstead High Street. It's where Mum always parks when we go shopping there.'

'I know. It's amazing, isn't it? I thought it would look good as part of your display.'

'It will. Thank you *so* much,' I said glancing at my watch.

'Sorry. Am I keeping you? It's just I was passing and I . . . well, when I made the connection, I couldn't wait to show you.' He reached into his rucksack again and got out more photos. 'Plus here's all the shots of houses where famous people lived.'

I took a quick glance at them and they looked fabulous. He'd clearly spent a lot of time going round photographing for me. I felt rotten. 'Steve, these are brilliant. Look, I'm so sorry I'm in such a hurry, but I've got to go. I'm supposed to be in Highgate at seven.'

Steve went to the door. 'No problem. I'll walk down with you.'

I felt like the Queen of Mean. I could see that he was

making a great effort to be cheerful, like he was cool about everything, but the atmosphere felt strained and unnatural. Mean, mean, mean, a voice in my head said. For a moment, I thought about calling Luke and cancelling. I didn't want to see Steve hurt, not for a moment, but Luke would have already left and I knew, that if I put our meeting off, it would only prolong the agony I was going through in my head.

When we got to the end of the road, I gave Steve an extra big hug. 'Speak to you later?' I asked. 'Maybe we can do something tomorrow.'

'Yeah, sure,' said Steve lightly. 'Yeah. See you around, TJ.'

And he walked off in the opposite direction. I could see by the way he hunched his shoulders up, that I'd upset him. Maybe Izzie has the right idea, I thought as he disappeared around a corner. Celibacy. Or maybe I should take a tip from Hannah. Become a nun. It would be a hell of a lot easier to opt out of the dating game altogether. It was painful no matter what side you were on.

I got to Pond Square at about ten past seven, but there was no sign of Luke. I checked my watch again and looked round. I waited until half past and still no sign. I didn't want to ring in case I sounded desperate but, by seven forty-five, I was freezing and my toes had turned to blocks of ice. I've been stood up, I thought. And it serves me right. I decided to give him another few minutes, then I called his number.

His mum answered.

'Er, is Luke there?' I asked.

'Yes,' she said. 'But he's asleep. Nodded off in front of the telly. Shall I wake him?'

Asleep? I thought, *asleep*!! 'Er no, don't wake him. I'll catch him later.'

'It's Sian, isn't it?' said Mrs De Biasi. 'I'll tell him you called.'

'No, not Sian. Er, no. Don't worry. It's not important. I'll catch him later.'

I clicked my phone off and sank on to one of the benches. I didn't want to talk to anyone while I was feeling this low. Izzie would probably say this was karma. She says that the law of karma is that what you sow, so shall you reap. In plain English, you get what you deserve. And I probably deserved this. I'd blown Steve out and now Luke had blown me out. But *asleep*! I couldn't believe it. And his mum knew Sian's name. She obviously called there a lot. Well, there's your answer TJ Watts, I thought. That's exactly how much this meeting mattered to Luke. So much that he fell asleep and forgot. I got up and wearily trudged down the road to the bus stop. God I hate feeling this way, I thought. Maybe I will be a nun or join those Hare Krishna people who renounce the world, shave their heads and hand people roses at airports. Anything, *anything* has to be easier than this.

Work was painted by the Pre-Raphaelite painter, Ford Madox Brown between 1852–1865 and depicts navvies digging sewers in Hampstead. It is currently hanging in the Manchester City Art Gallery in Manchester, England.

Chapter 15

Tempting
Trouble

When I got home the house was quiet as Mum and Dad were still at their concert at the Barbican. Mojo was curled up on the sofa in the sitting room and he looked up with a guilty expression when he heard me come in. He knew he wasn't supposed to sleep on the furniture as he had his own basket in the kitchen but, as soon as Mum and Dad went out, he always made himself comfortable on the sofa.

'Don't get up, Mojo,' I said as I sat next to him. He took a long look at me, then got up and licked my face. He let out a soft whine as if to say he understood, then curled up, leaning against my legs with his paw up over my knees. He's amazing when I'm feeling low. It's like he picks up on it, then likes to stay as close as possible to me as if trying to comfort me.

'Rough,' I said to him.

'Rff,' he agreed and sank his head on to my lap.

I switched on the TV and flicked channels for a while, but none of the programmes registered. My concentration was all over the place. After a while, I curled up with Mojo and closed my eyes and I must have nodded off because, the next thing I knew, I was awoken by the doorbell ringing. I checked my watch. Nine o'clock. Too early for Mum and Dad to be back, plus they never went out without their keys. I went to the window and peeked out from behind the curtain. My heart skipped a beat when I saw Luke standing there. Seeing a movement at the window, he glanced over as I darted back out of sight. The doorbell rang again. A long insistent ring. Then I heard his voice through the letterbox.

'TJ. *TJ.* I know you're in there.'

I tiptoed into the hall. The letterbox flicked open and I could see his eyes looking through.

'Go away,' I said.

'TJ. Let me in.'

'I don't want to talk to you.'

'Please TJ. Look, you've every right to be mad. I'm sorry I stood you up. I didn't mean to. I don't know what happened. I crashed out on the sofa and, the next thing I know, it was past eight. I tried ringing your mobile then, when you didn't answer, I came straight over. I'm *really* sorry. Let me in.'

By this time, Mojo had come to see what all the noise was about. He looked at me, then at the letterbox, then back at me as if to say, what kind of creature is so small they can look through a letterbox?

'*Ciao*, Mojo,' called Luke, causing Mojo to go over to the door and try and lick him through the letterbox. Then I heard him say, 'Ey*uck.*'

I had to laugh. Mojo's tail was wagging like mad, then he positioned himself on the mat inside so that he was eyeball to eyeball with Luke.

'Come on TJ, please,' said Luke. 'I'm down on my knees here.' Then he laughed. 'I really am too. And making eyeball contact with your dog, much as I like him, is *not* why I came over.'

'Five minutes,' I said firmly as I went to let him in. I felt genuinely mad with him. I'd had enough. More than enough, and now I just wanted my life and my sanity back. As always Luke was super-tuned in to how I was feeling.

'Mad with me, huh?' he said as he stood up with a big cheesy grin.

I wasn't going to give in easily. 'You could say that. I waited for ages. I was freezing.'

'I really am sorry. I meant to be there. Usually I'm Mr Reliable. I don't normally fall asleep early evening, but lately . . . dunno, I haven't been sleeping well . . . lot on my mind . . .'

'Tell me about it,' I said as I went back into the sitting room. Luke followed me in. 'TJ . . .'

'Your mum thought I was Sian. She knows there's someone called Sian all right, doesn't she?'

'Yeah, but I told you that's a one-way thing,' said Luke following me in. 'Totally in her head.'

I didn't ask him to sit down as I didn't want him staying, so we stood at opposing ends of the room, like boxers sizing each other up in the ring. 'I'm not so sure any more. I mean, how do I know if I can trust you? You play with people's feelings and I don't think you know how it affects them.'

'Hey, that's not fair. I never encouraged Sian.'

'You let her massage you, I'd say that's pretty encouraging.'

'Not in my house. Everyone's always giving everyone neck and back rubs. It means nothing.'

Oh, I thought, so did that mean that my giving him a neck rub meant nothing as well?

'So what about Nesta then? You've certainly encouraged her

and she has no idea that you plan to finish with her. If that's not playing with people's feelings, I don't know what is.'

'Yeah, but . . .'

'And you're a flirt, Luke De Biasi. I've seen you, holding girls' hands, playing the confidante to Sian. I think you probably like the attention.'

'Look TJ, I've told you before. There's nothing going on with Sian. *Nothing.*'

'Yeah, like you said it wasn't working out with Nesta, but I don't see you getting round to letting her in on it.'

Luke sighed. 'Ah, well that's difficult,' he said. 'I hate letting people down. And anyway, you're still seeing Steve, so you're one to talk.'

'Steve! *Steve?* What's he got to do with it? Why wouldn't I be seeing Steve?'

Luke looked directly into my eyes. 'Because of us!'

'Us! *Us?* What's that supposed to mean? What us?'

'You know that what's happening with *us* is on another level.'

That did it. I don't often lose my temper, but this time I saw red. 'Stop saying that! And what does it mean exactly? On another level? What level? It could mean *anything.* What am I supposed to *think*? You use expressions like that and it can be interpreted any *way*, it's no wonder Sian thinks you're into her. You probably told her that what you have with her is on another level as well.'

Luke sank down on to the sofa. 'Just going down to another level.' He grinned up at me.

I didn't laugh at his joke.

'I've never given Sian anything to go on,' he said. 'Honestly.'

'OK. Honestly then. What about Nesta? How do you feel about her? Really?'

'It's over. I know, I know I haven't told her yet, but how can I? You of all people know how difficult it's going to be.'

'There you go again. Why would *I* of all people know?'

Luke reached out, caught my hand and pulled me towards him. 'Come on, TJ, you can't deny it.'

'Deny *WHAT*?' I asked as I pulled away from him.

'Please TJ, sit down,' said Luke patting the cushion on the sofa next to him. I didn't want to look at him as, although I was still mad, I couldn't deny the chemistry in the room. The air was so thick, you could have cut it with a knife. Instead of sitting next to him, I sat on the floor to the right of his feet, with my back to him, and folded my arms.

He moved over so that he was positioned behind me, with me sitting between his knees, then he put his hands on my shoulders.

'Come on, Watts,' he said. 'You know that there's something pretty special going on between us. I know you do.'

He started to gently massage my shoulders and the back of my neck. I felt myself freeze, but when he began to play with my hair it sent warm shivers up my spine. It felt amazing and was starting to feel dangerous. I tried to shrug him off.

'Come on, relax,' he said softly. 'Let me give you a neck rub. You need to chill out a bit. Relax.'

What he'd just said to me about us having something special had caused my brain to fuse. I didn't know what else to say so I just sat there, letting him gently stroke my neck and my hair. It felt like my mind had gone totally blank, and everything had been turned off or tuned out except the sensation of him close behind me and the warmth of his hands on my shoulders.

After a moment, he got up and went over to the CD player. 'Got any good CDs?'

'Erghh. Not sure,' I said. 'Mine are all upstairs, but I think there are a few of my brother's somewhere about. He left them here when he took off on his travels. They're there on the right of the player.' Yes, I thought. Music. Good idea. Anything to distract me from the feelings that are running riot through me.

He picked out a CD, put it in the player and switched it on.

'I think you'll like this one,' he said as he sat behind me once again and resumed his gentle kneading on my shoulders.

As the CD began to play, I could hardly believe what I was hearing. I'd never heard the band before, but it was the perfect choice. Strings filled the room, then some piano, then the lyrics. All about dancing into the fire, eager to catch the flame. Tempting trouble, ready to play the game.

As the music filled the room, Luke's hands on my shoulders suddenly stopped massaging and he turned me round to face him and put one hand under my chin, so that I had to look up at him. As our eyes met, I felt myself start to lose resistance, like I'd turned to rubber. He leaned towards me, slipped his hands under my arms and pulled me up next to him. Then he leaned in again and it was like everything went into slow motion, his face gradually coming closer to mine. I felt like I was melting into him, then his lips touched mine. I so wanted to respond, but suddenly I saw Nesta's face in my mind's eye and Steve.

'No . . . *No*, Luke, we mustn't. There's Nesta and Steve to think about. Even if we do break up with them, this can only cause bad feelings.'

Luke let out a soft moan. 'TJ, you're *killing* me. *This* is killing me.'

He looked so sad sitting there. I hated to see him like that and realised that I hadn't thought about his feelings. He looked at me pleadingly and took my hand again. 'TJ, please. I can't go on like this.'

'But . . . Nesta . . .'

'I'll tell Nesta. I promise. I will. Come here . . .'

This time, as he pulled me towards him and put his arms round my waist, I reached up, put my arms around his neck and his face moved towards mine again and, at last, we were kissing properly. A long, deep, soft kiss. Nothing else existed. It was like everything went black and all I felt was the most sublime sensation of his lips on mine and his body close. Ecstasy.

After a few moments, he pulled away and smiled. 'I've wanted to do that for a very long time. You OK with this?'

I was more than OK. I felt like I was in heaven. All I wanted was more and I leaned forward and kissed him again.

We must have spent at least the next two hours with our arms around each other, cuddling and kissing until my jaw was sore. I'd never felt anything like it before, kissing Steve had never been like this. I wanted it to go on for ever and ever.

We were cuddled up with my head on his chest, holding hands listening to another CD, when we heard my parents' car pull up into the front drive. I leaped up in a panic. I'd completely lost track of time. I glanced at my watch. It was almost twelve. We'd been there for three hours.

'Oh God, they'll *kill* me.'

'Back door?' said Luke springing up and heading for the hall.

'Kitchen,' I said as we both legged it to the back of the house.

As I let him out into the garden, he gave me a quick kiss and both of us got the giggles then, as we heard the key in the front door, he sprinted across the garden. 'See you, Watts.'

'TJ, TJ? Are you there?' asked Mum coming straight through into the kitchen. 'What are you doing up?'

'Um. Just giving Mojo some fresh air in the garden,' I replied as I came in and began locking the back door.

Mojo chose this moment to come through from the sitting room so blowing my story. Mum looked at me, then at the dog.

'But . . .'

'Oh *there* you are,' I said, then giggled. I felt drunk. 'Bad Mojo. Come on, boy.' I began to unbolt the door.

Mojo wagged his tail and made for the garden.

'For heaven's sake, close that door,' said Dad coming through to join us. 'It's letting all the cold air in.' Then he looked at me. 'What's the matter with your face?'

'Face?' I said, putting my hand up to my chin. It did feel a bit raw. Oh God, I thought, I've got a snog rash. 'What do you mean?'

'Your face,' said Dad taking a closer look. 'It's all red round your jawline.'

'Oh, that!' I said, grinning like an idiot. 'Oh yeah. Er, I did a facial before. Got a bit carried away with the exfoliator and er, clearing any blackheads.'

Dad pulled a face and Mum was looking at me quizzically, as I made for the hall and stairs. I don't think she believed a word of it. Better get out of here quick, I thought, before they suss out what I've really been doing. Lying on the sofa snogging a boy who wasn't even my boyfriend all evening probably wouldn't go down too well in their book.

Later, when I lay in my bed in a mild stupor, still smiling all over my face, I thought, this can't be wrong. This is the real thing. It really is. And I, TJ Watts, for the first time in my life, am totally and utterly in love.

Email: **Outbox (1)**
From: babewithbrains@psnet.co.uk
To: hannahnutter@fastmail.com
Date: 12th December
Subject: True Love

Dear Hannah
It's one o'clock in the morning here and I can't sleep. I had
to tell you as I have to tell someone. I am in love. Really
really in love. It's official. Luke came over this evening and I
had the best night of my entire life. I think he is my
soulmate. And what is even better, he feels the same way. He
wasn't into Sian after all. It is awesome. I can't sleep thinking
about him. I am also going to email Steve as I think it's only
fair to him that I tell him as soon as possible and I don't want
him to hear from anyone else. Plus he is a nice guy. I will
follow it up in person as I know it's mean to dump someone
by email but I can't run the risk of someone else telling him
first and I'd hate that to happen.

Lots of love
TJ

Email: **Outbox (1)**
From: babewithbrains@psnet.co.uk
To: jamesblonde@psnet.co.uk
Date: 12th December
Subject: Us

Dear Steve
I'm writing to tell you that I can't go out with you any

more. I'm really sorry and I hope you won't be too upset. It's not you, I think you're fantastic. It's me. But I'm not going to insult you by explaining or trying to make excuses. It's never easy ending something and I'm keeping this short as it's about the hundredth version I've written and I couldn't find the right words in any of them.

I hope you will always be my friend as you genuinely do mean a lot to me and I really enjoyed going out with you and I'm sorry to do this by email, but will explain why I had to do it this way later.

Your friend
TJ

Chapter 16

Snog Rash

'God, what happened?' asked Izzie the next day at school as she stared at the rash on my face. 'Did something bite you?'

'Sort of, er, but not bite,' I replied sheepishly. I'd tried everything I could find in the bathroom when I'd got up. Mum's soothing creams, Germaline. Aloe vera gel. But my face was still inflamed and the creams only irritated it more.

Izzie looked puzzled.

'Snog rash,' I said.

'Oh! Steve not been shaving? I hate it when boys have that scratchy stubble. It can really hurt. I'll see if there's a balm or something in my essential oil book for you.'

I shook my head. 'It wasn't Steve.'

'So who . . . ? Ohmigod. Was it who I think it . . . ?'

I nodded. 'We couldn't help it, Izzie. We tried not to, but . . . it was too strong. He's going to tell Nesta. And I've already told Steve. Do you think I should tell Nesta?'

Izzie shook her head vehemently. 'No way. That's Luke's responsibility. Are you *sure* about this?'

'Hundred percent. I've never felt like this before. It is totally *totally* amazing. Everything was . . . just perfect. I think Luke's my soulmate.'

Izzie let out a sigh. 'Wow! Carumba! I thought you were the one who didn't believe in soulmates.'

'I know, but that was before Luke. It's like everything you and Lucy said . . . and more.'

'Double wow. What can I say?'

'Do you hate me?'

'No. Course not. If he's your soulmate, you can't argue with destiny, but hell, poor you, and poor Nesta. It's not going to be easy. I'd lie low if I were you in case Luke's told Nesta already. Stay out of her way until she's calmed down.'

Not going to be easy. That's an understatement, I thought as Izzie went off to the cloakrooms to hang up her coat.

Lucy wasn't as friendly when she arrived in the school hall five minutes later and confronted me straight away. 'Steve told me that you dumped him. On email too. That's a bit cold, isn't it? I'd have thought you could have at least told him to his face.'

I looked at the floor. She was right. I knew it had been a lousy way to dump someone, but then I wasn't thinking straight last night and it seemed the right thing to do at the time. In the light of the day, I wished I'd waited – like who was I thinking was going to tell Steve about Luke and me in the middle of the night? I guess love can make you go a bit doolally, I thought. I'd felt so high and so good last night that I thought everything would just work out, everyone would understand. It's true love and to be forgiven anything. When I woke up this morning, I cursed myself for having been so impetuous. If we lived in the old days of letters, I could have ripped it up but, with email, one press of the button and it's gone forever.

'I'm sorry Lucy. I know it wasn't one of my best ideas but I . . . I wanted him to know as soon as possible, in case he heard from . . . from anyone else.'

'Why? Why as soon as possible? Have you met someone else?'

I nodded. 'I am sorry, Lucy. I didn't want to hurt him more than necessary. Is he OK? How is he?'

'How do you think? He really liked you.'

'I know. I really liked him too. I still do. And that's why I thought it best he was told as soon as possible. It wasn't fair not to. The . . . er, the chemistry wasn't there any more and I didn't want to lie to him. Surely you agree with that?'

Lucy didn't look convinced. 'Whatever, but there are ways of letting someone down. So who's the new boy? You've been keeping him pretty quiet.'

'Oh . . . just someone . . .'

'Must be pretty special for you to end it with Steve by email.'

'He is. *Very* special, just . . . he was . . . is involved with someone as well and we don't want to go public until he's finished with his girlfriend as well.'

Lucy looked miffed. 'Fine. Whatever. Don't tell me then.'

'Lucy I *can't* tell you yet . . .'

'I *hate* secrets and I thought that we were mates . . .'

Just at that moment Nesta bounded up behind us. I felt myself cower inwardly. I didn't know if Luke had told her and, if he had, whether he'd have mentioned me or not.

'Hey,' she smiled, then noticed my face. 'Heyhey, TJ Watts. Do I see what I think I see? Uno snog rash. Hhmm. Looks like someone had fun. I didn't think Steve had it in him.'

'Snog rash?' said Lucy studying my face carefully. 'Oh yeah. Wow. You don't waste time do you?'

'What are you on about?' said Nesta. 'She's been going with Steve for ages.'

'Not Steve,' said Lucy. 'TJ's finished with Steve and got herself a new boyfriend. And she won't tell me who.'

Nesta raised an eyebrow. 'Oh really? Won't tell, huh?' she said, then leaned over and pulled my arm behind my back, like she was a policeman and she was arresting me. 'Ve have vays of making you talk, Miss Vatts. Come on, Lucy, we'll get it out of her someway or other.'

I laughed and tried to play along with her like everything was normal. Clearly Luke hadn't told her yet, but then it was only the morning after and he had probably decided that the right way to do it was face to face instead of email. As we were scuffling about in the corridor, Izzie came out of the cloakrooms and flew towards us.

'Hey, leave her alone,' she said, pulling us apart. 'She didn't mean to hurt anyone.'

Nesta let go of me and we all stared at Izzie for a moment. She quickly realised her mistake. From her angle, when she came out of the cloakrooms, it must have looked as if Lucy and Nesta were pushing me about.

'Izzie, they were only messing about . . .' I explained.

'Yeah. She has a new lover boy and won't say who,' said Lucy.

'And why on earth would we push TJ about?' asked Nesta. 'Are you on *drugs*?'

I shook my head at Izzie to try and tell her not to say. Unluckily, Lucy saw me.

'You know who, don't you Izzie?' asked Lucy.

Nesta pouted. 'So how come you told Izzie but not us?' she

asked. 'I thought we were all mates. Why can't we know as well?'

Izzie looked lost for words as Lucy and Nesta looked at her accusingly. Then Lucy looked at me and her eyes narrowed. I could see the penny drop for her.

'Oh no,' she gasped. 'Oh no. TJ?'

'What? *What?*' demanded Nesta. 'What *is* going on with you guys this morning?'

Lucy's expression grew cold. 'Nothing. Come on, Nesta, let's go.'

She linked her arm through Nesta's and pulled her away towards the assembly hall.

Izzie looked at me and grimaced. 'Hells bells and poo,' she said. 'The shitola has just hit the fan.'

I wanted to turn around and run. The warm glow that had been surrounding me since last night suddenly evaporated and was replaced by a cold feeling of doom. Why, oh why, does love have to be so complicated? I asked myself as Izzie pushed me gently in the direction of assembly.

Lucy hauled Nesta off as soon as assembly had finished and I saw them heading for the cloakrooms just as the bell for lessons went. I wanted to run out of the school gates and go home and hide, but how would I explain that to anyone? I can't exactly see my mum giving me a note to excuse me from lessons.

'Just tell her the truth,' said Izzie. 'She can only kill you.'

I nodded. 'I will. Should I catch up with them?'

Izzie nodded back. 'Best get it over with. Want me to come with you?'

'Please.'

As we made our way to the cloakrooms, I remembered a

scene from a film I'd seen with a condemned man walking to the electric chair. *Dead Man Walking*, it was called. 'Dead girl walking,' I said to Izzie as she put her arm through mine.

'Just keep breathing,' said Izzie, who looked as worried as I felt.

Nesta and Lucy had their heads close together in the corner of the cloakrooms and they looked up as I walked in. Luckily we were the only ones in there, which was a relief as I'd have hated anyone else from our class to have been there, earwigging it all then passing it round the school.

Lucy looked at me defiantly. 'I had to tell her, TJ. It's only fair. You said Steve deserved to know as soon as possible, so Nesta does too and . . .' at this point she gave Izzie a dirty look, 'and no one else round here was brave enough.'

I glanced at Izzie, who looked shocked, then at Nesta. 'I really am sorry . . .'

Nesta shrugged. 'Yeah. So am I. But no worries, TJ, I know it must be difficult for you and I'm sorry it's had to come out this way . . .'

I didn't understand and looked at the girls quizzically.

'She already knew,' explained Lucy.

'You *already* knew?' I asked. So Luke had told her? 'When? When did he tell you?'

'Oh ages ago, when you guys first started working on the project together . . .'

Whadtt? I thought. He never mentioned it to me. Last night he'd said he hadn't told her yet.

Nesta put her hand on my arm and looked at me sympathetically. 'It must be really tough for you . . .'

Tough for *me*? I thought. What the hell was going on? 'What exactly did Luke tell you?'

'Oh you know,' Nesta sighed. 'About you having a crush on

him. He told me all about it, as he didn't know how to deal with it. He said he didn't want to hurt your feelings as you were a mate of mine . . . And I didn't want to say anything to you as I didn't want to hurt your feelings either. I mean, it *is* kind of embarrassing, isn't it? I know you're into Steve, so fancying Luke? No way. I knew that you'd never make a play for him, in fact, I even wondered if he'd got the wrong end of the stick. You know, inflated male ego and all that.'

'I . . . I . . . So why did he say anything?'

'He said he wanted to let me know in *case* you got the wrong idea about him. He says it happens all the time, that girls misread the signals. He wanted to reassure me that your crush was all in your head. He told me that what he and I have is on another level and not to worry.'

I felt like someone had plunged a knife into me. 'But . . . but . . . I . . . Oh God. What a mess. I . . . So, you haven't spoken to him today then?'

'Today? No.'

'Oh God, I'm so sorry, Nesta . . .'

'No need to apologise. I'm glad it's all out in the open now and we can talk about it. And I totally understand. Luke is gorgeous, and as I said, loads of girls have crushes on him. I can't say I blame you . . .'

Lucy didn't look as forgiving and looked accusingly at my chin. 'But that doesn't explain . . .' She didn't finish her sentence and looked away, but not before Nesta had noticed where she'd been looking.

I saw confusion flicker in Nesta's eyes. Izzie looked horrified, not as horrified as I felt though. I felt mad with Luke. He'd given us both the same line. We were both on another level then? No. No. I knew it wasn't like that. Not after last night. It was special, a once in a lifetime thing.

Nesta sighed heavily. 'I'd forgotten . . . Steve didn't give you that snog rash did he?'

I didn't answer.

'I suppose he likes you because you're so clever,' said Nesta sadly. 'Beauty and brains, I always said it was a lethal combination.'

'But . . .' I started. Just at that moment, the door opened and Miss Watkins stuck her head round the door.

'Theresa Watts, Izzie Foster, Lucy Lovering, Nesta Williams. What are you doing in here? Didn't you hear the bell? Move yourselves. Now!'

As we filed out after her, my heart was thumping in my chest. I felt angry.

I need to talk to Luke, I thought, as soon as possible. Find out what he's been saying, and give him a piece of my mind.

I sat through Miss Watkins' class in agony. Lucy and Nesta were sitting behind and I looked round whenever I could to try and gauge what was going on in their heads. Lucy stared steadfastly in front of her and wouldn't let me catch her eye. Nesta looked upset and was doodling on her notebook. Izzie also kept looking round, then glancing over at me and rolling her eyes.

'Izzie Foster,' said Miss Watkins. 'What is so interesting at the back of the class today? Maybe you'd like to share it with the rest of us.'

'Er no, nothing, Miss,' stuttered Izzie. 'Sorry.'

'If you don't start paying proper attention, you'll stay behind and do detention. Understood?'

'Understood,' said Izzie and put her nose in her book.

I felt utterly miserable. Lucy and Nesta would probably never speak to me again and I'd managed to get Izzie in trouble, not only with Miss Watkins but also with Lucy. She'd made it very clear in the cloakrooms that she thought that Izzie should have said something to Nesta about Luke and me. My new best friends, I thought, and I was going to lose them. That is, if I hadn't lost them already.

At break, Nesta obviously had the same idea as I did. I watched as she dived out of the classroom, with Lucy in hot pursuit, then get her mobile out of her bag.

I waited until the classroom had emptied except for Izzie, who had hung back to stay with me. I quickly pulled out my mobile and dialled Luke's number. I had to warn him. Plus I had to find out what was really going on. I got his voice mail.

'Hell, voice mail,' I said. 'I think Nesta's got through first.'

'Try again,' urged Izzie. 'He might not be on break yet, so might have it switched off. Sometimes break-time is different in different schools.'

I sat there dialling. And dialling. And dialling again. Suddenly I heard the phone ring and Luke's voice at the other end.

'Luke,' I said.

'Hey, Watts,' he said cheerfully. 'Top night last night.'

'Yeah, right. I thought so too at the time.'

'Hey. What's the problem? Your voice sounds weird. What do you mean?'

'Have you said anything to Nesta yet about you breaking up with her?'

'Woah. Give me a break. It's only the morning after . . .'

'I think she knows . . .'

Luke's tone suddenly changed to serious. 'How?'

'Lucy guessed. It was bound to come out . . .'

I heard Luke sigh heavily at the other end. 'OK. Right. OK. Now calm down TJ.'

'Calm *down?!* She said she knew all about it. She said that you said I had a crush on you and you wanted to reassure her that it was all in my head. What's *that* all about?'

Luke was silent for a few moments. 'Oh that. Yeah. Listen, TJ. I was er . . . testing the water to see how she'd react. Look. Let me handle this my own way. I need time to think. Um. Yeah.'

'*Is* it all in my head?'

'You tell me, TJ.'

'Oh *please* don't start with all that again. What about last night?'

I could hear Luke sigh again. 'Don't start getting all heavy on me. It was a kiss. One kiss. No big deal.'

No big *deal?* I thought. How could he *say* that? A kiss that lasted almost three hours and now threatened to end my friendship with two of my best mates and had already ended my relationship with Steve. My mind was reeling and I was at a loss as to what to say next.'

'Look, got to go,' said Luke. 'Keep your chin up. I'll sort it.'

'No, *no* don't go,' I blustered. 'I need to know where I stand.'

Next to me, I heard Izzie take a sharp intake of breath and shake her head. I knew I'd broken the golden rule of, 'Thou shalt always be cool' and crossed into sounding desperate. I didn't care.

'Where you stand?' said Luke lightly. 'I don't know. Where are you?'

'In the classroom at school.'

'Well that's where you stand then,' he said, then laughed. 'Unless you're sitting that is.'

I didn't say anything. How could he be making jokes at a time like this? I thought.

'Hey, TJ,' said Luke. 'Lighten up. Don't be so heavy. I'll sort it and be in touch.'

And then he hung up. Izzie was looking at me with concern as I clicked my phone shut and burst into tears.

Cures for Snog Rash

Add two to three drops of rose, camomile, or both, to a bowl of warm water. Soak a face flannel in the water, then apply to the snog rash area for a few minutes.

Alternatively add a few drops of the same oils to your moisturiser and apply to the area.

Chapter 17

Fairweather Friends

The rest of the morning felt like eternity. I was dying to know if Nesta had spoken to Luke and what he'd said to her, but no way could I ask as she kept well out of my way and Lucy avoided Izzie and me, like we were the plague. Nesta looked as if she'd been crying, and it was all because of me. I felt so mean. And I felt sorry for Izzie, as she hadn't done anything.

'I am sooooo sorry,' I said in the lunch break, as Izzie and I sat by a radiator in the school hall. We both had sandwiches in front of us, but neither of us had any appetite. 'None of this is your fault and now it looks like Lucy's mad with you as well.'

'Well I'm mad with her now,' said Izzie. 'I mean, what is her problem? She's my oldest mate and she hasn't even *tried* to see things from my angle *or* yours. She just stomped off with Nesta and she hasn't given either of us a chance to explain anything. Some friendship, huh? It's like we're fairweather friends, pals if everything is hunky-dory. Friends are supposed to talk about things, weather the storms. Be friends, come what may.

Resolve problems. Not first sign of trouble and ooh, we're not talking to you. It's pathetic. And now I'm mad. And by the looks that Lucy's been giving us all morning, she is too.'

'I guess she's feeling protective of Steve and Nesta. I feel awful. Nesta looks really upset. She's been let down by two people, me and Luke.'

Izzie sighed. 'I know, it must be tough for her. But it wasn't as if you went out of your way to get Luke. He's the one that should be feeling sorry. From everything you've told me, you've tried to resist.'

'I did. I really did. I wish she'd let me explain. Anyway, it's all been an almighty waste of time. Looks like I've lost two of my best mates and finished with Steve and what for? One night with Luke and only a raw chin to show for it. Luke couldn't give a stuff about me. He was so weird on the phone, saying it was only a kiss and not to get heavy.'

'I'd like to show him heavy,' said Izzie. 'I'd like to knock some sense into him. And so should you, TJ. I mean, come on, the guy's been using the same line on you and Nesta and who knows how many others? He ought to take responsibility for his actions. And his words. But boys can be cowards sometimes and they *all* hate confrontation. It probably all came as a bit of a shock to him when you phoned. When they're under attack, some boys' first defence is to attack back. And who knows where he was when you called? You might not have got him on his own. If there were other boys around, he might have acted all cool because they were listening in . . . you know, keep up the macho, I'm-so-cool image. Pathetic.'

I glanced over at the other side of the hall where Lucy and Nesta were huddled together with their backs to everyone else.

'It's not Luke I care about right now,' I said. 'It's Nesta and Lucy. I really value their friendship.'

'And I thought that they valued ours,' said Izzie looking over at them. 'This is ridiculous.'

'You don't have to sit with me if you want to go over.'

'I know,' said Izzie. 'I *want* to sit with you. I'll speak to them when I'm good and ready.'

'I wish I could make it all right.'

'I think you should give Luke a piece of your mind. I think he's been getting away with murder. When's your next project meeting?'

'Tonight.'

'Are you going to go?'

'Dunno.'

During English in the afternoon, instead of working on the essay that Mr Johnson had set us, I wrote a letter.

Dear Sian, Olivia and Luke,

I'm really sorry, but I can't come to the meetings for the project any more. It's due to circumstances beyond my control as some problems have come up that I have to deal with. I hope that you'll understand and I really am sorry. I won't let you down though and will make sure that all the parts of the projects that I was doing get to you in time for the presentation. I've almost finished everything, it's just that I can't come to the meetings.

Best of luck with it all,
TJ.

As soon as school had finished, I raced out to the prefab and left the letter on the desk where one of them would see it.

Then I ran to the bus stop, praying that I wouldn't bump into one of them on their way in. I stood at the bus stop with my coat collar pulled up as far as it would go and my hair swept over my face in the hope that no one would see me.

Unfortunately, as I waited, a car pulled up and Olivia got out.

'Hey TJ,' she said. 'What you doing here? Not coming to the meeting?'

I shook my head. 'No, er . . . sorry, something's come up, but I have been working on the parts I said I would and I'll get them to you in time.'

'OK, cool,' she said. 'Is Sian in there already?'

'Um, don't think so. Why?'

Olivia shrugged. 'Oh, no reason specially. How's your mate Nesta?'

Ohmigod, does she know? I asked myself as panic flooded through me. But how could she?

'Um, Nesta's fine. Er . . . why do you ask?' I didn't want to say anything about her not speaking to me, as I intended to make things right with her if it was the last thing I did.

Olivia shifted uncomfortably. 'I . . . I don't know if I should tell you, but . . . see, I've met Nesta and I like her and well . . . I just wonder if one of us should warn her . . .'

My sense of panic was replaced by a sense of dread. 'Warn her about what?'

'About Luke. Remember I told you that he's a mate of my brother?'

'Yeah.'

'Is Nesta really keen on him?'

'I . . . yes, she is, was, is. Why?'

'I think Luke's ready to do his usual act. He's met someone new and Nesta's had her allotted time . . .'

'Really? Er . . . someone new? Who?'

'Not certain, but I have an idea. He told William that he's really fallen in love this time. Poor girl I say, as he only ever feels that way for about three months tops. Anyway, looks like Nesta might get dumped.'

I wondered if she knew anything about Luke and me, but was playing it cool. 'But why tell me?' I asked.

'Well I thought he might have talked to you. You know, about Sian . . .'

'Sian?'

'Yeah. Well it must be her, mustn't it? Who else? I know she's not his usual type, but she did let it slip the other night that something had happened between them. I must say I was a bit surprised, but Luke must see something in her. I wasn't sure whether to say anything, but I know that Nesta's a mate of yours and well . . . looks like she might get hurt. I've known Luke for a long time, remember I told you . . .'

I nodded. 'About his cut-off date. Looks like Nesta's not even going to make the three months.'

'Yeah. He knows he's got her, so needs to make a new conquest. I think he's still trying to prove that he is Mister Attractive and can make anyone fall in love with him.'

'So Nesta was just another conquest?'

'It's probably not that cold. I think he genuinely does fall for the girls he goes out with, but then he meets someone new and can't resist seeing if he can get them as well. That's when it all gets messy, as he isn't very good about coming clean that he's moved on and he leaves a trail of girls wondering where they stand with him. Bit of a coward when it comes to confrontation.'

And in the meantime, he doesn't realise the damage he does, I thought. The friendships he can destroy. Well, he's not going to destroy mine just to prove something to himself.

'I know it should be Luke that tells Nesta,' said Olivia, 'but, knowing him from the past, he'll avoid the situation so you can tell her if you want. Warn her so that she's ready for it. Anyway, better get going. See you next time.'

As she walked off, I felt more confused that ever. Was Luke still involved with Sian, or could this girl that Luke was smitten over be me? Or someone else entirely? Not that I wanted to have a relationship with him any more. No way. Losing my mates was too high a price to pay for a flaky relationship with a boy who didn't know what or who he wanted. I just wanted to find out what had been going on. As I stood there lost in my thoughts, I saw Luke appear around the corner and stride towards the school. My heart started beating in my chest. Maybe he'd come early in the hope of catching me on my own before Sian and Olivia arrived from their schools, I thought. Or maybe he wanted to speak to Sian? No, no, I told myself, he'd reassured me many times that there was nothing going on with Sian and I believed him. Maybe I shouldn't run away like a coward. Maybe I should talk to him and find out what was going on. Yes. He might be scared of confrontation, but I wasn't. I wanted to get my friends back, so I needed to be clear about what had been going on before I spoke to them again. I stepped out of the bus queue and started to walk towards him. As soon as he saw me, he veered off to the right, then called to a girl from Year Ten who had just come out of the school gates.

I couldn't believe it. He had *blanked* me. I felt myself crumble inside. Luckily my bus came round the corner a moment later, so I hastily rejoined the bus queue, dived on to the bus and sat there in a daze for the journey home. When I got back, I told Mum that I didn't feel well, didn't want any supper and was going straight to bed.

Once underneath my duvet, I tried to make sense of what

had happened. Why had he turned away from me like he hadn't seen me? Surely he'd have been expecting me to have been at the meeting, so why blank me in the street? Should I call him, have it out with him? I wondered. But the courage I'd felt earlier seemed to have faded and I felt weary of the whole business. Anyway, I told myself, he'd only tell me not to get heavy again. He said he'd sort it. Maybe I should let him. He'd probably call sooner or later and when he did I'd have my questions ready. I looked at the phone and willed it to ring. But then, he'd be in the meeting with Olivia and Sian. Or maybe he had a letter like mine to deliver, saying he wouldn't be coming to meetings either. I hoped not. What a mess. It would be a shame to blow the project after all the work we'd put in. Maybe I should call Nesta. She was probably at home in a similar state to me. Questioning everything. I felt awful about that. Maybe she was slagging me off to anybody who'd listen. My stomach knotted as I imagined her talking to Tony or with Lucy at her house, talking to her brothers and all of them hating me. How could I ever be friends with them again? They'd never let me. All of them would think I was a horrible person and maybe I was. A boyfriend stealer. And not just any boyfriend, I stole one of my best friends' boyfriend. Nesta was so brilliant when Hannah went out to South Africa last year and I felt like I didn't have a friend in the world. She'd gone out of her way to make me feel welcome in her home and her life, and how had I returned her friendship?

Oh God. I hate myself. I should have resisted Luke last night. Told him to go home. *Why* didn't I? Because I am the worst person in the whole world. Yes, they are probably all sitting round right now talking about what a rotten person I am. And Luke? Who knows what's going on in his mind. I'd been a complete fool? *Why* had I let him in last night? But after our marathon snogging session, I'd been so sure that he'd felt as strongly about me as I did about him and now, now I didn't know what to think. Am I desperate to have given in so easily? But it hadn't felt like that at the time, it had felt wonderful, perfect, meant to be. As the thoughts whirled round and round in my head, my mind began to feel exhausted. Is this what being in love is really like, I wondered as I recalled the conversation about it that I'd had with the girls only weeks ago. Feeling ill, like I wanted to curl up and die and yet, only last night, I'd felt on top of the world, in heaven. Now I was in hell, hell, hell.

Not long after I'd taken to my bed, Mum came in with a thermometer. She put her hand on my forehead and looked at me anxiously. 'Doesn't feel like you've got a temperature,' she said as she held out the thermometer, 'but pop this in your mouth and we'll see.'

I didn't object. How could I tell her that I had heartache. The love bug. It might be internal, but it hurts just as bad as any physical illness. If only there was a tablet I could take to ease the pain, I thought, make it all go away. It's so easy with a cold or flu, you just take a Lemsip and have hot drinks. With a broken leg, you put on a bandage but with a broken heart, what do you take? What can you do? There isn't an ointment or plaster that can mend it.

After a few minutes, Mum took out the thermometer. 'No, your temperature's normal, TJ. How are you feeling? What are the symptoms?'

I moaned and turned away from her to the wall. She was being so nice to me. If she only knew what a bad person I was. I felt tears in my eyes and didn't want her to see me crying.

'Sore head,' I said. 'Just need to sleep a while.'

'I'll bring you a paracetamol,' said Mum, 'then let me know if there's anything else you want.'

'Thanks. Got to sleep now.'

I waited for her to leave, but I could hear that she was still in my room. I could feel her looking at me even though my back was turned.

'TJ, is there anything you want to talk about? Anything bothering you?'

'No, just need to sleep,' I said. All I wanted was to be left alone so that I could have a good cry.

'Is it the move to Devon that's upsetting you because . . .'

'No. No, not that. I told you, I don't think I mind going now, in fact I think it will be for the best.'

Mum sat on the end of the bed and put her hand on my leg.

'So what then, love? You can tell me.'

'I can't. Just . . . just have you . . . have you ever wished that you could turn back time?'

'Millions of times,' said Mum softly. 'Could it be . . . something to do with a boy?'

I felt tears well up in my eyes. 'Yes. No . . . Just . . . I've made such a huge mistake . . .' I hesitated. I couldn't open up to her. I just couldn't. I felt too ashamed. She looked so worried, sitting there watching me, that I felt I had to say something. 'Oh don't worry, I'm not pregnant or on drugs or anything. It's just . . . a friend thing. I've . . . well, I messed up with my mates. But I'll . . . I'll sort it.'

Mum squeezed my leg. 'We all mess up from time to time, TJ. That's how we learn in life. It can be tough sometimes, but we can't always get it right. Thing is when you fall, you have two choices, to lie there feeling sorry for yourself or to get up and try and right whatever you've done. No crime in falling. The only crime is staying down.' She got up to go. 'Nobody's perfect. Maybe you shouldn't be so hard on yourself. Whatever you've done, I'm sure there's a way to make it come right. Sleep on it. Things always seem better after a good night's sleep.'

Email: **Inbox (2)**
From: mwatts@fastmail
To: babewithbrains@psnet.co.uk
Date: 12th December
Subject: Dresses

Hey TJ
I picked up the dresses ready for us to try tomorrow. I hope you like yours. I think you will. It's not too girlie.

See you soon,
Love
Marie

Email: **Inbox (1)**
From: hannahnutter@fastmail.com
To: babewithbrains@psnet.co.uk
Date: 12th December
Subject: True Love

Hasta la bandango amigo
Wow! Sounds like the real thing with Lukiemanukie. Please invite me to the wedding and I will buy a hat. Can I be bridesmaid?

Your friend
Hannah

Email: **Outbox (1)**
From: babewithbrains@psnet.co.uk
To: hannahnutter@fastmail.com
Date: 12th December
Subject: Love Sucks

Dear Hannah
No wedding. Except Marie's of course. No. No love affair
either. It has all blown up in my face and I have lost my
friends and Steve. Feel the worst I've ever felt in my whole
life (even worse than last time I felt my worst) and now I
have to go and play happy bridesmaids as we're going to
Devon for my dress fitting tomorrow. I think I will stand up
in the church and yell, DON'T do it. Love sucks. There
ought to be a government warning against it. Will explain
more later.

Lots of love
TJ

Chapter 18

I'm Going to Wash that Man Right Out of my Hair

The next day, I got up and ready to go to Devon but, when I got downstairs, Mum took one look at me and told me to go back to bed. I knew I looked bad, with bags under my eyes which were still bloodshot from last night. I'd tried putting in some eye-drops that I'd found in the bathroom cabinet, but they hadn't helped much. I still looked like I'd been awake most of the night. Which I had.

'You look awful,' she said. 'How are you feeling?'

'Not one hundred percent but I'll be OK.'

'You might be coming down with something. There's a lot of bugs around at the moment. My surgery is full of people with flu and coughs. Go back to bed for an hour or so as we're not leaving for Devon until mid-morning. If you're still not feeling right then, well, you'll just have to stay here.'

I didn't argue. I was feeling rotten. I got back into bed and managed to doze off for half an hour until I was woken by my mobile. Panic seized me. What if it was Luke? Or Nesta?

'Hello?' I said tentatively.

It was Izzie. 'Hey, how's it going?'

'OK. Except Mum thinks I'm ill.'

'Are you?'

'Not really, but I don't feel great. Have you spoken to Nesta and Lucy?'

'Lucy . . . Sort of.'

'What did she say?'

'Not a lot. I'm up at Costa in Highgate, as I'd arranged to meet her and Nesta here before this whole mad thing started. I thought that they might show up, but I doubt if they were still expecting me. Anyway, Lucy was waiting for Nesta and we had a row. She accused me of taking sides. Can you believe it? Like she hasn't with Nesta. So I accused *her* of taking sides. Then she said something like, what do I expect and that I should have told them what was going on, but if I had . . . well, I'd have betrayed your trust, wouldn't I? What was I supposed to have done? I couldn't win whatever I'd done, either way I was going to upset one of you. Anyway, I said I'd promised not to tell and you felt really bad about everything and she said, what like Nesta doesn't, as if I didn't care about Nesta's feelings at all. And that if we were all real mates and all trusted each other, then you or I would have let her and Nesta in on what was happening. And then she stormed off.'

'Oh hell, I'm so sorry Izzie. I should never have told you, then you wouldn't be in this mess.'

'I'm glad you did. You had to tell someone and I am your mate. And I understand why you didn't want to talk to Lucy or Nesta at the time.'

'God, I wish I could turn the clock back, Izzie. Just a few days. Delete. Skip back. I'm so sorry. I wish I could fix things.'

'Seems to me that you have a choice. Luke, or Nesta and Lucy. It's not too late to fix it with them. But if you choose Luke, then I don't think Nesta and Lucy will stay friends with you. Least not for a while.'

'I don't want Luke any more, no way. No boy is worth losing your friends for. Anyway, I don't think Luke even wants to talk to me now. I wanted to have it out with him but, when I saw him after school yesterday, he blanked me.'

'Ah,' said Izzie. 'But that could mean anything. Remember when I told you that the defence of boys, who feel that they're under attack, is to attack back?'

'Yeah.'

'Well the ones that don't use that tactic do the ostrich routine, you know, stick their head in the sand. Try and ignore the whole situation and hope it goes away.'

'So why was he coming to our school if he's trying to ignore things? He must have known he might bump into one of us.'

'There you've got me stumped. I suppose he can't get out of the project meetings as he's co-ordinator and the presentation is next week.'

'So what are you going to do now?'

'Wait for Nesta,' said Izzie. 'I refuse to play the we're-not-speaking game. We've been mates for too long. And despite what Lucy may think, I do care about Nesta's feelings. I think you should call her too. Don't give up.'

After she'd hung up, I lay on my bed and stared at the ceiling. I'd been staring at it so much in the last few weeks, I knew it intimately, every crack, every lick of paint. My choice, Izzie had said. My choice. My friendship with the girls or Luke? Luke, who I wasn't even sure of. Luke who, according to Olivia, had a cut-off date with all his girlfriends. There was no contest. We might have had an amazing night on Thursday, but it had come at too high a price and I wanted my friends back.

I took a deep breath and called Nesta's number. I got her voice mail so left a message asking her to call me.

Half an hour later, Izzie phoned again.

'I'm in the Ladies,' she whispered, 'so I can't speak for long. Bad news I'm afraid. Nesta arrived and I talked to her and tried to tell her that none of it was your fault and . . .'

'And?'

'And she's pretty cool. She's not mad with me like Lucy is. But she saw Luke last night after school and he didn't say anything about finishing with her. She says he still wants to see her and that she means a lot to him. Can you believe it? He's such a rat. In fact, he's coming to meet her here later.'

'Did she say anything about me?'

Izzie was quiet at her end of the phone.

'Please Izzie, even if it's bad. I need to know.'

'She said something about Luke saying that you got him when his guard was down and you sort of threw yourself at him.'

'*What?*' I felt my stomach churn. 'That's what he told me when I confronted him about Sian. Said she'd kissed him and he hadn't really wanted to kiss her back, but she threw herself at him. And Nesta believed him about me, huh?'

'Think so. I *am* sorry, TJ. I know you really thought he was The One.'

'Yeah, me and a long list of idiots by the sound of it,' I said. 'Does Nesta hate me?'

'Er . . . well let's just say that you're not up there with her favourite people right now.'

'Someone's got to tell her what Luke is really like, Izzie. I tried to call her but got her voice mail.'

'Do you want me to have another go?'

'You can try, but I think it's best if it comes from me. Are you going to stay and see Luke?'

'No way. I'd punch him if I saw him. I think he's a creep. He's playing both of you along in my opinion.'

After she'd hung up, I went and took a bath. It was like I wanted to wash the whole thing away. While I was lying there soaking, I could hear one of Dad's favourite CDs playing downstairs. It's the soundtrack to the film, *South Pacific*. There's a track that goes, 'I'm going to wash that man right out of my hair'. Too right, I thought as I reached for the shampoo.

The journey down to Devon took just under four hours and Mum tucked me up in the back under a blanket, so I managed to doze off for a while. The rest of the time I just watched the fields flash by. I thought about what Izzie had told me and I felt myself getting angrier and angrier. How could Luke have lied about me to Nesta? I wondered if he had a clue about the pain and confusion he was causing. I knew it was going to be hard, but I had to talk to Nesta and somehow get through to her that her boyfriend was a liar.

We arrived late afternoon and went straight to the cottage that Marie and Stuart had bought. It was a quaint little place, but in a mess as they'd only recently moved in and loads of stuff was still in boxes. Mum got busy straight away, putting the rubber gloves on and starting to clean out cupboards in the kitchen, while Dad went to check out the garden and a dilapidated old greenhouse, which was great because it gave me some time alone with Marie. Even though she's a lot older than me, I've always found her easy to talk to.

'How you feeling?' she asked as we took mugs of tea into her bedroom. 'Mum said you've been under the weather.'

'Sort of.'

'Flu bug?'

'Not really.'

'Boy trouble?'

'How did you guess?'

Marie smiled. 'I know the symptoms. Listless. Sad bloodshot eyes. Look like the weight of the whole world is on your shoulders. Going to tell me about it?'

'Not much to tell. Only that I've ruined my life, lost my friends, hurt a really nice boy and been let down by the only boy I ever loved, or thought I loved.'

'Oh. So nothing major then?' she joked.

I gave her a weak smile. 'How did you know that Stuart was The One, Marie?'

She sat on the bed and took a sip of her tea. 'Oh God. Loads of reasons. He makes me laugh. I love being with him. I can't imagine life without him.'

'Yeah, but how do you really know that he's The One?'

'He just is. It feels right. It's different to being with anyone else. I know that he's there for me. He'd do anything for me and I feel the same about him. Already he's like family in that I know he's a hundred percent on my side. I trust him completely.'

When she said the bit about trust, I felt my eyes watering.

'Hey,' said Marie. 'It can't be that bad. Are you going to tell me about it?'

'Promise you won't hate me?' I asked.

'Never,' she said, taking my hand and holding it as I filled her in on the whole story. When I'd finished she looked at me kindly. 'My poor TJ. Sounds like you need to talk to this boy. And to Nesta. Get a few things straight.'

I shook my head. 'Can't. Everybody hates me except Izzie. Nesta's not speaking to me and Izzie thinks that Luke is doing the ostrich routine. You know, head in the sand.'

'Then get him to take his head *out* of the sand. Talk to him. Ask him what the hell he thinks he's playing at.'

'I tried after school last night and he blanked me. It was awful. Anyway, what is there to say? When I tried to talk to him before, he told me not to get heavy and said that I was being demanding.'

'Well if he already thinks you are and, knowing you as I do, I can't imagine it as you're not a demanding kind of person, but if he *thinks* you are, then you've got nothing to lose. You want your mates back, so sort it with him. Be demanding. Ask him what his game is. If a boy has any respect for your feelings, he will give you the time, listen to how you are. Your feelings are as important as everyone else's in all of this and you've had a rough ride by the sound of it. I know people have got hurt, but so have you and you matter as well. Call Nesta. And call him.' She pointed to the phone by the bed, then got up to go. 'No time like the present. I'll keep the wrinklies busy and make sure no one comes in.'

I suppose I didn't look convinced as Marie turned back to me when she got to the door. '*Do* it,' she urged. 'You can't spend all weekend not knowing what's going on. Phone them.'

After she'd gone, I sat and stared at the phone for a few moments, then I picked up the receiver and dialled Nesta's number.

It was still switched off so, once again, I left a message.

Next I dialled Luke's number. He answered immediately.

'Hey Watts,' he said. 'I was just thinking about you. We got your letter about not coming to the meeting. What's that all about?'

He sounded so cheerful it took me by surprise. How could he sound so happy when I was in torment? I asked myself.

'Why did you blank me yesterday?'

'Oh *that*? I wanted to talk to you, but Nesta was about ten yards behind you. You had your back to her so you couldn't see her. I didn't want her to see us together. I didn't want to hurt her more than necessary . . .'

But it's OK to hurt me, I thought. 'So you did a runner?'

'*No*. Not exactly. In fact, when you'd got on the bus, I went and spoke to her. She was pretty mad with me.'

I decided to confront him about everything. Marie was right, I had nothing to lose. 'Yeah, so you told her that I threw myself at you. You *know* it wasn't like that.'

'I most certainly do,' said Luke in a low voice. 'It was fantastic.'

'So *why* did you lie?'

Luke sighed into the phone. 'Oh come on, TJ. Do we *have* to do this?'

'Yes. We *do*. I need to know what's going on. Izzie told me that you and Nesta are still an item. I thought you said that you were going to finish with her?'

'I am. I will, but I need to do it in my own time. I like Nesta and, as I said, I don't want to hurt her. Everything was happening a bit fast, so I thought I'd carry on seeing her for a while and let her down slowly.'

I couldn't believe that he was still keeping it up and, for a moment, was lost for words.

'TJ, you still there?' asked Luke.

'Yes.'

'Let's meet up next week. I really want to see you,' he said, making his voice go husky again. 'I've been thinking about you and Thursday night a lot. I can't wait . . .'

I could hear footsteps outside the door. 'Look, got to go. Bye Luke.'

It was Marie. She put her head round the door. 'I've brought you something to soothe your eyes,' she said, holding two slices of cucumber out to me. 'Everything OK?'

I wanted to scream. '*Nooooooo.* Not all right. I can't believe it. He still wants to see me. Says he's been *thinking* about me. Says he wants to let Nesta down slowly and he'll finish with her in his own time.'

Marie came and sat by me on the bed. 'Hhmmm. *That's* a familiar story. Do you really, really care for this boy?'

'I . . . I don't think so. No, I can't. It's a mess. It all feels way too complicated and I don't want to lose my friends over him.'

'Then tell him,' said Marie, 'and them.'

'What did you mean just now, it's a familiar story?'

Marie got up and made sure that the door was firmly closed. 'Promise you won't tell Mum or Dad?'

'Promise.'

Marie sat on the bed. 'When you asked me before how I knew Stuart was The One and I said trust, well, that's a lesson I had to learn the hard way.'

'How come?'

'Remember I was seeing a guy called Matthew for a while?'

I nodded. 'Vaguely. A couple of years ago? Doctor at the hospital where you worked in Bristol? I never met him though because you never brought him home.'

'Well, there was a reason for that, said Marie. 'See, what I didn't ever tell any of you is that he was married. That's why I said familiar story. I was such an idiot, TJ, talk about naive. He told me that he and his wife were unhappily married and that they were going to split up and they had no relationship to speak of any more and me, like a total fool, believed every word of it. He was always telling me that I was the great love of his life and that he would leave her in his own time as he didn't want to hurt her more than necessary etc, etc . . .'

'I never knew.'

Marie looked at the door. 'Nobody did. But at the time, it felt so right, I thought I really loved him, it was the real thing and he would leave his wife for me . . .'

'So what happened?'

'One day, I was asked to stand in for a colleague on the prenatal clinic and guess who was in the class? His wife. His five-months-pregnant, very sweet wife. So much for their relationship being over. When I asked him about it, he said it was just one night and he still intended to leave her after the baby was born. I could tell from meeting her that she didn't have a clue and she was looking forward to the birth of her child.'

'I'm so sorry Marie, you must have been gutted.'

'I was. Heartbroken and I felt like such a cow. I wouldn't have got involved if I hadn't thought his marriage was as good as over. He made his wife out to be this unfeeling monster, but she was a lovely woman. But he made me realise that if he was stringing his wife along, at a time when she needed him most and telling lies behind her back, then he might do the same thing to me. It made me realise that the most important thing in any relationship is trust. Oh I know it's different with you, TJ. You're much younger and I'm sure that this Luke is nothing like Matthew, but I just wanted to warn you that there are men out there like that and, what Luke is doing to Nesta, he may well do to you. It sounds to me like Luke doesn't know what he wants, either that or he's a coward like Matthew was.'

'So what happened to Matthew?'

'Still with his wife last I heard. I finished with him as soon as I realised that he was lying to me, but it took me a long time to get over it. I felt awful. Evil. I kept seeing his wife in my mind and I felt so mean.'

'I know. That's how I felt when I saw how upset Nesta was, when she realised that Luke had cheated on her with me. But now he's talked her round again and instead of being mad with him, she thinks I threw myself at him and she's mad with me.'

'Is he worth it, TJ?'

I shook my head. 'Absolutely not. No way am I going to give up two of my best friends for someone who, a few months down the line, might decide that some other unsuspecting victim is the love of his life and I'll find myself on the scrap heap.'

'Exactly,' said Marie. 'But the bottom line is, do you trust him?'

I shook my head. 'Not any more.'

'Do you trust Nesta?'

I nodded. 'One hundred percent. She couldn't lie or keep a secret if she tried.'

'Then there's your answer,' said Marie getting up, going to the wardrobe and pulling out two stunning dove-grey dresses with tiny white snowflakes embroidered round the hem. 'But, in the meantime, we've got a wedding coming up, so let's forget about Luke for a while and try these dresses on!'

Aids for Bloodshot or Tired Eyes

1) Soak two camomile tea bags in hot water. When the water has cooled, squeeze the tea bags out, lie back and apply the bags to your eyes.
2) Cut two thin slices of cucumber. Lie back and apply to the eyes.

Chapter 19

Confrontations

'Hi, can I speak to Nesta?' I asked.

It was Saturday night and Mum and Dad were finishing supper with Marie and Stuart in the kitchen. I hadn't much appetite, so I'd excused myself and made a beeline for the phone in Marie's bedroom. All I wanted to do was get on the phone and get my friends back.

'Hold on, I'll just go and call her,' said Tony, who had picked up the phone. He came back a few minutes later. 'She says she's not in.'

Next I tried Lucy. Her mobile was on voice mail, so I left a quick message saying that I needed to talk to her. Then I called Izzie. Luckily she was there, so I filled her in on my latest phone call with Luke.

'I told you so,' she said. 'He's telling you one thing and Nesta another.'

'I'm going to tell Nesta,' I said. 'That is if I can get to speak to her.'

'And I'll tell Lucy,' said Izzie. 'That is if I can get to speak to her. I'm going over there tomorrow and I'm going to sit in the front porch if she doesn't let me in.'

'Maybe I'll come and join you depending on what time we get back. I could bring a banner saying sorry.'

On Sunday, we didn't get away as early as I'd hoped in the morning, as Dad wanted to check out estate agents and Marie and Mum still had wedding plans to go through. I went with Dad to look in estate agents' windows. It might have been my imagination, but he didn't seem as enthusiastic as he had been in the beginning and it was me who seemed the more eager of the two of us, although I was beginning to regret having told Mum that I was happy to move. On the one hand, it would be a new start for me – a new chapter was just what I wanted after I'd put the record straight with Lucy and Nesta. Down here, no one would know me or what I'd done. On the other hand, if I could make things right with my mates, the last thing I'd want to do was leave them.

After a lunch of Marie's spaghetti bolognese (it's her speciality and the only thing she can cook. I wondered if Stuart's realised yet that unless he cooks, he's destined to eat takeaways or the same meal for the rest of eternity), everyone wanted to do some Christmas shopping in a market that was held in the local scout hut. I saw loads of things there that were perfect for presents for Nesta and Izzie and Lucy. As we browsed and I bought a few items (including a recipe book for Marie), I thought I couldn't imagine life without the girls even after we'd moved to Devon. I would always think of Izzie when I saw a crystal or aromatherapy kit. Glittery make-up and bath gels would always remind me of Nesta and any romantic type of fashion or lovely fabric would always make me think of Lucy and her passion for design. I felt sad as I bought them presents thinking that this might be our last Christmas in the same city. I couldn't bear to think it might all end on a sour note. I bought a silver and amethyst bracelet for Izzie, a red velvet scarf for Lucy and a tiny handbag with a fluffy trimming for Nesta. I hoped that they'd accept my gifts and still be my friends, and we could spend the coming holiday together as we'd planned before this whole fiasco with Luke had started. I'd made up my mind, Luke was history. I just hoped that Lucy, Izzie and Nesta would be a part of my future no matter where I lived.

I made sure that I got to school early on Monday morning and was waiting at the gates to catch Nesta and Lucy on their way in.

Lucy was the first to arrive. She looked confused when she saw me as if she didn't know how to react.

'Lucy,' I called. 'Can I speak to you?'

She hesitated for a moment, then came over.

'I wanted to say that I'm really, really sorry,' I blurted. 'I never meant for any of this to happen and want you to know, *please* will you be friends again? I'll do anything, and I know I've messed up badly and handled everything the wrong way. But it's all over with Luke and me. I promise. I've been such a fool.'

Lucy looked embarrassed. 'I saw Izzie yesterday. She came over and wouldn't leave until she'd told me everything.'

I smiled. 'Did she set up camp in your front porch?'

Lucy smiled back. 'Something like that. She said she wasn't going until we'd talked everything through, and that she'd brought sandwiches and a sleeping bag and was going to sleep in the shed if I didn't let her in. Anyway, she told me everything about you and Luke and everything that's happened, and . . . and . . . I guess I was a little hasty in judging you.'

'Does that mean we can be friends again? I know it's only been a short while, but it's felt like an eternity. I've missed you so much and it's been hell not being able to talk to you.'

Lucy nodded. 'I've missed you too – like this weekend, it felt like something wasn't right. But . . . look TJ, I do want to be friends, but let's get one thing straight, friends put each other first and tell each other everything. You should have said something about fancying Luke.'

I nodded. 'I know. I really *really* know, but . . . I was afraid that you'd hate me.'

'I don't hate you. You can't help who you fancy, but you can help what you do about it.'

'I know, and nothing like this will *ever* happen again. I promise that from now on I will tell you everything, *everything* . . .'

'Deal,' said Lucy, smiling.

I wrapped my arms around her and gave her a huge hug. 'I really honestly truly didn't mean it to happen,' I said. 'I've been *sooo* stupid . . . and unhappy . . .'

'I guess love makes us all a bit stupid sometimes . . .'

'It's made me realise a lot . . .'

Just at that moment, Nesta came round the corner. She looked taken aback to see me being so pally with Lucy and turned to walk the other way.

'Nesta,' I called after her.

'Later,' she said as she walked off towards the assembly hall.

It wasn't going to be easy winning Nesta back, I thought.

'Any ideas?' I asked Lucy.

'Grovelling might work,' she replied. 'If that doesn't work, try bribery, a lifetime's supply of chocolate or something. And I'll try and talk to her in the break.'

At break, Lucy made a beeline for Nesta as she headed out of class and I prayed that she might get through to her. However, when we went back into class fifteen minutes later, Lucy looked over at me and shook her head.

'I'll try at lunch,' said Izzie. 'If nothing else, she has to realise what Luke is really like.'

'Thanks, Iz,' I said. 'But I think it should come from me.'

'Well let's just hope she doesn't shoot the messenger,' said Izzie with a grim look, 'or try to strangle you. But then again, it might give us a chance to practise our first aid skills.'

I lightly punched her arm. Thank God for Izzie, I thought. She's kept me sane through all this.

At lunch, I was first out ready to confront Nesta. As she came out of the classroom, she saw that I was waiting and headed in the other direction. Lucy and Izzie came out soon after and gave me a nod to go after her, so I followed and caught up with her.

'Nesta,' I said. 'We have to talk.'

'Nothing to say,' she said.

'It's about Luke . . .'

'I *said* nothing to say. He told me about how you threw yourself at him.' Then she stopped and turned to me. 'How could you, TJ?'

I took a deep breath. 'I'm sorry, Nesta, I really am. But it wasn't how he said it was.'

She waved her hand as if dismissing what I was saying. 'Yeah, yeah. Whatever.'

'No. *No*. Nesta. Not whatever. It wasn't all in my head, you have to believe that. Luke has been lying to both of us.'

She shook her head. 'You just don't get it, do you?' she asked. 'He's into me. End of story. Now get your own boyfriend.' And she started to walk off down the corridor.

I couldn't let her go off like that. It was going to be the hardest thing I'd ever done and I knew it would hurt her, but she had to know the truth. 'I spoke to him after he'd told you that story about me throwing myself at him and . . .'

I saw her slow down, so I caught up with her again. 'Listen Nesta, I'm really sorry to have to tell you this and . . . and . . . I'm sure Luke *does* like you. He told me that he likes you, but he's also told me that he's going to finish with you.'

Nesta stopped. She didn't look at me, but I could see that she was listening.

'He . . . he said he wants to be with me and doesn't want to hurt you, so he's going to go out with you a bit longer and let you down slowly. I don't even know if that's true, but I think you ought to know what he's saying behind your back.'

Nesta didn't say anything.

'I'm really really sorry. And I didn't throw myself at him, honestly. There was one time when we kissed. *One* time . . . and it wasn't me forcing myself on him. It really wasn't. He was with me for three hours . . .'

Nesta finally looked me in the face. Her expression was one of anger and hurt. 'He told *you* that he's going to finish with *me*?'

'Yes. Can't you see what he's doing, Nesta? He's telling us both different things . . .'

'And . . . when he kissed you, he was with you for three hours?'

I nodded.

Nesta ran her fingers through her hair and looked agitated. 'OK. OK . . . Let me get my head round this. So you're saying that Luke lied to me about you?'

'Yes. Remember my snog rash?'

'I asked him about that, and he said that Steve must have given you that.'

'No way. And anyway, you've seen Steve. He hardly has to shave. I know it's hard to hear, but it was Luke.'

'And you say that he's planning to dump me?'

'That's what he said.'

'OK. OK. So . . . if he *does* dump me, are you going to go out with him?'

'*Noooo.* No way. I can't trust him. Neither can you. That's why I'm telling you all this. But you *can* trust me, Nesta. I'm being totally honest with you now. I don't think we're the only girls he's stringing along either. Sian thinks he wants to be with her as well.'

'Sian? That blonde girl?'

'Yes. He told me that he didn't fancy her. Not his type he said, but then she told me that he'd kissed her and when I confronted him about it, he gave me the line he gave you about me. That she threw herself at him.'

Nesta looked shocked. 'Sian? I can't believe it.'

'Well who knows what's really going on in her head, but I don't think it's entirely her fault that she thought she stood a chance with him. He can't bear to tell anyone the truth. I think he wants to know that he can have all of us. But I've had enough of him. I don't want any more misunderstandings, not knowing what's going on. I want to be with people who are totally on the level, who I can trust and who trust me. I want us to be friends again more than anything in the world.'

Nesta gave me a long hard cold stare. 'I'll kill him,' she said then turned and walked away.

I stared after her, wondering if I should follow her, when Izzie came up behind me. 'Leave her,' she said. 'She probably needs to be on her own for a while.'

Email: **Outbox (1)**
From: babewithbrains@psnet.co.uk
To: hannahnutter@fastmail.com
Date: 15th December
Subject: Love

Dear Hannah
God I miss you. So much has been happening here and I've learned so much mainly that the most important thing in any relationship is trust. I really liked Luke a lot but I can't trust him, not like I can my friends. I really hope I can win them back.

Love
TJ

Email: **Inbox (1)**
From: hannahnutter@fastmail.com
To: babewithbrains@psnet.co.uk
Date: 16th December
Subject: Love

Ma petite TJ
Methinks you are very wise and I just want you to know that even though we are many miles apart now that I trust you completely. Friends are forever and I shall pray from afar that they all see sense and make it up with you.

Love and stuff
Hannahalulu

Presentation

'He's just come in,' said Izzie coming over to the stand where I was busy with Olivia pinning up our work for the project. It was the afternoon of the presentation and anyone involved had been let out of school for the afternoon to go to the Institute in Highgate to prepare for the evening. The hall was buzzing with teachers and pupils rushing about, making last minute adjustments, all busy trying to show their work to its best advantage in its own screened-off area.

'Time to face the music, I guess,' I said as I glanced over my shoulder and saw that Luke was heading straight for me.

'Let me know how it goes,' said Izzie and pointed to the other side of the hall, 'and I'm only just over there if you want me to come over and knock his lights out.'

'What happened to your Buddhist philosophy about not harming any living creature?'

'I wouldn't *kill* him,' she said with a grin, 'only maim.'

'Thanks, Iz,' I said, then turned back to the board and began to pin up my poster detailing all the people who'd lived in

Hampstead. Our area did look impressive. On one side were all the photographs that Steve had taken for me before we broke up, colour blow-ups of the houses we'd visited. On the right were my posters of all the famous people who lived in the area, a map of where they'd lived and Luke had picked a selection of quotes from the writers and photos of some of the paintings of the area. Sian had done some fabulous illustrations of streets, shops and houses and Olivia had done a great job on the lay-outs of all the titbits of information in between. The whole effect was very professional and glossy.

'It's beginning to take shape,' said Olivia standing back as Luke came to join us. 'I think it's going to look good. Don't you think, Luke?'

Luke looked at me and not the work. 'Yeah. Looks great. Sorry I'm late. Er . . . Olivia,' he said as he reached into his pocket and pulled out his car keys, 'could you start getting the boxes in my boot out of my car. I've got a load of brochures on the houses that people can take away if they want. I need to just check a few things in here then I'll come and help you unload.'

'Sure,' said Olivia and headed off for the door.

I carried on pinning up the work.

'So why haven't you returned any of my phone calls?' asked Luke. 'I've been going out of my mind.'

'Oh I think you know *exactly* why,' I said, without turning to look at him.

'Actually I don't,' he said. 'I think we need to talk.'

I couldn't resist. 'Oh do we have to do this now?' I asked.

'Yes. I need to know what's going on . . .'

'Oh don't get all heavy, Luke,' I said, turning to him at last. 'Tonight's the big night.'

'You know I've finished with Nesta, don't you?'

'I know that Nesta finished with *you*,' I said. 'Lucy told me.' Apparently she didn't waste any time and finished with him the same day that I'd spoken to her about his lying.

'So that means it won't be a problem with us any more.'

'*Whadt?*' I couldn't believe his cheek. 'Er . . . reality check, Luke. I think there's a *major* problem with us, a few in fact. One, that you're a liar. Two, that you seem to have some kind of problem being alone and three, that I can't trust you. Oh. And four, I wouldn't go out with you if you were the last person on the planet.'

Luke looked taken aback. 'But . . . I thought we had something special.'

'And so did Nesta, and so does Sian and God knows how many other idiots. Now, if you'll excuse me. I think I'll go and give Olivia a hand with those boxes.'

At that moment, Sian came over and looked coyly at Luke. You're welcome to him, I thought as I made my way across the hall.

Izzie caught me up at the door. 'Everything OK?'

'Sure. How about you? Is your stuff up and ready?'

Izzie nodded in the direction of her stand. She'd managed to get loads of posters of the leaders of all the different religions and a big statue of the laughing Buddha took pride of place on a table at the front and good old Steve had photographed all the churches in the area for her. She'd even persuaded Trevor to dress up as a swami although he didn't look too comfortable about it as people kept going past him singing, 'Hare Krishna'.

Suddenly Izzie's eyes swivelled to the door. 'Ohmigod,' she said. 'Major babe alert. Ding dong. Eyes left. Which school is that divine apparition from?'

I turned to where she was looking and saw that a tall boy had come in behind Olivia. He was striking, like he could have been Orlando Bloom's younger brother.

'Don't know but he's definitely a five star hubba hubba,' I said as I checked him out. 'Is Nesta here yet?'

'Down the end of the hall helping Lucy,' said Izzie pointing to the far right of the hall where Lucy was busy dressing a mannequin while Nesta gave instructions. Then Izzie laughed. 'Looks like they've clocked boy babe as well.'

I glanced over and saw that both Lucy and Nesta were looking in the boy's direction. Lucy saw us looking and gave us a wave. As we waved back Nesta looked over, then turned away when she saw me.

'How is Nesta by the way?' I asked.

'She's been pretty quiet all week,' said Izzie. 'She still not speaking to you?'

'She did speak to me yesterday,' I said, 'when we came out of maths. Only to say that she'd never speak to me again though.'

'Ah,' said Izzie. 'So there's hope then.'

'How do you see that?'

'No one can ever say never say never. She said yesterday that she'd never look at another boy as long as she lived and look at her now. She's definitely checking the hubba hubba boy out. If she can break her vow never to look at another boy in the short time of twenty-four hours, she may come round to being mates with you again.'

A few moments later, Lucy made her way through the throng to join us. 'Hey, have you checked out the boy over there.'

'Oh yes,' said Izzie. 'Mucho tasty.'

'That's what Nesta said,' said Lucy. 'I think she may be on the road to recovery.'

Luke walked past on his way to the door and took one look

at Lucy, Izzie and I, then glanced down the hall at Nesta.

'Got to get some last-minute photocopying done,' he gulped and disappeared fast.

For the next half-hour, we kept busy with the preparations. I stayed away from Nesta. I felt that the ball was in her court and there was nothing more I could say or do to win her back. In the meantime, Izzie came over to see me, then went to check on Nesta and Lucy. Then Lucy came over to me while Nesta watched from the fashion stand and I watched her from the history stand. After about half an hour of this, I glanced over at her and caught her looking at me. She stuck her tongue out at me and made a silly face. Then she gave me a look with one eyebrow raised that was like a challenge – as if to say, what are you going to do about it? I pulled my worst face back at her. I'd perfected it in the mirror years ago. I put an index finger on my nose to make it snub, stretched the corners of my mouth out with the little fingers of both hands, stuck my tongue out and crossed my eyes.

Just at that moment, who walked by but hubba hubba boy? He stopped and stared at me. Behind him, I saw Nesta totally crease up laughing.

'Hmmm. Very ladylike,' said the boy.

'I do try,' I said. 'I've been told that it's a very seductive look.'

The boy grinned. 'Unforgettable,' he said then moved on.

'On the pull again, huh?' said a familiar voice a few moments later.

It was Nesta.

'Yeah, but I don't think he fell for my super sexy look,' I said with a laugh.

'Slut,' said Nesta. But she was smiling as she said it.

'I'm really, really sorry . . .'

'Boooring,' yawned Nesta. 'We've been there done the

apologies and stand-offs. Look. Bottom line is, I miss you. And on top of that, Lucy and Izzie can't spend their lives going between us.'

I held my breath for a moment. Was she making up?

'OK. No more saying sorry but you have to know that I know I've been totally out of order, but I would never ever have dreamed of doing what I did if I hadn't thought that Luke was really special. Remember weeks ago, when we talked about soulmates. I . . . I thought Luke was my soulmate. I know it sounds major stupid now that we know that he's such a liar, but . . . I had all the symptoms that Izzie described. Sick, stupid, ill, couldn't sleep, couldn't think straight. I did think it was a once in a lifetime thing.'

Nesta didn't say anything for a few moments. 'The One, huh?'

'Yeah. Bummer.'

'Yeah. Major bummer.'

For a moment I thought she was going to get mad at me for saying I thought Luke was my soulmate. I decided to change the subject. 'So you were saying. Poor Lucy and Izzie. If we don't talk, it would be cruel to them.'

'Yeah, why should they suffer when it's really Luke who's the rat-faced, pig-goat-poo person in all of this. Where is he, by the way?'

'Out the back somewhere. Keeping out of the way. Once we got the stand up, he made a load of excuses to disappear. I think being in the same room as both of us is difficult for him, never mind Lucy and Izzie glowering at him from their stands.'

'Good,' said Nesta. 'If I never see him again it will be too soon.'

Lucy and Izzie came over. 'Hey, you're talking.'

'Yeah,' said Nesta. 'We thought we owed it to you and Izzie.

You're going to wear yourselves out going between the two of us, so for your sakes and *only* that, yes, we are going to make up. OK, TJ?'

'Double OK,' I said.

'Excellent,' said Lucy.

'Now, more importantly,' said Nesta. 'You guys may be stupid enough to believe in finding The One and doing your head in in the process but I, the only sensible person here, know better and that there are many Ones out there. So. Who's that boy babe cruising the hall?'

'I saw him first,' said Izzie.

'No, I did,' said Lucy as she gave Izzie a slight shove.

'TJ, you want to stake your claim before battle commences?' asked Nesta.

'Do you fancy him?' I asked Nesta.

'D'oh, *yeah*. Just what I need in my time of grief.'

'Then he's yours,' I said.

'Chicken,' laughed Nesta. 'Anyway, we don't even know who is yet. But I intend to find out.'

'I thought you were through with boys,' said Izzie.

'Nope,' said Nesta. 'Just ones like Luke. There's plenty more fish in the sea and not *all* of them are razor sharks.'

'Very wise,' said Izzie. 'And if at first you don't succeed . . .'

'Try try try again,' Lucy finished for her.

'No,' said Izzie. 'If at first you don't succeed, skydiving is not for you.'

We all cracked up. Lucy looked at the three of us and grinned widely. 'God I'm so glad we're mates again. This last week has been hell. I'm so glad you managed to see things from TJ's angle, Nesta . . .'

'Yeah,' said Izzie. 'She's had a tough time too and there are two sides to every story.'

'Or three if you're involved with Luke,' said Nesta.

I was about to say four if you included Sian, but bit my lip.

'Yeah,' said Izzie. 'It's like that saying, before you criticise someone, walk a mile in their shoes.'

'Oh very wise, Obi-Wan Kenobi,' said Nesta. 'But there's another bit to that saying. Before you criticise someone, walk a mile in their shoes. That way, when you do criticise them, you'll be a mile away and you'll have their shoes.'

We all laughed again. I felt great. Out of the corner of my eye, I saw Luke come back through the doors. He took one look at us and turned on his heel. I didn't care, in fact I felt relieved he'd disappeared. I could hardly believe it. Here we all were, me, Izzie, Lucy and Nesta together, having a laugh like we used to. There was only one more person I needed to make things right with and that was Steve. I'd noticed him as soon as I'd arrived at the hall, he was up on the left busy arranging his photographs on his stand. He'd kept his head down the whole time as if he was in a world of his own. Lucy saw me looking in his direction.

'He's OK,' she said. 'He was cut up, but he'll be OK.'

'I feel bad about him,' I said, 'really bad. He deserved better than the way I broke up with him.'

'He'll get over it. Steve's not one to mooch about.'

I winced inwardly as I thought about how he must have felt waking up, turning on his computer and finding my message there. Like – good morning and you're dumped. Love TJ. How could I have had such disregard for his feelings?

'There has to be some right way to finish with people,' I said. 'It's like I went to one extreme with my stupid email charging in with my "must be honest, right now" policy. And Luke went to the other extreme by avoiding confrontation and not telling anyone anything but what they wanted to hear. We both ended up hurting people. There has to be a middle way to do it.'

'Apparently there are fifty ways to leave your lover.' Lucy laughed, then began to sing the song, 'Fifty Ways to Leave Your Lover' by Paul Simon. I tried to muffle her as her voice got louder and louder.

I so wanted to go over and talk to Steve, go back to how we were, mates, having a laugh, because even though I didn't want to get back with him, I did miss his company. For a moment, I understood why Luke found it so hard to end relationships. So maybe someone isn't the *great* love of your life, your soulmate, The One, but like with Steve, you still like them. You certainly wouldn't want to hurt them. You can love people in different ways, I thought, as Luke would say – on different levels. It's hard knowing that you're going to hurt someone or, in my case, *have* hurt someone. I guess for Luke not saying anything must have seemed like an easy option. But people still do get hurt, I reminded myself. It's damaging to string someone along under false pretences, giving them hope where there is none. It only prolongs the pain. But as I watched Steve, I thought, maybe Luke wasn't so much a rat as a coward. It's a biggie facing up to the responsibility that when you have a relationship with someone and they really like you, you hold their heart in your hand. I don't want to be a coward. One day very soon, I'm going to call Steve and talk to him honestly about everything that's happened. I just hope that I can find the right words and that he'll still be my friend. Not boyfriend. Friend. Even though things hadn't worked out with Luke, I couldn't deny that what I'd felt on the night he came to my house had been really special. I wanted more of that lovely feeling of being hopelessly in love, but without the complications of people getting hurt and secrets and lies.

At six-thirty, everyone was ready and there was a hush of

anticipation as Mrs Allen showed Susan Barratt, the school governor, and Sam Denham, the journalist, around. The hall looked wonderful as some Year Eight pupils had dressed a huge Christmas tree on the stage and the room smelled wonderfully festive with the delicious smell of cinnamon and clove coming from the mulled wine on the refreshments tables set up ready for the public.

Both Sam and Mrs Barratt seemed very impressed and stopped to speak to just about everyone on all the stands, Sam spending a little longer on the fashion stand talking to Nesta. She looked well pleased and looked over at me and winked after he'd moved on. When Sam and Mrs Barratt had done their rounds, the doors opened and in flooded everyone's friends and families.

Mum and Dad seemed genuinely interested in all of it and after Dad had been round to look at all the stands, he came back and spent a long time studying ours.

'You love living here, don't you?' he asked as he looked at my map of Hampstead.

I nodded. 'There's so much to do and see. Remember that famous saying by Samuel Johnson: Tire of London and you're tired of life.'

'He was right,' said Dad. 'This last few weeks, I've realised how much I love London too. I love to go to the Barbican to the concerts. I love to walk on the Heath. I love the theatres, the cinemas, restaurants. It's all here on our doorsteps.'

'So why are we moving then?'

Dad smiled. 'Good question. And one that I've been asking myself over and over these last few weeks. And so has your mother. So we've decided. We're not moving. Not just yet. We're not ready to give up our London lives yet. No. The new plan is that I still go part-time at the hospital and use my days off to enjoy London. We've lived here so long but there's still so much we haven't done. Too busy working! I don't want to go to some quiet place and have nothing to do but potter in a greenhouse all day. Nope. We're staying put. So . . . How do you feel about that?'

I looked over at Nesta, Lucy and Izzie. 'How do I feel?' I gave him a big hug. 'That's how I feel.'

When Mum and Dad went over to get some mulled wine from the refreshments table, I noticed a couple who had just come in to the hall. With them was hubba hubba boy. I wasn't the only one who had seen them either because, as they made their way towards our stand, suddenly Nesta, Lucy and Izzie all appeared beside me.

'Mine,' said Lucy.

'No, mine,' said Izzie.

'Nope, mine, mine, *mine*,' insisted Nesta.

I laughed to see them jostling, when Olivia stepped out to greet the couple. 'Hi Mum, Dad,' she said, then turned to me. 'This is TJ, who's been working on the project with me.'

'Hi,' I said.

Then she turned towards hubba hubba boy. 'And this is my brother, William.'

I felt my jaw fall open.

'Another of your alluring looks,' he said, smiling, as I shut my mouth.

'I have a whole range,' I said, as he moved behind me to join his parents who were looking at Olivia's work. I quickly turned to the girls, who were all standing to the right of the screen. I pointed at the boy.

'Olivia's brother,' I whispered. 'Olivia's brother as in Luke's *best* friend.'

'William?' asked Nesta.

I nodded.

'I heard Luke mention him but we never met,' she said.

The boy turned back and gave Nesta a long look.

'Contest over,' said Lucy. 'No doubt who *he's* interested in here.'

Izzie cracked up laughing. 'William as in Luke's best friend. Cool.' She nudged me to look over at the stage where Luke was sitting with Sian. He looked as if he was going to be sick. He caught my eye and I felt an electric current run through me. There was such a sadness in his eyes as he looked at me and, for a brief moment, I felt a twinge of regret that things hadn't worked out differently. He'd said he thought we had something special. I think we did, but . . . how could I believe him? That's the trouble with liars, you can never know if they're telling the truth or spinning you a line. I made myself look away.

Nesta also glanced over at Luke, then turned back and fluttered her eyelashes in William's direction.

'Hhhmmmm,' she said, smiling at us. 'Luke's best friend. Now *this* could be very interesting.'

Wedding Announcement

On Wednesday, December 24th, Marie Watts
was married to Stuart Callaghan in Bigbury Bay,
Devon. Wedding guests travelled on a sea tractor to
Burgh Island Hotel where they were snowed in for
several days due to unforeseen blizzards.
Bridesmaid TJ Watts (15) said, 'My parents
are delighted. My sister had a white wedding after all!'

*Mates,
Dates &
Great
Escapes

Thanks to Brenda Gardner, Yasemin Uçar and the ever fab team at Piccadilly. Also to Rosemary Bromley at Juvenilia.

And to Steve Lovering for being such a patient listening ear when working out outlines, and for accompanying me to Florence to research the locations in the book (although I don't think he minded too much). Also to Laura Denham for good advice for overcoming fear of flying.

And to Scott Brenman, Edward Jeffrey, Olivia McDonnell, Alice Elwes and Natalie Reeves for giving me the low-down on school trips from a teen's point of view.

And big thanks to all the lovely readers out there who buy the books and send me their letters and e-mails.

Chapter 1

Turning Scarlet

A light above the surgery door flashed on and a few people in the waiting room looked up expectantly.

'Mrs Harper,' called the nurse at the reception desk. 'Go on through.'

A blonde lady who had been sitting next to us got up and made her way through to the surgery.

'Let's get out of here, Lucy,' said Nesta. 'I thought you were joking.'

'Yeah. Seems a bit drastic to me,' said TJ looking about nervously. 'Giving blood is not my idea of a fun way to spend Saturday morning.'

'I know, but hey, drastic situation, drastic measures,' I said. 'And I'm not asking any of you to do it. I think it's a good idea regardless of my problem and why I first suggested coming here. It may save a life.'

Izzie pointed at a poster on the wall. 'Yeah,' she said, 'it's a way of giving something back to the community. Says there that only six per cent of people donate blood.'

Nesta put her hands into the prayer position. 'St Lucy and St Izzie, out to save the world. No way I'm doing it. Can't we just put a quid in the donation box instead?'

We were sitting in the waiting room at the blood donor clinic. I'd seen the poster outside the Tube on the way home from school last night and dragged my mates in here this morning. *Save a Life by Donating Blood*, the poster read. Save my life, I thought as I had a brainwave. It could be the answer to the curse that follows me everywhere I go. Blushing. Giving blood could be the solution. One pint less, one pint less to blush with. The girls thought I'd gone barking mad and laughed their heads off when I told them. I guess it was a bit bonkers to think that it would solve my blushing problem, but I got to thinking that even if it was a daft idea, giving blood can save a life (as the poster said), so no harm done and I'd manage to do a good deed in the bargain.

'And I don't think blushing is a problem,' said TJ. 'I think it's sweet when you turn pink.'

Yeah right, I thought. I know different. It makes me look like a kid and it's embarrassing and a half. I blush so easily at the maddest things. Like if anyone says *any* word with the slightest sexual connotation, I turn purple. Like in biology last Wednesday, we were doing the reproductive behaviour of frogs. Frogs! How unsexy are they? But in the course of the lesson, our teacher, Miss Aspinall, said reproductive organs and, baboom, I turned scarlet. I *hate* it. It's not like I'm a prude or even really embarrassed, but some out of control part of me has decided that if I hear a sexual word or I'm talking to a boy I fancy, blood will flood to my face. It's weird – if I'm in the dark and no one's looking at me, I'm fine. I can hear anything, watch anything, the rudest most disgusting thing, and I know I won't blush, but, if the lights are up or people are looking at me, I turn pink at anything. Of course, my brother Lal is well aware of the fact and uses any excuse to get me going. Like last night he said, 'Pubic hair', turned to me and waited with a great stupid grin on his face. I could have thumped him. Course, I turned red on cue. How pathetic is that? I can't control it. No *way* am I embarrassed by pubic hair. Everybody gets it. But say the words and look me in the eye and off I go. Pink, red, scarlet. Stupid, stupid, stupid.

'Next,' called the nurse at the reception desk.

I stood up and walked towards her.

'Name?' she asked.

'Lucy Lovering.'

'Age?'

'Fourteen. Fifteen in May.'

The nurse peered over her glasses. 'Not old enough,' she said and looked beyond me at the waiting queue. 'Next.'

Not old enough. Story of my life, I thought as I went back to join the others. Nesta, Izzie and TJ. My mates. My mates that are all the same age as me, but look like they're eighteen, whereas I look like I only just crawled out of junior school. Nesta's five foot seven, TJ's five foot seven and Izzie has had a spurt of growing recently and is the tallest of all of us at five foot eight. Me, I've had my own growing spurt too, bringing me up to the grand height of five feet. Woopedoop. Not. It causes no end of trouble, like if we ever want to go and see an adult film. They all sail in, no questions asked at the cinema ticket counter, then they get to me and it's no go. Last time we tried it, Izzie was ahead of me in the queue. 'Can't let your little sister through,' the sales person said to Izzie and everyone in the foyer turned and stared at me. I could have died, and went bright red as usual. Well, my mates might look older than me, taller than me, they might be ahead of the game in many areas, but there's one major part of growing up where I may just pip them all to the post.

Blushing Tips

Wear pale make-up, although this can also make you look ill. *Nesta*

Only go out in the dark (bit limiting, but it is an option). *Lucy*

What you resist persists, so if you stop fighting it and even announce when it's going to happen – 'I'm going to go red' – it will probably go away. *Izzie*

Um. Wear very bright red lipstick; that way when you blush, your face will match your lips. OK. Not my best idea. I dunno. I think it's sweet when people blush. *TJ*

P.S.: Donating blood isn't going to help one bit. *Dr Watts (TJ's mum)*

Chapter 2

Be Prepared

We were back at Izzie's when I brought the subject up. We were up in her bedroom and she was on the internet on her favourite astrology site, downloading our horoscopes for February.

'Hey Nesta, this is true,' said Izzie scanning the print out of Leo. 'Says you're in for some foreign travel.'

'And for you and TJ,' said Nesta. 'Our school trip to Florence.'

'I know. I can't wait,' said Izzie. 'Mum's been plying me with books about the place. She's all for me getting a bit of culture smulture – art galleries, taking in the talent of centuries gone by.'

'I was thinking about a different kind of talent,' said Nesta, 'like all those gorgeous Italian boys. I've been brushing up on my Italian so I'll be able to chat to them in their language.'

'And you could all pass as Italians,' I said. Unlike me with my short blond hair, Nesta, TJ and Izzie have got long dark hair. I could just see them swanning through the streets of Florence, looking cool in big black sunglasses. 'The local boys won't know what's hit them.'

'I thought you'd be through with Italian boys after he who shall not be named,' said Izzie.

Nesta flicked her hair back. 'You mean Luke? He was a minor blip. Not all boys are like him.'

I noticed that TJ looked uncomfortable and was staring at the floor. Luke De Biasi. Love rat extraordinaire and the first boy to almost split us up as friends. He was going out with Nesta, then declared undying passion for TJ, who I think did genuinely fall in love with him. It got a bit messy for a time. Nesta was devastated; TJ was confused as hell. I took sides with Nesta and Izzie took sides with TJ. It was horrible. In the end, we all decided that losing our friendship over a boy, a boy who told lies no less, wasn't worth it and he got dumped. I think it affected TJ more than she lets on though. I think she really thought that Luke was her soulmate. Nesta's not a soulmate kind of girl. She collects boys' hearts like other girls collect handbags. She wants to experience as many as possible she says and, with her stunning exotic looks (she's half-Italian, half-Jamaican), she's never short of admirers.

'What does mine say?' asked TJ.

Izzie looked at the screen. 'Hhmmm. Sagittarius. New horizons will open up to you.'

'It will be my first time in Italy, so I guess that counts as a new horizon,' she said.

Izzie looked at me sympathetically. 'I wish you were coming Luce,' she said.

'Yeah,' said TJ. 'Isn't there any way? I heard there are a couple of places left. Apparently Alice Riley and Georgia Watson have dropped out.'

I shook my head. 'No chance. My family can't afford a bus ride to Scunthorpe at the moment, never mind a trip to Italy. What does my horoscope say, Iz?'

Izzie punched in a few keys and brought up the horoscope for Gemini. 'Oh. Hhmm. Sounds ambiguous. Something you have been considering for a time is about to come to a head and you have to decide which way you want to play it. Dunno. What do you think that means?'

'Tony,' I said.

I've been dating Nesta's older brother on and off for a while now, and lately we've settled into being a proper couple. Regular dates. Regular phone calls. Regular snogging sessions on the sofa when our parents are out. I first saw him crossing the road in Highgate outside his school. Cute, dark, wide gorgeous mouth. It was love at first sight. The reason I wouldn't let things get serious before now was because he always wanted to take things further – further in the sense of from the sitting room and in to the bedroom. I didn't feel ready, plus he may be the love of my life, but I'm not blind. He can get any girl he wants and he likes a challenge. I've been a challenge as I've been fending him off. It wasn't my intention to get so involved at this stage in my life. I wanted to be like Nesta and play the field a bit. I'm not fifteen yet and thought there would be plenty of time for serious relationships later, but you can't help who you fall in love with. Along came Tony and it all started happening. Still is all happening. But he's three years older than me; he wants to sleep with me and he's not going to wait forever.

'What do you mean? Tony?' asked Nesta.

'Well, I do really really like him, so I'm thinking about going to number ten.'

TJ looked up from one of Izzie's books that she had her nose in. 'Number ten?' she asked. 'You're going to see the Prime Minister with Tony?'

I laughed. Sometimes I think TJ is on another planet. 'No, dummy. As in go all the way.'

'All the way? Wow,' said Nesta. 'Woah.'

Izzie turned away from her computer. 'This is a bit sudden,' she said. 'Are you sure?'

'Yes. No. I mean, why not? And it's not really sudden. I've been thinking about it a lot. You have to do it sometime and I've known Tony a long time now and we really do like each other . . .'

'Yeah, but you always said you didn't want to rush things,' said Izzie.

'But we haven't,' I protested. 'We've been going together for ages now. So why not do what he wants? I have to get it over with sometime.'

'Yeah, but with *Tony*?' said Nesta, making a disgusted face.

'And you make it sound like a chore,' said Izzie, 'saying you have to do it sometime. Like it's on a must do list. Must clean bedroom, must do homework, must have sex with boyfriend.'

I sighed. I couldn't deny that it did feel a bit like that. Like an exam looming in the future. I can't say I was looking forward to it that much, as I don't know if I'll be any good at it. It was bad enough worrying if I was an OK kisser, but everybody has to do it sooner or later so why not with someone I like as much as Tony?

'When?' asked TJ.

'I don't know. I haven't totally decided, I mean . . . I haven't even told him that I'm thinking about it.'

'Where?' asked Izzie.

'Where? I don't know. Give me a break. I told you, I haven't decided definitely. I wanted to talk to you guys first.'

'Well I don't think you should,' said Nesta. 'You're not even fifteen yet, and he's eighteen.'

'Yeah, but if she is thinking about it,' said Izzie turning to Nesta, 'she has to be ready. Like she doesn't want her mum finding her and lover boy in the nudie pants on the sitting room sofa. She'd have a fit.'

'Er, excuse me,' I said. 'I am in the room here.'

Izzie turned back to me. 'But seriously, Lucy,' she said. 'Have you really thought this through?'

'Yes and no. The time and the place maybe not, but with love how can you plan it? Surely the right moment will present itself. We'll just know it and if we're in a place where it's OK, then . . .'

Nesta folded her arms. 'No,' she said. 'You're too young.'

Izzie snorted. 'You sound like my mum,' she said, then put on a voice like the queen. 'Lucy Lovering. You're *far* too young.'

'Yeah, but Lucy, you are,' said Nesta. 'I read somewhere that the average age that most people lose their virginity is seventeen.'

'So?' I said. 'Who wants to be average? Anyway, *I* read in one of mum's magazines that a quarter of teenagers have lost their virginity by the time they're fifteen. So there. I think you're just saying I shouldn't because you want to be the first.'

'Am not. I don't want to do it until I've been with someone for ages and I really, really love them.'

'But I do love Tony.'

'I agree with Nesta,' said Izzie. 'Really Luce, you're not old enough. I think you're doing it just to keep him happy.'

I sighed. 'Here we go again. I'm so sick of hearing that, not old enough. It's the story of my life. Not old enough. Not old enough. Why shouldn't I do it? Why not? It's not like I haven't known Tony for ages and why shouldn't I want to make him happy? He does loads of things for me . . .'

'Condoms,' interrupted TJ.

'What about them?' I asked.

'You'll need them if you do it. Have you got any?'

'No. Why?'

'D'oh. Safe sex, dummy, and you need protection from STDs.'

'What are they?' I asked.

'Sexually transmitted diseases,' said TJ. She's our local medical expert. Both her parents are doctors, so she picks up loads of information about diseases and stuff. 'My mum said that loads of people she sees at her surgery who have had unprotected sex get chlamydia.'

'What's chlamydia?' I asked. 'Sounds like a posh girl's name – like Lady Chlamydia Armstrong Wotnot.'

TJ laughed. 'Yeah, but it's not a name. It's a disease which is very common, apparently has few side effects so many people don't even realise that they've got it, but if untreated it can lead to infertility.'

'Chlamydia, condoms, STDs, unwanted pregnancies,' I said. 'What happened to *romance*?'

Nesta sighed. 'See,' she said. 'Head in the clouds.'

'Yeah. You have to be responsible,' said TJ. 'You don't want to get pregnant.'

'Since when did you lot become such . . . such killjoys?' I asked, as the rosy glow around my fantasy began to fade.

'We're not being killjoys,' said Nesta. 'We're your mates. We're looking out for you.'

'Hmf. Feels more like you're ganging up on me.'

'No, we're not,' said Izzie. 'It's just best to be prepared. To know what you're getting into. Tell you what, let's look condoms up on the internet. I'll go into one of the search engines.'

She pressed a few keys and, a moment later, a whole list of website addresses came up. After a few seconds, she started laughing.

'Ohmi*god*! You can get anything and everything on here. Here. Here's the one for you! I'll read it,' said Izzie as she studied her screen. '*Surprise your partner and add a new dimension to your love life with a glow-in-the-dark condom. It will make it a night to remember.*'

We all cracked up. The image of Tony wearing a glow-in-the-dark condom was hysterical.

'There's loads more,' said Izzie as she scrolled down her computer screen. 'Ohmi*god*! I never realised there were so many types!'

'What like, small, medium and liar?' I asked.

'All sorts . . .' Izzie said, laughing, as we crowded round the computer to have a better look.

We were so busy scanning the pages and laughing our heads off at all the types that came up that we didn't notice that the door had opened and Izzie's mum had come in.

'What's so funny?' she asked.

Izzie almost jumped out of her skin.

'*Mum*! I've *told* you to knock!' she said as she quickly closed the site, went back to her desktop and assumed her best innocent look.

As Mrs Foster eyed us suspiciously, I felt myself starting to blush and prayed that it wouldn't give the game away. Mrs Foster can be really intimidating when she wants to be. She's so different to my mum, who is easy-going and looks like an old hippie. Mrs Foster looks like a proper grown-up, always in high heels and immaculate clothes, never a hair out of place.

'What could you possibly be doing that you wouldn't want me to know about?' Mrs Foster asked, lifting her nose to the air and sniffing. 'You haven't been smoking in here, have you?'

'Mum,' groaned Izzie. 'I don't smoke. Won't smoke. Give me a break.'

Mrs Foster shrugged. 'Ah well. I'm going to the supermarket and wanted to know if any of you were here for a late lunch or early supper?'

'No thanks,' chorused Nesta, TJ and I.

'No,' said Izzie, looking pointedly at me. 'We've got some very important window shopping to do.'

'What for?' asked Mrs Foster. 'Italy?'

Izzie tapped the side of her nose. 'Something we learned from the Girl Guides,' she said. 'You know their motto: Be prepared.'

That set us all off laughing again.

Mrs Foster looked mystified. 'Right,' she said. 'Suit yourselves.'

Girl Guides motto: Be prepared.

Chapter 3

The Pros and Cons of Toothpaste

First stop was a pharmacy in East Finchley to get some nail polish remover for Izzie.

'Seriously though,' said TJ, as we made our way up the High Street, 'you do have to think about birth control. You can't expect the boy to take all the responsibility.'

'I guess,' I said. I was still feeling like the girls had put a major dampener on my mood. Part of me could see that they were right – I hadn't really thought it through properly, but another part felt like they just didn't want me to be the first to do something for once.

'I guess it wouldn't hurt to check out what they sell in the chemist's,' I said. 'As you said, be prepared, and I certainly can't buy them off the internet.'

'OK,' said Izzie. 'Where do you want to look? The pharmacists in Cootes are really nice. I'm sure they'll be very helpful.'

'No way,' I said. 'My mum shops there. I can just imagine her popping in for shampoo or something and them letting on that her dear virginal daughter had just been in looking at condoms.'

'There are loads of other chemists,' said TJ. 'There's one right at the end of the High Street. That's usually pretty quiet and we wouldn't want anyone seeing us checking out the selection.'

We made our way up to the last row of shops and hovered outside the chemist's, pretending that we were looking at the window display, that is until Izzie pointed out that we were all staring at a promotion advertising ointment for piles.

'Hhhmmm. Fascinating, not,' she said.

'Nesta, please will you go in and check them out for me?' I asked. 'The shop assistant will take one look at me and come out with the you're-not-old-enough line.'

'But you're not buying any,' said Izzie.

'Even so,' I said. 'I can't bear to hear that you're-not-old-enough line once more, and you do look the most grown-up out of all of us.'

'Sure I'll look for you,' said Nesta. 'I'll pretend that I'm a character in a film and I'm about to go away with my lover on a romantic weekend to Paris.'

'Whatever,' I said. I was used to Nesta acting out scenes from films in her head. She wants to be an actress when she leaves school and believes in practising at every given moment. 'The rest of us can come in with you and look at the make-up or something.'

We shuffled our way into the shop and, while the assistant was serving a customer, we scoured the shelves.

'Over there,' said Izzie after a few minutes, 'to the left of the cash till.'

We waited until the customer left and the shop became empty, then Nesta straightened herself up as tall as she could and walked over to the cash till. She looked at the condoms on display, then came over to us at the other side of the shop.

'They have all sorts: gossamer, extra lubricated, extra safe, ribbed, sheer . . .'

I pulled a face. 'They sound horrible. Like old ladies' tights.'

'And they come in packs of three or twelve.'

I felt myself turning pink. '*Twelve?* Gimme a break. I wonder how much they cost. The three-pack, I mean. They've probably got a price written on them or you could ask the assistant.'

'OK,' said Nesta and made her way back to the counter. She was just about to pick up a pack, when the shop door bell binged to indicate another customer had come in. Nesta's face was a picture. Her jaw fell open when she saw who the customer was and she quickly withdrew her hand from the condoms. At the back of the shop, Izzie, TJ and I darted behind a large display of spectacles and sunglasses.

'Mrs *Allen!*' said Nesta, putting on a big cheesy grin. 'What a lovely surprise. Um, er, yes, menthol or whitener? It's always such a hard decision, don't you think?'

She picked up a tube of toothpaste and held it in front of our headmistress's face. Mrs Allen looked at her quizzically.

'Yes, Nesta, I suppose it is,' she said, picking up a packet of aspirin. 'Now while you debate the pros and cons of toothpaste, do you mind if I go ahead of you? I'm in a bit of a hurry.'

'Oh no, I mean, yes, please, go ahead,' stuttered Nesta, losing her cool for a moment and glancing back at us. 'I've got to get a few things.'

She raced back to our side of the shop and looked mystified when she couldn't see us.

Mrs Allen paid for her purchases and headed for the door. 'Behind the spectacle counter,' she said whilst looking straight ahead.

'What? Who?' asked Nesta, trying her best to look wide-eyed and innocent.

'Your mates,' said Mrs Allen. 'Lucy Lovering, Izzie Foster and Theresa Watts. For some reason, they're cowering behind the sunglasses stand.'

Nesta turned and looked in the direction of the spectacle display. Izzie, who had put on a large, black pair of sunglasses, poked her head out and gave Mrs Allen a half-hearted wave as she went out of the door.

'I swear she didn't even glance in our direction,' said Izzie as Nesta raced over to join us. 'It must be a job requirement for being a headmistress. Eyes in the back of your head.'

Nesta went and peered out of the window and down the High Street. 'She's gone into the hairdresser's,' she said. 'Coast clear.'

'Can I help you girls with anything?' called the shop assistant, who by now was eyeing us suspiciously.

'Um, yes. Just getting some make-up remover pads,' Nesta called back.

She was about to make her way back to the counter again when, once more, the door chinked that there was another customer.

'Not our day is it?' said Izzie, as we all darted back behind the spectacle display.

'No,' I said, then indicated the spectacles on sale. 'We can't be seen to make spectacles of ourselves.'

TJ started giggling, then and that set me off, then Izzie.

'Keep it together, you guys,' hushed Nesta.

'Who is it?' I asked. 'Can you see who came in? Best check it's not Mrs Allen back for some eye drops for her extra set of eyes or something.'

Nesta poked her head round the corner of the display. 'Ohmigod, get back,' she said. 'It's Candice Carter.'

'Oh *no*,' I groaned. Candice is a mate in our year, but she's one of the biggest gossips in the school. Tell her anything and it spreads like Asian flu.

'She's probably come in for more of that colour she puts on her hair,' said Izzie. Candice was always experimenting with her hair colour. Lately it had been a bright raspberry red.

'No. No, I don't think so, as the hair colour is at the front of the shop,' said Nesta. 'She's . . . oh, I think she may be buying condoms – she looks pretty nervous. She's looking round to check that no one's watching.'

We all stayed very still while Nesta tried to see what was going on.

'Oh Lord,' she said after a few minutes. 'You'll never guess what she's bought.'

'What?' I asked, as at last the door chinked that Candice had gone.

'A pregnancy test!' said Nesta.

'You're kidding,' said Izzie. 'Candice?'

'Ohmigod,' I said. 'I wonder if she is. Pregnant, that is. She has been going with Elliot, a boy from Wood Green High, for months now. I wonder if they've done it.'

'I'd say most definitely from the look of things,' said Nesta.

We stared at each other in silence for a few moments.

'Girls,' called the shop assistant suddenly appearing round the corner of the display, 'have you made your minds up yet? Do you want to buy something or not?'

Nesta looked at me and raised an eyebrow. 'Lucy?'

'Yes,' I said. 'Um, do you sell chastity belts?'

Position of Headmistress: Only those with
an extra set of eyes need apply.

Chapter 4

Mrs Finkelstein

I was on the Jerry Springer *show, trying to balance my three giant babies on my knees but wasn't succeeding, and one of them kept slipping down on to the floor. I looked terrible. Haggard, pale and spotty with bedraggled, unwashed hair.*

'What are the babies' names?' asked Jerry.

'Nesta, Izzie and TJ,' I sobbed. 'I named them after my mates at school.'

'Even though the babies are boys?' asked Jerry.

I nodded sadly.

'And when exactly did you turn to drink, Lucy?' asked Jerry.

'When the father of my babies deserted me for a Hollywood starlet and left me living in a dustbin,' I whispered and the studio audience gasped in horror.

'Well, tonight, we're going to hear from Tony,' said Jerry. 'He's been waiting backstage to tell his side of the story. Come on out, Tony.'

Tony appeared at the side of the stage and the audience booed loudly. He looked gorgeous, clean, radiant, at his most handsome. I began to hit him round the head with one of the babies, which had now turned into a pillow.

'Lucy,' said Jerry. His voice sounded strange. Feminine. 'Lucy . . .'

'Wha . . .?' I opened my eyes to find Mum leaning over me.

'Come on, love, get a move on. It's time to get up,' she said. 'Bathroom's free.'

'Urggh,' I said from the depths of my duvet. I took a deep breath and willed myself to wake up properly. It took me a moment to realise that I'd been dreaming. It was such a relief to wake up and find myself safe and babyless.

'Lucy, you're miles away,' said Dad at breakfast. 'What's going on in that head of yours?'

'Oh, nothing,' I said, turning pink. I couldn't tell him about my dream. No way.

'It's not possible to think about nothing,' said Steve, my swot-box brainy brother, as he tucked into a slice of toast and peanut butter. 'I've tried. Even if your mind goes blank, you still think the thought, my mind is blank.'

'Whatever,' I said. I pushed away my half-eaten bowl of muesli and got up from the table.

'Aren't you going to finish that?' asked Mum.

I shook my head. 'Not hungry.'

'Then take an apple to school,' said Mum as she went to collect the mail that had just plopped on to the mat in the hall.

Dad looked at me kindly. 'Is something bothering you, Luce? You're very quiet this morning.'

'No, not really, that is, well . . .'

'I knew there was,' said Dad. 'So spill. What is it? You're on drugs, become a compulsive gambler? What?'

'Yeah, right.' I smiled weakly. 'No, er . . . just had a bad dream and . . . there's the school trip next month to Florence. Nesta, TJ and Izzie are going and I wish I was going with them, that's all.' That should put him off asking about my dream, I thought. I have to be careful with Mum and Dad sometimes. Both of them love to analyse dreams and they have a way of getting information out of you before you know it. Mum – because she's a counsellor and works all day getting people who don't want to talk to open up, and Dad – because he's so chilled and unjudgemental. Like Mum, he's a bit of an old hippie with his ponytail and liberal views about everything. This time however, I didn't think he'd be so liberal. Dads can come over all protective of their daughters when it comes to boys. And having triplets.

Mum sighed as she came back in with the mail. 'Did I hear you talking about the Florence trip? I am sorry you can't go with the others, Lucy, but you know how things are at the moment. Steve needs a new winter jacket, Lal needs trainers, the car insurance is due this month, the mortgage payments have just gone up, we've had a ginormous phone bill . . . It's never-ending, so I'm afraid money for school trips is out of the question.'

'I know. That's why I haven't gone on about it.'

'Our school is going on a skiing trip,' said Steve. 'I'd love to do that one of these days, years, lifetimes.'

Dad didn't say anything; he just looked at Mum, rolled his eyes and shrugged his shoulders.

Mum sat down at the head of the table and started to go through the post. 'See,' she said, holding up the wad of envelopes to us, 'nothing but bills, bills, bills.' She put the pile in front of her and sifted through until she came to one that looked like a personal letter. 'Oh, what's this one?' She opened the envelope and read. 'Oh dear,' she said after a few moments.

Dad got up and looked over her shoulder. 'What is it, love?'

Mum glanced anxiously at Lal. 'Mrs Finkelstein.'

'What?' said Lal, as Dad read the letter, then also looked in his direction. 'Whatever it is, I didn't do it.'

'It's from Mrs Finkelstein's solicitor,' said Dad.

Lal went white. 'But . . . but . . . it was *ages* ago that I broke her window. Last year. And I went and apologised. Even paid for it out of my pocket money. Remember?'

Everyone knew Mrs Finkelstein. And her house. She'd lived in the large detached one at the end of our street as far back as I could remember. It was a dingy, spooky-looking place, straight out of a horror film, with an overgrown garden at the front and shabby curtains at the windows. Curtains that never opened. She never had visitors. In all the time I'd lived in this area, I'd never seen anyone, except for her cat, go in or come out. When I was in junior school, Izzie and I used to think her house was haunted and that Mrs Finkelstein was a witch. Instead of taking the short cut to school through the alley to the right of her house, we used to walk the longer way to avoid passing in case she came out and put a spell on us and we were never seen again. I used to have nightmares about her. She was almost bald and always dressed in a faded black coat and her slippers, and pushed a battered old pram. One day, Izzie and I decided to be brave and made ourselves walk close so that we could see what was in the pram. It was full of old newspapers. Sometimes you'd see her in the shopping area shuffling around, putting discarded papers in the pram. Weird. As I grew older, I realised that she was a harmless eccentric and she didn't scare me so much. Even so, I kept out of her way if I saw her approaching on the same side of the pavement as me.

'So what does her solicitor want?' asked Steve.

'He doesn't say,' said Mum. 'Just that Lal should be at his offices with one of his parents on Friday.'

'Are you sure you haven't done anything, Lal?' said Dad. 'I won't get angry if you tell us, but we need to know what we're dealing with.'

'No, honest,' said Lal. 'I haven't done anything, *honestly*. I know she's a mad old bat, but I never hassle her. In fact, last time I had anything to do with her was on the High Road. Some kids were laughing at her and calling her names and I chased them off. Remember how she always used to shove old newspapers in the pram she pushed around? Well, after I'd seen the kids off, I gave her a few old papers that were lying on a nearby bench. Weird,

I know, but it was the first time I'd ever seen her smile. After that I never had anything to do with her. Honest.'

'Nothing?' asked Mum. 'Think. Think carefully. Something you've forgotten?'

Lal was quiet for a few minutes. 'No. I saw her around, but that was the last exchange we had, if you can call it that. I do talk to her cat though. I always stop to talk to him when I pass her house. He likes to sit on the wall in front and is always up for a tickle under his chin. He's a sweet old boy, blind in one eye with a gammy leg. I feel sorry for him.'

Dad took the letter from Mum, folded it and stuck it behind the clock on the dresser. 'Maybe something's happened to her cat,' said Dad. 'And she's seen you talking to it and, oh I don't know, thought you might have had something to do with it. Who knows what goes on in her mind. Look, don't worry, Lal. Whatever it is she thinks you've done or haven't done, we'll deal with it on Friday. I know what these old timers can be like sometimes. They get an idea into their head about someone and there's nothing you can do to dissuade them. Maybe some other lad has been messing around and upset her. Whatever, we'll put it straight.'

He meant to be reassuring, but Lal looked worried. Clearly I wasn't the only one in our neighbourhood who'd been spooked by Mrs Finkelstein in the past. As I watched him sweat, I wondered if, like me with my mad dream, there was something that he was keeping to himself.

Chapter 5

Candice

News about Candice was all around school by break time on Monday. Candice had told her mate, Jade Wilcocks, who had told Mary O'Connor, who had told Mo Harrison, who told Izzie, who told Nesta and TJ, who told me.

'Apparently she's ten weeks gone already,' said Izzie, as we made our way to the cloakroom.

'Oh God, poor thing,' I said. 'I wonder what she's going to do.'

We didn't have to wait long to find out as she was huddled in the corner of the cloakroom surrounded by her mates. Her eyes were the colour of her hair, red, as she looked like she'd been crying.

Nesta went straight over to her and gave her a hug. 'Hey, Candice. You OK?'

Candice shook her head and looked at the floor. 'I suppose you've heard the news?'

Nesta, TJ, Izzie and I nodded.

'Is there anything we can do?' asked Izzie.

Candice sighed. 'Wave a magic wand and turn back time a few months.'

'What are you going to do?' asked Nesta.

'Nesta!' I said as Candice began to sob. Nesta was never one for subtle questioning.

'I don't know,' she sighed. 'I don't know. What would you do?'

'Well, do your parents know? What do they think?' asked Nesta.

'No,' wailed Candice. 'I haven't told them yet. I mean, what do you say? I got a B in English and oh . . . by the way, I'm having a baby.'

'Yeah. Tough call,' said Nesta, 'but you're going to have to tell them sometime.'

'Not necessarily,' said Mary O'Connor. 'She could always . . . you know . . .'

'Have an abortion, you mean?' asked Nesta.

'That's what I'd do,' said Mo. 'That way no one need ever know about it.'

At this, Candice broke down and started crying properly. 'How can I decide something like that? How can I? I don't know if I could do it. Oh God, my life is *over*. What am I going to do? I *can't* have a baby. I'm only fifteen. I can't believe this is happening. I want to go to college. How am I going to do that with a baby? I won't even be able to get a job.'

'I guess it's a bit late for the Morning-After Pill,' said Izzie.

'Yeah, like ten weeks too late,' groaned Candice. 'You have to take it within seventy-two hours after . . . you know . . .'

'That's what I'd have done,' said Mary. 'I'd have been straight down the birth control clinic and got that pill in time.'

'You could have the baby adopted,' said Jade Wilcocks, 'then you could go to college.'

Candice sniffed. 'But I'd still have to give birth. And it would *hurt*! And everyone would know and say things about me behind my back. Do you think abortion is bad?'

'God, I don't know,' I said. 'I mean, people have them all the time . . . for all sort of reasons.'

'And who can say what's bad or not?' said Izzie. 'I mean, people use all sorts of birth control. If you're going to be really philosophical, you could say that that prevents a baby even having a chance. I don't know. It's a real biggie. I wish God had e-mail sometimes and we could ask him about this sort of thing.'

'My parents are totally against it,' said Mo, 'but I think that it is an option. I mean, if you're not ready to have a baby and you have no support system set up to look after it, why not? Babies cost money and if you're not able to look after it and you don't really want it, then that's not very kind to the baby, is it? So why have it?'

'Does Elliot know?' asked Izzie.

Candice sighed. 'Yes, he knows.'

She looked so sad, drained. I felt really sorry for her. This wasn't the Candice we all knew, always up for a laugh, life and soul of any party.

'But how did it happen?' asked Nesta.

'Duh. We had sex, dummy.'

'Yeah, but didn't you use anything?' Nesta persisted.

Candice nodded. 'Yes. Yes we did. But safe sex isn't always so safe. I think that maybe he didn't put it on in time. I don't know. I don't really know how it happened. We thought we were being so careful. We *were* careful. I bet you all think I'm totally stupid.'

'No way,' said TJ. 'I was a surprise baby. And my parents are both doctors. You'd think if anyone knew all about contraception, it would be them. These things happen.'

'Yeah,' said Izzie. 'It could happen to anyone.'

'Not if you don't have sex,' said Candice. 'Now I wish I hadn't.'

'Was it the first time?' asked TJ.

'No. We'd done it before a couple of times. I don't know what went wrong this time.'

'What does Elliot say?' asked TJ.

Candice leaned over the sink and looked at her face in the mirror. She began to dab her eyes with cold water. 'God, I look a state.' She turned to look at TJ. 'Elliot says it's up to me. It's my decision. He says he'll stand by me whatever I decide, but I don't know if I want to be with him for the rest of my life. But what's the option – be a single mum? I don't know if I could do that either. It's not something you really think about when you're only dating. But what if I do decide to have it and we stay together? How long is he going to hang around? He's only sixteen. If I have the baby, I'll have ruined his life as well. How are we going to pay for it? I don't know. Oh God, I just don't know.' Her eyes started to well up with tears again.

'It might not be so bad,' said Nesta, reaching out and taking Candice's hand. 'Hey, come on. Your parents might be brilliant about it. They might help out and it might turn out to be the best thing that ever happened to you.'

'You don't know my dad,' wailed Candice. 'He'll kill Elliot. He'll kill *me*.'

Nesta squeezed her hand. 'No, he won't. Course he won't. Come on, worst thing he can do is ground you.' She attempted a smile and Candice tried to smile back but couldn't hold it.

Poor, poor Candice, I thought, as I watched her sobbing into the sink. I'd hate to be in her shoes. For me, having babies had only been a dream. For Candice, it was a reality.

Chapter 6

Role Playing

On Thursday night I had a date with Tony. Not a going-out date, I was going over to his parents' flat and we had planned to watch a DVD and chill out. He knew that I was gutted about not being able to go to Italy with the others, so he said he'd get the movie called *A Room With a View*. Some of it is set in Florence and he said he wanted to get it for me so that I wouldn't miss out altogether. I'd been looking forward to it all week but, by the time Thursday came round, I felt sombre. Preoccupied. I kept thinking about Candice crying at school on Monday. What would I do if I were in her shoes? Probably like her, I'd cry a lot. But then what? Being pregnant wasn't something that went away because you didn't want it to be happening. Candice was going to have to deal with it. And make a decision.

It was lovely to see Tony and to snuggle down in his arms to watch the movie. Nesta had gone out to see a musical in the

West End with her parents so we knew we'd be alone for a few hours. All I wanted to do was cuddle up and forget the world, so I hoped he wasn't going to try anything. I wasn't in the mood.

Tony, on the other hand, was in the mood and seemed more interested in snogging than watching the film. When it had finished, he put on Nesta's chill-out compilation and came to sit next to me on the sofa. He put his arm round me and gave me a long smoochy kiss. A few moments later, one of his hands strayed round to my front. I pushed him away. He carried on kissing me, then tried again. Again I pushed him away.

After a few more tries, he pulled away and sat up. 'OK, so what's up, Luce?'

'I'm sorry, Tony, I just not in the right frame of mind . . .' I said.

He faked shock horror. 'Not in the right frame of mind to make out with me? Hhmmm. Must be losing my touch. Here let me try a more subtle approach.'

He threw me back on the sofa, then dived on top of me, nuzzling into my neck and tickling my waist. 'Not in ze mood huh? Ve have vays of getting you in ze mood.'

I laughed and reached back, grabbed a cushion and hit him over the head. 'And ve have vays of fighting back.'

He sat up, raised an eyebrow and grinned wickedly at me. 'Hhhmm. So you vant to fight do you?'

I stood up, armed with my cushion. 'Try me,' I said. I was pretty good with a cushion. I'd had years of training with my two brothers. 'Choose your weapon.'

Tony grabbed a cushion and we went into a great cushion-bashing fight. After a few minutes, he lay back on the sofa and gasped. 'OK, OK. You win. I surrender. I am your slave. I am at your mercy.'

He pulled me on top of him and began to kiss me again. The pillow fight had dispersed the black cloud that had been hovering over me all week and reminded me of why I liked Tony such a lot. He could always make me laugh so, this time, I responded. Once again, after a few moments, he started with the wandering hands. I let him do it for a while and tried to relax, but I couldn't get the image of Candice out of my mind so, after a while, I pushed him off.

'Oh *Lucy*,' he moaned as he sat up. 'What is it with you? Usually you like us being together like this.'

'I know,' I said. 'I'm just not in the mood tonight.'

Tony sighed. 'So when *are* you going to be? There's nothing wrong with it. We've been going together for ages and you know I hold back a lot as it is.'

I sighed. Just what I didn't want to talk about.

Tony sat up for a moment, then looked at me searchingly. 'I need to know what's going on, Luce. You know I want to sleep with you. How long are you going to make me wait?'

I sat in silence for a while, wondering what to say to make it right. 'Don't know,' I said finally.

'Don't know. What's that supposed to mean?'

I felt confused. One part of me wanted to give in to him, another part felt like running away. 'Don't know.'

'Come on, Luce, be reasonable.' He leaned over to me and

snuggled in. 'Give me a break.' Then he sniffed and began to talk in an American accent. 'I'm just a poor lost boy who needs some tender loving care, mam. I've been on the road for many a year now and I'm tired, I'm cold and I'm lonely. What I need is the love of a good woman to restore my faith in mankind.'

We both started to laugh.

'That is a crapola American accent,' I said.

He sat back and grinned up at me. 'Good game though, huh? I saw it on one of those late night sex programmes on TV. They said that in some relationships, it helps to role-play sometimes.'

I rolled my eyes back at him in way of an answer. Tony was always watching stuff like that and reading 'How to be a better lover'-type books. It made me laugh, as he studied them as though he was swotting for a degree in the subject.

He wasn't about to give up. 'Come on, Luce. Let's play that you're a lonely woman out on the prairie and I'm an old experienced cowboy who's been out on the road . . .'

'Who wants to seduce me . . . ?'

'Yeah, you got it!' He smiled.

Nice try, I thought as he sat up and twirled an imaginary moustache.

'How about we play, I'm a very prissy school ma'am,' I said, 'and you're a very naughty boy.'

Tony laughed. 'Yeah. OK. Whatever,' he said. 'As long as I get to seduce you.'

I shook my head and he sighed heavily. I felt mean. It wasn't his fault that I wasn't in the mood for cuddling, never mind having sex. It wasn't him that got Candice pregnant. I decided to try and lighten the atmosphere by making him laugh. I stood up in front of him. 'OK, I've got a role-play for you.' I put one hand on my hip, then bent my other arm and stuck it out at an angle.

He looked bemused. 'Er not sure I get it . . .'

'I'm role-playing. Don't you see? Yoo hoo I'm a teapot.'

Tony cracked up laughing. 'You're bonkers, Lucy Lovering. Hmmm. Yeah. Yoo hoo, I'm a teapot. Yes. Very alluring. Don't think that was one of the examples suggested on the programme, though.'

I sank back on to the sofa and we sat holding hands for a while listening to the music.

After a few moments, Tony turned to me. 'Now, I can't really imagine this for a moment, not unless you're suffering from total brain damage. But . . . are you going off me?'

'No. *No.* Nothing like that,' I reassured him quickly. Even though he'd phrased his question to sound as if he was cool about it, I could tell by his eyes that, behind the bravado, he was feeling insecure and vulnerable. I decided to tell him what was really bothering me. 'This girl at our school has just found out she's pregnant.'

'What's her name?'

'Candice Carter.'

'Wasn't me.'

I punched him. 'I can't stop thinking about her,' I said, 'and what I'd do if it was me. I don't want to end up the same way and, let's be honest, we're definitely heading in that direction.'

Tony sat up and looked at me. 'Just because one girl gets pregnant doesn't mean that you will.'

'I don't want to risk it, Tony.' I snuggled back up to him. 'Why can't we carry on the way we are? Just kissing and cuddling?'

Tony sighed.

'Why not?' I persisted.

He sighed again. 'Because . . . because . . . Oh you know why not.'

'I can't do it, Tony. I'm sorry. I thought I was ready, then . . . well, I'm just not and especially not tonight.'

'Then I don't know if I can carry on like this.'

I sat up. 'Meaning what?'

'Meaning, I don't *want* to carry on like this. It's really difficult. You know I want to take things a stage further and I thought you were into it as well.'

'But . . . oh, Tony, it's not just taking things a stage further. There are risks involved.'

'I've bought condoms,' he said. 'It doesn't have to be a risk.'

'Condoms can split or leak sometimes.'

'I promise I'd be careful.'

Careful, I thought. Just what Candice thought she was being. I shook my head. 'No, sorry Tony, but no. You know I like you more than anyone I've ever met, but I'm not ready. Like, what would you do if I got pregnant?'

'But you won't.'

'You can't guarantee that. What would you do?'

Tony ran his fingers through his hair making it stick up. 'Jeez. I don't know. Don't get heavy about it. We're dating, not starting a family here.'

'But we do have to consider the risks.'

Tony leaned back and chuckled. 'Honest, Luce, I swear that you sound like my mother when you come out with stuff like that.' He began to mimic my voice. 'We have to consider the risks.'

I tried to smile, but it annoyed me that he wasn't taking me seriously. 'I really like you, Tony,' I said. 'You know that don't you?'

'And I like you,' said Tony. 'So why not? It's the most natural thing in the world.'

'Maybe. Yes. Probably. But for one, it's risky and two, it's illegal. You have to be sixteen to have sex legally.'

Tony sat up and took a deep breath. 'I'm eighteen,' he said sadly. 'I'm way legal.'

'I know.'

We sat in silence for a few minutes and the atmosphere felt heavy and uncomfortable. After a while, he reached over and took my hand. 'So what are we going to do?'

'Dunno.'

'How about we take a break for a while, hey?' he asked.

'What do you mean?'

'Well, we've come to the end of the road for us for the time being.'

This wasn't what I wanted to happen. This wasn't what I wanted to hear. 'But why?'

'Because you've just made it very clear that you don't want to go any further with me, so what are we supposed to do? Relationships need to progress and ours isn't doing that. *Can't* do that. We take a step forward, we take a step back. It's not working, Luce, and I'm going out of my mind with frustration.'

I felt numb with disbelief. It was all happening so fast. One minute we're having a pillow fight and cuddling and now . . . he's ending it? It couldn't be happening.

'I don't see why we can't go on as we are,' I said.

He shook his head. 'I don't think I can do that. You and me, well, we've lasted longer than with any other girl I've dated, but I've been holding back for a long time now and I've tried, I've really tried . . .'

'So what are you really saying?'

'Well, actually, you said it first. You're not old enough.'

'I'll be fifteen soon, then sixteen and . . .'

'That's like a year and a bit, Lucy. I can't wait that long. If you're going to make me wait that long, then I'm going to go crazy. We've had a good time, but I feel that if we go on like we have, then we'll start getting at each other. Destroy what we had and that would be a shame because it's been good. I'm sorry, Lucy, but . . .'

'You want to finish?'

He nodded, then sighed. 'It doesn't have to be like this, Luce. I would be really careful. I have done it before.'

'Too much information,' I said, holding up my hand and trying to smile as I said it, but actually I felt like crying. The last thing I wanted to hear about was his other conquests. But then, he was older than me. He had done it before. Maybe it would be OK. Only a few days ago, I'd been seriously considering it, trying to convince myself that there was nobody more perfect to do it with the first time. Then I thought about Candice again. No way, no *way* did I want to be in her shoes.

Tony took my hand and looked at me pleadingly. I felt tears spring to the back of my eyes as I shook my head. We sat in silence again and the atmosphere felt like lead. So much for my great romantic evening, I thought. I couldn't think of anything else to say. There *wasn't* anything else to say. Tony wanted our relationship to progress and it had come to a thundering halt.

'Guess I'd better go, then,' I said.

Tony looked sad, but nodded in agreement. 'I'll walk you home,' he said as he got up.

Nesta called at ten past eleven that night.

'You still awake?' she asked.

'Well, I am now,' I said, sleepily.

'What happened?'

'We broke up.'

'What?! *Why?*'

'I wouldn't go all the way.'

'I'll kill him. Honest, Lucy, I had such a fright. You should have seen me. After what you said the other day about thinking about doing it with Tony, I wondered what you were up to while we were at the theatre. All the lights were off when we got home and no sign of you or Tony. I thought you might be in his room doing the deed. I wanted to give you warning that we were back and ran round switching on lights and the TV, then announcing as loud as I could outside Tony's room that I was going to the bathroom. Mum and Dad thought I was on drugs or something.'

'Had Tony gone to bed?'

'Yeah. I knocked at first in case you were still in there hiding in the wardrobe or something, then, when I realised that you'd gone, I asked where you were. He just muttered, "Gone." When I tried to get more out of him, he told me to go away and shut the door. So, did you really break up?'

'Yeah. We did. The sex thing came up and I decided I wasn't ready.'

'Because of Candice?'

'Sort of. Partly. Plus . . . I don't know, I'd been thinking about it a lot over the last few days. I know not everyone gets pregnant and I know loads of other girls at our school have done it, but I wasn't sure I wanted to be one of them. It all began to feel so complicated and *serious*. I wasn't at all sure what I was feeling and why I was considering going ahead with him. Was it because I was feeling pressured or because I wanted to do it? Plus all the birth control, STD stuff to think about. I don't know, Nesta. No way am I ready for all that.'

'So you're still a virgin?'

'Pure as.'

'Are you OK?'

'Yeah. I will be.'

'I think he's a total creep dumping you because you won't put out.'

'No. It wasn't just that. It really wasn't. He's probably right. He's eighteen. I can't blame him for wanting to take things further. It's more like . . . I don't know, bad timing. He wanted one thing for us, I wanted something else. It wasn't working any more. I'll be OK. It's not like he dumped me because he was bored and had gone off me. To tell you the truth, he looked gutted.'

'I still want to kill him.'

'Look, I want to go to sleep now. See you in school tomorrow.'

'OK. Night.'

Actually, I didn't want to go to sleep. I wanted to think about what had happened. It felt weird. I wasn't sure how I felt. Sad of course, but another part of me felt relieved, like I'd had a close escape. Tony and I had been going with each other on-off for over a year and the sex thing was always at the back of everything, like an unspoken pressure. As Izzie said, a chore on my must-do list. I felt relieved that, for the first time in ages, I had a reprieve. I didn't have to think about any of it for a while – no condoms, no contraception, no planning the right time or place. As I snuggled down in my duvet, I decided I wouldn't be all freaked out about it, like oh, I've been dumped. I've been dumped, poor me. I would move on. I would be positive. Make a new start. All the same, it felt strange. Life without Tony. I was a singleton again.

I got out of bed, got down on my knees and rooted round at the bottom of my wardrobe to find Mr Mackety, my old teddy bear.

'It's you and me again, pal,' I said, as I found him, then got back into bed with him for a cuddle.

Comforts for the Newly Single

Chocolate
Ice cream
Comedy movies
Getting out your old teddy bear
Mates

Chapter 7

Lal and the Lawyer

'I put salt in his coffee this morning,' said Nesta on the way into assembly the next morning. 'You should have seen his face. Served him right.'

'Yeah,' said Izzie. 'And you could sew a few fresh prawns into his duvet and wait for them to go off. He'll be looking everywhere for the smell.'

I laughed, but I didn't think Tony deserved that. I still liked him and he had looked upset at us breaking up. I didn't want him to suffer. 'Give him a break, Nesta. He was being honest, that's all.'

TJ linked her arm through mine. 'Not all boys are like that. You got to move on, Luce. Find a boy who isn't only after one thing.'

'Do they exist?' I asked.

'Yeah. Course,' said Izzie. 'Loads of them.' She didn't look convinced, however.

'Yeah. Boys will be queuing up for you,' said TJ.

I didn't care. I didn't want another boy or another relationship. In fact, I wondered if I'd made a huge mistake last night. Tony must have thought I was such a baby. And pretending to be a teapot? How mad was that? What had I been thinking of? I felt empty. An empty teapot. What if I never found another boy I liked as much? What if I did find a boy and he turned out to be the same as Tony and I was destined to play out the same scene with the wandering hands over and over again? Were all boys only after one thing? And what if Tony started dating soon and I had to hear about it from Nesta? How would it be when I saw him round at her house? As TJ, Nesta and Izzie tried to make me laugh by coming up with more and more outrageous ways of making Tony's life miserable, I found I couldn't join in. I didn't want to talk about him any more.

'From now on, I declare this a Tony-free zone,' I said. 'Let's talk about something else apart from boys, boys, boys.'

Big mistake, I thought, as they all started chatting about their forthcoming trip to Florence. What they were going to take? What outfits? The galleries and museums that they'd be visiting. I couldn't help but feel envious. I so wished I was going with them, but I knew that there was no way. Sometimes life sucks, I thought. They're all going to be off in Italy and I'm going to be home alone with a stuffed toy, watching holiday programmes and wishing I was there.

After school, I raced home as fast as I could as I wanted to make a treat for Lal when he got back. It was the day that he and Mum were going to see Mrs Finkelstein's solicitor and I was worried about what might have happened. I wanted to have something special waiting for him to cheer him up in case it was bad news. I decided to make him his favourite – cheese and tuna melt with a dash of chilli sauce.

I hadn't been back long and had just let the dogs out into the garden when I heard keys in the front door.

'How did it go?' I asked, going out to the hall.

Lal looked at the floor and sighed. 'Bad,' he said. 'Really bad. I have to go to court next week and maybe have to go to prison. The solicitor said I might get five years!'

'What!' I gasped. 'But *why*? What did you do?'

Lal sank on to the stairs and put his head in his hands. 'It's *too* awful.'

Mum slapped Lal lightly over the head. 'You stop that. No, he's not going to prison, Lucy. Nothing like it. He's winding you up. But there is news. Some bad, some good. Is your dad home? And Steve?'

I nodded. 'Dad's out the back in the garage and Steve's in his room. Why? What's happening?'

'Call Steve down, will you, Lucy?' asked Mum as she took her coat off. 'And I'll get your dad. Lal and I have got something to tell you.'

What on earth could it be? I wondered, as I took the stairs two at a time to get Steve.

Five minutes later, we were all gathered around the kitchen table. Even Ben and Jerry had sensed that something was going on and scraped at the back door to come in from the garden. Steve got up to let them in and Ben ran in and came to sit with his head resting on my knees while Jerry took his place next to him, his head resting on Lal's.

'Right,' said Mum. 'Everyone's here. Anyone want a cuppa tea and a bicky before we tell you? I'm famished.'

'*Mum*,' I groaned. 'If you wait another second, I swear I'm going to explode. What's happened?'

Mum looked round at all of us. 'What do you want first? The good or the bad news?'

'Bad news,' said Dad. 'Let's get that over with.'

'OK,' said Mum. 'The bad news is that Mrs Finkelstein died just after Christmas.'

Lal couldn't contain himself any longer. 'And the good news is that she left *me* some money.'

'How much money?' asked Steve.

Lal beamed back at him. 'Rather a lot, actually.'

'Yes. But there is a condition,' said Mum.

After about five minutes, I was wrestling Steve for the phone. Both of us wanted to phone round and tell our mates the good news. He won so I raced upstairs to use my mobile. I couldn't wait to tell Nesta, Izzie and TJ.

'How much?' gasped Izzie.

'Fifty grand. Yeah. I know. Amazing isn't it? It's like winning the lottery.'

'And it's from Mrs Finkelstein? I can hardly believe it.

Remember when we used to think she was a witch?'

'More like a good fairy it turns out. Apparently she was totally loaded. Like mega doshed up. She left most of her money to a cat charity, apart from this one bit to Lal. I'm so happy I could dance.'

'Yeah, but she left it to Lal.'

'I know. But on the way home, he had a chat with Mum and later Dad said it was OK as well. He wants to give every member of our family two grand each as a special pressie. The rest Mum and Dad want him to put in a savings account to see him through college. That's going to be brilliant as well, as Mum and Dad have been trying to put money by ready for when we all go to uni or college or whatever and I don't think they've managed to save much at all.'

'So what are you going to do with yours? Savings account?'

'Some,' I replied, 'but isn't it obvious what I'm going to do with the rest?'

'Hire a killer for Tony?'

'No, dummy. Think.'

'Oh yeah! Course! Florence.'

'Yessss! And I know that those spare places are still going as I heard Miss Watkins telling someone this afternoon.'

'*Brilliant*. Oh Lucy, that will be so top. It wouldn't have been the same going without you. Now our whole gang will be there.'

'I'm going to phone TJ now and tell her. Will you phone Nesta for me? I don't want to risk Tony answering. I'm not ready to play out that scene yet.'

'Yeah, course.'

Next I called TJ. Like Izzie, she was over the moon when I told her the news and realised that I could go to Italy with them.

'So what's the condition on Lal getting the money?'

'He has to look after Mrs Finkelstein's cat. It's so funny as we were all worried that Lal'd done something to upset her when, all along, she'd put him in her will. Dunno how Ben and Jerry are going to feel about having an old cat around but, hey, no one's going to say no to fifty grand are they? We'll get them some luxury dog food or something to soften the blow.'

'But why did she leave it to Lal?'

'He used to talk to her cat on his way home from school sometimes. She must have seen him and clocked it. Lal's a real softie on the quiet you know, especially where animals are concerned. He buys dog food with his pocket money sometimes and leaves it out for the fox. Since we got wheelie bins in our neighbourhood, Lal has been worried that foxie couldn't get leftovers from the rubbish any more. But Florence, I'm coming to Florence. It's amazing, isn't it?'

'Totally,' said TJ. 'Just shows that you never know what's round the next corner.'

'But we do this time. Florence!'

Life *is* full of surprises, I thought after she'd hung up. Only this morning, I'd thought there was no way, no how I could go on the school trip and now, not even twenty-four hours later, everything's changed. Not only can I go, but I'll have some spending money as well. Perfect, perfect way to get over Tony. *Viva*, I'm off to sunny . . . um, . . . Italy, *viva* um, *Italia*.

Revenge Ideas

Sewing fresh prawns into his duvet. *Nesta*

Sewing up the ankles of his trousers. *TJ*

Tie his shoelaces together. *Lucy*

I don't think revenge is good for the soul. Forgiveness is better. But then, if I was pushed for a suggestion, I reckon you can't beat getting hold of his mobile phone, then phoning the automatic time in Hong Kong. *Izzie*

Chapter 8

Take-off

'Passport?' asked Nesta.

'Check,' chorused Izzie, TJ and I.

'Lip-gloss.'

'Check,' we chorused again.

'Condoms.'

I hit Nesta over the head. 'No, definitely not. No condoms. I don't want to see them, hear about them or think about them for some considerable time. Or boys for that matter. Time off. I'm having a holiday from all that stuff.'

Nesta pulled a face. 'Yeah sure, until you meet some cutenik on the plane . . .'

'Nope. I'm serious. Not interested.'

I looked out of the coach window at the dark February morning. I didn't care that it was wet and gloomy or an unearthly time to be up on a Saturday. I didn't care that we were stuck in traffic. We were on the M4 heading for Heathrow airport. On our way. I felt so excited. I'd hardly slept a wink last night thinking about it. Italy. It was actually happening. A whole week in Florence with my mates. OK, so our teachers, Mrs Elwes and Mr Johnson, and twenty-one other pupils were with us, but that didn't matter. A week without school, sharing a room with TJ, Izzie and Nesta. Bliss. I'd never been to Europe before. I'd never even been on a plane before, as our family usually took holidays in England in Devon or on the south coast somewhere. This was to be my first time abroad. As we turned off the motorway on to the exit for the airport, I heard a roar to my left: a plane was taking off, up, up and over the cars on the motorway and into the sky.

And then it hit me. In about two hours, I would be on one of those great metal contraptions. Strapped into a seat. My first time. I made myself breathe. I can't do it, I thought as I felt myself go hot, then cold. I can't. It's not natural. I mean, how does a thing that size and that weight even get off the ground? Suddenly the floodgates in my head opened and every bad news story about planes from the past five years decided to replay in my head. Oh not now, not now *please*, I told myself. No. I'm cool. I *must* be cool. The others will think I'm a big scaredypants if I suddenly announce that I'm frightened of flying.

'You OK, Luce?' asked TJ. 'You've gone kind of quiet.'

'Um, yeah. Just thinking . . .'

'Aren't you excited?'

'Yeah. Yeah. Course, I will be when we get there, but . . . but

I've never flown before and . . .'

'Piece of cake,' said Nesta. 'No worries. Lovely, up in the air and the clouds beneath you. Fab.'

'How high up exactly?' I asked.

'About thirty-five thousand feet.'

I felt myself shiver. Oh dear, that's high, I thought. And once you're in and up, no chance of getting out. It's not like the Tube or the bus where you can get off at the next stop if you feel wobbly.

TJ reached over and put her hand on mine. 'Don't worry,' she said. 'I used to be scared of flying, but statistics show that it's safer than crossing the road. I read that somewhere. The journey's only a few hours. We'll be there before you know it.'

I attempted a weak smile back. 'Hope so,' I said.

The airport was heaving with people of every age, shape and nationality. Some irate and in a hurry, some looking apprehensive like me, others stretched wearily over chairs checking the monitor about delayed flights, others aimlessly wandering about clutching their hand luggage and waiting for their flight call. People eating, drinking, shopping, changing money, spending. I'm glad I'm travelling with a group, I thought, as Mrs Elwes led us to the check-in desk. The number of people travelling was overwhelming. I think I'd have found it all too much on my own.

At the check-in, an old couple were causing a commotion, as they didn't seem to know what they were doing or where they should be.

'What airline are you flying with?' asked the flight attendant behind the desk.

'Pardon?' the old lady shouted. 'You'll have to speak up, I'm a bit deaf.'

'Airline?' repeated the flight attendant. The old lady looked confused so the flight attendant raised her voice. 'WHO ARE YOU FLYING WITH?'

At this the old lady smiled and pointed to an even more ancient looking man with her. 'UNCLE BERNARD,' she shouted back.

I got the giggles and Mrs Elwes turned round and frowned at me. Luckily, the old couple finally realised what the flight attendant was really asking and soon our group was checked in, our luggage labelled and sailing away on a conveyer belt.

After that, it was through Passport Control and security where Mr Johnson was stopped and searched. At the sight of the young female security officer feeling up and down our bald and bespectacled teacher's trouser legs, our whole group started giggling.

'Probably the most fun he's had in years,' whispered Nesta.

'I hope you girls are going to behave on this trip,' said Mrs Elwes, trying to shush us up by waving her hands, but I could see that she was having a hard time not cracking up as well.

We nodded back at her. 'Best behaviour, promise,' said Nesta.

'Right then,' she said, once the last of us was through and had collected our hand luggage. 'We have some time before departure, so you can have a wander if you like. You can either meet Mr Johnson or myself here in half an hour precisely or listen out for any announcements saying that our flight is ready for boarding and make your own way. If for any reason anyone gets lost, check the monitors and make your way to the departure gate posted. In *plenty* of time. You're Year Ten so I expect you to act like responsible adults. Never forget that we're travelling as a school and we represent that school. Understood?'

The twenty-five of us nodded, then took off in various directions to explore the shops. We knew what to do when the time came to board. Mrs Elwes had been over it all enough times in class, plus she'd handed out leaflets on the coach about procedure.

The departure area was brightly lit with shops and cafés and took my mind off flying for a while. We tried on perfumes in Duty Free, dabbled with make-up samples, bought mags in WH Smith, explored the bookshops, tried on jewellery in Accessorize, mooched about in the clothes shops, had Cokes and before we knew it an hour had passed.

'Oh Lord,' said Nesta, as she checked her watch, then glanced up at the monitor.

'Oh poo,' said Izzie. 'Our flight started boarding ten minutes ago.'

'Will the following passengers please go to Gate Number 12,' came an announcement over the intercom, 'where their flight to Florence is ready to depart. Isobel Foster, Theresa Watts, Nesta Williams and Lucy Lovering.'

'Ohmigod, that's us,' said TJ. 'Oh crapola and a half.'

She began to run to a passage where there was a sign saying

which gates were where and we raced after her at top speed. The sign also said that some gates were five minutes away, some ten minutes and some twenty. Of course, Gate 12 was one of the last.

'I don't think we're going to make it,' panted TJ, as we pelted along the tunnel almost knocking over passengers coming the other way.

'We have to,' said Nesta. 'We can't get this far . . .'

'Mrs Elwes is going to kill us,' said TJ.

'What's she going to do?' I asked as I ran along side her. 'Tell us we're grounded when we're thirty-five thousand feet up in the air.'

Izzie started laughing and had to stop and hold her sides. '*Don't* make me laugh when I'm running a marathon.'

After a breathtaking sprint down long corridors, in the distance, I spotted a familiar tall blonde woman.

'I can see Mrs Elwes,' I called over my shoulder and at last we were there. We hurtled into the small seating area by the Gate as the last passengers were making their way into the tunnel leading to the plane. Mr Johnson was pacing up and down by the desk and looking at his watch.

'Sorry, sir,' said Nesta, as she raced up to him and used the excuse guaranteed to work with most male teachers. 'Er . . . girls' thing, period problem . . . Had to get last minute supplies . . . I can explain . . .'

Mr Johnson immediately looked at the floor and waved us ahead of him. 'Right. Right. No need to explain. Um. Carry on.'

'Yes, sir, sorry,' said Izzie as she overtook him.

'You girls will be the death of me,' he said, shaking his head and mumbling as he followed us on to the plane. 'I don't know why I got talked into this trip. Madness. I should be going to Scotland for a bit of quiet fishing. On my own. Yes, madness, madness to have agreed.'

Once on the plane, he settled down and put his newspaper over his head and Nesta found our seats on the left-hand side of the cabin at the back.

'He's just stopped smoking,' said Mo Harrison as she shoved her coat into the overhead compartment. 'Best keep out of his way for a few days.'

'Do you want to sit in the window seat or aisle?' asked TJ pointing at the seats in front of Nesta and Izzie. 'You choose as it's your first flight.'

'Oh, sit at the window,' said Nesta, 'then you can look out.'

I did as she said, but I wasn't sure about it. Once on board, my panic had returned. The inside of the aeroplane looked too small to have so many people tightly packed in. It felt airless and I felt suffocated. I just wanted to get the whole thing over with.

As soon as everyone was seated, the plane began to taxi along the runway and a female voice on an intercom welcomed us aboard.

'OK, Luce?' asked TJ.

I nodded and gripped the sides of my seat.

'Eyes right,' Nesta whispered from behind us. 'Looks like we're not the only school doing a trip to Florence.'

I glanced over to my right and sure enough there was another group. Boys. About twenty of them and, as we were eyeing them, they were eyeing us back. They looked well pleased to have spotted a group from an all girls' school on their journey.

'Let the holiday commence,' said Nesta.

'In case of emergency . . .' continued the female voice over the intercom as the flight attendants went into the safety procedure at the top of each aisle.

One dark-haired boy with a cheeky face, who was sitting opposite us, introduced himself as Liam and took it upon himself to give a running commentary along with the voice-over. He leaned over to us. 'What she's saying in short is, we crash, you die.'

'Oh thanks a lot,' I said, but TJ laughed.

Later when the flight attendant gave instructions as to what to do if we went down over water, Liam leaned over again.

'The light is to attract any sailors, as in "Hello, sailor" and the whistle is to attract the attention of any passing sharks.'

TJ laughed again and they got chatting. I, in the meantime, was having a religious moment and had decided to appeal to higher powers. Dear God or whoever's up there and whatever you like to be called, I prayed, please let this plane go up and down without any problems. I know I probably could have been a better person and prayed more often, but I promise that if only you let this plane take off, and land, and fly, I will be positively saintly and do no end of good deeds.

mous thrust and roar from the engines and we were
r. I gripped my seat tighter. I glanced out of the
window. Big mistake as landmarks beneath us began to look
smaller and smaller, and in minutes it was like looking out over
a toy town as the houses and cars became dots as we took off
into the sky. Suddenly we hit cloud and I couldn't see anything.

'Ohmigod, we're going to crash,' I gasped, clutching TJ's arm.
'The pilot won't be able to see. What if there's another plane in
the sky? He won't be able to see it.'

'They fly by their instruments,' said TJ. 'Don't worry. All other
traffic will show up on his monitors.'

'I don't like it,' I said and shut my eyes tight, then opened
them again.

Unluckily, Liam noticed and, as soon as the announcement
came on saying that we could undo our seat belts, he came over
with his mate and leaned over our seats.

'Your mate chicken, then?' Liam asked TJ.

'Chicken!' chortled Nesta behind us. 'I'd stay away from her
if I were you, sonny. Don't let her hear you saying things like
that. It can get her mad and that's not a pretty sight. She may be
small, but she's lethal. Think *Charlie's Angels*. Think *Kill Bill* . . .'

Think *Winnie-the-Pooh*, I thought, but I didn't like to
interrupt her when she was on a roll.

'In fact,' she continued, 'we're on our way to an anger
management convention to see if they can help her. We had to
sedate her for the flight in case she took a dislike to anyone on
board. So take my advice and push off.'

As soon as Liam's mate clocked Nesta, his eyes lit up. 'Now this flight is getting interesting,' he said and moved down the aisle to chat to her.

'Some boys just can't take a hint, can they?' asked TJ, glancing over her shoulder.

Izzie leaned forward from behind us and handed me a small bottle. 'Here's some Bach Flower Remedy,' she said. 'Put a few drops under your tongue.'

'Thanks,' I said.

'What's it for?' asked TJ.

'Anxiety,' whispered Izzie. 'It helps people chill. It's totally natural. It's from Lucy's dad's shop.'

I took the bottle and dropped a little on to my tongue. I'd seen it on the shelves at the shop but never tried it before. It tasted of alcohol.

'See,' said Nesta in a loud voice. 'I *told* you we had to sedate her. Something's upset her and we're having to up her medication.'

I felt myself turning bright red as all the boys in the middle aisle turned and stared at me with my bottle of Bach Flower Remedy.

Suddenly the plane took another lurch upwards and my stomach went with it.

'It's going to be OK,' said TJ as I clutched her arm again. 'Listen. You have to trust that the pilot knows what he's doing. He's trained. Millions of planes take off every day all over the world without incident . . .'

I put my fingers in my ears. 'Don't like it . . .'

'Those noises are good. It means that the plane is doing what it's meant to do,' said TJ. 'If you understood the mechanics of it, you wouldn't be scared at all. It's only because you don't that you're frightened but, honestly, there's nothing to worry about.'

'Have some more Bach Flower Remedy,' said Izzie. 'And if that doesn't work I've got some lavender essential oil that you can dab on your forehead to relax you.'

'Nah. Forget that New-Age mumbo jumbo,' said Nesta. 'Check out the boys. Nothing like a cute boy to distract the mind.'

I decided to do as Nesta instructed and glanced over at the boys to do a quick scan. Nope, not one I fancy, I thought. Not one of them was a patch on Tony, but then he was exceptionally good-looking. I felt sad that things had ended the way they had. He had tried to phone me last night, when Nesta, TJ and I slept over at Izzie's ready for the early flight this morning. Nesta had told him to pick on someone his own age as she was still mad at him on my behalf, but I couldn't help but wonder what it was he wanted. Probably just to say goodbye as he's nice like that and we've always been good friends, I thought.

After half an hour or so, we were served a breakfast of a stale croissant and a cup of bitter-tasting coffee. Instead of eating, the boys seemed to think it was funny to start a food fight and began chucking their croissants around until they got a telling off from one of their teachers. They soon chilled out as the teacher looked scary – a bit like Professor Snape in *Harry Potter*.

He didn't put our girls off, however, and as the flight went on, most of our group got chatting to the lads. Nesta moved over into the middle aisle and was soon surrounded by admirers, all fighting for her attention as usual. A handsome Indian boy took Nesta's place and seated himself next to Izzie. TJ moved off to talk to Liam and I could hear her laughing down the aisle. At one point, a dark-haired boy looked over at me and raised an eyebrow as if to say how about it? He was handsome in an overblown way that doesn't appeal to me. Big mouth, big eyebrows. He looked well sure of himself.

'Hi. I'm Chris,' he said, then winked at me.

I made my eyes go cross-eyed. That put him off. He wasn't my type. Not one of them was my type. It would be a long time before I saw some one who could compare to Tony.

'Practise,' mouthed Nesta from the centre of the plane.

I shook my head. I wasn't even in the mood for practice flirting. What was the point? I refastened my seat belt, put my head in my magazine, then let myself drift off thinking about Tony. I let myself imagine what it might have been like going away with him, how he'd hold my hand when the plane took off, how he'd put his arm round me to reassure me when the engines got noisy . . .

'Lucy, Lucy, we're here,' said TJ's voice in my ear. 'Wake up.'

I sat up and rubbed my eyes. 'What? Where? Where am I?'

'Italy!' announced Nesta.

I glanced out of the window to see airport buildings and the runway. 'What we've landed and everything?'

'Yep, and you snored and dribbled all the way through it,' said TJ. 'The whole plane was laughing.'

'Did not.' I punched her.

'You were well gone. I tried to wake you, but you just took my hand, put your head on my shoulder and called me Tony.'

'Sorry,' I said. 'It must have been because I didn't sleep much last night, then we had to get up at the crack of dawn.' I was glad I'd slept through the landing. It was the part I'd been dreading most. But now it was over, we'd landed and were well and truly in Italy.

It didn't take long to get through Customs and pick up our luggage, and soon we were outside the airport where the girls were full of gossip about the boys and who'd said what to whom.

'Guess I missed a lot when I nodded off,' I said, as Mrs Elwes marched us towards the exit.

'Nah, not really,' said Nesta. 'Anyway the boys are staying at the same hotel as us so you can soon catch up.'

'Oh no,' I groaned. 'So am I going to be Billy Loner for the trip while you all get off with the boys on the plane?'

'No way,' said Nesta. 'There was no one there I liked, but it looks as though TJ and Izzie have scored.'

TJ grinned. 'No one serious,' she said. 'Not on holiday. The guy I was talking to was a laugh, but he's a bit of a show off and the group he's with seem a right load of plonkers.'

'Boys in a group,' said Nesta. 'They always act tougher than they are.'

'And more stupid,' said Izzie. 'But the boy who sat next to me, Jay, he was nice.'

'Oh God,' said Nesta, as we got outside the airport building and Mrs Elwes stopped at a battered-looking bus and started talking to the driver. 'I thought Florence was the city of style.'

'It is,' I said, as I noticed an elegant black limousine that had just drawn up behind the bus. 'I see my private transport has arrived. Excuse me, girls. I'll see you back at the hotel, that is if your old jalopy makes it.' I flounced off towards the limo doing my best cat walk strut.

Nesta coughed loudly. I turned back to look at her and she pointed at a pillar to my left, behind which was a tall boy with floppy blond hair who was watching me with an amused look on his face.

He stepped forward. He was cute, dressed in jeans, a black parka and baseball cap. It was hard to judge how old he was, maybe sixteen, maybe seventeen.

'Your car awaits, ma'am,' he said in an American accent, then doffed his cap. 'Can I give you a ride?'

'Why sure you can, young man,' I replied in my best American accent.

As he opened the back door for me, the chauffeur turned from the driver's seat and gave him a quizzical look.

I looked around for the owner of the car. I didn't want to get into trouble before we'd even left the airport. 'Hey, whoever owns this car might not like us messing about with it,' I said, 'and the chauffeur doesn't look too pleased.'

The boy grinned. 'Oh he's cool. The car's for me. My dad sent it for me. Allow me to introduce myself. Teddy Ambrosini Junior.'

Oh Lord, he really is an American, I thought as I went scarlet. 'Lucy Lovering. Junior. Um. Sorry. Didn't realise.'

'Why would you? So can I give you a lift some place?'

'Um. No. Only joking. Here with . . . friends.' I indicated our group with a sweep of my hand.

He glanced over at the group from our school, who were all standing staring. Izzie, Nesta and TJ were laughing their heads off.

'You got a lot of friends,' he said.

'Yes. I um, like people. Lots of them.'

'Cool. Me too. So. Your first visit to Florence?'

I nodded. 'Sightseeing. Can't wait. You?'

'Funeral.'

Oh God. I felt myself blushing. 'Oh. Sorry. I just assumed . . . Um . . .'

'It's OK. You weren't to know.'

'Someone you knew?' I asked, then I wanted to slap myself. What a dumb question. Why on earth would he be attending a funeral of someone he didn't know?

'My grandmother.'

I felt really awkward. 'Oh. A relative, then?' Oh God. More stupid. Stupid me. Course she's a relative. 'I mean . . .'

Teddy smiled. 'Yeah. She was a relative. My father's family live over here. My gran was here in Florence. My dad's based in Milan though. I come over a few times a year since my folks broke up. Where are you staying?'

'Hotel Renoldo or Revoldo or Revanoldo. Somewhere. In Florence. You?'

'Hotel Villa Corelli.'

'Lucy Lovering,' called Mr Johnson, 'on the bus now.'

The boy grinned. 'Looks like one of your friends wants you.'

I grinned sheepishly. 'Teacher. School trip.'

'Thought so,' he said. 'Well have a good trip, Lucy Lovering Junior. Maybe see you around.'

'Yeah,' I said. 'Maybe.'

What a great name and what amazingly white teeth, I thought as I got on the bus with the others. And what a fab voice. Low and sultry. Shame I totally blew it by acting like the dumbest person to arrive from Dumbland.

Flight Tips

Bach Flower Rescue Remedy to steady nerves.

Lavender oil for calming. (A few drops on a tissue then inhale, or rub a few drops into the temple.)

Eucalyptus oil (a few drops on a tissue then inhale. Eucalyptus is a natural antiviral and can kill any germs circulating in the cabin and help prevent getting other people's holiday viruses.)

Take earplugs and an eye mask if you want to sleep.

Chapter 9

Firenze

'Keetchen closed,' growled an acne-pocked man behind the reception desk at our hotel.

'We only wanted a sandwich or something,' insisted Mrs Elwes. 'A snack? These girls have been travelling since early this morning.'

'Keetchen closed,' he repeated and turned away.

Mrs Elwes turned to us and rolled her eyes. 'OK. Line up girls and get your room keys from Mr Johnson. I suggest we go and dump our bags. Have a quick wash, then meet back here and we'll go straight into the centre for a bite to eat.'

'Fantabuluso,' said TJ as Mr Johnson handed her a key.

'Now we'll get to see the real Florence,' said Nesta. '*Firenze*. That's Florence in Italian!'

I hoped we would, as my first impressions of Italy from the bus had been disappointing. Motorway, building sites, traffic, and the hotel looked like any other hotel in the world on the outside – a five-storey building in a busy suburb. The weather was grey like back in the UK and it was nothing like the Florence I'd seen in the film *A Room With a View*.

I followed the girls up to the first floor, which is where our room was, and wondered what Teddy's hotel was like. If it was anything like the limo, it would be spectacular.

'Oh,' said Izzie, as TJ unlocked our door and we stepped inside a room the size of a broom cupboard. There were two bunk beds crammed in on either side, a tiny wardrobe, an ancient-looking TV on top of a rickety cabinet and a set of drawers. The only nice thing in the room was an antique lamp with red beading around the shade.

'Bagsy the top,' I said as I slung my rucksack on the top bunk on the left of the room.

'OK,' said Nesta as she headed straight for the cupboard under the TV set. 'At least it's got a minibar.'

Two minutes later, she was handing round pieces of chocolate she'd found in the minibar. I munched on my bit, then got up on to my bunk and lay back to enjoy our new surroundings.

'Ah, luxury,' I said as I gazed up at the ceiling. The paint was peeling off in places and the shadow in the right corner looked distinctly like damp.

TJ slid open a door to the side of the room and stuck her head in. 'Well, at least we've got a shower and loo. That's something.'

'As long as we're not expected to sleep in it,' I said. 'Although it might be more comfy than this. These pillows are really lumpy.'

'Never mind,' said Nesta through a mouthful of chocolate. 'We won't be spending much time in here.'

Izzie peered through a small window behind the TV. 'Oh the beauty of Italy,' she sighed.

I got down to go and look. I laughed when I saw that all that was visible from the window was a brick wall opposite. 'So much for a room with a view.'

A moment later there was a knock at our door.

'Reception in five minutes, girls,' Mrs Elwes called through.

'But we haven't unpacked,' said Izzie.

'We won't need much,' said Nesta as she threw her hand luggage into the minuscule wardrobe. 'I've got a few Euros that Dad gave me – enough to last us this afternoon, then we can change the rest of our money later.'

'Shall we take mobiles?' I asked. I was really chuffed because Nesta's dad had had all our mobiles upgraded so that we could use them abroad. I was dying to phone someone on mine, even if it was just Izzie in the next bed.

Izzie pulled a face. 'Mine's at the bottom of my bag. Let's leave them. We'll all be together so we won't need them.'

I pulled a few things out of my rucksack and threw them in the wardrobe with my hand luggage.

'Why have you brought that load of stuff?' asked Nesta as she spotted my sewing basket on top of my clothes. 'We're supposed to be on holiday.'

'A true artist never travels without the tools of her trade,' I replied. 'You never know when inspiration will strike. I might see some fab fabric and, according to the schedule Mrs Elwes gave us, we haven't got much on in the evenings.'

'You're here to *relax*,' said Nesta as she locked our money up in the small safe that she found in one of the drawers. 'Give yourself a break and buy some ready-made stuff. I've heard that the markets are full of fab stuff.'

Ten minutes later, we were back on the bus and on our way into the centre. As the bus made its way over the River Arno, down busy streets lined with shops, Florence started to look more interesting. I felt my eyes popping out of my head as I took in the brightly-lit windows displaying gorgeous-looking clothes and designs, and I couldn't wait to start exploring. The bus stopped on a street in the centre and we got off and headed straight for the nearest pizzeria. After a Coke and a slice of pizza, Mrs Elwes and Mr Johnson announced that it was time to start the tourist trail.

'First stop, the station,' she said and marched us off down a busy street.

'She's been before,' said Mr Johnson, who took up the rear of our group. 'Knows her way round.'

I'm glad one of us does, I thought as we followed her down a busy street.

As I battled to keep upright in the jostling crowds, I couldn't help but feel that there must be more to the place. I'd seen great shops, great window displays, loads of cafés, but I wondered what the fuss about Florence being a magical romantic place was all about. It looked like any big, bustling city to me.

At a kiosk, Mrs Elwes bought tickets for an open-topped sightseeing bus and we all piled on and upstairs.

'Fantastic,' said Nesta, as the bus chugged off and we sat back to take in the sights.

'Easily the best way to see the city on the first trip, even though it is a tad chilly,' said Mrs Elwes, who took a seat in front of us and wrapped her coat tightly round herself. 'When I first came with my husband, we wore ourselves out walking all over the place. This way, you can see it all, get your bearings and you cover more ground than you ever could on foot.'

'Nice one, Mrs Elwes,' said Izzie, who was never one for long walks.

The bus tour was definitely the way to do it, especially for a shortie like me. On the street, I felt like I was going to be crushed at any minute but, up on the bus, I could see clearly. Every street seemed to have something worth looking at. We'd turn a corner and there would be a glorious building, a group of amazing statues or work of sculpture. This is more how I imagined it, I thought, as I sat back to take it all in.

'That's the Duomo,' said Mrs Elwes, as we passed an enormous golden cathedral with beautiful carvings on the doors. 'It dates back to 1294. And that marble building in the square opposite, that's the Baptistry. Look to your right as we go past at the stunning door. It's called the Gate to Paradise.'

'Oh, wow!' said Nesta. She pointed down towards the Duomo. 'Definitely a place to investigate.'

I looked to where she pointed, and saw that she wasn't looking at the magnificent doors or the architecture, but rather at the steps where there were hoards of teenagers hanging out.

'Over there, over there,' said Nesta waving madly at a bunch of cute-looking boys who looked up and waved back.

'Ding *dong*,' said Izzie and gave her the thumbs up. 'Magnificent examples of early twenty-first century sculpture, I do believe. Why, they almost look alive!'

Mrs Elwes looked at Izzie and smiled approvingly. 'I'm so pleased that you appreciate art,' she said.

'Er . . . um, yes,' said Izzie. 'Art.'

'Imagine how it must have been before the traffic and the tourists,' said TJ. 'It must have been fab.'

Nesta pulled a face. The tourists, of the male variety, were clearly what she found most interesting.

After a while the bus passed back over the River Arno where Mrs Elwes pointed out a bridge with houses on it in the distance. 'Ponte Vecchio,' she said. 'That's where all the jewellery shops are.'

'Lead the way,' said Nesta, smiling. 'Sounds like my kind of sightseeing.'

The bus wound its way up a hill, past stunning old villas in shady grounds and up to a square that Mrs Elwes told us was called Piazza Michelangelo. The hilltop view was panoramic. Stretched out in front of us was the river, the Old Town, the Duomo, towers and churches, red-roofed buildings. It looked wonderful. The light was just starting to fade and the whole city was bathed in a rosy glow. Now this is more like a scene from the movie, I thought as I gazed around me. It's just a' question of finding the right places. Like in any city, there are the old interesting bits and the new bland bits, like the area we drove through on the way to the hotel from the airport.

'From here, it looks like a place from a different era,' I said.

'It is,' said TJ. 'The Renaissance.'

'Old you mean,' said Izzie, but she looked well impressed.

'Anyone seen the movie, *A Room With a View*?' asked Mrs Elwes.

I nodded.

'Remember the scene where the Helena Bonham Carter character, what was her name in the film? Can't remember! Anyway, she opens her window in the beginning and we see Florence for the first time?'

I nodded again.

'Well that was filmed from somewhere around here,' said Mrs Elwes, pointing to the left of the square. 'From just down there, I think.'

'I *thought* so,' I said.

On a plinth in the middle of the square, gazing out over Florence, towered a giant statue of naked man. It looked as though whoever made it set out to create a perfect face and body.

'He looks like he worked out,' said Nesta as she took in the fabulous muscles on his legs and arms.

'That's Michelangelo's *David*, but not the original,' Mrs Elwes told us. 'There are two copies of it, in fact. One here and

437

one in one of the squares in the centre. The original is in the Galleria dell'Accademia.

Nesta looked the statue up and down. 'Nice butt,' she said and took a photo.

Mrs Elwes rolled her eyes. 'You're looking at one of the greatest works of art in the world and all you can comment is "nice bum".'

'Well it is.' Nesta shrugged.

Mrs Elwes looked again. 'Yes,' she said, grinning. 'I suppose it is.'

'This is my favourite bit of Florence so far,' I said as I looked around. 'It's how I imagined it would be.'

'What looking at David's bottom?' asked Nesta.

'No stupid, the view, the sense of history. You can really feel it up here.'

'Ah, but there's so much more,' said Mrs Elwes with a smile.

I took a deep breath. So much more, I thought. I hoped so. I'm almost fifteen and I've hardly seen anything of the world and yet there is so much to see. Cities like this in Europe, America, the Far East. Places filled with people all living their lives in locations so different to my familiar one in North London.

As the bus continued its tour, it took us back down the hill past more stately old houses and villas in their own grounds. I pointed to one that looked like a grand country house with shuttered windows and beautiful terraced grounds with statues and fountains and trees.

'That place looks the business,' I said as we passed by.

'Villa Corelli it says on the sign,' said Izzie. 'Someone very posh must live there.'

'Villa Corelli?' I asked. 'I think that's where Teddy said he was staying. Is it a hotel?'

'Grand Hotel Villa Corelli. One of Florence's finest,' said Mrs Elwes. 'I went there for cocktails once. That was all we could afford. I can't imagine what it costs to stay there.'

I looked to see if I could see Teddy anywhere in the grounds, but there didn't seem to be anybody about. 'Maybe we could sneak in for a Coke one day,' I suggested.

'A Coke?' asked Nesta. 'Somehow I don't think it's just a Coke that you want there.'

I punched her. 'I told you. I am not interested in boys on this trip and, anyway, we'll probably never see Teddy again.'

'Teddy,' Nesta said with a laugh. 'What kind of name is that?'

'I like it,' I said. 'It's a cuddly name.'

Nesta raised an eyebrow at me.

'Stop it,' I said. 'His name is cuddly. It doesn't mean I want to cuddle him.'

'Yeah right,' said Nesta and gave me one of her knowing looks.

The bus drove back over the river, into the centre and let us off outside an ice cream shop.

'Now this is what I really call art,' said Izzie as she took in what was on offer. There was every flavour imaginable described in English and Italian – pineapple, banana, strawberry cheesecake, raspberry, kiwi, pistachio, vanilla, coffee, chocolate to name only a few.

'Fab, fab, fab,' I said as TJ handed me a double pecan fudge and I took a lick. 'Art. Culture. History. Statues with great bums. Fashion. Great ice cream. This place is growing on me.'

'It will if we keep eating these ice cream gelato thingees,' said Izzie. 'Literally, it will grow on your bum. But . . . well, I can't resist. Yum.'

'And now to my favourite place,' said Mrs Elwes. 'Just a quick look before we go back to our hotel as we've had a long day.'

Mr Johnson didn't have an ice cream and I saw him looking longingly at a man at a bus stop who was smoking a cigarette. Why want one of those, I thought, when you can have ice cream instead? They smell disgusting and make you ill and make you miserable if you can't have one. I hoped I'd never get addicted.

Mrs Elwes led us down a street, then turned a corner and we found ourselves in a large square lined with open air cafés. To the far right, there was a collection of statues. They looked unlike so many of the statues back in England, where the subject was still. These looked animated – arms reaching towards the sky and limbs bent as if ready to take off at any minute.

'This is Piazza Della Signoria,' said Mrs Elwes. 'It's where the Uffizi museum is and is my favourite of all the squares. The Uffizi is over on the right near the statues. We'll visit there tomorrow. Now, Mr Johnson and I are going to get a drink in the café over there and you girls can either join us or have a wander. Don't go out of the square as there's enough to see here for now. Meet back here at six on the dot. Have those of you who have upgraded mobiles got them?'

'Oh no, I left mine at the hotel,' I whispered. 'It's in my hand luggage.'

'So did I,' chorused TJ and Izzie.

'And me,' said Nesta. 'They barely gave us a minute to get organised. Just nod and smile. We'll be fine. We won't need them.'

As Mrs Elwes and Mr Johnson headed off for the café, Izzie, Nesta, TJ and I made for the statues. On the way we passed a gold statue of an Egyptian mummy.

'Strange that this is here,' said TJ going up close to get a better look. 'All the other statues are white and look Roman.'

The statue turned and winked at her.

'Woah,' she cried and leaped back in shock.

'A mime,' I said.

'Brilliant,' she said as she recovered. 'I don't know how they keep so still.'

'Must be very boring,' said Izzie, 'standing like that all day.'

The statue gave her a deep bow, then clapped. Whoever was behind the costume must have understood English.

After the mummy, we went to look at the statues. Like *David* in the Piazza Michelangelo, they were all enormous and naked. It was awesome to gaze up at the great, sculpted bodies towering into the sky.

'*Perseus* by Benvenuto Cellini,' said TJ, who had brought along a guide book. '*Rape of a Sabine* by Giambologna, *Hercules and Cacus* by Bandinelli . . .'

I couldn't resist it. 'Um . . . I wonder if she was,' I said.

'Was what?' asked TJ.

'Bandy. You know, Nelly. I wonder if she was bandy. Bandy Nelly. Not a very kind nickname.'

TJ patted my head. 'Just keep taking the tablets, Lucy,' she said, then went back to her guidebook. '*Judith and Holofernes* by Donatello.'

'I wonder if Bandy Nelly had a sister. Knock-kneed Nellie,' I said and I began to walk about as if I were knock-kneed.

Nesta and Izzie cracked up, but TJ rolled her eyes and went to look at a statue that looked just like the one we'd seen in the square earlier in the afternoon.

'The second copy of Michelangelo's *David*,' she said as she gazed up. 'These statues are so old. Don't you think they're impressive? Some were done in the fourteen hundreds, some in the fifteen.'

'Not exactly shy back, then, were they?' asked Izzie as we stared up at the statue of *Poseidon*, to the left of *David*.

'Not exactly well-endowed either,' said Nesta staring at the statue's willie. 'At least not in proportion to the rest of him.'

'Maybe the artists weren't allowed to make the willie big in the old days,' said TJ. 'I mean if it was in proportion to the rest of him, it would be enormous.'

This set us off laughing which attracted the attention of a group of Italian boys who came over to us.

'*Bella occhi*,' said one to Izzie.

'What did he say?' she asked Nesta.

'Shhh, I'm listening,' she whispered back.

The boys were burbling away in Italian and, even though I didn't understand any of it, I could tell by their expressions and body language that they were talking about us. What they didn't know was that Nesta understood. Having an Italian dad, she's been to Italy to visit his relatives here a few times and, though she says she doesn't speak the language fluently, she says she can make out what someone is saying. When they'd finished, she put her hand on her hip and said something to them in Italian. They scurried off like mice.

'What did you say?' I asked.

'I said that we were nuns and that our mother superior was watching from the other side of the square.'

'Brilliant,' I said.

'Shame,' said TJ. 'One of them was quite cute.'

For a short time, we sat on the side of a fountain by the statue of *Poseidon* and watched the world go by.

'The Italian women have such style,' said Nesta, as an elegant woman dressed in head-to-toe black walked past with a white husky dog. 'I think I'm going to dress in black from now on.'

I glanced over at the café where Mrs Elwes was. I could see her sitting at one of the outside tables and, like us, happily taking in the view.

'What's the time, Nesta?' I asked.

She glanced at her watch. 'Almost five.'

'Loads of time,' said TJ, who had been gazing up at a sombre-looking building with a tower behind and to the right of the fountain. 'Let's take a quick look in here.' She got up and soon disappeared into a door.

Izzie, Nesta and I wandered in after her and found ourselves in an elegant courtyard with pillars and stone steps leading upstairs.

TJ consulted her guidebook. 'This is the Palazzo Vecchio,' she said. 'It's where the Medici family lived in the fifteen hundreds.'

'Shall we take a look upstairs?' I asked, pointing at the steps.

'You have to pay to go in, I think,' said Nesta. She got out her purse and counted her euros.

'Still OK for time?' I asked.

Izzie glanced at her watch again. 'Loads.'

Nesta went over to the kiosk to enquire about entry. She turned back and gave us the thumbs up. 'Just got enough. Shall we do it?'

We nodded back at her.

Moments later we were up the stairs, exploring. The rooms were awesome, as all the walls and ceilings were covered with detailed paintings. Vast battle scenes in an enormous hall and seasonal country scenes in smaller rooms. There was something on every available surface and to see so much colour and design packed into one area was breathtaking.

'Maybe this is what they did instead of using wallpaper,' I said, as we reached yet another painted room and gazed out of the window over Florence. 'You know, you get a mate to come over and do a mural instead. It looks so ordinary from the outside but, inside, they must have spent millions doing all this.'

'Maybe we should do our rooms like this when we get back,' said Izzie. 'You know, paint scenes from our lives. Maybe not. I don't think my mum would be too pleased if I painted a pic of you lot over her posh Sanderson wallpaper.'

'She doesn't know what she's missing,' I said. 'I couldn't paint as well as this, but maybe I could see if any of Bandy Nelly's relatives are still alive and hire them to come over and do me a mural and a naked statue. Look lovely on the back patio with our garden gnomes and potted petunias.'

TJ gave me a look of despair. Sometimes I think she finds it hard that we don't all share her love of history.

From the window we could look out into the square, so I glanced over to the café to find Mrs Elwes. I couldn't see her.

'Can't see the teachers,' I said. 'What time is it? Maybe we'd better get going.'

'No,' said Nesta. 'We've only been in here about twenty minutes. We'll be fine.'

'It's about half five,' said Izzie.

'Is that all? I feel like we've been here ages,' I said.

Suddenly TJ slapped her forehead. 'Ohmigod,' she cried, then looked at her watch. 'Time. Did any of you guys put your clocks forward when we got off the plane?'

We all shook our heads. Then it dawned on me. 'Oh no,' I said. 'No wonder time seemed to be lasting forever. We're still on English time. Italy is an hour ahead. Remember Mrs Elwes told us to do it when we got off the plane.'

'Oh God! Yes, I remember,' said Izzie. 'We were too busy watching Lucy chat up the Teddy bear.'

We raced down the stairs, through the courtyard and across the square to the café. We scoured the customers sitting at the tables. No sigh of Mrs Elwes. No sign of Mr Johnson. No sign of any of the other girls in our class.

'Oh poo,' said Izzie.

'What do we do now?' asked Nesta.

'Get a cab,' I said. 'We know the name of the hotel.'

Nesta got her purse out and turned out the money in there. There were only a few notes left. 'No way is this enough.'

'Bus?' suggested TJ.

'There were a million at the station we passed. How would we know which one to get?' I asked.

'We could walk,' said Nesta. 'Does anyone remember the way back?'

Izzie, TJ and I shook our heads.

Stranded on our first day in Florence. A fine start to our holiday, I thought as I looked around and tried not to panic.

Chapter 10

Busking It

'When the going gets tough, the tough get going,' said Nesta.

'Meaning?' I asked.

'We come up with a solution,' said Nesta. 'It's not a problem. We'll find our own way back.'

'No,' said TJ. 'Phone. We ought to phone and let them know where we are.'

We looked around for a phone box. Not one in sight.

'Policeman,' I said.

We looked around for a policeman. Not one in sight.

'We could go and look for one,' suggested Izzie.

TJ shook her head. 'I don't think we should leave the square, in case one of the teachers is still looking for us.'

'Next great plan anybody?' asked Izzie.

'It's a sink or swim situation,' said TJ. 'I say we swim. We earn our cab fare.'

'And how exactly do you propose that we do that?' asked Izzie. 'Get a job? At this time of day?'

'When in Rome do as the Romans do,' said TJ.

'But this isn't Rome,' I said. 'It's Florence. What do you mean? Do as the Florentines do?'

'Mime,' said TJ and pointed over to where the Egyptian mummy had been only an hour earlier. 'Like the mummy. It can't be difficult.'

'Top idea,' said Nesta. She pulled off her woolly hat and gave it to TJ. 'OK, you go and stand in the square and us guys will keep an eye out for weirdos, as you won't be able to move your eyes when you get going.'

'But . . . but why me?' asked TJ. 'You'd be loads better at it.'

'Your idea,' said Nesta.

Izzie, Nesta and I went and sat back on the edge of the fountain while TJ positioned herself a few metres away with Nesta's hat in front of her. She made her body go rigid and positioned herself as though she were a dummy in a shop window with one arm out as though pointing and one leg slightly up. Not bad, I thought as the first group of tourists went past and stared at her. Then the Italian boys we'd met earlier spotted her and came over. They did everything they could to get her to react – waving their hands in front of her face, doing mad dances, one even started singing. TJ managed to keep a straight face until they all lined up in exactly the same posture as her. It was funny to watch and, in the end, TJ couldn't resist and started laughing.

Eventually the boys moved off, when they realised that TJ wasn't into being chatted up, and she went back into her pose. She stayed still for a good five minutes, but no one walked past. Then she started wobbling and almost fell over. She quickly resumed her position. Finally an old man with white hair passed by and dropped a few coins in front of her.

'*Muchos gracias,*' she said. The man gave her a strange look.

'That's Spanish,' called Nesta.

'I'm doing a Spanish mime,' TJ called back.

A few minutes later and she couldn't keep it up any longer. She dropped her posture and came over.

'It's *really* hard,' she said. 'My arms began to ache being in the same position for so long. It's like your muscles begin to shake. And it's boring, not so much keeping still but not being able to look around and move your eyes. One of you guys have a go.'

'Yeah, Nesta,' I said. 'Why don't you do something?'

'Like what?'

'Um . . . fortune-telling,' I said.

'No way,' said Nesta. 'I'm not a fortune-teller.'

'Oh come on. We need to get back to the hotel,' I said. 'I'm starving. Go on, try it. For us. Pleeeease. Just think, there's probably a lovely supper waiting for us and comfy beds and . . .'

'Lumpy pillows,' said Izzie.

'And two fuming teachers,' added TJ.

Izzie unwound her scarf from her neck and handed it to Nesta. 'Wrap this around your head. You are no longer Nesta. You are now Madam Rosa.'

'But it's you who's into all that heeby-jeeby, Iz. I don't know the first thing about it.'

'Ah,' said Izzie. 'But you're the only one of us that speaks any Italian, plus you are an actress. You don't know what parts you're going to have to play in your career. It will be good practice. Improvise. Say general things – the sort of things that will have happened to everybody, then you can't go wrong. Come on, I know you can do it.'

'Hmmm, I'm not so sure,' said Nesta, but she began to wind the scarf around her head like a turban. 'I don't think I should stand out in the square and do it. I'll sit at the end of the fountain near the pillar and you can send people to me. I'll tell you how to say, "Have your fortune told" in Italian.'

'Good idea,' said TJ.

While Nesta took up her position by a pillar, we called out what she'd told us to say into the square. *'Per la chiromante, da questa parte. Per la chiromante, da questa parte.'*

Most people walked by and looked at us as though we were mad, but a couple of women in their twenties came past and looked interested. One blonde, one brunette, they had backpacks on and looked like tourists.

'Per la chiromante, da questa parte,' I called to them, then decided to try it again in English. 'Fortune-telling, this way.'

'Oh fortune-telling,' said the blonde one in an Australian accent. She turned to her friend. 'How about it, Marie? See what the future has in store?'

Her friend laughed and looked over to where I was

pointing at Nesta. 'She doesn't look very old,' she said.

'Ah,' said Izzie, 'but she is from an ancient family of gypsies and has had the gift of seeing since birth. Age doesn't matter with the Oracle.'

Nice one, Iz, I thought as the women gave us ten euros and went over to Nesta. She really got into her part. She took the blonde woman's hand and then touched her cheek, looking deeply into her eyes. She then rolled her eyes up and swayed about. I thought she looked as though she was going to be sick, but I guess it was acting. And if there's one thing Nesta likes to do, that's act.

'You have travelled far . . .' she began in a deep husky voice.

Marie nodded.

'You are at a crossroad in your life . . .'

Again Marie nodded.

'You have known love . . . but you have also known pain . . .'

More enthusiastic nods.

'I see a tall, dark man . . .'

Marie looked up at her friend. 'Ian,' she said.

Nesta nodded. 'I see good things . . . a bright future . . .'

Marie's friend grinned. This was obviously what they wanted to hear.

'I see many children . . .'

At this Marie's face crumpled and she burst into tears and rushed off. Nesta looked shocked. 'What's the matter? What did I say?'

Her friend looked dismayed. 'We came on holiday because

she found out that she can never have children. She's worried her boyfriend Ian wants them and will choose someone else that can give him them. What you've just said confirms it.'

With that, the lady rushed off to join her friend.

'Oops,' said Izzie. 'OK. Cut that out of the act. Too risky. Don't mention babies. Talk about love, marriage and that sort of thing.'

'*Per la chiromante, da questa parte,*' TJ called out to two elegantly dressed men who strolled by. '*Per la chiromante, da questa parte.* Fortunes told in English and Italian.'

'Go ahead, Ryan,' said one in an American accent. 'It would be fun.'

'Why not?' said the blond one and TJ led him to Nesta.

Nesta looked at his hand and into his eyes. 'You are a very handsome man,' she said. 'I see much love in your life.'

Ryan turned and grinned up at his friend.

'I see a blonde girl. I see love. I see marriage . . .'

The expression on Ryan's friends face turned cold. 'Blonde girl?' he asked. 'What does she look like exactly?'

'Um. Very pretty. Um. Very nice lady,' said Nesta.

'I knew it . . .' said the friend and, before we knew it, he had stormed off.

'*Now* what?' I asked nobody in particular.

'Wh . . . what did I say?' asked Nesta.

Ryan sighed and ran to catch up with his friend.

Nesta shrugged. 'What was the problem?'

'Obvious, you dingbat,' said Izzie. 'They're gay and now,

thanks to you, one of them thinks the other has got something going with a pretty, blonde girl.'

We looked over to the other side of the square where we could see the two men having a row.

'Oops,' said Nesta. 'I guess this wasn't such a good idea after all. Fortune-telling isn't as easy as it looks.' She unwound the scarf from her head and gave it back to Izzie. 'So Lucy . . .'

All three of them turned and looked at me.

'What?' I asked.

'Your go,' said Izzie.

'I can't do anything. I can't sing, can't act. Only thing I can do is make clothes and that's not really an option.' I said.

'And we need some more money to get back to the hotel,' said Nesta.

'Try the mime thing,' said TJ. 'A cab can't cost that much. We probably only need a few more euros. Someone might take pity on you.'

'Thanks a lot,' I said, but I knew there was no getting out of it. We were mates and I couldn't let them down.

I went into the middle of the square and tried to copy the pose of one of the statues near the Uffizi with my arms reaching up in the air, legs slightly crossed. I stood as still as I could, eyes fixed upwards.

I could hear the girls cracking up laughing behind me. Not fair, I thought. I didn't laugh at them. I was vaguely aware of someone standing in front of me, but I kept my eyes fixed skywards. I didn't want to ruin my pose by looking at whoever was there.

'You OK?' asked a familiar American voice.

I let myself look ahead. It was Teddy standing there with an amused grin on his face.

'I was doing mime.'

'Mime? Oh right. OK,' he said. 'I thought you looked kind of uncomfortable. Like you needed the bathroom.'

I felt myself blush scarlet. So much for my career as a mime artist, I thought.

'Oh God,' I heard Izzie say behind me. 'Here comes trouble.'

'Lucy Lovering!' cried a voice to my left. 'Izzie Foster! Nesta Williams. TJ WATTS!'

We turned to see Mr Johnson advancing towards us. He was smoking a cigarette and had a face like thunder.

Things to Do if You Get Stranded With No Dosh

Pray
Cry
Beg
Busk
Sing
Do a mime act

Slightly more sensible options are:

Call someone you know and reverse the charges (preferably someone in the same country!).

Get a cab to someone or somewhere you know. Get them to pay the cab fare at their end, then settle up with them later.

Ask a police officer for help. (But make sure he is a policeman and not someone *miming* being a police officer, as you never know.)

Chapter 11

International
Woman of Mystery

'I'm going to be an international woman of experience and sophistication,' I announced the next morning.

'Me too,' said TJ through a mouthful of the sponge cake that was served for breakfast. I'd wanted my usual toast or muesli, but it wasn't on offer on the buffet table. There was cake, ham, cheese, tomatoes, croissants, tinned pears, prunes and yogurt – nothing I fancied in the morning so I made do with a roll.

'And what exactly does that entail?' asked Izzie.

'It entails travelling a lot, staying in the best hotels,' I said, 'knowing all about art and culture, having love affairs with interesting, talented men and looking divine at every occasion.'

'OK,' said Izzie. 'I'll be one as well, then. Nesta you in?'

'I already am one,' said Nesta, who was wearing sunglasses even though we were indoors. She'd borrowed them from her mum especially for the trip. Big, black Gucci ones. They looked fab.

'I see Mr Johnson has abandoned his no-smoking resolution,' said Izzie with a sideways glance at the table where he was sitting and puffing away. At least he seemed in a better mood this morning. He'd been hopping mad the previous night, even though we'd done our best grovel act and tried to explain about the time difference and how we'd forgotten to put our watches forward. Apparently he thought we'd wandered off and had gone looking for us in the adjacent squares. Before he calmed down, he threatened to put us on the next plane back to England, but then he must have realised that it wasn't such a great idea as either he or Mrs Elwes would have had to go with us, leaving the rest of the group with only one teacher.

Our journey back to the hotel had turned into a bit of a farce, as at first Teddy had offered to give us all a lift in the limo, which of course Mr Johnson refused. 'We'll get a cab,' he said loftily and ushered us away. Only there were no cabs and, after traipsing around for half an hour, who drove past, but Teddy, who offered us a ride again. This time Mr Johnson gave in and so we drove back in style. Teddy seemed really nice. I sat next to him and got chatting while the others tried to calm Mr Johnson down. Teddy said he came over at least once a year, usually in the summer holidays, to visit his dad in Milan, but had been allowed time out of school to attend his grandmother's funeral. His parents were divorced and he lived in the States with his mum and he didn't see his dad's side of the family very much. His dad remarried and worked in textiles and had factories all over Italy. I told him that I wanted to be a fashion designer and he promised to show me some of his dad's fabric samples. He asked where we were going sightseeing and, when I told him that we'd be going to the Duomo the next morning, he'd said he might see me up there. He wanted to take some photos from the top for an album he was making in memory of his grandmother's life and where she'd lived.

When I was lying in bed later, going over the day, I decided that I'd like to get to know him better. As Florence was so different to North London, he was different to the boys I met back home. I wanted to be open to new experiences on all levels and it wouldn't hurt to broaden my horizons on the boy front as well as seeing a new country. Besides, I was only in Italy for a week, too short a time for things to get complicated. No harm in just getting to know him.

As we resumed our sightseeing after breakfast, it was obvious we were in the doghouse with Mr Johnson and Mrs Elwes, who insisted on keeping us within their sight. I hadn't envisaged having two teachers on my tail as part of my new role as international woman of sophistication and experience, but I didn't mind too much as there was so much to see and Mrs Elwes was a great tour guide. First we did the Uffizi Gallery with a million other tourists and school parties on half-term, so it was difficult to see anything in the long corridors and rooms there. It was easier for the others as they're tall but, when you're short like me and there are twenty people crowding round a painting or piece of sculpture, it's hard to see over their heads. I found myself only getting glimpses of the art on display in between people's armpits. TJ was in heaven as she loves history and we had to drag her away from some of the rooms. Nesta and Izzie seemed more interested in taking in what the tourists were wearing and eyeing up boys than becoming experts on Renaissance art.

After the Uffizi, we explored the interior of the Duomo, which was awesome. The domed ceiling was painted with some very strange-looking paintings. Some of heaven, which were OK, but the ones of hell were seriously gruesome. People being swallowed head first by demons or having their limbs or heads cut off. Yuck. Not my idea of spiritually uplifting. I began to feel a tingle of excitement at the prospect of seeing Teddy again, though. This is a new chapter in my book of life, I thought as we wandered round the vast cathedral. My cosy life in North London seemed a million miles away. Tony seemed a million miles away. Teddy, on the other hand, might only be a few steps away at the top of the Duomo.

At the end of the tour of the interior, Mrs Elwes called us all over to her. 'For those of you who want to go to the top, you're free to do so. There is a fantastic view from up there, so join the queue if you wish to go up. Mr Johnson will be at the back of the group and I'll stay down here to meet you on your return.'

'Well, I want to go,' said TJ.

'And we all know that Lucy will,' said Nesta. 'Isn't that where you said you'd meet Teddy?'

I nodded. 'If he's there. We didn't say an exact time.'

I got out my mirror and applied a slick of lip-gloss, then we went outside to join the long queue that wound itself halfway around the side of the Duomo. After about fifteen minutes, we were inside again and being directed to a small door where we could see stone steps leading upwards. I really hoped that Teddy would be at the top when we got there. It would be so romantic, like Meg Ryan meeting Tom Hanks up on top of the Empire State Building in the movie *Sleepless in Seattle*. Only this is Italy. And there's no lift up.

'Last one to the top's a sissy,' said Izzie as she sprinted up the first spiral of steps.

We raced after her and kept up a good pace for about five minutes, after which we had to stop and catch our breath. The stairway was very narrow, going round and round and round and *round*. I felt myself getting dizzy and Nesta was feeling the same.

'Don't know if I can do this,' she said. 'My head's spinning.'

We looked behind us, but there was no way we could turn back as the stairway was too narrow and already we could see the next lot of tourists coming up behind us.

'This has to be what hell is like,' said Izzie as we set off again. 'Stuck on a tiny stairway for ever with a million people behind you pushing you upwards so that you can't rest.'

'No, we can do it,' said TJ. 'We're young, we're fit . . .'

'We're gonna die . . .' said Nesta as she puffed her way ahead.

On and up and on and up and *on* and *up* we trudged.

'We have to be almost there,' I said, after what seemed like an eternity of climbing.

Suddenly the stair opened out to a small landing and we could see people coming down.

A boy with his mother went past us and grinned. 'You're about halfway up,' he said.

'Oh noooooo,' groaned Izzie. 'I thought this trip was supposed to be fun. This is a nightmare.'

We made our way up more steps and more steps and more steps. By now, no one was speaking. It took up too much energy. It must be about five hundred steps to the top, I thought as I stopped for a moment to catch my breath. Now I understood why Mrs Elwes hadn't wanted to accompany us. She must have done it before and knew what was involved. I hope Teddy's not up there, I thought. I might have looked OK when I was down at the bottom, but I could feel that my face was now scarlet and I was out of breath and sweating like mad. Not my most alluring look. As I panted my way up, suddenly there was an opening and a ladder, and I prayed that this might be the end of the steps. Izzie went up the ladder first, then TJ, then Nesta, then me. Then at last, we were at the top and Florence stretched out in front of us. It was an amazing view and, as it was a bright day, we could see for miles. It felt like we were on the top of the world looking out. I edged my way over to the metal barrier to look down.

'Woah,' I said, stepping back quickly. We were very high up and people on the streets down below looked like ants. Everything went blurry and, I felt as if I was going to fall. 'Don't go to the edge.'

Izzie stepped forward and like me, quickly stepped back. 'High! ET wants to go home. Don't like it.'

'You big bunch of girls,' said TJ, who was happy close to the edge and looking over. 'Let's walk round.'

I followed her along the narrow landing around the top, but I made sure that I kept as far away from the barriers as possible. Even though they were waist-high, I didn't feel comfortable at all.

There were about a hundred people up there and I quickly scanned them to see if I could see Teddy, but there didn't seem to be any sign of him.

'He's not here, is he?' asked Izzie as she too scanned the crowd.

I shrugged. 'Well I guess it was a bit of a long shot as he might have come earlier.' I did feel disappointed though. It would have been great to have seen him up here at such a great location. And, with a bit of luck, he could have carried me back down.

After lunch of ciabatta, mozzarella and tomatoes in a café near the Duomo, our bus took us back up to the Piazza Michelangelo, the square with the statue of *David* and his bum that we'd been to the day before. We got off the bus to explore the market stalls there, where everyone bought aprons with a picture of the torso of the statue of *David* on them. I bought six as I thought they'd make fun presents and they were only eight euros each. The aprons were hysterical as they showed David's willie and all the girls on our tour put them on and lined up for a photo in front of the statue. Sadly, Mr Johnson didn't seem to find it very funny, especially when Nesta tried to get him to wear one. After the market stalls, we went up to a church and a fabulous old cemetery to the right of the square. Some of the gravestones were like works of art, with statues of people and ornate sculptures of flowers and swords. Of course we all had to have our pictures taken pretending to be angels standing over the graves.

At about three in the afternoon, Mrs Elwes announced that we were allowed an hour to explore or have a coffee or just relax.

'And you girls,' she said, looking at Izzie, TJ, Nesta and me, 'what time do you have on your watches?'

'Three, Mrs Elwes,' said TJ. 'We've put our watches on the right time.'

'And don't forget we have our mobiles,' said Nesta. 'My dad had them upgraded for us to use in Europe as a holiday present.'

'Switched on?'

'Yes.'

'OK, I've got the numbers so I'll give you a second chance to go off and explore but, if you're not back in an hour, you're in *deep* trouble. Understood?'

'Understood,' said Izzie.

As soon as she'd wandered off a short distance, Nesta turned to the rest of us.

'Hotel Villa Corelli,' she said. 'It's only down the road. Remember, we saw it from the bus.'

'But we can't go in there,' said TJ. 'We're not guests.'

'No problem,' said Nesta. 'Just walk in like you own the place. No one will ask. Remember Mrs Elwes said she went for cocktails? We'll have a Coke and, anyway, we know Teddy. We can say we're visiting him if anyone asks. Oh come on, TJ. I've always wanted to look in one of those really swanky hotels.'

Normally I'd agree with TJ. I'm not very brave about going in very posh places as I feel intimidated, but Florence was having a weird effect on me and I felt like I wanted to try everything and no one was going to stop me. Plus, if I was going to be an international woman of experience, I needed to have some. Experiences, that is.

'And maybe we'll see Teddy again,' said Nesta. 'It's important for Lucy to help her get over my dumb brother.'

'Lead the way,' said Izzie.

'It's neoclassic,' said TJ as we walked up towards the hotel's entrance.

'Neo-posh,' said Izzie as we walked inside.

Even Nesta was fazed when we walked into the hotel lobby. It was fabulous with a very distinctive smell. Money. Marbled floors, marbled walls, humungous displays of exotic flowers. No one was about and it was clearly not a place where four teenage girls could hang about without looking conspicuous. And no way was it a place that you could just pop into for a Coke. The others were about to turn away, when I took a deep breath and marched straight up to the reception desk and rang the bell. A moment later, a blonde lady appeared from a back room.

'Er . . . excuse me. Do you speak English?'

'Yes, madam. How can I help?'

'We're here to see Teddy Ambrosini Junior, please.'

'Just a moment,' she said. 'Who should I say is calling?'

'Lucy Lovering. Um. Junior.'

She gave me a funny look, then went to her phone and dialled. A few moments later she glanced up. 'He's coming down,' she said.

'Cool,' I said. 'I mean, thanks.'

Five minutes later, Teddy appeared in the lobby. He looked delighted to see us all.

'Hey,' he said. 'I'm so sorry I couldn't make the Duomo this morning. My aunt turned up to check I was OK.'

'Why are you staying here,' asked Nesta, 'if you're family lives in Florence?'

'They don't,' said Teddy. 'That is, some of them do. My dad has a place in Milan. It was my grandmother who lived in Florence, and her place is packed out with assorted relatives so Dad thought I'd be more comfortable here.'

'I'll say,' said Nesta.

'We're very sorry to hear about her death,' said Izzie. 'Were you close to her?'

Teddy shook his head. 'Yeah. She was a great lady. I didn't see as much of her as my American grandmother, but I used to see her once a year when I was over visiting Dad. He's arriving tonight with my stepmother. Say, would you like to see my room?'

We all nodded and trooped after him up a flight of stairs and into a room on the first floor. I say room, but it was more like a suite. It must cost a bomb to stay here, I thought as I took in the richly coloured rugs on the floor and heavy drapes at the window.

'Nice place,' said TJ.

'It used to be a private residence,' said Teddy. 'Royal folks' pad.'

'Cool,' said TJ.

'I was just putting some photos on the computer,' said Teddy, 'ready to send back home to my mom.'

'Brilliant,' I said. 'Can we see?'

We all crowded round the laptop, which was set up on a writing desk. Teddy pressed a button on his keypad and lines of photographs appeared.

'God, I wish I could send photos,' said Nesta. 'I'd love to send pics home.'

'I can do that for you,' said Teddy and reached over to his camera.

We spent the next fifteen minutes larking about and taking pictures. Izzie in a Buddha pose on the bed. Nesta sprawled like Cleopatra over the bed with her sunglasses on and a glass in her hand. Me peeping out from behind one of the curtains. Izzie insisted that I had one taken with Teddy, and it all got a bit silly as he pulled a rose out of an arrangement on top of the TV and knelt on the floor and held it up to me. Course, I went red and grinned like an idiot.

'*Romeo and Juliet*,' said Nesta.

'Only that was in Verona, not Florence,' said TJ.

'Who cares?' said Nesta. 'Verona, Florence. It's all Italy and it's all romantic.'

It didn't take Teddy long to transfer the pictures on to the computer, take down our e-mail addresses then, with a ping, send them off to our computers in England.

'The Renaissance folk might have been whizzes at art,' said TJ, 'but we have digital cameras and e-mail.'

After cups of tea in delicate china, we took our leave and ran back up the hill to the square. We didn't want to be in trouble with Mrs Elwes and only just made it in time.

'You going to see him again?' asked TJ as we got back on the bus.

I nodded. Before we'd left, Teddy had asked for our itinerary, so I'd given him a rough idea of where we'd be going in the next few days in case he could get time off from his family duties. I felt brilliant. This place may be full of art and history and fantastic stories of who'd lived here in past times, I thought, but the past has gone. I'm here now. I'm alive and my story's still unfolding.

Back at our hotel, we had supper and a bit of a laugh with the boys from the other school, then went back to our rooms and got into our pyjamas. We raided the minibar for goodies – one bar of chocolate, two chunks each. We tried watching the telly, but it was all in Italian so we decided to phone home. We took turns and Nesta was last to go.

She put the phone down and sighed.

'What?' asked Izzie.

'I should have thought . . .'

'What?' asked Izzie again.

'We share our Inbox back home. Tony saw the photographs.'

'So?' asked Izzie.

'The one of Lucy and Teddy. Mum said he flipped and stormed out of the flat.'

'Serves him right,' said Izzie. 'I mean, it was him that finished with her and all because she wouldn't have sex with him.'

'It wasn't just that . . .' I began to protest.

'Apparently he came back later,' continued Nesta, 'packed his rucksack and said he was going off to some rave in Devon.'

'So?' asked TJ.

Nesta glanced at me. 'With Andrea Morton,' she said.

'Who's she?' asked TJ.

'You don't want to know,' said Nesta.

'I do,' I said.

Nesta sighed. 'Andrea Morton's this girl who's been after him for ages. I didn't say anything about her before, Lucy, because, for one thing, he was smitten with you and, for another, he didn't seem interested. She was doing all the chasing.'

'How old is she?' asked Izzie.

'Seventeen,' said Nesta. 'Why?'

'Obvious, isn't it?'

'No.'

'Seventeen. Legal. We all know what Tony wants,' said Izzie.

Nesta lay back on her bed. 'Well, good luck to him.'

'Exactly,' I said. I felt a twinge of jealousy, but I knew that he'd move on sooner or later. He had to. I couldn't expect him to stay single just because we'd split up. I mustn't mind, I told myself. I have to move on as well and I knew just the person I wanted to do that with.

'Um. Do you think that room service will deliver chocolate?' asked Izzie, who was on her knees on the floor with her face in the minibar. 'We're all out here.'

'Yeah,' said TJ. 'Who needs boys when you can have chocolate?'

'Ah, but maybe we do need them when we *haven't* any,' said Nesta. 'Let's call the boys in their rooms. Maybe they haven't eaten their supplies.'

There are four hundred and sixty-three steps to the top of the Duomo.

Take water and sandwiches. And oxygen.

Chapter 12

Exploring

'Maybe Teddy's gay,' said Izzie as we got ready for bed on Thursday evening.

'Maybe,' I said, 'or maybe he's just come out of a relationship and is off girls for a while.'

'No way,' said Nesta. 'I've seen the way he looks at you and I'm never wrong about these things. He fancies you big time.'

'So why hasn't he kissed me, then?'

I'd seen Teddy every day since Sunday in his hotel. I got the feeling he was a bit lonely as, although his dad and stepmother had arrived to join him at the hotel, once the funeral was over, his dad left Teddy to his own devices as he had business in Florence to attend to and his stepmother wanted to go shopping. He came over in the evenings for an hour or so and we sat in the lounge downstairs and chatted. We found we had loads in common as he was interested in design and wanted to do it when he went to college, though he wasn't sure whether to do furniture or fabric. He brought samples of his dad's fabrics for me to look at and they were stunning, all the vibrant colours of Italy. At the end of the evening, I'd walk him back to the limo, which always waited for him in the car park.

As the week had gone on, I could tell he liked me, but he never made a move, not even to hold my hand, and I began to wonder if he liked me only as a friend; if there was something wrong with me or I'd misread the signals. All the other girls from our school were having a whale of a time and just about everyone had got off with someone.

Izzie spent every moment she could with Jay and it looked like they were getting serious. TJ hung out with Liam, although she said it was platonic as she didn't fancy him. He did look a bit odd, as one of the boys in their group had shaved off one of his eyebrows when he was asleep on the first night in Italy as a joke. Not a great look. Nesta however, for the first time ever, was having a hard time pulling. Loads of boys on the school tour fancied her, but she'd set her sights higher. She fancied Marco, one of the waiters. He was well fit. Tall and dark with deep brown eyes. She found out from one of the other waiters who spoke good English that Marco was a musician who was working at the hotel part-time. Sadly though, no matter how hard she flirted, he played it cool and treated her as though she was one of his customers. Nothing more. Of course that only made him more attractive in Nesta's eyes, and it could only be a matter of time before he succumbed as Nesta, like her brother, liked a challenge.

And then there was me. Every day at breakfast, Chris, the boy who'd given me the eye on the plane, sauntered past and made some stupid comment or tried to get my attention by throwing bits of croissant at me. Not a very impressive way of getting attention in my book. No way was I interested in him. I liked Teddy, but I wasn't sure what was happening with him. I thought he fancied me, but nothing. Not even a peck on the cheek. It was weird. After all the anxiety about Tony trying it on all the time, now I was worried about a boy who didn't want to try at all. I tried to tell myself that it didn't matter. Nothing could come of it anyway and I'd had a brilliant week exploring some of the places around Florence with the school.

We'd spent Monday touring the churches and palaces in Florence, and then on Tuesday we'd been out to Siena which is a medieval town built on three hills. Nesta got in trouble there as it was an unusually warm day for the time of year and she went into one of the churches in a tiny tank top. The man on duty gave her a filthy look, then handed her a sort of paper pinny to wear to cover herself up. Course, she had to have her photo taken in front of one of the churches with it over her head like a mad nun. The place I liked the best there was the Piazza del Campo. It's a huge square built on a slope in the middle of the town and, twice a year, they hold a famous horse race there called the *Palio*. Horses race round the outside of the square while up to thirty thousand people stand in the middle to watch. Don't think I'd like to be there for that. I'd get squashed and wouldn't see a thing.

On Wednesday we visited Lucca, which was a lovely quiet place. It's surrounded by a high wall and you can only get in through one of six enormous gates. Inside, people tend to get about by bicycle as cars aren't allowed, and we hired bikes and rode round the track on top of the city wall. It was a great way to see it all and much more relaxing than Siena which was hard work because, being on a hill, some of the streets were very steep. The bike ride also made a nice change from yet another church. They were beginning to blur in my head and I couldn't remember which church or cathedral was where.

My favourite trip was to a place called San Gimignano on Thursday morning, and it was there that I felt like I'd really fallen in love with Italy. Like Lucca, cars weren't allowed in and the only way in was through one of two great gates in a ginormous wall. TJ told me that it was nicknamed the Medieval Manhattan because there were thirteen towers there, and that there used to be seventy towers in the old days. Apparently people used to build them to show that they were rich and successful. The higher the tower, the richer you were. It was smaller than Siena and Lucca and only had two squares, but I really liked the atmosphere. You could really imagine how it must have been in the past. Narrow streets lined with shops led to the main squares and, in one of them, there was a lovely church with stunning frescoes. TJ told me that some of the movie *Tea With Mussolini* had been filmed in there. We went up a tower in the centre of the town and from there was the most wonderful view of the Tuscan countryside. San Gimignano is on a hill so we were high up before we ascended the tower but, once up, we could see for miles in all directions. Rolling green hills, cyprus trees stretched out in front of us with the occasional dot of a farm or villa. It looked magical, like a painting. I felt as though I was standing on the threshold of my whole life, looking out on the beginning of endless possibilities. I really, really want to travel, I decided. See as much as I can while I can.

'I'm totally frescoed out,' said Izzie, as we travelled back from our Friday trip to a winery and yet another church on the outskirts of Florence.

'Me too,' said Nesta. 'I've got art coming out of my ears.'

'Yeah right,' I said, laughing. I hadn't noticed Nesta or Izzie taking too much notice of the art as we visited places. The boys from our hotel had done all the same tours as us and they'd spent all the time they could hanging out with them.

As we got off the coach, Mrs Elwes announced that we were to be allowed an evening out on our own as long as we stayed in groups.

'Call Teddy and let him know,' said Nesta. 'We can all go out. We'll cover for you as Mrs Elwes and Mr Johnson will think that you're with us.'

'I want to go out with Jay,' said Izzie, 'so can you cover for me too?'

'No prob,' said Nesta. 'TJ and I had planned to hang out with the boys anyway. We can say we were all together.'

Half an hour later, the girls escorted me to the Ponte Vecchio, the bridge where I had arranged to meet Teddy.

He was already waiting for me when I arrived and I agreed to meet the girls back there after two hours.

At first, it felt strange to be on my own with him, wandering round unfamiliar streets in the dark and there wasn't a whole lot to see as the shops were closed. After a while, he asked if I'd like to drive around some of the surrounding area. I nodded. Even though I'd only known him under a week, I could tell that he was trustworthy. Besides the girls knew where he was staying and had my mobile number, if he decided to kidnap me and sell me to the slave trade.

As we sat back in the leather seats in the limo, I longed to reach out and hold his hand, but I didn't want to seem forward and I certainly didn't want to feel an idiot if he wasn't into it. The driver drove us out of Florence and up to a little town called Fiesole in one of the hills, where we got out and strolled along the lanes until we came to some steps. At the top of the steps, we sat on the wall and gazed out over the lights of Florence, twinkling away in the distance. He stood behind me and, for a moment, I thought he was going to put his arms round me. But he didn't. It was beginning to drive me mad. I wondered if Izzie was right and he was gay. He did seem like a sensitive person and he dressed beautifully, in simple but well-cut clothes, the way a lot of gay people do.

'Have you seen that film *A Room With a View*?' he asked.

'Yes. I saw it before I came out here.' I had a quick flash of the night I'd watched it, wrapped in Tony's arms before he got his attack of the wandering hands. For a moment, I felt sad and wished he was here with me looking out at the view, standing behind me and snuggling into my neck.

'And do you remember the scene where Helena Bonham Carter's character is in the poppy field and sees the boy she likes?'

'I do.' It was a really romantic scene – probably what got Tony going, I thought.

'It was up here that it was filmed,' said Teddy and at last he put his arms round me. 'Do you remember the name of the character that Helena Bonham Carter played?' he asked as he turned me round to face him.

I shook my head. 'No.'

Teddy smiled. 'It was Lucy. Her first time in Florence. The film was in the classic collection on the plane coming over here, so I thought I'd give it a watch seeing as it was set here. Then the first girl I meet when I get off the plane is called Lucy. Her first time in Florence. Kind of like fate or synchronicity or something.' And then he kissed me.

After a few moments he leaned back. 'I've been wanting to do that all week but, bit mad I know, I wanted to wait until I could bring you up here. Even though it was a sunny day in the movie and it's dark now, I wanted our first kiss to be up here just like the movie.'

I felt really touched. It was the most romantic thing anyone had ever done for me. Tony may have got the DVD out for me, but wanting to play out a scene from it in exactly the same location, that's cool. For a moment, I felt sad that it wasn't Tony that I was sharing a kiss with, then I made myself focus back on the present. Tony's moved on, I told myself. He's doing God knows what with Andrea Morton in Devon. It's over between us and I mustn't let memories of him ruin what could be a perfect moment with someone new. Teddy wrapped me in his arms again and I snuggled in and pushed any thoughts of Tony away.

'So what about the second kiss?' I asked. 'Where should that be?'

'Anywhere you like,' he said with a smile.

So we kissed in the lane going back to the square, in the square, in the car driving back into Florence and again on the Ponte Vecchio. He was a really good kisser and I felt like I was in a movie. Maybe not *A Room With a View* as that was about Edwardian times, but it felt every bit as special.

By the time the girls came to collect me, I felt as though I was floating on air.

A Room With a View (1985)

Directed by James Ivory
Written by Ruth Prawer Jhabvala
Based on the book by EM Forster
Starring: Helena Bonham Carter,
Julian Sands, Simon Callow
Denholm Elliott, Maggie Smith,
Daniel Day-Lewis, Judi Dench

Chapter 13

Outsider

'I've heard of love making you feel weird,' said Nesta as I retched into the loo the following morning, 'but this is taking it a bit far.'

'Oh ha ha,' I said weakly as another spasm of nausea hit my stomach.

'Must have been that seafood pizza you had last night on the way back from the bridge,' said Izzie as she leaned over the sink and soaked a flannel. 'I told you you should have had the four cheeses.'

The mention of food brought on a fresh wave of sickness and I had to bend over the loo again. This is not the view I had in mind when I came to Italy and certainly not how I envisaged spending my last day, I thought as I gazed at the white bowl beneath me.

'Don't . . . talk . . . about . . . food . . .' I groaned.

'I'll go and get Mrs Elwes,' said TJ, offering me a glass of water while Izzie put the wet flannel on my forehead.

Food poisoning, Mrs Elwes declared fifteen minutes later and I was put to bed with some tablets for my stomach and strict instructions not to get out of bed.

Izzie put her coat on ready for the trip. 'I'm so sorry you'll miss Pisa,' she said.

I felt myself wanting to retch again. 'Ugh. Please. Don't mention pizza.'

'No. Pisa. Pisa, where we're going today,' said Izzie.

I waved her away. 'Pisa, pizza, whatever. I never want to see food again.'

I was hardly aware of the girls slipping out of the room and I must have dozed off as, the next thing I knew, it was eleven o'clock and I was alone in the room. I lay there for a while staring at the paint peeling off the ceiling, then climbed off the bunk and tried standing up. I definitely felt better. I looked at myself in the wardrobe mirror. A little pale, but it seemed like the worst of the sickness had passed. I climbed onto Nesta's bed, lay down and flicked on the TV, but it was all in Italian. I attempted to have a shower, but the water was freezing. I tried to read, but it seemed like a waste to be in bed when I was on holiday so I decided to explore the hotel and see if anyone was about. The corridors were empty and the only sound was the hoover behind closed doors. Cleaning ladies were busy in the lounge, so no chance of hanging out there. In the end, I decided to go back to my room and call Teddy and see if he was free to act out more scenes from *A Room With a View*.

He wasn't in his hotel so I tried his mobile.

'Come and join me,' he said after I'd explained why I wasn't in Pisa with the others. 'I'm at the station waiting to meet my stepsisters, Arianna and Cecilia. They're on the train from Milan and I promised Dad that I'd meet them.'

'You didn't say you had sisters.'

'They're not my dad's. Not blood sisters. They're my stepmother's kids from her previous marriage.'

'Are you sure I won't be in the way?'

'Course not. You'll like them. I'll send the car for you.'

When I got out of the limo at the station, I began to feel ill again and wondered if going out had been a good idea. The station was heaving with people, dashing to get their train or meeting passengers. It felt overwhelming. I was about to turn back to the limo when I spotted Teddy by the ticket office.

'Train should have been in ten minutes ago, but it was delayed,' he said, as he took my arm and he led me towards the platforms. 'Should be here in a moment though.'

I started to feel faint being among so many people who were all in a hurry and for a moment felt like I was going to fall over.

'I'll sit back here,' I said as I spied a bench, 'and catch you up in a moment.'

'Sure you're OK?' asked Teddy. 'You look kind of green.'

I nodded. 'It's the new fashion. Green is the new black. I'll be OK. Go. You don't want to miss your stepsisters.'

I watched him make his way over to the platform as a train

came in and, as its doors opened, people started spilling out on to the platform. I looked among them for two young girls, but couldn't see any that were unaccompanied. Then I realised that he hadn't told me how old they were. Maybe they were older than him.

A couple of blonde girls in jeans wandered down the platform. They walked straight past Teddy, so not them. Then a very fat girl and her skinny friend with frizzy hair, but no, not them. Then, oh no, I thought, as two stunning girls in tip-to-toe black got off the train. Hope it's not them. They're way too glamorous and I feel such a mess. They walked past Teddy, although one turned back to check him out. But no, not them. I felt a sigh of relief. Suddenly I heard someone call out Teddy's name and he waved. Coming towards him were two tall girls who looked about eighteen. If the two previous girls had been stunning, these two were super stunning. As in mega. They looked like they'd just walked off the pages of one of my Italian *Vogue* magazines. One of them had wild, curly black hair almost down to her waist. She was wearing a pair of black jeans (with diamanté down the seams – it looked as if she had sprayed them on) and the highest pair of pointy boots I'd ever seen. Men were turning their heads to look at her. She kissed Teddy on both cheeks and he grinned back at her. The other girl held back a moment, then took her turn at the two kisses. She was classically beautiful with fabulous cheekbones and silver-blond hair pulled back in a high ponytail. Like her sister, she had high pointy boots on. It was hard to tell which was the oldest as they both looked so grown-up and self-assured.

'Hey, I want you to meet someone,' said Teddy, beckoning me to come forward. I stood up and shakily walked towards them. I felt like a midget peasant in my scruffy trainers, baggy jeans and unwashed hair. The girls towered over me and looked at Teddy quizzically.

'Arianna, Cecilia, this is Lucy,' he said. 'She's . . .' He grinned at me. 'What are you? A friend of mine. Yeah. She's here on a school trip from England.'

'Oh how fantastic,' said Arianna, the dark-haired one. 'You're English. I *love* the English. Where are you from?'

'London.' I felt tiny compared to her. Pale. Uninteresting.

'I know London well,' continued Arianna. 'Chelsea. Kensington. Mayfair. And Harvey Nichols. I love it. And the hotel we stayed in was divine. So quaint. Browns. You know it?'

I shook my head.

'Which part do you live in?' she asked.

'Muswell Hill.'

She looked at her sister who shrugged.

'Muswell Hill?' asked Cecilia. 'Where's that?'

'In the north.'

'Ah. We didn't go there.' Arianna put her arm through mine. 'So you come with us back to the hotel? We can talk all about England.'

They plied Teddy with their luggage and he grinned sheepishly at me as the girls pulled him away towards the exit where the driver was waiting to take the bags.

I trotted along with them, feeling more and more like a child who was with grown-ups.

Once in the car, the girls began chatting away in Italian to Teddy. Just as they had perfect English accents when they spoke to me, he seemed to have a perfect Italian one when he spoke to them. I decided to make an effort to join in.

'You speak great English,' I said to the girls. 'And you speak great Italian,' I said to Teddy. 'Do you speak other languages?'

'French, German . . .' said Arianna.

'Spanish and a little Russian,' said Cecilia. 'How about you?'

I was beginning to feel more and more inadequate and wished I hadn't asked. 'Um. Double Dutch,' I offered.

The girls looked at me with a puzzled expression.

'She's joking,' said Teddy. 'It's like slang.'

'Oh, OK. Double Dutch. Cool,' said Arianna.

'You speak Italian?' asked Cecilia.

'A little . . .' I said, praying that she wouldn't ask me to say anything. 'Where's the loo?' was about as much as I'd learned.

'But how rude of us,' said Arianna. 'Speaking in Italian. We must speak English.'

She's a nice girl, I thought. She can see that I can't understand a word of what they were saying in Italian and is trying to include me. Beautiful *and* nice *and* sophisticated *and* speaks a load of languages. As they chatted about England in an attempt to include me, I realised that the England they knew was not the same as the England I inhabited. Private schools. Private cinemas. Private parties. Polo matches in Windsor. Ascot. Restaurants I'd never heard of. They were like the girls Nesta met when she went out with a rich boy last year. Girls who move in different circles. Circles with lots of money. I felt like a complete outsider and at a loss for anything to say. Asking if they knew Marks and Spencer on the Broadway in Muswell Hill just wasn't an option.

This isn't good, I thought, I feel excluded when they speak Italian and even more excluded when they talk in English about England. I mean, Ascot. I haven't been to Ascot. Or shopped in Joseph in Knightsbridge. I'm out of my league here I thought, and I want to go back to my crumby hotel and crawl under the sheets. As the limo drove on, I couldn't stop staring at the girls as they chatted away. They eventually gave up on me and reverted back to their native tongue. They were everything, I thought I wanted to be. International women of sophistication and experience. I could never be like them, I thought. Not on the pocket money I get and this being my first time abroad.

As we drew nearer their hotel, we drove down a narrow street with a few shops and a restaurant where Arianna asked the driver to stop.

'Oh, do let's go in there,' she said. 'I read about it in *Harpers*. They have a new chef who is apparently the best in Florence. Everyone's talking about him. Are you hungry, Lucy? Want to give it a try?'

I was beginning to feel hungry, as I hadn't had a bite to eat all day and my food poisoning had pretty well disappeared. I nodded my head.

Arianna said something to the driver, then we got out of the car and made our way into the restaurant. It was very chic with a simple décor of white walls, abstract paintings in vibrant reds and purples, and flowers that looked like birds' heads on stems. The headwaiter came forward to greet the girls as if they were lifelong friends, took their coats and swept them away towards a white linen covered table. As an afterthought he came back and looked at me as if I had just crawled out from under a stone.

'Yes, I am with them,' I said and handed him my parka. I reminded myself of Nesta's favourite quote – no one can make you feel inferior without your permission. I was determined not to give my permission. OK, so I hadn't been to many places like this. Well, it's about time I started to, I thought.

Morsels of tasty bites arrived one after the other on enormous white plates. Each course was beautifully arranged as though there was an artist in the kitchen arranging each leaf, and it almost felt a shame to ruin the design. All of it tasted delicious and, although I hadn't got a clue what I was eating, I did my best to join in and enthuse with the girls and Teddy.

After lunch, I still felt hungry as the portions had been tiny and I found myself hankering for a cheeseburger and chips. I must be feeling a lot better, I thought as Teddy asked for the bill, then went off to find the driver.

Arianna got out her wallet so I followed her lead and pulled out my little Chinese purse.

'How much?' I asked.

She looked surprised. 'It's OK. I can pay. You are our guest.'

'No, no,' I insisted. 'Let's split it.' I didn't want her to think that I was hanging around with Teddy because he was rich or anything.

She looked at the bill. 'OK. This should cover our share,' she said as she put down a wad of euros. 'Now I must go and visit, as you say in English, the Ladies.'

Cecilia got up to join her. 'See you in a mo,' she said with a smile.

I smiled back. These girls were OK and really making an effort to be friendly, although I had noticed Cecilia eyeing up Teddy a few times and hanging on his every word. Clearly she doesn't see me as competition, I thought. She probably thinks that Teddy is hanging out with me because there was no one else around. I wonder if they're talking about me in the Ladies, asking each other what on earth Teddy's doing with a scruff-pot like me?

I picked up the bill to work out my share. One hundred and sixteen euros. A quarter of that would be? Ohmigod. I felt my heart sink. Twenty-nine euros. If only I hadn't bought so many of those mad *David* aprons. I only had twenty-five euros left and I still had to pay for my share of the chocolate the girls and I had eaten from the minibar.

As I was counting out my money, Teddy came back and pulled out his wallet. 'Here let me get that. You're my guest.'

I put my purse away, but I felt mortified.

I felt doubly bad as Arianna and Cecilia came back and witnessed Teddy paying my share of the bill as well as his, but neither of them said anything.

Best Thing for Food Poisoning

Drink plenty of fluid. Rest. Don't eat anything until the stomach settles and then eat only light food for a day or so. *Dr Watts*

Rest. Drink fluids. Have cheeseburger and chips, not posh titbits that cost a fortune. *Lucy*

Chapter 14

Cinderella

'Wow, get you,' said Nesta as I got out of the limo in front of the hotel. 'You won't be speaking to the likes of us mere mortals soon.'

The school bus had arrived back at the same time and everyone was getting off. Mrs Elwes looked surprised to see me up and about, so I quickly thanked my driver and hotfooted it back to the room with the girls before she did an inquisition and I found myself in trouble.

'Oh yes I will,' I said. 'Especially after the day I've had.' I'd never been happier to see my mates. People who understood me. Dressed like me. Spoke like me. Liked me. Not that Arianna and Cecilia didn't like me but, as the afternoon had gone on, I felt more and more inadequate. They'd insisted that I went back to the hotel with them after lunch and hang out. As it was my last day, I'd just wanted to be alone with Teddy, but he had some errands to run for his dad and so had to take off for a few hours.

He wouldn't hear of me going back to my hotel until the others were back so, in the end, I had no choice but to stay with the stepsisters. I suppose it did make sense in one way, I mean, why hang out in a drab hotel when you can luxuriate in beautiful surroundings. I just wished I'd felt more at home there.

As they'd unpacked cases of the most stunning clothes, Prada, Gucci, Fiorucci, they discussed a concert with some famous Italian rock band that they had tickets for that evening. As they'd said about the restaurant, anyone who was anyone was going to be there. Teddy included. I wondered why he hadn't mentioned it. Maybe now Arianna and Cecilia had arrived he wanted to hang out with them and, like most of Florence, I was history. 'Oh you'll be able to get a ticket from your concierge,' Arianna had said.

Not likely, I'd thought as I pictured the miserable being that inhabited reception at our hotel. We can't even get a glass of water from him. I wasn't bothered about going to a concert. I had hoped that Teddy might come over to my hotel like on the other evenings, but he phoned late afternoon and said that he wouldn't be back at all as he had something he had to do and would arrange for the car to drop me off. He didn't say anything about the evening. End of story, I thought. So much for my holiday romance. He wasn't even coming back to Hotel Corelli to say goodbye. Now that the girls had arrived maybe he'd realised that I didn't belong in his world. I'd served my purpose and was no longer needed.

'Rubbish,' said Nesta after I'd filled her, TJ and Izzie in.

'Yeah,' said Izzie. 'You're Cinderella, they're the ugly sisters and you shall go to the ball.'

'Ugly is one thing they're not,' I said. 'Believe me. They are geogorgeous with a capital G. And they were nice. Genuinely. So polite and . . .'

'I bet they have spotty bottoms,' interrupted Nesta.

'And bad breath,' said Izzie.

'And three nipples each,' said TJ. 'In fact, they sound so perfect, I bet that they're robots.'

I laughed. It was mad that I'd allowed myself to get so intimidated. I wouldn't have done if TJ, Nesta and Izzie had been with me.

'I want to go to the concert,' said Nesta. 'Everyone was talking about it on the bus and Mrs Elwes and Mr Johnson seemed cool about our lot going too. Liam and Jay got tickets on the internet before they came out here and Professor Snape, their teacher, is going too with a load of other boys from their school. Mrs Elwes said that if Snape was going, then we could go, as long as we stayed in a group. So . . . all we need are some tickets.'

'We need an insider,' said TJ. 'Some Italian who knows where we might get some.'

Nesta's face lit up. 'I know just the man. I'm going to go and ask Marco if he knows anything about it. I saw him go into the dining room when we got off the bus.'

She disappeared out of the door and, while she was gone, TJ and Izzie filled me in on their day out. It sounded like they'd had a great time and I wished I'd been with them, where I belonged, instead of feeling like an outsider in the Hotel Corelli.

Nesta returned fifteen minutes later looking flushed and happy. 'He spoke to me. At least, I spoke to him. He doesn't speak much English. God he's *so* gorgeous . . . Italian boys are so hot. He has the most amazing brown eyes . . .'

'Tickets, Nesta?' interrupted Izzie. 'Can he get us any?'

'Oh. Yes. He's playing with one of the warm-up bands tonight so he's got some complimentary ones.' She fished about in her pockets and produced tickets. 'So we can go. He's almost finished his shift and then his band are coming to pick him up. He said we could go with them and squeeze in the back of the van with the equipment. Not exactly a flash limo like you're used to, Lucy, but us lesser beings have to bum it sometimes.'

I thought I detected a note of sarcasm in Nesta's voice. I couldn't bear to think that they might have felt left out because I'd been swanning about in a limo and going to posh places. The last thing I needed was to be made to feel excluded by my best friends. 'You *know* it's not been like that, Nesta. I'd much rather have been with you today and I don't mind going in the back of a van. You know I don't.'

'Er, yes. But . . . um, one small problem . . . Marco only had three tickets.'

Izzie and TJ looked at each other, then at me.

'Well you obviously have to go, Nesta,' I said. 'You got the tickets and you like Marco.'

'Maybe we could all go and get all of us in,' she said. 'Maybe we could get tickets on the door.'

I shook my head. 'Doubt it. Arianna said it's been sold out for weeks. No. You guys all go. I'll stay here.'

'No,' said TJ. 'You can't do that. Nesta, you go on your own.'

'Noooo. Please. In a van with a load of strange boys? I might be mad, but I'm not that stupid. Oh come on, I can't go on my own. One of you come at least. Maybe we should put names in a hat or something.'

'We don't need to do that. I can stay with Lucy,' said Izzie. 'TJ, you go with Nesta.'

'No honestly,' I said. 'You three go. I'm really not bothered about going. Not now. I might see Teddy and the girls there and I've had enough humiliation for one day, thank you very much. It would be awful to go and see him there and he'd get all embarrassed because he'd know he didn't mention the gig to me. I'd hate to end the holiday on a sour note. So no. You go.' I held my nose up and tried to do what Nesta does when she's being melodramatic and trying to be noble. 'No. I shall stay here alone with my memories. With my broken heart and broken dreams . . .'

It took a bit more persuading but, in the end, the girls gave in and agreed to go. The room became a flurry of activity with hairdryers, make-up, clothes and shoes scattered all over the place as they got ready. Half an hour later, they looked fabulous. Maybe not decked out in Prada, but I reckoned they could give Arianna and Cecilia a run for their money.

'You sure you're going to be OK?' asked Nesta as she put her coat on ready for the off.

'Totally,' I said. 'I'll walk you out.'

At the back of the hotel, the van was in the car park where Marco had said it would be. The girls piled into the back with the other band members whose faces lit up when they saw that three stunning young girls were travelling with them.

'Now don't stay out too late,' I said, putting on my croaky old grandma voice. 'Don't take any drugs. And TJ, don't go licking strangers' ears. We know what you can be like when you're allowed out.'

'OK, Ma,' said TJ, laughing. 'Now you go get some cocoa and get back to your knitting.'

'Okee dokee,' I replied, trying to look as cheerful as possible.

After I'd waved them off, I went back to my room and lay on the bottom bunk. I couldn't help but feel low. Sometimes I don't feel that I belong anywhere, I thought as I flicked on the TV. I don't like it here in this crumby hotel and yet I felt uncomfortable at the Grand Hotel Villa Corelli. Where do I belong? I wish Tony was here, I thought. He'd make me laugh and get me out of this weird mood. Maybe my period's due and that's why I'm feeling emotional. Still, at least I know it is due. If I'd had sex with Tony, I might be here wondering if it was going to come at all. I wondered what Tony was doing over in England. If he'd gone to the rave and slept with Andrea Morton. I felt tears sting the back of my eyes. So much for me wanting to be a grown-up, a woman of experience and sophistication, I thought. I've never felt so young and so inexperienced in all my life. Pathetic. My one try at getting over Tony has turned out to be a disaster. My first holiday romance and here I am on the last night on my own. Dumped the moment Teddy got a better offer. How humiliating. I might try and kid myself that I can wing it in the world of grown-ups, but all those people in the past who've said 'You're not old enough', maybe, just maybe, they were right.

Just at that moment, I heard a rustling sound at the bottom of the door and saw an envelope being pushed through. As I got up to see what it was, I felt a stab of anticipation. Maybe it was a note from Teddy. It had my name on it, so I ripped open the envelope and went over to the lamp so that I could see better. Inside was a condom and a note, saying: *For a night to remember, my room, Number 14. 8.30. Chris.*

OK, Chris, I thought. Yeah. I'll give you night to remember.

'I thought you might take up my offer,' he said with a smirk when he opened his door five minutes later.

'Did you?' I said, putting on my most alluring smile. 'Yeah. How could I refuse an offer like that? But . . . I thought you might need a bit of cooling down first.' I produced the condom from behind my back. I'd filled it from the taps to make it into a water bomb so I bashed him over the head with it. 'But you know the awful thing about condoms? Well, they can burst.'

Water dripped down his face as it burst over his head. 'Your loss, you . . . you're so . . . childish,' he moaned as he ran back into his room. 'Anyway, you're . . . you're probably too young for me.'

Story of my life, mate, I thought as I made my way back to my room. Why fight it? I asked myself. Anyway, sometimes it's fun to act childish. Trying to be grown-up and mature, it stinks.

I lay back on the bed and giggled to myself. Yeah, condoms, they make brilliant water bombs. I must tell the girls when they come back. A moment later, the phone rang.

'I suppose you think you're *so* clever,' said Chris's voice.

'Well medium clever,' I replied. 'I don't like to boast.'

'You ought to grow up and act your age . . .'

'So you said. Don't you have anything new to say?'

'Just that I think you're a lesbian.'

'Oh. OK. Cool.' I said and put the phone down.

A moment later, the phone went again.

'Look, give me a break will you?' I said into the receiver. 'Just bog off and leave me alone. I don't fancy you. I never will and you can take your stupid condoms and stick them up your bum.'

'*Lucy* Lovering,' said Mr Johnson's voice. 'Who on *earth* do you think you're talking to?'

'Oh! Er . . . well, not you,' I gasped. 'Sorry sorry, oh God . . .'

'The dining room is about to close for supper,' he said in a clipped voice. 'If you're eating, you'll need to be there in five minutes.'

'Yes, Mr Johnson. Sorry, Mr Johnson.' Oh bugger, Mr Johnson, I thought as I put the phone down.

And then the phone went again.

'Hello . . .' I said cautiously.

'Hey Lucy,' said Teddy's voice. 'Phew. I thought I'd missed you.'

'Oh Teddy. Missed me? How? Why?'

'I tried your room about ten minutes ago, but no one picked up. Then it was engaged when I tried again. What are you doing?'

'Oh, going to have supper in a minute, then this and that. There's a whole crowd of us here, yeah, having a great time . . .' I was determined not to give away how much he'd hurt me. 'Why? What are you doing?' As if I didn't know, I thought.

'I was going to go to the concert.'

'Yeah, Arianna told me about it,' I said breezily. 'Well. Have a good time, must dash. It was nice meeting you.'

'Nice meeting me? Hey Lucy. Are you OK? You sound a bit weirded out.'

'No. I'm fine,' I said. 'Absolutely fine. Couldn't be better. Anyway, got to go now. Got a million things to do. Leaving tomorrow. So. Yeah. Have a great time at the concert.'

'Oh,' he said and I could hear disappointment in just that one word. 'Yeah. OK. Shame. See, I got you a ticket. That was why I couldn't get back to the Hotel Corelli to see you. I didn't want to say anything and get your hopes up in case I couldn't get one for you, but I managed it. Last one I think. But . . .'

'You got me a ticket?'

'Yeah.'

'But aren't you going with Arianna and Cecilia?'

'They're making their own way. Meeting a bunch of mates there. And just between you and me, I can only take so much of all their girlie stuff. It gets a bit boring after a while. It's like they can only ever talk about clothes and who's the latest in-person. I'd much rather have gone with you. At least I can have a decent conversation with you.'

I started to laugh. 'Is that all?'

'I think you know very well that's not all . . . but you know what I mean. Oh come on, you're going back to England tomorrow. We *can't* not spend our last night together. Who knows when we'll see each other again. Just . . . please, Lucy . . . I . . . I've never met anyone like you before. I really like you. You're different . . .'

'Like good or bad different?'

'Good. *Really* good, really, really . . .'

'I will come,' I interrupted.

'You *will*? Oh fantastic. I was so disappointed when I couldn't hang out with you today, but it was really hard getting that ticket. I had to go all over the place. I'll come and get you. Half an hour?'

Cinderella shall go to the ball, I thought when I put the phone down. Then I panicked. I had nothing to wear. I'd lent Izzie the only decent top I'd brought with me and all that was left were T-shirts I'd worn in the week. Oh God. I had half an hour. What was I going to wear? If I was Cinderella, wasn't my fairy godmother supposed to appear with the perfect dress? So where was she?

I opened the wardrobe but, nope, no fairy godmother in there or perfect dress. All I could see was a pile of dirty laundry.

I pulled out my black jeans. They would be OK if only I had something to wear with them. But what? I stared round the room looking for inspiration. Some of the girls' clothes were still scattered over the beds, but there was nothing there that fitted me. Izzie, Nesta and TJ are all so tall. With breasts. So what? Maybe I could do a Julie Andrews from *The Sound of Music* and make something out of the curtains. I'd brought my sewing kit with me. Mad idea, I thought. The curtains looked even dirtier than our laundry. So what? What? Arianna and Cecilia will probably be decked out in some fabulous little designer numbers, and Izzie, Nesta and TJ had all left looking like rock chicks. I don't want to turn up looking like some boring loser. I'm a designer, I thought. If I was at home, I could knock something up in a moment. There must be something I can use. I went back to the wardrobe and pulled out what was in there to see if anything could be adapted. T-shirts. More T-shirts. A frumpy old woolly. Couple of fleeces. Bags with assorted souvenirs in. The aprons with David's naked torso on them that we'd bought in the market up at Piazza Michelangelo. Yeah, Teddy would definitely think I was different if I turned up in one of those.

Then I had an idea.

I could make this work, I thought as I pulled an apron out of the bag and held it up against me. OK, so it might not be Prada or Versace, but they're not my style anyway. I might not have a fortune to spend on clothes, but I do have ideas. If I go to the ball, I want to go in a Lucy Lovering one-off creation.

How to Make a Water Bomb

Take either a balloon or a condom. Fill with cold water. Tie the end. *Voilà*. Bombs away!

Chapter 15

Concert

A spray of perfume, a last slick of lip-gloss and I pulled on my parka and went out to the reception to wait for Teddy.

'Off to the ball?' asked Mrs Elwes, appearing from the dining area and carrying a large glass of red wine.

I nodded. 'That American boy, Teddy, he got me a ticket. And we're meeting the others there.'

Mrs Elwes smiled. 'So what have you got on under there?'

'Um, top, jeans, the usual,' I said, then looked down at my sneakers. 'Shame about the shoes though. I didn't bring any glam ones as I knew we were going to be walking so much.'

'What size are you, Lucy?'

'Thirty-four. Why?'

'Give me a tic,' she said and ran off to her room. She was back minutes later with a large carrier bag. 'Somebody left these on the bus. I've been round everyone in our group and Nesta said they weren't yours. I think someone from the last school trip must have left them.'

She produced a pair of shoes from the box and I gasped. They were perfect. Black, high and strappy.

'But won't someone write to reception and ask for them?' I asked.

Mrs Elwes took a sip of her wine. 'Huh. I tried handing them in. The concierge just looked at me, waved me away and said, "No polish, no polish" . . . I give up with that man. He's been completely unhelpful since day one.'

I looked at the shoes. 'Can I really?'

Mrs Elwes smiled again. I think she was feeling a little happy from the wine. 'Sure, go ahead,' she said.

I quickly pulled off my trainers and stepped into the shoes. They fitted perfectly.

'Cool,' said Mrs Elwes.

I felt like hugging her. 'Anyone ever tell you you were their fairy godmother before?'

'That's me. Cinderella you shall go to the ball,' said Mrs Elwes. She waved an imaginary wand, then tottered off towards the lounge.

Five minutes later, my carriage arrived and I was on the way to the ball, er . . . rock concert. Teddy was so sweet on the journey and held my hand all the way. We didn't say much and I felt a stab of sadness as I watched the lights of Florence flash by outside the window. This was our last night together and maybe I'd never see him again. I got the feeling that he was thinking the same thing.

The concert was being held in an old hall on the edge of town and already there were crowds waiting outside when we arrived. They all stopped and stared when the limo pulled up.

'Who is it, who is it?' I heard a few of them ask.

Someone in the crowd said, 'Nobody,' in a disappointed tone. I laughed as Teddy handed our tickets to one of the men on the door and we were ushered through.

'I'm going to leave my coat in the cloakroom, then see if I can find my mates,' I said.

'And I'll look for Arianna and Co,' said Teddy. 'Meet you back here in five minutes?'

I nodded and went to the cloakroom to get rid of my parka. I felt a brief pang of nerves as I discarded the jacket and hoped that I hadn't made a huge mistake in my outfit.

'*Da paura, il tuo* top,' said the girl behind the desk.

I looked at her quizzically and shrugged. 'English, no understand.'

She smiled, looked me up and down, then gave me the thumbs up. Maybe my top would be OK after all.

'Lucy,' a voice called behind me. I turned, and there were Izzie and TJ making their way towards me through the people swarming inside the main hall.

'Wow,' said TJ and pointed at my top. 'Where did you get that?'

'Er . . . it's a Lucy Lovering special. Do you like it?'

'It's brilliant,' said TJ. 'I want one.'

I'd cut the bottom of the apron, hemmed the top, then cut

the black ties off three more of the aprons and I'd quickly sewn on six hooks so that the ties could be laced up my back. When I put it on I had the perfect halter handkerchief top with black straps at the back.

'But the choker,' said Izzie. 'That's gorgeous. I've never seen that before.'

I grinned. 'Oh yes you have. It was Velcroed round the lamp in our room, remember. I'll stick it back later.'

The choker was my last moment of inspiration. The lamp was the only half-decent thing in our room, red with a red velvet fringe from which dripped red beads. It made the perfect choker when I took it off and tied it round my neck.

'Lucy, you're a genius,' said Izzie. 'And will you make me one of those tops too when we get back?'

'Sure,' I said. 'Only we need to get down the market before our flight tomorrow and buy up some supplies, and I . . . I'm sorry, but I cut the straps off three of the aprons.'

'No worries,' said TJ. 'They didn't cost much and anyway, we can easily sew them back on.'

Teddy appeared a moment later with his stepsisters. He gave me a long appreciative look up and down and I felt myself blushing.

'Lucy,' said Arianna as she came over to me and gave me the two-cheek kiss. 'You look fab. Who's it by?'

'It's an original,' I said. 'An LL creation made specially for me.'

'LL,' she said. 'Yeah. I think I've heard of them.'

'She made it herself,' said TJ. 'She's LL.'

Arianna looked well impressed.

'It's so cool – Italian and cheeky at the same time,' gushed Cecilia. 'Oh please could you make two, for Arianna and me.'

'Sure,' I said. 'And these are my friends, Izzie and TJ. Hey, where's Nesta?'

'Oh somewhere draped all over Marco,' said Izzie. 'I think he finally gave in.'

'I knew it was only a matter of time,' I said.

After that, the evening was great. The bands were wild and the music even wilder. It felt brilliant to be bopping away, even though I didn't understand a word that anyone was singing. And my *David* top went down a storm. By the end of the evening, I had twelve orders from girls at our school, plus the two from Arianna and Cecilia. So much for it being a one-off original, I thought.

'LL Designs branch out to Italy,' said Nesta, when she took a moment to detach herself from Marco. 'I think we should go into business.'

'Yeah,' said TJ. 'Lucy can make them. I'll do the advertising, Nesta can model them . . .'

'And I'll sing about them,' grinned Izzie. 'Oh cor blimey, very rum, the statue of *David*'s lost his bum . . . Hhhm. Maybe not. OK, I'll work on the lyrics.'

Teddy offered to give us all a lift home after the gig and we had to drag Nesta away from Marco. She was in tears when she got into the car.

'He promised he'll write, but I know he won't,' she sobbed.

'It's too sad . . . I meet the love of my life and we're destined to part . . .'

'Love of your life?' asked Izzie. 'Hey come on, you've hardly said two words to each other as he doesn't speak good English.'

'But I speak some Italian. Anyway, we don't need words. We speak the language of love,' she said and looked wistfully out of the window.

Teddy glanced over at me and gave me a sad smile. I wonder if you are going to make false promises to write, I thought. Or if we'll ever meet again.

When we got back to the hotel, the girls very sensitively made themselves scarce and left Teddy and me alone. We walked around the car park, then went and sat on a wall at the back where Teddy pulled me close to him.

'Guess this is it, then, Lucy Lovering Junior,' he said as he tucked a strand of hair behind my ear.

'Guess so, Teddy Junior.'

He leaned forward and gave me a long, lovely kiss, then he pulled back.

'I will write if you'd like,' he said. 'I know I want to stay in touch. We can e-mail. And I can send you photos from back home.'

I nodded. 'I'd like that. And, with the profits of my *David* tops, the first thing I'm going to buy is a digital camera so I can send you photos too.'

'Cool. I'd really like to see where you live and your family and all. And send me pics of some more of your designs. I'd really love to see them if tonight's creation is anything to go by.'

'I will. And send me some of your designs. I'd really like to see them too.'

And then there didn't seem to be anything else to say. We kissed a little longer, but we both knew that at some time we had to part. I walked him back to his car and we held each other for a few moments. Then he got in and gave the driver the nod. I felt so sad as I watched the car start up, then make its way out of the car park, on to the street and out of my life.

How to Make an LL Handkerchief Top
Out of an Apron

Cut off the part of the apron that would hang below the waist.

Put on the top part and measure how long you want the top to be (i.e. to the top of your jeans or, if you have a fab midriff, cut to a few inches under your bust).

Sew four or six loops on to the side of the apron front. Two at the bust, two at the bottom (and, if you want more lacing at the back, two in between the bust and bottom).

Cut off the straps that would have gone round your waist and use them to lace in a criss-cross across your back.

If you have any strap left, use it to edge the hem for a neat finish. If not, sew a hem on the bottom so that you have a neat line.

And there's your top. If you lace it tight, it will look really cool.

Chapter 16

Homeward Bound

'I can't wait to see Mojo,' said TJ as she strapped herself into her seat belt ready for the flight back to London. 'I've missed him like mad.'

I felt a stab of guilt. I hadn't thought about our dogs, not once. And I'd hardly thought about my family at all. There had been too much going on. But now we were settled on the plane and our goodbyes had been said, I realised that I was looking forward to going home. Back to my own bed. Peanut butter and honey on toast for breakfast and a decent cup of tea. Soon Florence and Teddy would be a distant dream, and London my reality once more. I wondered how things would have been if I'd met Teddy in my everyday life. Had it felt so special because of where we were? No, it wasn't only the location, I decided. We'd have got on wherever we were. He was a genuinely nice guy. But back to normal, back to school. Ugh. And Tony.

Hhmm. I wasn't sure how I felt about that. The school trip had been the perfect distraction from him, but now I was going back and I'd have to face him sooner or later round at Nesta's.

'You feeling OK this time?' asked TJ, as the plane started up its engines and we began to cruise down the runway ready for take-off.

I nodded. I did feel fine. Completely different to the journey out. I felt calm. I'd done it before. Maybe there were some aspects of my life where I had become a woman of experience.

Everyone seemed quiet as we took off. Girls were staring out of the windows, each of us lost in our private memories of Florence.

It didn't last long. As soon as we were up in the sky and the seat-belt sign had been switched off, people started swapping places, girls going to sit with the boys, boys chatting up the girls, the teachers looking weary and glad it was all almost over.

'Life goes on,' I said to TJ. 'And time waits for no man ... or woman or something like that.'

She laughed. 'Feeling philosophical, are we?'

'Sort of.'

'You OK about leaving Teddy?'

I nodded. 'Sort of. Yeah. No choice had I?' I had felt a little sad, but was fine about it in the end. He'd rung our hotel early this morning and asked if he could see me off at the airport. I'd told him no. For one thing, it would have been awkward having everyone there and staring at us, and we wouldn't have been able to snog properly, not under the eagle eye of Mrs Elwes and

Mr Johnson, who was now, according to some sources, back on twenty cigarettes a day. I wanted to remember the concert as our last time together and Teddy had understood. He'd also promised to come over to England sometime. And I'd promised I'd go to visit him in the States when I was older. I really meant it too. I had the feeling that Teddy and I would be friends for a long time.

About an hour into the flight, an announcement came on asking everyone to return to their seats and fasten their belts.

'Why's that?' I asked TJ. 'We're not landing yet.'

'Probably going to run into some turbulence,' she said. 'It happens all the time. Nothing to worry a . . . a woaaaaaah . . .'

A sudden lurch and it felt like the plane was falling out of the sky. A scream went through the back of the cabin. Mainly from the girls from our school. And Liam.

'You OK?' asked TJ, clinging on to the seat rest as the plane steadied itself. 'It will probably only last a minute or so.'

The plane took what felt like another dive and books and magazines went flying. 'Er . . . yeah.'

Only the turbulence didn't last a minute. It went on and on, as if the plane had suddenly been put in a washing machine. On spin. Bump bump theewump. My new-found calm disappeared as a voice in my head said, ohmigod, we're gonna diiiiieeeeeeeeee.

I wasn't the only one who looked freaked. Liam, who was sitting in the middle aisle opposite TJ and me, threw up all over Chris who was next to him.

'Eeew,' cried Nesta. 'Gross.' She'd never make a good nurse, I thought as Liam turned greener and greener. A flight attendant attempted to clean him up, but she was swaying all over the place and eventually gave up, reassuring him that she'd be back in a minute.

'Hold hands, hold hands,' said Izzie from the seat behind. She and Nesta leaned forward and TJ and I leaned back and we joined hands over the tops of our seats.

'It's g . . . g . . . going to be OK,' said Nesta. 'Just a storm or something.'

'Oh *no*,' moaned Izzie, as the plane lurched up, down and sideways. 'That means lightning and that means it might hit the plane.'

'Oh thanks a *lot,*' I said. 'But, look, you guys, I just want you to know that you're the best friends I've ever had and I really, *really* love you.'

'And I want you to know that I really, *really* love you as well,' said Nesta.

'Try meditating,' said Izzie as she took a deep breath. 'It will help calm us down.'

'No way,' said Nesta. 'If I'm going to die, I'm not spending my last moments chanting om shanti wotnot or whatever.'

'Then what do you suggest?' asked Izzie.

'Praying. Begging. I dunno.'

'Let's sing,' said TJ. 'Hmmm. Let me think. Songs for plane crashes . . . Hhmmm. *Ah ah ah ah, Staying Alive . . .*'

'Hhhm, good choice, TJ,' said Izzie.

'We're not going to die,' I said. 'And we're not going to crash.

Cut it out, TJ. You said it would only last a few minutes.'

'I lied,' said TJ, who by now was almost as green as Liam. 'Sometimes it can go on for ages.'

I shut my eyes tight and, as the plane rattled and bounced along, I prayed that we'd make it home. Please, please God, let me see my mum and dad one more time. And Steve and Lal. And . . . and Tony. I wanted to see Tony one last time. Oh God. I really, really did. So we might have had fallings-out, but now, when it came to the crunch, it was his face I saw in my mind, not the lovely Teddy. We'd been through so much together. Oh God, oh God, I thought. I'll be ever so good if you get us through this and I promise I won't only pray at exam times or when I'm travelling. I promise, God. I'll pray in between when everything's all right.

As suddenly as it had started, the turbulence ended and everyone breathed a huge sigh of relief. An announcement came over the intercom that we were through the bad weather and it was going to be plain sailing from then on. Only we're flying, I thought, then looked out the window just to check that the pilot hadn't actually been correct and we'd landed in the sea and were plain sailing. Or a plane sailing. But no, fluffy clouds were all that I could see.

'I still mean it that I love you guys,' I said.

'Ditto,' said Nesta. 'Now where's our lunch?'

That's one thing I love about Nesta. She can go down fast, but she can come up even quicker.

The rest of the flight went smoothly and, before we knew it, we were starting to descend into London. It was grey and cold as we got off the plane, but it did feel good to be back on solid ground and not thirty-five thousand feet up in the air being thrown about. We were through Passport Control quickly enough, then it was off to collect our luggage before getting on to the coach for the last leg of the journey back to school where Mum or Dad would be waiting. Well, hello London, I thought as we walked through Customs and through the arrival gates. Crowds of people were waiting behind the barriers for friends and relatives, some with names on cardboard, one family with a banner saying, 'Welcome home'. It felt nice and festive watching all the eager faces waiting to greet their loved ones. And it felt good to be able to understand everything that was being said all around us again.

'*It's nice to go travelling,*' sang Mr Johnson as he wheeled his trolley past us, '*in winter, summer or rain, but It's so much nicer, yes it's so much nicer to come home.*'

Izzie laughed and nudged me. 'He seems happy,' she said with a grin.

'I wonder why,' I said. 'I mean, most men would be happy to go away with twenty-five gorgeous young girls.'

'Ah . . . look,' said Izzie, pointing to the end of the line of people waiting for arrivals. 'So sweet.'

I glanced to where she was pointing and there was a boy dressed in jeans and a black coat. I couldn't see his face as it was partly obscured by the most enormous bunch of white roses. How romantic, I thought. He's come to meet his girlfriend and, judging by the size of that stunning bouquet, she means a lot to him.

'Oh. My. God,' said TJ, then nudged me. I turned to look at her and saw that her face registered surprise. She pointed at the boy with the flowers again.

I looked back at him.

Now I could see his face.

It was Tony.

The complete
Mates, Dates

The MATES, DATES series

1. Mates, Dates and Inflatable Bras
2. Mates, Dates and Cosmic Kisses
3. Mates, Dates and Portobello Princesses
4. Mates, Dates and Sleepover Secrets
5. Mates, Dates and Sole Survivors
6. Mates, Dates and Mad Mistakes
7. Mates, Dates and Pulling Power
8. Mates, Dates and Tempting Trouble
9. Mates, Dates and Great Escapes
10. Mates, Dates and Chocolate Cheats
11. Mates, Dates and Diamond Destiny
12. Mates, Dates and Sizzling Summers

Companion Books:
Mates, Dates The Secret Story
Mates, Dates Guide to Life
Mates, Dates and You
Mates, Dates Journal
Mates, Dates and Flirting
Mates, Dates and Saving the Planet

Cinnamon Girl

First impressions count. A few weeks after moving to London, India-Jane has managed to convince boy-of-her-dreams Joe that she is an artistic, nit-infested stalker who takes things to extremes. It's not quite the new life she was looking for.

But a fresh start is never easy – starting a new school in Year 11 without looking like a No-mates Nellie, finding real friends who'll share everything with you, discovering what the people you fancy are really like - it's all just a fraction of the mad whirl that is India-Jane's life.

Cathy Hopkins explores, with her trademark wit and wisdom, deeper issues for teens – but with all the humour and cringe-making situations that fans can't get enough of!

The CINNAMON GIRL series

Truth Dare Kiss Promise

What would you do if you had to tell the complete **truth** for a day? Would you **dare** enter a national singing competition? Could you cope with what happens when you **kiss** the school heart-throb? Could you **promise** to be faithful, whatever form temptation takes?

Becca, Cat, Lia, Squidge and Mac all enjoy playing the *Truth, Dare, Kiss or Promise* game to liven up their lives – but they can never predict where it's going to lead them!

The TRUTH, DARE, KISS, PROMISE series

www.cathyhopkins.com

Like this book?
Become a mate today!

Join **CATHY'S CLUB** and be the first to get the lowdown on the LATEST NEWS, BOOKS and FAB COMPETITIONS straight to your mobile and e-mail.

PLUS there's a FREE MOBILE WALLPAPER when you sign up! What are you waiting for?

Simply text MATE plus your date of birth (ddmmyyyy) to 60022 now! Or go to www.cathyhopkins.com and sign up online.

Once you've signed up keep your eyes peeled for exclusive chapter previews, cool downloads, freebies and heaps more fun stuff all coming your way.